Exposed

by

Karyn Good

Aspen Lake Series

Exposed

Cover Art by *Kim Mendoza*

The Wild Rose Press, Inc.
PO Box 708
Adams Basin, NY 14410-0708
Visit us at www.thewildrosepress.com

Publishing History
First Crimson Rose Edition, 2015
Print ISBN 978-1-5092-0246-1
Digital ISBN 978-1-5092-0247-8

Aspen Lake Series
Published in the United States of America

Splinters of wood, shards of glass, and Kate's last remaining scrap of poise crumbled under the heavy tread of his steel-toed boots. Seth eyed the broken lock, gave the door a yank, and sent it crashing to the floor.

Kate jumped back.

Next, Seth ripped off a shattered section of doorframe and tossed it into a growing pile. "They knew to take it out close to the deadbolt. Knew the doorjamb would give way. These old deadbolts only extend so far and presto you're in. Would have taken some heft to do it though."

So, a hefty axe-wielding maniac with a thing for women's clothes. Perfect. That didn't make her want to chug a giant rum and coke at all. "Can you fix it?"

"Sure." He dug around in a couple of pockets before pulling out a measuring tape.

Good Lord, his cargos had more pockets than she had good intentions. But at least he was giving her some good news. "Today?"

"The door? Yeah. I'll need to go back and get supplies: a door, new locks. Obviously." When she didn't smile back, he nodded his head in what could only be defeat. "Right. I have a couple of things I need to finish up there, and then I'll be back." He fingered a torn wire. "Nothing I can do about the alarm. You'll have to contact the company. But you'll have a door in by the end of the day. The rest of it is going to take some time."

He dived back into his pockets and came out with a little pencil. More searching for what she assumed was paper to write on with no luck. She flipped open her organizer, pulled off a piece of paper and handed it to him. "How much is all this going to cost me?"

Dedication

For Rachael,
who always keeps me guessing.

Chapter One

Kate Logan pushed aside the yellow crime scene tape. She didn't waste time pondering her options. Not many to consider. Her fingers tightened over the shattered wood frame of her boutique's backdoor. It was going to take divine intervention to make things right in time for the festival. She didn't need the nasty splinter stabbing into her thumb as confirmation.

"Darn it." Finger in mouth, the metallic taste of blood on her tongue, she navigated the destruction in search of the tissue box. Files, catalogues, and broken shelving units littered the floor. Her desk was a ruined mess. Hacked apart. By an axe.

An. *Axe*.

Nothing terrifying about that. She shuddered. So was the thought of paying to fix it all. With her bank account sitting next to zero and her line of credit tapped, repairing the break-in damage was an expense she didn't need and couldn't afford. Sure, she had insurance but collecting took time, hassle, and energy she didn't have. Tissues found, she ripped one free and pressed it against her fingertip.

An axe.

Aspen Lake was a small prairie resort town, a treed oasis in the middle of farming country boasting three thousand year-round residents. During the tourist season, the numbers swelled due to the influx of cottage owners and seasonal campers. Break-ins happened, not frequently, but often enough. But this? This was extreme. And big news.

This was tasty enough to coax any small-towner out of his or her comfiest lazy-chair. They would come. The curious and well meaning. The gloaters. The haters. The ones certain she was a designer handbag short of a full closet. All with a varying degree of poor, poor, pitiful Kate plastered on their faces. Here's hoping the gawkers were also spenders. So long as they walked out with a black plastic bag emblazoned with her string of pearls logo and the words Kate's Closet what did she care? Respect wasn't a purchase requirement.

"Kate?"

"I'm back here." *Hiding.* With nowhere to toss her used tissue, she stuffed it into a pocket and twisted around to face her assistant, Grace Bighill. One of two women who held the dubious title of her best friend. The other, Lily Porter, was on a plane headed out of province to take care of her recuperating mother.

"There's someone here to see you." Grace's face was full of apology, her long black hair swinging out to the side. She offered up a sorry-to-bother-you shrug. "Your dad sent him over from the lumberyard."

"Thanks. I'll be right there." Kate dredged up a smile.

"No problem. Take your time." Her words trailed away.

She stepped out onto the small loading platform to compose her thoughts. Her dad coming to her rescue was old news. She'd decline. Like all of the other times she'd refused his help in the last two years. She glanced up. Black clouds bubbled and toiled overhead. At least, it wasn't storming.

Yet.

Kate hated rainstorms. She rubbed the late September chill from her arms and tried to concentrate on the most troubling problem first. Looked for the answers in the old, pitted brick buildings lining the back alley. Nothing but normal. From the battered Dumpster to the few parked vehicles to the coo of pigeons. There was no sign of the person who'd come in the dark intent on doing damage. She closed her eyes and tipped her head to the heavens. No answers came. Only more questions.

What else was new?

Bottom line, she couldn't afford the disruption. Not with so much at stake: the fate of her business, the success of the town's annual Gothic Revival Fair, her hard-earned sobriety. Two of which were in serious doubt. The fair would go on even if the head organizer was a mess.

Her heart ached over the trashed vintage-style display case she'd spent weeks refurbishing. The worst part was destruction when she craved order. A successful fair weekend could make all the difference to her bottom line. Sales equaled income. Independence. Redemption. If that didn't happen…

Well, she'd survived worse she supposed.

Grace's low laugh floated in from the boutique area. Kate frowned, then remembered she had a visitor. She skirted the remains of her shattered back door. After an obligatory glance in the tiny mirror, the only thing to escape the frenzied demolition, she smoothed a finger over an eyebrow. The mirage of self-confident business owner wavered. She stuck out her chin, straightened her shoulders.

Two steps into the main area of the boutique Kate faltered. She should have paid more attention to Grace's "Take your time." Grace wasn't flirting. Grace didn't flirt. She had her reasons. That didn't mean she wasn't appreciative of the opposite sex. Just discriminating. She made any interested parties work for her attention. But this guy encouraged a little rule breaking.

Strike one.

Kate acknowledged the little catch of breath, like the kind that came with finding the exact perfect pair of shoes. You knew they were going to cost you. That there was going to be plenty of hurt before things got better, if they ever did. But even with all that you knew you had to have them.

Strike two.

Good thing she had plenty of practice obliterating those kinds of thoughts. She was immune to scarred work boots, long legs, and Pearl Jam wearing handymen. She lifted a brow. Great hair though. Six feet plus in height. His loose-limbed stance made it clear he didn't give a crap about any of it, which added a little bit of wild to Mr. Long and Lean. Her fingers twitched. That made her nervous. And nervous didn't project the right image.

Strike three. He didn't know it yet, but he was out of here.

"Can I help you?" She plunged into the Kate Logan act. Relished the comfort of the fit. The shaky Kate disappeared behind the strut that had made her famous.

He said something to Grace before turning toward

her, and the full impact of the whole package hit her square in the chastity belt. She beat down the urge to smooth a hand over her skirt. Instead, she put one stiletto in front of the other and advanced.

"You must be Kate." He held out a hand. "Seth Stone."

Behind him Grace offered up a wicked smile. "He works for your dad. He sent him over to fix the damage. Seth's a carpenter. As well as an artist."

Wow, that was a lot of information. How long had she stood brooding out her busted back door? Kate eyed his outstretched hand and the ink on his arms with great reluctance. Set her hand in his with even greater trepidation. Hers was engulfed by rough, long fingers. She spared a second to appreciate his great bone structure before she extricated her hand.

His grin was shock therapy to her dormant libido. Great. Could this day get any worse?

Grace put a hand on her shoulder and squeezed. "If you have other stuff to deal with, I can show Seth the damage to the back. He's already had a look at the display case."

"No, that's fine." She smiled at Grace knowing her offer had nothing to do with wanting to keep his attention. She was worried. Everyone worried, even though they tried to hide it. Waiting for anything that would cause a backslide. "We need to get things rearranged in here and ready for tomorrow morning."

Kate retrieved her day planner, in which her life was organized one careful bullet point after another, so she could scan the notes she'd jotted down earlier and motioned for Seth to follow her. "Through here."

"Yes, ma'am." His soft tread echoed the click of

her heels. "So, what happened?"

"Someone broke in early this morning. The alarm went off around four a.m. Grace has been here ever since. I was out of town." Saturday nights she attended sobriety meetings in the city. Safe in the knowledge she wouldn't bump into any other attendees in the line-up for gas, or at the café, or selecting fruit at the grocery store.

A two-hour drive each way meant she usually stayed overnight at her aunt's house. But this time she and Lily had shared a hotel room and a rare girls-only weekend. She'd dropped her off for her early morning Sunday flight and rushed home. "I didn't get back until just a little while ago. The police have come and gone."

She stopped inside the doorway and gestured at the mess.

"Wow." He ran a hand over the damaged frame. "What did this?"

"An axe."

"No shit." He spared her a glance. Gave her a questioning lift of his chin. "How are you holding up? You okay?"

"I wasn't here." That's all he, or anyone else, needed to know. "As you can see, the place is a disaster. The door, doorframe, the shelving units, the display case out front are the worst of it. I'll need a desk." She didn't bother mentioning the missing inventory. All of it in the same one or two sizes, which meant they were looking for someone with a thing for size eight female clothing.

Splinters of wood, shards of glass, and Kate's last remaining scrap of poise crumbled under the heavy tread of his steel-toed boots. Seth eyed the broken lock, gave the door a yank, and sent it crashing to the floor.

Kate jumped back.

Next, Seth ripped off a shattered section of doorframe and tossed it into a growing pile. "They knew to take it out close to the deadbolt. Knew the doorjamb would give way. These old deadbolts only extend so far and presto you're in. Would have taken some heft to do it though."

So, a hefty axe-wielding maniac with a thing for women's clothes. Perfect. That didn't make her want to chug a giant rum and coke at all. "Can you fix it?"

"Sure." He dug around in a couple of pockets before pulling out a measuring tape.

Good Lord, his cargos had more pockets than she had good intentions. But at least he was giving her some good news. "Today?"

"The door? Yeah. I'll need to go back and get supplies: a door, new locks. Obviously." When she didn't smile back, he nodded his head in what could only be defeat. "Right. I have a couple of things I need to finish up there, and then I'll be back." He fingered a torn wire. "Nothing I can do about the alarm. You'll have to contact the company. But you'll have a door in by the end of the day. The rest of it is going to take some time."

He dived back into his pockets and came out with a little pencil. More searching for what she assumed was paper to write on with no luck. She flipped open her organizer, pulled off a piece of paper and handed it to him. "How much is all this going to cost me?"

"No worries." Seth didn't glance away from his inspection of the frame. "Boss said to say it's taken care of."

"My father doesn't pay my bills. I do." Trust Bill Logan to send over the new guy with a message he knew would upset her. Kate's chin went up as she clutched her scheduler to her chest. She wasn't sure how, but she'd come up with the money. She'd find a way to pay Seth and pay back her father for overstepping.

Pencil scratching on borrowed paper Seth shrugged. "I'll let you work that out with him."

It might mean another humbling appointment with the town's one and only loan officer willing to deal with her. According to him, she was a high-risk client. He was doing her a favor where others wouldn't. He'd given her detailed and thorough business plan the barest skim, then he'd offered an alternative repayment schedule. A joke, of course. No harm done. She'd misunderstood his intent, overreacted. After she'd suggested they share the details of his generous offer with his wife.

Her skin heated in humiliation at remembering his "Who do you think she's going to believe, Kate? Her husband, a pillar of the community? Or you?"

As in her, the subject of more nasty accusations than she had shoes. And she owned a lot of shoes.

Didn't matter, she was going to make good on the loan. And not on her back. Or her knees. Or whatever position the creep had in mind. She could tell his tiny mind had swirled with possibilities by the way he'd shifted in his seat.

God.

She really needed a drink.

"You okay?" The concern in Seth's voice snapped her out of it.

"Yes." She put a hand to her throat. She was here. She was sober. She was going to stay that way.

He stepped out onto the small loading dock and studied the overcast skies. "Before I leave I'll take some measurements and put up some plastic sheeting to cover the opening."

"Sounds good. Thank you." She sighed with relief and avoided searching the dull sky for signs of worse weather. No need to add more drama to an already crappy day. Not when she was expected to spend the evening at the local bar with a group of people who knew it was the last place she should be hanging out. But she'd chosen the location to prove a point. She was in control, temptation be darned. She could handle this. Had handled it for the last two years.

Seth shook his head. "No need to thank me. You give me a chance to design a new display case? I'll be the one thanking you."

Against her will, her lips twitched and she nodded. "Why don't we see how the door goes first?"

"Fair enough. I'll do my best to amaze." He grinned. A heart-stopping, slow-spreading, deadly kind of grin. A slight lift of the corners until it gradually widened to reach all the way to his eyes. Eyes that hid a hint of jungle cat in them. The kind of smile that took forever to get where it was going, but when it got there you felt like someone had forgotten to yell "Clear!" before they used the paddles.

When she committed to getting sober, booze wasn't the only thing she'd given up. If you didn't count the one night of insanity and crushing loneliness she'd succumbed to, it meant she hadn't had sex in over a year. She battened down her hatches as a lovely rush of hormones washed through her. He wasn't her type. She didn't go for younger men, and she put him somewhere in his early twenties. She was twenty-nine going on eighty. No, he was not for her. But that didn't stop her from squirming in her high heels.

"I'll leave you to it." She slipped her ice queen persona back into place, stiffened her spine and her resolve as she tried not to ooze pheromones. Or desperation. Then she decided to ignore all of it and him and hoped any potential fantasies died from lack of cultivation. She had enough problems. She didn't need gorgeous. Or intense. Or broad shouldered. It was time to give older, stable, and established a try. A gentleman by choice. One who looked like Gregory Peck and owned a suit. Someone respectable. She did a quick scan of Seth's back view. Not a guy who looked like summertime at the beach. Were those leather bracelets? With beads?

And what? She was doing inventory now?

So…he was hot. Her life was a mess. She didn't need it to become a hot mess. On that thought she bolted. She changed into her favorite pair of jeans, a designer blouse, was there any other kind, and swapped her stilettos for a pair of low heeled, but still fabulous, boots. Then she concentrated on putting her boutique and herself back together. She and Grace filled trash bins with broken lumber and shattered glass, repeating the trek to the back alley Dumpster over and over.

As promised, Seth measured, hung plastic, and returned by early afternoon. He spent the rest of the day doing whatever it was he was doing to the music of power tools and the worst of grunge rock. Both were loud, but only the latter was annoying. By midafternoon

Kate changed her mind and had Seth set up a temporary counter. At five o'clock, she pushed an exhausted Grace out the door.

Grace caught her eying the boiling thunderheads. She put a hand on Kate's arm. "I can stay."

Kate gave her a reassuring hug. "I'll be fine. I'm going to plug in some headphones and concentrate on paperwork. Try to find a way to replace the lost inventory. But thanks."

"It's weird about the missing stock, don't you think?"

Kate shivered. "This whole thing is insane. Can you even remember the last time something like this happened in Aspen Lake?"

Grace winked. "At least, you've got the hunky carpenter for company."

"Right." She rolled her eyes. "I don't think catering to my neurosis is part of the job description. You should get home before it starts to pour."

"You could ditch the fair committee meeting tonight, come home with me. We'll have a girls' night."

"I'll be fine." Cold air rolled in the open door and she pointed Grace out the door. "Rain check on the pajama party?"

Grace's umbrella snapped open. "Okay, see you tomorrow."

When her bright red umbrella turned the corner, Kate shut the door.

"If all your doors are as old as the one out back, I'm thinking we should replace them too." Seth strolled in from the back of the boutique. He'd tied a faded bandanna around his head to hold back his hair. Add in the tool belt, the scent of cut wood, and her womb contracted.

She swallowed. "Probably a good idea."

He pulled off work gloves that had seen one too many jobs. "I can take a look if you'd like?"

"Um...sure." The first slow rumble of thunder shook the sky, and Kate couldn't help it. She looked to the big window at the front of the shop. She waited. Flinched at the fleeting flash of lightning. She started to count and got to three Mississippis. Deep breath in, hold for three seconds, deep breath out as she fought off the panic.

"You okay?" His words sounded a long way off.

"I'm fine." *Get it together, Kate.* She looked away from the window and unclenched her fists, swiped sweaty palms over the back of her jeans. "We can take a look—"

Flash. Ground lightning, like that day three years ago. She froze, then remembered to count. She put a calming hand to her forehead. Two Missis—

Boom.

"Kate? You okay?"

She shut her eyes tight and prayed. But the sensation of entering the swerve in her car came anyway. She was out of control, and there was no getting it back. She gave up breathing altogether.

"Kate." Callused hands framed her face. Seth's voice registered, she tried to concentrate. It didn't work. "Look at me."

She couldn't pry her eyes open. A sharp crack of thunder rattled the windows. She grabbed for his wrists and hung on.

Inhale. Hold. Exhale.

"Okay. That's good. Breathe." His hold tightened.

"Because here comes another one."

He didn't let go. More, he gathered her in. Her cheek rubbed against worn cotton. Strong arms wrapped around her. She huddled into him. Counting down, she soaked up his warmth. Three seconds later, when the crack came, it was less intense. She pried her eyes open and met soft amber eyes narrowed in concern. Then it happened again. Louder.

"I've got you."

Flash.

Her arms banded around his waist. Her fingers knotted into his shirt.

Boom.

"No. No, no, no." Not again.

"Breathe." His order didn't stop her muscles from tightening or her brain from seizing.

The window rattled. Light flashed, and a hushed moan escaped against her will.

He smoothed a hand over her hair and whispered words that didn't register. All she heard was the crack of thunder.

She let go of him to cover her ears. Squeezed her eyes shut tight against the impending flash. More thunder. More stroking of her hair as he cocooned around her. When the bursts of light and the roll of sound faded, she realized her arms were not only holding onto him they were pushed up under his shirt pressed against his skin.

She pushed her sanity to the edge by smoothing out the tortured fabric covering his back and shoulders. Then she broke away. "I'm sorry."

"Don't be." Rough hands caressed her neck, his thumbs were at her jawline coaxing her to look up at him. She didn't want to meet his searching eyes. He didn't let that stop him. "Happens to the best of us."

"I doubt that." She brought her hands between them, settled them against his chest, and she gave a gentle push, stepping back. "But thanks."

His hands slipped from her neck to hook into the front pockets of his cargos. He'd ditched his tool belt. It was on the floor by his feet along with his work gloves.

She spared a second to assess her mental state. Not great, but not bad either. She blew out a discreet breath, tried to let go of the fear still clinging to her insides. So weak. So…embarrassing.

"Sorry about that. I promise I'm not a neurotic mess as a rule." Such a lie. But he didn't need to know that.

"No need to explain." He shot a thumb over his shoulder, his grin long gone. His lips were a stiff line, along with his posture. Everything about him screamed escape. "I should get back to work. Couple of things to finish up, then I'll be back in a couple of days."

Head bobbing, she waved him off with a bit too much enthusiasm. "Great. I'll see you then."

With a reluctant nod, he did one more scan for cracks. She hoped she didn't look as shattered as she felt. "Are you going to be okay here by yourself?"

"Yes, of course. I have a meeting to get ready for, so…" Awkward. So very, very awkward.

The door flung open and the last man on earth she wanted to see charged into her boutique. Water spilled off his black Stetson and mucked up her floor.

Well, crap. Clearly, bad things did happen in threes. "Tyler, what are you doing here?"

Tyler Bodnar stopped short at the sight of Seth. His

eyes narrowed, taking in the otherwise empty room. Nothing subtle about Tyler. Her ex-high school sweetheart glared at Seth.

****

That morning Seth Stone had been convinced things were looking up. His decision to move to a small town solid. New job within a week. Studio set up. He'd even gotten a new commission for a customized carved beam from a northern hunting lodge doing a major renovation. Eight hours later? Not so much.

"Tyler." Her attitude matched her harsh clothes. So many buttons locking up her wrists and neck and marching down the front of her fancy shirt. Even her pockets had buttons. No one was penetrating that fortress. "What are you doing here?"

"What do you mean, what am I doing here? There's a storm outside. You hate storms." Tyler hooked his thumbs behind his enormous belt buckle.

The ice princess cocked a hip, and it was a face-off.

Wonderful.

This was exactly the kind of stuff Seth had moved out to the middle of nowhere to avoid. Females. Drama. And the resulting volcanic eruption. He'd helped her through the whole storm thing. Done his good deed. His random act of kindness. He was done. Time to clock out. Except…

"With the storm and everything, I figured you could use some company." Tyler glanced around, zeroed in on the ugly short-term display case and winced. "Or, you know, a little help putting things back together."

"Actually, Seth's helping with all that. But thanks

anyway." A low roll of thunder sounded in the background. She crossed her arms, lifted her chin a notch.

Seth knew it had more to do with the storm than offering up a challenge. Tyler didn't seem to clue into the fact even though he was here because of the storm. Seth extended a reluctant hand and an insincere smile. "Seth Stone."

"Tyler Bodnar." After a not-so-friendly shake, he let go.

"Good to meet you." Observing the need for social niceties didn't usually set his teeth on edge. But the negative energy rolling off the guy was eating away at his depleted supply of good humour. Still, he made an attempt at conciliatory. "I work at the lumberyard. Kate's dad sent me over."

"Helping out how?" demanded Bodnar, turning to Kate.

Her artic freeze plunged to a polar vortex. "I hired him."

"You hired him?" repeated Tyler, with a little too much stunned emphasis on the "him," like he wasn't standing right there.

No way was he leaving Kate here with this asshole.

"It's none of your business, but yes." Pretty soon they were all going to be battling frostbite.

Bodnar scowled. Seth figured lifelong exposure must have rendered him immune to hypothermia. Not put off, Bodnar grabbed hold of Kate's arm. "Can I talk to you for a minute? Alone."

Was this guy for real?

Kate yanked her arm free before Seth could get a demand in. "There's no need."

Tyler shifted closer. "Kate."

The way he said her name grated on Seth's very last nerve. He didn't need this crap. Or want anything to do with it. But this guy was crossing way over the line. He stepped forward, hands clenching. His personal rules against using physical force to handle disputes did not stretch far enough to include assholes who manhandled women.

"You need to step back," suggested Seth. Way, way back.

The ice princess shot him a wintry glare. Like he was the problem. She pointed a finger. "Stay out of this."

Bodnar concurred, "Yeah, Stone, butt out."

Was this guy five years old? What was next? Sticking out his tongue? A temper tantrum?

"Tyler." With a warning glare at Seth, she switched her attention back to the cowboy. "I'm fine. You don't need to worry about me. It's under control, and I'm sure you have things to do."

"Are you kidding me?" Kate's eyes narrowed, but Bodnar was oblivious. "Your dad can't mean for you to *hire* this guy?"

Again, he was standing two feet away.

"Who I hire is none of his business. And it's definitely not yours." Done with subtle she marched to the door. She opened it to the pouring rain. "Thanks for stopping by."

"Kate, the last thing you need to do right now is make another poor decision." Warning offered, Bodnar stuffed his hat back on his head. "I'll be in touch."

Of course, he would. He seemed like that kind of guy.

"I'm sorry about that." Kate avoided looking at him, concentrated instead on shutting and locking the door.

"Don't worry about it." He was tempted to melt a little of the chill off her. Wondered what happened when she warmed up. He wanted to see some of the worry leave her eyes. Wanted to know what would happen when she smiled. He offered up one of his own, one calculated to charm. "I'll do a mock-up of what I have in mind for your display case. You won't be disappointed. I'm very good at what I do."

"How reassuring." No smile, and he figured the raised brow was a warning.

He wanted to smooth a thumb over it. Bad sign. Besides, she was his boss. Worse, she was his other boss's daughter. He needed to leave and not look back. Knew it right down to the soles of his feet. But he was full of ideas for her new display case, and it was going to kick ass. He would keep things professional. *Be* a professional. "I'll see what I can put together."

"About earlier…the storm. It threw me a little off kilter." She lifted her chin and looked him straight in the eye, daring him to contradict her.

A little off kilter? Yeah, right. But who was he to argue with the boss? "About the other doors? You want to leave that for another day?"

She nodded, relief easing some of her stiffness. "That would be great."

"You going to be okay here on your own?" Because he was honor bound to ask, even knowing her answer.

"Absolutely." He wasn't sure he believed her, but her eyes were clear, no sign of another panic attack beating at the back of them. The rain bashed at the large display window, but the worst of the storm was moving off with only the odd rumble and faint flash.

"All right." He dug her shiny new set of keys out of his pocket. "The back door is done. I need to check in with my other boss. Eight o'clock Thursday morning work for you?"

"Eight is fine." Keys in hand she walked him through to the back of the shop, waited while he shuttled his gear out to his truck. She lifted a hand. "Thank you."

"Thursday." He lifted one in return and hopped into his truck to escape the rain.

Soaked to the skin he steered his truck in the direction of his grandparents' cabin. Hard to think of it as home, but he was trying. On the outskirts of town, it was secluded without being isolated. It gave him room to be creative. To think. To be. It was a connection to his past, his dad, his real family, as he worked to cut the cord on a different set of family ties.

Through the slashing of the windshield wipers, he navigated the wet gravel road. His head was full of preliminary sketches for Kate's display case, the newly commissioned beam. A burl of wood sat next to him on the bench seat. He'd rescued it from a co-worker's stump pile. It was a rare find, large enough for two gallery-worthy pieces. Brain working overtime to the pounding rain and the wipers working to keep up, he checked his rear view mirror.

Jesus. Really?

Through the rivers of rain, he got a look at the driver of the truck tailing him. His black cowboy hat pulled low, Tyler Bodnar sat on his bumper's ass. His fingers tightened around the wheel. Okay, so the guy was officially crazy. Good to know. At least, he wasn't hanging around Kate's. She'd had enough. And why was he even going there?

Feeling protective was not conducive to keeping their relationship professional. No reason at all to think she couldn't take care of herself. Other than thunderstorms. He'd never view one quite the same way again. No more wonder and awe at nature's might. Till he died he'd see Kate, terrified and clinging to him. Smell her too. Spice and terror.

He turned off the main road onto his driveway, and Bodnar kept driving. Brooding didn't change the facts. He was better off out here. In the quiet. With his art for company and the woods for inspiration.

****

After a couple of hours of trying to sketch out his ideas and failing, Seth changed his mind. Familiar enough with his process to know he needed a break, some food, and, yes, people. The hum of voices welcomed him the second he opened the door to the Back Forty. The welcome smell of beer and fried food had his stomach growling in anticipation of the biggest roadhouse burger on the menu.

Neon signs buzzed, dartboards waited, and two big-screen televisions played Monday night football. A couple of women were showing off their skills at the pool table. He wouldn't have minded a game. Instead, he chose an empty stool at the long log bar and offered a nod to the old guy next to him.

"Hey, there. What can I get you?" His favorite kind of bartender, pretty and smiling. She leaned in and flashed some very appealing dimples.

Seth grinned back. "A bottle of Bud would be great. Also a cheeseburger with the works?"

"You want fries?"

"What's a burger without fries?"

She gave him a wink. "Coming right up."

He swiveled in his seat to scan the sparse crowd. To his surprise, he saw a familiar face. A stunning one. She was surrounded by a mix of people. All of them were talking at once. Kate rubbed a hand across her forehead before holding up a hand. She looked tired. And tense. Good thing she wasn't any of his business. No need to run through ways to loosen her up. No need, at all. He turned back around.

"Here's your beer. The food will be out in a little while."

"Thanks."

Her dimples made another appearance. "You're the new guy."

"Excuse me?" He paused, bottle halfway to his lips.

"At the lumberyard." Very, very pretty. She grinned some more. "News travels."

He didn't know what to do with that so he nodded. "I thought it was time I checked the place out."

She snagged her bottom lip. "Glad you stopped by."

He tilted the bottle in her direction. "I'm Seth."

"Hey, Seth." Her voice dipped to flirty. "I'm Brittany, but my friends call me Britt."

The older gent seated next to him lifted his empty glass. "Hey, Brittany-you-can-call-me-Britt, you think I could get another drink sometime this decade?"

"Coming right up, Stan." She rolled her eyes at

Seth before grabbing a bottle, blonde ponytail swinging behind her. His kind of uncomplicated in faded, filled out jeans, a tight t-shirt with the words Keep Calm I'm Sexy printed in rhinestones across her impressive chest. She glanced back over her shoulder. "I'll just check on your order. Be right back."

Add in a very nice ass.

"You always get that kind of reaction from the opposite sex?"

At the sound of her dry-as-the-desert voice, any buzz he'd acquired fizzled. He turned toward his long legged boss. She ran a hand over her tucked back hair. There was nothing of the day's earlier upset in her eyes. Not that she was relaxed. She couldn't be in the curve hugging, knee length, black skirt or the same white, buttoned up shirt she'd worn earlier. Don't touch me all the way down to the fuck me shoes.

He shifted on his seat. "Not always, no."

But often enough that it made sex easy.

Her smirk suggested she was also a mind reader. "Out for a night on the town?"

"Just a beer and burger. You?"

"Wrapping up a meeting." She gestured toward her group. "The Gothic Revival Fair committee."

He stifled a laugh. "Seriously?"

"Very serious. It's an annual thing." She rested a hand on the bar and smoothed another over her hip.

Britt sauntered back into view, dimples gone. She plunked down a little wire basket containing cutlery, napkins, ketchup, mustard, salt and pepper. "Another round, Kate?"

"Thanks, Britt." Kate spared her a glance then pointed to a poster tacked to the wall. "The fair's the last weekend of October. This year it's an Edgar Allen Poe theme. The whole town goes all out with street vendors, readings of the tarot and palm variety, as well as literary ones."

"'Once upon a midnight dreary, while I pondered weak and weary...'"

"Impressive. You know your Poe." Kate squirmed closer as a guy squeezed in to give Britt his order.

"The first couple of lines, anyway. I can't say as anyone's found that impressive before." Seth worked at not inhaling her scent, but it wafted out to surround him. Everything hot and sultry, like bazaars, spices, and colorful scarves. Desert heat in September on the Canadian Prairies. Sweat dampened the back of his neck, the palms of his hands. The unexpected reaction had him grabbing for his beer.

"Well." She gave the bar a pat and straightened up. "See you Thursday."

She headed back to her table. Hips swaying, curves covered but impossible to hide, and calves accentuated by the killer heels. Her father, his boss, would smite him down for noticing. He hadn't needed to hear Bill Logan's "I'm trusting you, boy," on his way out the door to know it.

So, it was a good thing she wasn't his type.

"You've met our local celebrity." Britt set his meal down in front of him.

Food, exactly what he needed. He grabbed for the ketchup bottle and lifted the bun off his burger. "Celebrity?"

Britt didn't try to disguise her glee at Seth's ignorance. She rested her arms on the bar and leaned in, kept her voice low. "Kate Logan. Used to be a big deal model until the accident. Driving too fast on bad roads in worse weather. She wrapped her car around a lamppost. Rumor was she'd been drinking, but nothing ever came of it so I guess rumor was exactly what it was."

"Britt, don't you have better things to do besides gossip." The man beside him shifted on his seat.

"Oh hush, Stan. It's not like it's a secret." She eased in closer. "Anyways, didn't seem to matter to her husband, who left her. Or her agent, who dumped her. She went off the rails for a while, did a couple of stints in rehab, and now she's back in town. Owns Kate's Closet on Main Street."

Seth shrugged and stuffed a French fry into his mouth. So, the ice princess had a past. Didn't everyone? Not wanting to encourage her, he concentrated on his burger.

"God's honest truth." She grinned, and either she didn't care or couldn't take a hint.

To save himself from a reply, he indulged in another mouthful of burger. He offered a thumbs up and kept chewing hoping she'd leave him alone to eat in peace. Luckily, there was a hail from down the bar, and Britt left to fill orders. Seth stuck another fry in his mouth.

He knew enough not to believe every word he heard someone speak. Still…interesting. Didn't hurt to know who you were working for. Plus, it explained a couple of things. He swiveled on his stool to steal another look at his sexy boss. She caught his look, and he swore the corners of her mouth lifted. Then the door opened, and Tyler Bodnar strode in with a couple of other guys. It didn't take Bodnar long to pick Seth out of the crowd. He was a little slower spotting Kate, but when he did he frowned and flashed a look back at Seth. Clearly less than impressed at finding them both in the same place.

Seth could relate. He wasn't thrilled to see Bodnar anywhere near Kate. Bodnar pointed to a table in the corner, and he and his friends headed in that direction. Seth's appetite died, but he refused to let the rest of his burger go to waste. Then he picked up his beer and didn't even try to stem the urge to swivel on his stool and watch the room. Was Tyler here because he knew Kate would be? He chanced a look at Kate, who was oblivious. She was busy with the other members at her table, gesturing in a circle, eyes on the paper in front of her.

The table full of guys placed their order. Then with his eyes on Seth, Tyler threaded his way through the half-empty tables and came to stand behind Kate. He put a hand on the back of her chair. He leaned in, his mouth by her ear. She jerked in surprise, placed a hand on her heart, and fought for a few inches of space. Undeterred Tyler put his other hand down cutting her off from the rest of the table.

Seth shifted in his chair. A heavy hand landed on his shoulder warning him to stay in place. "She wouldn't appreciate a scene."

Seth stayed where he was watching her tight smile, taking in her tense shoulders, her hands smoothing out the papers in front of her. He didn't read lips so he had no idea what she said to him. Tyler's hand moved from the table to her shoulder, and with his eyes back on Seth he kissed the top of her head.

Seth tracked his path until Bodnar was back at his

table. He leaned in and grinned at his two companions. They shared a laugh and looked in Seth's direction. The man next to Tyler slapped him on the back. Seth shook his head, the edge of his teeth rough under his tongue. He raised his beer and finished it off.

Again. None of his business.

More loud laughter sounded from the back of the room. Fuck that shit. When the old guy next to him left to use the head, he signaled to Britt for another beer. Maybe some more information wouldn't be a bad thing. When she set his beer down in front of him, he asked, "What's the story on the guy at the back with the black hat?"

"Tyler?" She shrugged, then frowned in concentration. "Rode the circuit for a while, now he runs the family ranch."

"Not ringing any bells." Seth refused to feel guilty for prying. "Maybe I know his girlfriend?"

Britt snorted. "He doesn't have a girlfriend. Not that he lacks for offers. But he's too busy pining away for Kate."

"Really?" He rested his elbows on the bar and leaned in inviting confidences.

"It's not a secret. Thing is, lots of nights he doesn't pine alone, which would be part of the reason she doesn't take him seriously." She shook her head in disgust, and once again lines creased her forehead. "If you ask me, he gets a little too into the act. Know what I mean?"

Yeah, he did.

"But it's not just Tyler. She shuts them all down the minute they get any bright ideas about parking their boots under her bed. For Tyler, that challenge is the equivalent of flapping a red flag at an ornery bull."

"Sounds like he's got a problem understanding the word no?"

"If I thought such a thing, which I don't, I wouldn't be spreading that fact around. I've got better survival instincts than that." Head down she started pushing her rag around on the counter she'd just finished wiping down. "He's got a lot of friends around here who wouldn't take kindly to those type of things being said."

Britt and her wipe cloth moved down the bar. His neighbor was back on his stool. A few more locals wondered in, and it didn't take Seth long to figure out there was a kind of hierarchy to the place. They either stopped in with Bodnar or the old guy to his right, sometimes both.

Turning sideways he held out his hand. "Should have introduced myself earlier, Seth Stone."

"I know who you are." The old guy sized him up before taking his hand. "Stan Knight."

"Can I buy you drink?" offered Seth.

"At my limit." He held up an almost empty glass. "Any more, Britt will blab, and Ruth will find a way to bust my balls for it."

"Rain check then."

Stan turned away to stare straight ahead, and Seth figured that was it. He'd been shut down. Then Stan said, "Knew your dad. Back in the day."

"Yeah?" If he lived to be a hundred, he'd never get tired of hearing stories about his dad.

He gave Seth a sideways glance. "Good man."

Seth nodded in agreement. "He was."

"Your grandparents are good folks too."

"The best." The cool taste of beer eased the

tightening of his throat. "I'm living at their place."

"Way I hear it, it yours now." It wasn't accusatory, but it wasn't friendly either.

Seth decided honesty was the way to go with Stan Knight. "I think they knew I needed a place of my own, so they made it happen."

"Know that too."

"Come again?" Seth twisted to look at him. Stan picked up his glass, sipped, set it back down.

"I know all about you." He turned to face Seth. "We live down the road from you. Next place over. Your grandad and I are old friends."

Seth smiled. Kind of. "Well, always nice to meet the neighbors."

"Ain't it just. Hear you're working for Bill Logan?"

"Yep."

"Another good man."

Seth decided on a little conversational scouting. "Taking a little detour to help out his daughter."

"So, that's what that little pissing display was all about."

"Was it?"

"Word of advice, Seth." He downed the rest of whatever was in his glass, plunked it down. "Leave Kate be."

Why was it the more someone told him to leave her alone the more he wanted to do the opposite? "I've got no plans beyond fixing a couple of doors."

Stan stood and slapped a light hand down on his shoulder. "Nice meeting you. Ruth's been on me about seeing your studio. Fancies herself a bit of an amateur collector."

Proof he did know things. "Anytime she wants to come by she's welcome."

That earned him a hint of a smile and a tilt of Stan's chin. "I'll let her know. Night."

Seth returned the chin lift. "No problem. See you around."

Then he decided it was time to head home. The bar was starting to feel a tad overcrowded, and he needed his studio. He had some thinking to do. He tossed some bills on the bar, enough for a generous tip, and stood up as Kate did the same. He paced out his leaving to meet her at the door. For no good reason he decided on a little pissing of his own.

"Calling it a night?" he asked, as he held the door open.

She tucked a portfolio under her arm. "Yes, meeting's over. Time for some beauty sleep."

Like she needed it. "After you."

"Thanks." She slipped past him to stand under the bright lights of the covered entrance.

The rain had stopped, and the air was damp and dark. A smear of cloud fogged out the moon, but nothing menacing. He could even make out a few stars. She'd be okay tonight, free from storms.

She stepped out into the night. "How about you? On your way home?"

His breath puffed out in the chill air. "Busy day tomorrow."

She stopped and put a hand on his forearm. "I really do appreciate you helping me out."

"No problem." Without thinking he linked his fingers through hers. "See you Thursday. Bright and early. I wouldn't want to disappoint the boss. I hear she's a stickler for punctuality."

"Really. What else did you hear?" She tugged her fingers free and rubbed her arms.

He pretended to consider it. He wanted to see her smile. A real one this time. "That she's as dedicated and hard working as she is beautiful."

It didn't work. Unimpressed, she began her walk across the parking lot. "That's what you're going with?"

He beat her to opening her car door, a four-door silver Audi. His whistled low. "Nice ride."

"Goodnight, Seth." She gave him a stern look, keys in hand she slipped into the driver seat. "Eight o'clock, sharp."

"I'll be there." He rested one arm along the roof of her car, the other along the top of the open door. He leaned in. His voice dipped, carrying more suggestion then he intended or wanted. "Wouldn't want to disappoint the boss."

She tugged her door shut in response. He waited while she backed up and drove out of the lot. Stan Knight was right, he needed to leave her be.

After all, she could fire his ass and no doubt influence her father to do the same. Seth couldn't afford to be out of work. After his last and final cash infusion to his stepmother, he was broke. He had bills to pay, supplies to buy, a fridge to fill. Here's hoping the couple of pieces he had out on commission sold soon. He had one other piece of sculpture almost finished, a savage, winged raven struggling to escape a barbed wire trap, that still needed…something extra. Blinded by a sudden solution Seth didn't notice Tyler Bodnar lounging against the side of his truck until he was almost on him.

The guy was like a bad stain on an ugly shirt, all he did was make things worse. Seth sighed. "Something I can help you with, Bodnar?"

"Just here to offer a little piece of advice, seeing as you're new in town." Tyler tipped his hat back and pushed away from his resting spot against Seth's truck. "Stay away from Kate Logan. She's off limits."

Like Seth gave a shit. "That might be a challenge since I work for her. Plus, I'm guessing Kate's capable of setting her own limits."

Asshole.

"It'd be wise to quit, you know, while you're ahead." The crunch of boots on gravel sounded behind Seth, and he shot a look back to see two men behind him.

He refused to let the odds intimidate him. "How about we let Kate decide who she wants to hire or fire."

Stepping forward, Tyler let lose a harsh laugh. "Here's the thing, Kate's been through an awful lot in the last little while. She doesn't need any more problems."

"And you're assuming I'm going to be a problem based on what?"

"Based on the fact that I don't like you, Stone." He leaned in to whisper, "Around here that's a bad thing."

"And I'm not in the mood for your kind of crazy tonight. So, if you'll excuse me…" He went to push past Tyler but got shoved back into the two men behind him. They each grabbed an arm. Struggling did no good; he was pinned in place.

"That's not the answer I was looking for. Let's try this again." Tyler smiled. Seth knew what was coming and tried to brace for it.

"Stay away from her." The punch caught him square in the gut. He sucked in air as he doubled over as far as he could go with his arms pinned behind his back. Forced back and upright he stared down Tyler Bodnar. It earned him a second blow to the stomach.

"It's good advice. Make sure you take it. Or we're all going to find ourselves right back here. And we don't want that? Do we?"

He managed to wheeze out a breathy, "Fuck you."

A fist to his eye had him seeing stars. The solid right hook to his jaw hurt like hell. The taste of copper filled his mouth. He turned his head to spit out the accumulating blood and spit. The men holding his arms let go, pushed him away. Seth had no choice. He hit the ground, his knees buckling.

Tyler grabbed a fist full of his shirt and yanked. "Don't make me tell you twice."

Seth spit out a laugh along with more blood. "Should warn you…my hearing's not that great."

Tyler let go after a savage twist. The kick caught him in the ribs. "You are one stupid shit, you know that? Get smart quick, or we'll talk again."

Biting back the bile working its way up the back of his throat, he glared after Bodnar and his honky-tonk band of assholes. Heard their laughter. Their back slapping congratulations. Shifting so he was sitting propped up against the side of his truck, he ran his tongue along the inside of his split cheek. Using the solid surface as leverage, he managed to slide his way up to standing.

His stomach rolled. Egged on by pain and adrenaline, the heated urge to retaliate sank its claws in deep. He swiped a hand across his mouth. It came away bloody. He clenched his fist, focused on breathing through the pain.

His father's favorite mantra floated through his brain: *Hate cannot drive out hate: only love can do that.* How many times had he heard that one as a kid? Many. He'd been small, wiry, tough. The impact of his father's words hadn't sunk in until he was thirteen years old. After he'd pushed Billy "The Kong" Donnelly into the dirt, and worse, for calling him out at home plate when he'd clearly been safe. All because Seth kissed Sophie Calidori first.

Somehow, his father had found out about the beating. Seeing his disappointment, sensing his despair of ever getting through, worst of all watching him walk away, hadn't been worth the satisfaction of besting The Kong in front of all their friends. It marked the last time he'd resorted to violence to prove a point. Therefore, he'd learned early on karma was indeed a bitch. It hadn't taken The Kong long to take advantage. There were others who'd used his newfound reluctance to deliver retaliatory beat downs. He'd survived. He'd also learned black eyes and bloody noses healed a lot faster than the humiliation of being bested.

But making his father proud had been worth it. It still was. He wrenched open his truck door and hoisted his ass inside. This time would be no different. He grabbed the sun visor and yanked it down. Took stock of his face, reached for a discarded hoodie to clean up the blood. He needed to get home, to his studio. To his art. To things that made sense.

At the end of the day, he needed to see a man who kept his promises. Kept them again the next day. And the day after that. No matter the personal cost. He did not want to see a man who caved in another man's face because he wasn't strong enough to deal with him in a smarter way.

He would exorcise the part of him sniffing for blood. The need to feel his fist on flesh. Ignore the mind numbing, crazy high of inflicting pain on a fellow human being. It was about taking control. Not giving it up. He dug his keys out of his pocket. He hadn't escaped crazy to end up drowning in it again.

Chapter Two

Kate did a shocked double take when Seth stepped through the door to Kate's Closet at quarter to eight Thursday morning. The early morning light highlighted his split lip, the ugly bruising, his tight, closed off features. She put a hand to the base of her throat. Then she made sure the rest of him was in one piece. "Oh my God, what happened?"

He pushed past her, his usual loose gait a bit stiffer this morning. "Nothing."

"It doesn't look like—" He didn't slow down. She planted her feet, cocked her hip, and called, "Hey."

His body went solid, and then he pivoted to face her, all male attitude, his spread hands asking his question for him.

"You know *what*." She didn't think, she went to him, didn't even try to resist the urge to touch gentle fingers to his face. "Last time I saw you, you looked a little less battered."

"Ouch." He tilted his head to the side to escape her fingers. "Careful."

"Sorry." She settled her hands on her hips, in an effort to stop embarrassing herself and him. He was glaring at her like a caged zoo cat. Besides, physical contact was the last thing she needed. He'd invaded her dreams last night. Plenty of skin, skimming fingers, and tangled sheets. This morning she vowed to keep their contact to a minimum. That didn't mean she didn't want to know what the hell was going on. "You want to tell me what this is all about?"

He looked her straight in the face. "Nope."

She narrowed her eyes. "Can you at least reassure me this kind of thing doesn't happen often?"

The cat in him went still. The dark in the back of his eyes shifted.

"Nothing to say?"

He tapped his watch. "I gotta get to work."

She wasn't stupid, contrary to popular opinion. She was familiar with the idea of probabilities. "And if I were to go find Tyler and ask him?"

Seth pursed his lips, gave a slight nod of his head. "You do that. Tell him I said hey."

"Uh huh."

He cocked his head. "Anything else?"

She put a hand on his arm to stop him from leaving. "If I find out Tyler is responsible for that split lip and those bruises because he's got some mistaken idea in his head that you and I are more than…working together, I won't be happy."

"It's done." His jaw locked, but his tawny eyes softened. "Leave it alone."

Something clutched in her belly. "You want me to put anything on that lip?"

The answer hit them both at the same time. Her lips parted. His pupils dilated. They both backed up a step.

"I'm fine. Don't worry about me."

It wasn't worry that consumed her. Or robbed her of the ability to think rationally. But she could take a hint. She'd leave him be, then maybe she'd settle down into her average, everyday confused state.

She gave it her best effort for the entire morning. And was supremely annoyed her best wasn't good enough. If he was close, her eyes wandered in his direction. When he was out of sight, she was conscious of the sounds coming from the back room even though she refused to step foot back there. Her armpits damp, her mind distracted, she had no idea what it was about him? She didn't go for younger men. Or carpenters. That sounded snooty. It wasn't. Her dad owned a lumberyard, worked hard, earned the respect people gave him. She just always pictured her perfect man wearing a suit and tie. What was Seth wearing today? She stole a peek, like that was necessary. A Nirvana t-shirt. It looked as old as she felt.

Seth was measuring her front door jamb, squatting, flexing, and stretching. It was driving her mad. She couldn't remember the last time a man made her panties damp. Sexual desire had drowned a boozy death. Her next drink more important than anything else, especially sex. Ask her ex-husband. He'd told anyone who would listen. Or pay for an interview.

Seth jimmied the old door off its hinges. She was keeping her vintage-style door, which was actually pretty solid considering its age, but it needed to be rehung and a new deadbolt system put in. It all required repairs and fill-ins and other stuff that made her eyes glaze over.

She'd rather think about his hair. Or his face. Or his tattoos. She recognized Northwest coastal art when she saw it, with its thick lines and geometric shapes of black and red escaping out his sleeve all the way down to his wrist. She tilted her head to get a better look at his ass. Did women swoon anymore?

And how shallow was she? Had she learned nothing? Valuing appearance over everything else led to heartache. Or worse, rehab.

"He's good for business." Grace came to stand beside her. Contemplative, a little sad, she was Aspen Lake's modern day gothic beauty. "Did he tell you what happened?"

Her boutique was full. Women browsed, chatted, and did their best to catch a glimpse of the new guy in town. Half the female population had passed through the doors of Kate's Closet before lunch. So far she'd crushed the urge to snap her fingers in front of more than one ogling face. Maddie James had slipped him her phone number. She made a mental note to scratch her name from the guest list to Kate's Closet annual pre-Christmas Crush party.

"No, he did not." Kate glanced at her assistant. "You think he's noticed?"

Grace shrugged. "Hard to say."

"If he does, he's not letting on." Nor was he letting the attention distract him. He was polite, made the appropriate responses, laughed when required. But Kate sensed he was holding back. Not aloof. Careful.

"He's too preoccupied keeping track of you." Grace winked at her.

"Do you have this in a size eight?" asked Mrs. Carlisle, holding up a cashmere sweater. "It's Misty's birthday, and I'm thinking this would be just the thing."

"Oh, that would be perfect on her. Hang on, I'll check. If not in this color, maybe a dark gray?" suggested Kate.

"I'll go." Grace headed in the direction of the clothing racks suspended from the ceiling by steel cables, Mrs. Carlisle trailing after her.

She frowned after them. Out of the corner of her eye, she caught Seth's stretch. His t-shirt lifted just enough to let everyone know he was a Joe Boxer kind of guy. A hush settled over the crowd of women. Kate rolled her eyes.

Grace was wrong. What would he see in her? A washed-up model with a failed marriage behind her and too much emotional baggage to be considered stable. If he was noticing, he wouldn't stay interested for long.

The sound of her father's voice shook her loose and got her moving in Seth's direction ready to do damage control.

"Staying out of trouble, I hope." With his big, rough hand still resting on Seth's shoulder, Bill Logan examined Seth's work. His voice carried through the whole of her tiny boutique. "How are the repairs going?"

"Dad." She offered up her cheek for a kiss. As Seth's temporary boss, it was her job to spare him the public interrogation.

Seth shrugged, concentrating on the door. "They're going."

Like that answer was going to appease her father. Kate tugged her father out into the crisp September sunshine. Proving Seth had zero survival skills, he followed them out.

Kate offered a welcoming smile to a woman giving them curious glances. She maneuvered them one door down until they stood in the nowhere land next to Calamity Claims Insurance. "What are you doing here?"

Bill Logan ignored her. "You measuring twice,

cutting once?"

"I know what I'm doing." Seth yanked off his work gloves and stuffed them into his back pocket.

"Now, don't take offence." Satisfied, her dad gave Seth's shoulder another slap. "Just checking in to see how things are going."

Before she could open her mouth, Seth went over everything, kind of like he was reporting in when the person he reported to at the moment was her. But she wasn't about to explain it in the middle of Main Street. Instead, she changed the subject. "It's the last Thursday of the month. Shouldn't you be on your way to the town council meeting?"

Her father passed a hand over his brush cut. "Not leaving until those lunatics aren't on my girl's doorstep."

"What lunatics?" Spotting the group of people congregating on the other side of the street, she sighed. "Oh, those lunatics."

Wearing nineteenth century peasant gear, the women stood out in their ankle-length, long-sleeved dresses and pinned up hair. The men were equally noticeable in their thick, black pants, dark button-down shirts, and squarish dark hats. Members of the newly congregated Valley of the Shepherd Church huddled together clutching bundles of paper while hassling shoppers who crossed the street to avoid them.

She frowned. "What are they doing in town on a Thursday? They usually show up on Saturdays."

Her father snorted, waved his hand in dismissal. "They're protesting the fair. Claiming we're inviting Satan into our midst. That it'll bring the wrong sort of people into town. Etcetera and so on. We should go inside."

"Wait. What?" Kate raised a brow at the pointing, protesting finger pointed in her direction from across the street. "What wrong sort? The paying kind."

The owner of the finger broke away from the rest of the group and stepped into the street. Bill Logan put a protective hand on her arm. "It's not a joke, Katie. They're serious about shutting it down."

She stiffened. The rest of his followers moved in behind him like a migrating flock of Canada geese. Seth pressed against her side. Her father stepped in front of her. "Better you go inside. Let me talk to them."

Not likely. She pushed past him while the flock was forced to wait for a break in traffic. "I'm not going anywhere."

When she didn't hustle her butt out of there, he glared at her. "You're heading up the committee this year. Your information is on a lot of the promotional material. Your name's come up in their correspondence."

Typical. "So, why am I just hearing about this now?"

"For once, do as I say and get." Kate didn't budge and he puffed out his chest, his face set in rigid disapproval.

"That look didn't scare me when I was ten, it doesn't scare me now."

"Save me from stubborn females." Thwarted, he appealed to Seth. "Help me out here, son."

"Kate." Seth shifted his stance. "Unless you want a scene right here in front of your place?"

Too late.

"Good day, friends." Tall and gaunt, smile too

smug, eyes over bright, the gentleman known as the Shepherd held out his hand to her father. He made an encompassing sweep of Main Street. His smile beaming when passers-by hesitated. In pulpit mode, he announced, "I'm Matthew Parsons, Shepherd of the Valley Church."

Her dad's hand stayed plastered to his side. "Bill Logan, owner of Logan's Lumber." He nodded toward Seth and then Kate. "Seth Stone, and my daughter."

Parsons kept smiling, a pointer scenting his trail. He dropped his hand and zeroed in. "Miss Logan, if I could have a minute of your time?"

"Yes, of—"

Her father butted in. "She's busy. Best you move along. You can take your concerns up with the council."

Kate counted to ten.

Matthew Parsons preened. "Oh, we intend to, but we feel we need to meet with Miss Logan in person. She is, after all, spearheading the committee for this travesty of a fair."

Despite his age, her dad was still a formidable presence with a temper he kept under wraps until he needed to do otherwise. "Seth, why don't you take Kate inside."

Ten wasn't a high enough number, but she didn't have time to count to a bazillion. People were staring, clustered together straining to hear. Parsons' followers either closed in behind him or persisted in handing out flyers to anyone who walked by and would take them. One young boy was sticking them under the windshield wipers of parked cars.

Enough theatrics. "What is it you think I can help

with, Mr. Parsons?"

Seth lurked closer. Undeterred Parsons placed a piece of paper in her hand. She gave it a cursory scan not bothering to read past the headline: The Devil's Mark in Aspen Lake. She handed it back opting for cool disdain. "You obviously have strong feelings about our fair and a misguided concept of what happens and the reasons behind it. If you attend, you can see for yourself it's all harmless fun."

"Unleashing the devil isn't something we take lightly, Miss Logan."

Okaaay.

He pressed on. "Perhaps your personal experiences have numbed you to the devil's influences, and now you're a gateway for him."

"Wait just a minute." Her father blustered and stepped forward.

Seth growled low in his throat.

Matthew Parsons raised his voice. "We can help with that if you wish." Louder still, knowing he had the eyes of the gathering crowd. "Perform an expulsion."

"That's enough." Seth, looking like he put the grim in reaper, reminded the Shepherd of his presence. "Show's over. Time for you all to move along."

Thankfully, six feet two inches and one hundred and eighty plus pounds of menace proved too much for the Shepherd to overlook. He backed up into the street stopping traffic. He shot Kate a look and raised his arms to the honking of angry drivers. "I can see we've much work to do here. We won't rest until it is done."

Some of the shepherd's flock were slower to cross the street, lagging behind shoving flyers at people. A young girl separated from the rest. She knocked into

Kate, then sprinted off.

"You okay?" A strong arm wrapped around Kate's waist and, for no good reason, she wanted to lean into Seth. Take comfort, breathe in his warmth, and his calm. Hardly the self-sufficient image she wanted to project so she stepped back. The loss of contact made her knees wobble.

"Yes," she remembered to answer, almost forgetting the question. The girl stood across the street staring back at Kate, eyes huge, gnawing on her bottom lip. Kate frowned. The girl ducked away.

"Katie, you sure?" Her father's worried face obscured her view of the street.

"I'm fine." It came out harsher than intended. She was so tired of the cotton wool treatment. Of the people she loved searching for signs of distress, monitoring her moods, stepping in to make it all better. She deserved, had fought for and earned, a second chance to prove she could handle herself.

Seth's fingers were warm against her lower back. "Why don't we go inside? Catch our breath."

"I said I'm fine." There were whispers and pointed glances. She hated it. The attention. The wondering. The hasty conclusions. She channeled the strong, competent woman she knew was inside her.

"I'm not saying you aren't. But the sooner we're inside, the sooner everyone else will move on."

She stepped away from what she heard in his voice, saw in his eyes, felt at the small of her back.

"Katie, how about I take you to lunch." Her father looking, she could tell, to gather her up.

"No." She put a hand on his arm, stole a patient breath. "You have a meeting you need to attend. I promise, I'm fine." She planted a kiss on his cheek. "I'll talk to you later. Besides, I want to know exactly what was in those emails."

Bill Logan ran a hand over his hair. Stubborn denial etched into the lines of his face.

"I have a right to know," she insisted. Then she pointed a finger at Seth, steeled her voice, and gave in to the bitchiness of feeling three inches tall. "Don't you have work to do? So I can have a door to lock tonight?"

His two words of rebuttal said it all. "Yes, ma'am."

He marched off.

Fine, he was upset. She could work with upset, far easier than concerned.

Matthew Parsons was another matter. How did one dim the spotlight of an attention-seeking, religious zealot? It was times like this she remembered the taste of whiskey on her tongue, the slide of it down her throat, the warmth of it in her belly. Problems solved sip by sip by sip until oblivion wiped the memory of them away.

Desperate for a distraction, she made her way behind the makeshift display counter and dug around for her stash of breath mints. She popped four in her mouth. The taste of mint flooded her system making her eyes water. One look at her To Do List settled her down. Another customer wandered in. Seth went back to work without another word to her.

She'd make things right with him later.

Curious customers kept her busy the rest of the afternoon. She didn't forget about Matthew Parsons. Ideas came, most were dismissed. She recorded the better ones. Organization was her saviour. Seth said very little to her, preferring to go through Grace. Like they were still in high school. He'd also gone from stoic to giving out flirty replies or aiming that ridiculously sexy grin of his at more than one overjoyed shopper.

She wished it wasn't a pleasure to watch him run a hand over a piece of wood. And, of course, her newly minted dirty mind went there. What was wrong with her? Her ovaries were screaming like twelve-year-old girls at their first boy crush concert. Even if he was acting like she was the biggest bitch on planet earth.

Grace nudged her side. "Here's a radical idea, ask him out?"

"What? No." She rolled her eyes.

"Why not?"

"Um…in case you missed it, he's not speaking to me." And who could blame him? "Second, I'm his boss and there are rules about that kind of thing. And third, he's not my type."

"What type? You don't have a type. Take a prowl on the wild side. Indulge in a little extra-curricular activity. It'll be good for you. He'll be good for you."

"Like that wouldn't lead to a whole lot of trouble." Trouble she didn't know she could face sober. "And for your information it's called sexual harassment."

"Oh, please."

Kate ignored her scoff. "And I do so have a type."

"And what would that be? Imaginary? It's been almost two years since you've gotten any. Tyler doesn't count." Grace's face was a study in earnest delusion. "Here's a great guy, a hot guy, one who can't keep his eyes off you. I say go for it."

"You're a fine one to talk. When's the last time you had sex?"

"This way one of us would be getting some."

"You go get yourself some. I'll live vicariously through you."

"Right. I'll just thumb through the blank pages of my little black book. See who's available." Kate opened her mouth, and Grace held up a hand. "Do not say his name. Do. Not."

"Why not? He fits your good guy/hot guy criteria."

"It's just...it would never work. He's a cop."

"Yeah, so."

"It's a little hard to get past seeing a guy cuff your sister. He knows too much stuff." She shuddered. "Bad stuff. Anyways, we're talking about you. You're interested. He's interested. Do something about it."

"I've known him for less than a week. Besides, he might have been interested, but after my drill sergeant act that ship has sailed."

"So apologize. Make it right. Then crook your little finger and reel him in."

"How optimistic of you." Kate left the barest of spaces between her thumb and pointer finger. "Not to mention a little insulting."

"Like I'm wrong."

She sighed in defeat. If you couldn't admit the awful truth to your best friend you were lost. "I am interested."

So very interested.

"Okay then." Grace gave her a little push in Seth's direction. "Talk to him, start with an apology and work your way up to an invitation to dinner. Wait, you can't cook. Out to dinner."

"Very funny." Kate smiled, like the idea of a public date didn't terrify her. "One step at a time. First an apology."

Grace put a hand on her arm and squeezed. "Kate, this isn't AA."

"Grace, give me a break. I've known him for four days. I need to know a little more about him before I *reel him in*."

"Fair enough. But remember, this is the twenty-first century. If you're interested, walk up to him and ask."

"Yes, Dr. Phil. Now that we're done discussing my sex life, let's talk about yours."

Grace glanced down at her bare wrist. "Would you look at the time? Gotta go."

Kate called after her, "I know where you live."

Grace flashed a fake grin. "That's harassment. I hear there are rules against that kind of thing."

Kate stuck out her tongue, then turned back to her list. Nothing made Kate happier than checking items off. She added apology to the top of it and bided her time.

By late afternoon, and despite a still silent Seth, she was downright giddy. Phone calls made, paperwork done, and she'd sold the poppy red wrap dress, the most expensive in the shop. She and Grace high-fived each other as it walked out the door wrapped in tissue and stowed in a Kate's Closet bag.

"Oh, wait." Kate motioned Grace back and fished a pink message slip out of her pocket. "Here's that web address for that craft boutique in the city I promised you."

"Thanks." Grace held out her hand as another piece of paper tumbled out of Kate's pocket. Grace picked it up and exchanged it for the phone number. "I'm going to work on my website tonight and I need inspiration."

Kate unfolded the scrap of paper Grace had handed her. Her heart stuttered. Childish letters printed with a blood red permanent marker: HE'S A BAD MAN. BE CAREFUL. She turned it over to examine the back, saw nothing, and turned it back around.

"What is it?" Grace put a hand on her arm. She leaned it to get a look at it. "What's wrong?"

"I don't know. Probably nothing." Kate handed it over.

Grace scanned the paper. "Creepy."

"A girl bumped into me. Earlier, on the sidewalk." She gazed through her shop window to the street. She pictured the scene, tried to remember the face of the girl and failed. "One of the Shepherd's followers."

"Why would one of them slip you a note?" Grace's tone was sharp, suspicious.

Kate shook her head. "I don't know."

"A prank."

"What if she's in trouble?"

"That Shepherd of theirs is a lunatic. He could be behind this, wanting to start something. Stir things up." Grace rubbed her arms. "Maybe with everything else going on you should show it to the police?"

"Maybe. It's probably nothing." Except it didn't feel like nothing. She scanned the words again. "It's just...either way, whether she's warning me or he's using her to mess with me—she's in trouble."

Grace brushed her arm and whispered out of the side of her mouth, "Hot guy alert."

"What's going on?"

"Nothing." Kate folded the piece of paper and stuffed it back into her pocket. She wasn't going to ask him out on a date, but that didn't mean she didn't have

Karyn Good

things she needed to say to him. "Can I talk to you for a minute?"

"Sure." Even though it looked like it was the last thing he wanted.

"I'll just find something to do somewhere else." Grace flashed her a thumbs up and headed for the back of the shop.

When you screwed up, you admitted it. Or you were supposed to. She'd always had problems with the admitting it part. "About earlier? That thing with Matthew Parsons threw me off, and I took it out on you. I got pissy. I'm sorry."

Seth went on wiping his hands with a rag. No eye contact. No great smile. Blank. "That guy is not going to back off."

"I know." Was the note burning a hole in her pocket? Did she smell smoke? Or was that the blaze of sexual attraction turning to ash. "I appreciate the fact you wanted to help. I do. But I can handle him. I just…need to do it my way."

"Okay." He shrugged a flannel-covered shoulder and finally, *finally*, looked her in the eye. "We're good."

She had her doubts and gave another try at sounding contrite. Or, at least, human. "I didn't say it earlier and I should have. Thank you."

"You're welcome." He tipped his head in the direction of her front door. "Come on, let me know what you think."

Message received, back to business. She ran a hand over the resurfaced wood, the brand new knob, and deadbolt. What could she say? It looked like her door. But she wanted forgiveness and a smile. "It looks great.

I can't tell a difference. You do amazing work. Really—you do. Fabulous."

She tacked on a babbling "It's perfect," for good measure accompanied by a megawatt smile that hurt her cheeks.

It worked. Sort of. He maintained eye contact. But no flirty grin for her. No casual with an undercurrent of sexy.

She lost the smile, but the crazy she'd tossed around like confetti cluttered the air between them. "I'll stop now."

"Appreciate it. It's just a door." He stuffed his rag away and dug out a paper. "I gotta go. But I figured I'd give you this first."

"Sure." She nodded. "What is it?"

"An invoice for the work already done and a quote for the rest of it."

"Right. Of course." She made a show of unfolding the paper and studying it. It wasn't unreasonable. In fact, it was probably on the low side. "Everything looks to be in order."

"So, we're good?"

"Yes." The need to smooth things out overwhelmed her. "And thanks again. For agreeing to do the job."

He left on a nod without a backward glance. It hurt. Which was ridiculous. She didn't need the distraction of mutual attraction. The one-sided kind was bad enough. It took focus to get a business up and running, along with drive, dedication. No room for flirting, or…other messy, silly things.

She was his boss. It was her boutique. Her livelihood. She had the right to demand excellence. To give orders. She squared her shoulders. He liked the silent treatment? Fine. He was about to find out she was the queen of the cold shoulder.

****

What the hell was wrong with him? Beyond a door or two and her display case, Kate was none of Seth's business. His life, his agenda, wasn't any of hers. He squinted into the setting sun. The only thing they had in common was the desire to keep things professional. He was done with female drama. D.O.N.E.

The scene in the street came to mind. Her cool detachment. So what if Seth didn't trust Parsons or his soapbox? If he saw through him so did Kate. She had the brains and the icy attitude to cut men like Parsons off at the knees. God only knew what she'd do to a lowly carpenter who dared step over her line. Cut off something he valued a whole hell of a lot.

Deflating thoughts of future emasculation did the trick. So, he'd spun a few fantasies? So what? Plenty of women out there who didn't shoot frost from their fingertips. He'd pick one of them to fantasize about. The job wouldn't last forever and putting up with her attitude meant cash for insulating his studio. If she'd looked gut punched when he'd handed her his invoice? Not his problem.

He cranked the radio and let the music do its job. Sighting the cabin—his cabin—centered him. Caroline couldn't touch it. Couldn't sell it, pawn it, or steal it. His grandparents' legacy was safe. He was free.

His relaxed, happy feeling evaporated at the sight of his other boss's truck taking up space in his driveway. Bill Logan climbed out of his truck. He did the same. Seth frowned, not getting a good feeling.

He'd overheard Kate's failed attempts to get a hold of her dad. Nope, he didn't have to be psychic to know nothing good was coming next.

"Seth."

"Bill, what can I do for you?" Had he caught Seth leering at his daughter? Did fathers' have a sixth sense about that kind of thing? Seth had been thinking some pretty dir—

"Can we talk?" He motioned toward the cabin.

"Sure." Seth liked his boss. He was a good guy to work for. He liked the job. Enough to want to keep it. So, he led the way and prayed Bill Logan wasn't a mind reader. He raised his brows at Seth pulling out keys to unlock the two sets of deadbolts. No small town policy of open doors for him. He kept things locked up tight for good reason. "Come on in. Can I get you anything to drink?"

"I won't say no to a beer. It's been a hell of a day." Kate's father accepted the chilled bottle and eyed the bargain basement brand with misgiving. "Thanks."

"Glass?"

"No, thanks."

Seth motioned to a chair at the kitchen table and pulled one out for himself. Might as well get this over with. "What's this about?"

"I'm worried about Kate." Bill Logan worked real hard at appearing casual. "And this whole thing with those fanatics from the Valley Church. Bad enough they've got it in for the fair, but Matthew Parsons is putting Kate in the center of it."

Which didn't have a thing to do with him. And wasn't going to if he could help it. "She's a big girl. Going by what happened this afternoon, she can handle herself."

Bill smoothed his hand over the tabletop, avoided looking Seth in the eye. "I wish I was that sure."

He refused to react. Instead, he waited. Sipped his beer. Prayed this wasn't going where he thought it was going.

"You saw that preacher today. He's crazy." He tapped a finger in time with his words. "And he thinks Kate is possessed and doing the devil's work."

He didn't want to know but he had to ask. "What's this got to do with me?"

Bill Logan went for the kill. "I need someone to keep an eye on Kate."

"No." Seth snorted out a laugh, not a good laugh, more like a geezus-God-not-in-a-million-years kind of wheeze.

Bill Logan narrowed his eyes, anything but casual now. "I can make it worth your while."

Seth got serious fast. "No, end of discussion."

Bill switched gears again. "Don't go getting all offended. She's my little girl. I just thought maybe you could help me out. What happened today? That's only a little bit of what she's up against."

Seth refused to feel guilty about wanting to keep distance between him and his boss's needy daughter. But he also wanted to keep his job at the lumberyard. "It's not that I don't want to help out. I just don't think I'm the right person for the job." The last thing he needed was an excuse to spend more time around Kate. "Maybe this is something you should be asking Tyler Bodnar."

"Tyler's a little overzealous where Kate's concerned." Bill eyed the fading bruise around his eye, no doubt making connections Seth wanted to avoid. He lifted his chin and cut to the chase. "Did Tyler have a hand in that?"

"It's settled," said Seth. Hoping like hell it was the truth.

"Sure it is." But Bill set it aside in favor of his overall objective, trapping Seth between a rock and a hard place. "I need someone she won't suspect. Someone who's not her type. Someone who's got more sense than to hit on his boss." For all his stressing it was a good idea, the last bit was a clear warning. "Someone she won't look twice at hanging around. Someone who will keep me apprised of what's going on."

Someone motivated to keep his job. And not her type? That was a tad offensive. Not to brag but he was kind of irresistible when he wanted to be. He had a reputation. It was warranted. Not that it was relevant to this screwed up conversation. The whole idea was a no go. "Can't do it. I'm not spying on your daughter."

"Don't go getting all dramatic. It's not spying. Just a word in my ear if trouble comes her way. Simple."

Seth clarified. "So, in other words, spying."

"No." He shook his head. "More like being proactive and running interference should things get ugly."

"No." That was where he drew the line. This awkward tête-à-tête was over. "I'm not bodyguard material. I gave up using physical force a long time ago."

Bill Logan spread his hands in victory. "That's exactly why you're the right man for the job. Low key. Level-headed. The last thing Kate wants or needs is a scandal. She's finally recovered from the mess that bastard of an ex-husband created for her. I'll be damned if I'll see her backslide."

Level-headed? If he only knew how much effort it took to maintain that illusion. "I'm sorry, man. I just don't think I'm the guy for the job."

Bill sighed, not that Seth was deceived into thinking he'd given up. He was good at reading people. It was in the eyes, the determination to get one's own way. Anyway they could manage.

"It's a suggestion only." Bill smiled. It signaled a change of tactics. Seth was getting whiplash. "You already know I knew your father. That we were friends back in the day. He was quite the man, your dad."

"Yes, he was." Seth still missed him. Missed his influence and the part of him that calmed the beast in Seth.

Bill Logan stood up. "Come on, I want to show you something."

Seth went on alert but it didn't stop him from following his boss out the door. He put his reservations on hold desperate to hear more about his dad.

The drive to the Logan place lasted five minutes. Bill regaled him with tales. Seth couldn't help it. He lapped up the old summer campfire stories like wood soaking up stain. It was obvious Bill Logan and Sam Stone had been good friends. Seth knew his boss was playing him. Could sense it. Living with Caroline had taught him well. But he also sensed how much his boss missed his old friend.

They hopped out of his truck and headed for a large storage shed. Bill pushed open the doors to reveal a tarp-covered vehicle.

"This was your dad's pride and joy." Bill yanked off the cover to reveal a mint condition 1972 Dodge Demon.

"She's gorgeous." Seth brushed a reverent hand over the car's backend. He had no problem picturing his Dad in it. He'd had a thing for cars. "Does it run?"

"You bet." Bill dug out a set of keys and tossed them to Seth. "And it's yours."

Seth snagged the keys out of the air. The shock dissipated as warning bells rang. "I don't understand."

"Once your dad stopped coming out here as often, we still kept in touch." While he came to grips with that revelation, Bill made his way to Seth's side, clamped a hand on his shoulder. "He asked me to do him a favor. To keep the Demon out here. He was planning on giving it to you for your sixteenth birthday. Course, things happened. I made a couple of attempts to get in touch, left messages with your stepmother. I'm guessing she didn't pass them on to you. After talking to your grandparents, we agreed I should keep her here and wait for the opportunity to give it to its rightful owner."

It didn't surprise Seth. His stepmother was a total bitch. The only one who hadn't seen it was his father. Had she found out about the car she would have sold it. Like everything else. Like she wanted Seth to sell the cabin to pay off her debts.

He ran a hand over the roof. The cool exterior and the warm memories didn't stop him from being suspicious. "I don't know what to say except thank you."

He gave Seth's shoulder a squeeze. "No need to thank me. We look after our own around here. This needed looking after, so I did."

Of course, he had. And Bill Logan had someone he needed looking after. Seth felt the noose tightening.

"Your father was a good man. One of the best. You take after him." He pointed at Seth's black and purple eye. "You keep that in mind."

If he only knew.

"Anyways, consider her passed down. She's gassed up and ready to go."

Seth closed his eyes. Took a deep breath. You paid your debts. He'd learned that from his father too. "As far as Kate's concerned...I'll let you know if anything happens. But once the fair is over I'm done."

"Good enough."

"And then we're even."

The old man waved in agreement and walked away pretty damn confident he'd gotten what he wanted. Then again, there was a reason they cautioned against wishing for stuff you had no right to ask for. He'd stick close to Kate. As close as he could get without going up in flames.

He opened the door to his dad's car and breathed in the scent of misuse and open road. He thought of his dad, and blocked the flood of memories threatening to take him where he didn't want to go.

Chapter Three

Kate smiled brightly for the host of a public television show. Acting normal was exhausting but imperative to restoring her tattered reputation. Born stubborn her grandmother used to say. It was true. She used it to meet her objective of poised, efficient, and smart. To make it all look effortless and not a terrible sham.

Her shoulders slumped; she straightened them. Bad posture was forbidden. No showing cracks in the façade. No admitting to any less than honorable traits. Like how many pieces of herself she'd given away for countless bottles of scotch. How a single soul-sucking one-night stand still haunted her. Memories like those caused the perspiration rings under her arms to widen.

But she pulled it off. So well she was now scheduled for another interview closer to the fair, possibly involving a tour of the town. It was a badly needed win, and she intended to run with it.

Back in her car she caught up on her emails and text messages. One from Lily. Another from Grace. Two from Tyler. A missed call from her father. All leading with the same question, some version of: *Just wondered how you were doing*? She ignored them all in favor of stopping for an extra-extra-large black coffee and stole a few moments alone to mainline caffeine in peace.

She massaged the end-of-the-day ache centered in the middle of her forehead. Another sleepless night stretched out before her. One starring inked men with tool belts and cat eyes. Oh, the things they'd done together. Who knew she had such a vivid imagination? It was a bit disconcerting.

Enough of that. Upward and onward. It was the only path that mattered. She put her car into gear and headed home. Arms full of binder, tablet, and purse she pushed in the backdoor of Kate's Closet expecting solitude.

Seth set down his hammer and pulled out his earplugs. "You're back."

"Um...yes." And nope not a dream. Still, she blinked a couple hundred times to make sure. But no, one hundred percent happening right in front of her, ink, tool belt, cat eyes. Bad thoughts, very bad thoughts, joined the coffee pulsing through her system. Why was he here? It was late. Past dark out. And of course, the first thing to come out of her mouth was a demand. "Is something wrong? Or did I miss a last minute meeting request?"

Seth gave her a look she failed to decipher. "I spent some time last night working up a plan for your new display case and counter. Since the project is time sensitive I figured we could go over it tonight? If you've got the time? Make any changes that need to be made so I can get started."

So he could be finished with it. And her. She got it. Understood his reasoning. Still...

She juggled her armload, her earlier guilty thoughts heating her cheeks a slutty red. Even though she was an adult with adult needs. Obviously, too long ignored. It wasn't like he could read her mind. "Of course. The sooner things are back to normal the better."

He moved to catch her slipping binder. "It would help to know if I'm going in the right direction."

The sooner he was done and out of sight the better. "Good idea. Do you mind if we go up to my apartment and look things over? I jotted down a couple of ideas."

"Give me a moment to clean up." He jerked a thumb toward the back bathroom.

"Go ahead. I'll lock up. Come up when you're done."

She detoured to the front of the shop to pick up the file with her notes and met him by the door at the back leading up to her apartment. It was an old brick building. One of the first built way back when and the stairway was steep and narrow. She headed up the steps ignoring the claustrophobic effect of Seth, citrus soap, and sawdust.

She hustled aware of Seth following behind her eye level with her butt and those twenty extra pounds. Not that it mattered. He wasn't interested in her derrière. Not when he could have his pick of younger, firmer derrières.

She should stop it. Really. That kind of self-talk was pathetic and beneath her. Those twenty pounds looked good on her. She had a great ass. Who was he to judge? He should be thankful for the excellent view.

Problem solved. On to the next one. Discounting relatives, no male had stepped foot over her threshold since she'd moved into the tiny apartment above her boutique two years ago. Enough space for one. No room for more. In line with her five-year plan.

"It's small, only one room, but it's handy." And

cheap. As in free. Which was important when one had no money to speak of. Although probably not something you confided to your employee. But, darn it, he was making her nervous and that freaked her out.

He shrugged. "I like it."

For some strange reason she was relieved. She hesitated, but he stepped around her heading for the one thing in the teeny space that would interest him. The one thing she'd fought for in her divorce settlement, a five by six foot original work by Nathaniel Dossantos. It took up a third of one wall and was worth a small fortune. She prayed she wouldn't have to sell it to pay the bills.

She came to stand beside him. "We met at a charity event. Became friends of sorts, as much as you can be friends with a man like Nathaniel." She studied Seth's profile, the line of his jaw as it jumped. "Tell me, are all artists so temperamental?"

His eyes met hers for a brief second before he turned back to the painting. "Passion. Creativity. Sometimes it equals temperamental."

She was no judge of passionate. The last couple of years had been about survival. That's what she saw in the painting. The promise of it. It reminded her every day of the need to push forward.

"Why don't you spread your stuff out on the table? Have you eaten?" She was starving and possibly a little faint, judging by the light-headedness plaguing her.

"That would be...good. I guess. But really, you don't have to go to any trouble." He looked a little panicked. Good. They were a matched set.

"I'll see if I can find some food." She needed to eat. Breakfast was a long time ago and lunch had consisted of a granola bar she had stashed in her glove compartment and a couple of Tic Tacs she'd found at the bottom of her purse.

He must have sensed her hesitation, he asked, "I don't mind running across the street and picking something up?"

"No. Thanks anyway. I'll think of something." Anything to avoid ordering dinner for two from Mary's Café and Rumor Mill. Trouble was she hated to cook. Which wasn't quite true. More like she was terrible at it, as in legendarily, preposterously, laughingstock bad at it. Unless you counted popcorn. She popped a mean bowl of popcorn.

Then she forgot about cooking and food. Seth shrugged out of his flannel shirt revealing a tight white t-shirt and every wicked thought bubbled back to the surface fighting for first place. His hair now loose was finger-combed into a tousled, sexy mess. She'd been on photo shoots where that look had taken an hour to create.

"Anything I can help with?" She turned from surveying the contents of her fridge to find him right there. He had a knack for catching her unawares. Like a big, tawny jungle cat. Silent and gorgeous. Who could blame her if food preparation was the second thing that came to mind? "Can you cook?"

"Sure. I don't mind cooking."

"You don't mind cooking?" she echoed.

"Not at all."

He was gorgeous. He cooked. He was good with his hands. *Don't think about his hands.* And he was staring at her like he wanted to run. "Um...that would be great."

"What do you feel like?"

To avoid answering, she slipped her aching feet out of her pumps and lost a good four inches. Having to look up into those amber eyes threw her off. She forgot the question. "What?"

He cleared his throat. "To eat. What would you like to eat?"

"I'm easy." Oh my God, she hadn't just said that? "I mean, anything goes." *What? Wrong. Wrong, wrong, wrong. Try again.* "With food, that is. What I mean is I'm not picky. About *food*." She was such an idiot.

She ducked around him and rubbed her hands together determined to add some maturity back into her conversational style. "But I'm an excellent sous chef. So, put me to work."

"Let's see." He stuck his head into the interior of the fridge and pulled out a carton of eggs and a bunch of green onions. "Why don't you start by chopping up some of these? I think we'll go with omelets. A bowl? Whisk?"

She gave him a brief tour of her four cupboards and two drawers. Small quarters in her miniature galley kitchen led to brief seconds of physical contact. It couldn't be avoided and she gave up trying. It was nice. Doing this with him. Too nice. Addicting.

"Here. Let me show you." He stepped behind her. Surrounded her. Fireworks went off in her womb. "Hold it like this. Gripping the end of the metal part and the handle at the same time. Tuck the fingers of your other hand. Yep, curled in just like that."

"Okay." One word was all she managed, her neck arching toward the warmth of his breath.

"You're less likely to cut your finger off this way."

The knife sliced through the onions with sharp, crisp strokes. All she wanted to do was lean back into him. His hand stopped prompting hers. Then he was gone.

He looked back from his new position at the stove. "Tell me more about the fair. How did it start?"

She picked up a block of cheese, the grater, and raised her eyebrows at him in question. He nodded, adding oil to a hot pan. Hands busy, it was easier to shift into neutral. "The town council was looking for a way to increase Aspen Lake's exposure and to bring back some of the business we lose once tourist season ends. The first year the town sponsored a pumpkin-carving contest by local artists, a local farmer created a corn maze, and the churches got together and hosted a fall supper. Every year it keeps evolving."

"With you at the helm." He slid the whisked egg mixture into the pan.

"For this year." She eyed the mound of cheese and judged it enough. She ran her hands under the tap and grabbed a towel. "It's a great time. Lots of fun. We've added a couple of new events this go around."

"Such as?" He reached around her for the cheese, and she held her breath when his arm brushed a little too close to her breast. Her nipples contracted in appreciation. She offered a silent prayer for the concealing power of padded bras.

She grabbed a couple of place mats and some cutlery and set the table. "This year we're adding a beer tasting on Friday night. On Sunday, Kate's Closest is hosting A Woman's Affair: Tea, Cakes and Couture."

"Can't go wrong with beer. Or cake. Not sure about the rest of it."

She bit down on her lip to stop the smile fighting to

lift. "No appreciation for fashion?"

"If we're talking about what women wear under their clothes, then yeah. Otherwise, not so much." He glanced up from his chopping, eyes full of mischief. "You ever, ah, do a Victoria's Secret show?"

"No. Sorry to disappoint. No Sports Illustrated either. But lingerie on the runway, sure." She stole a piece of pepper off his cutting board and popped it in her mouth. He was going to pay for that wicked look. She leaned back against her small island and gave a wee stretch. "Going almost naked becomes second nature."

The knife in his hands stilled.

That's right. Take a minute to visualize. There you go.

She was so bad. And it felt so good. So good she laughed as she reached past him for a couple of glasses out of the cupboard. On to the sticky business of what to offer him to drink and how to explain the lack of choices. "Sorry, I can't offer you any alcohol as I'm sure you've heard."

"Water's fine with me." He set a couple of plates down on the table. Her mouth watered and it had nothing to do with food.

He pulled out her chair, waited for her to sit. In four years of marriage, she and Drew had never achieved this level of domesticity.

"What else happens?" He came back with the salad.

She broke off a small piece of her omelet, tasted it. "Over the years we've added street vendors, tarot, and palm readings. Saturday night is the Mad Man's Ball." Another small bite and she sighed in appreciation.

"This is a delicious."

He chewed, swallowed. "Mad Man's Ball? You're kidding, right?"

"When you think about it, nothing says dark and imposing like the end of fall on the prairies. The temperatures dip, the sun sets early, the wind blows. Very melodramatic."

"All you need is a crumbling castle."

"Actually, we hold the ball at a place called the Abbey. It's on the outskirts of town. Three stories of wood, brick, and huge windows with lots of interesting nooks and crannies."

His fork stopped in midair. "I've driven by it. Always wondered about it."

She sampled another forkful. "It's very popular. There's a restaurant on the first floor that serves the best pizza around, a cabaret hall on the second floor, with living quarters on the top floor. It's even haunted by the original owner. Lots of clanging and banging and flickering of lights reported."

"Sounds perfect for something called a Mad Man's Ball. What else?" He scooped more food into his mouth.

"The readings are always popular." The pitch dark outside gave the room a cozier feel. If they'd lit candles, dimmed the lighting, this would have date night written all over it. Good thing it was a business dinner. She wiped her clammy hands with her napkin. "This year it's Poe's work. But we've done Byron, Radcliffe, and the Bronte sisters. It brings in a lot of tourists."

He poured water into her glass. "Sounds fun. And profitable. No wonder you need your display case done by the end of October."

Yes, this cozy dinner was about work. Not intimacy. Or sex. Or friendship. But work. Plain, old, sensible work. "If it's possible? Although, I'm not sure how all the extra work and time away from the lumberyard is going to go over with your other boss?"

Seth shifted in his chair. "That's not going to be a problem."

She raised her eyebrows. "That doesn't sound like my dad."

He lowered his fork and moved his half-eaten plate of food to the side. "I guess he knows how important this is to you."

She rolled her eyes. "I'm sure he has an ulterior motive. We just haven't figured it out yet."

Seth pushed his chair back, and she glanced up surprised. More so when he rose to clear the table. "About the display case? Maybe we should go over my plans."

She put a hand on his arm. "I don't think the chef is required to do dishes too. How about we sit over there and I'll clean this up later?"

He didn't argue. Or waste time. He produced a sheaf of papers posthaste and got done to business. "I've got the plans right here."

Um…okay. She was no rocket scientist, but she could take a hint. They settled down beside each other on her one love seat. His plans were very thorough, detailed. That was so sexy. Bonus, she loved the concept. A curved top in dark wood with a glass front showcasing the display drawers that slid out allowing for easy access from behind the counter. Ample space while not taking up too much room. They spent half an hour bent over the plans, tweaking things she thought might benefit the workspace/showcase.

"I love it. It's going to be perfect." Engrossed in their discussion she'd slid closer until they were hip to hip on the two-seat sofa. She faced him, a huge grin of approval aimed right at him. He watched her, his amber eyes serious, careful. She tilted her head. He was so close. So different than anyone she'd come across. And solitary confinement had lost its appeal the minute she'd laid eyes on him.

His eyes flashed. She didn't imagine it. Didn't think either. She simply reacted, leaning in with the certainty he'd meet her halfway. Instead, he withdrew a fraction of an inch. Not far but undoubtedly a retreat.

Oh, God.

"I…" She closed her eyes in horror. Or denial. But no, it was happening. She knew this because she opened her eyes and he was still there. Close enough to smell the sweat of humiliation pooling out of her pores. He was staring at her in ear shattering silence. With nowhere to go, she stood up. Wiped her hands down the side of her skirt.

Pull it together, Kate.

She refused to gasp out an apology like a fish. "I shouldn't have done that. I crossed a line. I'm sorry."

"Kate." He got to his feet. "It's not that I don't want to—"

"No need to explain." *Please, do not explain.* "It won't happen again." So, so, so not happening again. "I promise."

Why was he moving in closer? He smoothed a knuckle over her cheek. Her skin tingled in response, proving humiliation didn't kill desire. It was merely trampled and ready to rear its ugly head again. Then he shoved his hands in his pockets. "It's not that I don't want to kiss you. I'm just not in a position to right now."

"You're involved with someone." Relief washed through her. It wasn't that she was a horrible person. He had a good reason. One she could live with. "I understand."

He shook his head. "I moved here with the intention of concentrating on my art. I can't afford to get involved with anyone right now. No matter how beautiful or appealing. You don't seem like the sex and forget it type. And that's all I have in me right now."

Wasn't that the story of her life? Men wanting to have sex with her but not interested in getting to know the real her? All they saw was the face.

She knew how to deal with men like that. She froze them out. "Well, thank you for being honest with me."

Really, it was for the best. Did she want him to get to know the neurotic, insecure woman she'd become in the last six years? Did she want this beautiful man to see the real her? She should back away. Put more than two feet of distance between them.

"Tell me I'm wrong." His Adam's apple bobbed. "Then ask me to stay and I will."

"No, you're not wrong." She looked away. Too tempted by far to risk being carefree enough to sleep with him. To kiss him goodbye afterwards. To work with him the next day like nothing had happened. Wished she didn't believe in consequences. Or guilt.

"I should go." He ran a hand over the stumble forming along his jawline before retrieving his shirt. At the door, with his back to her, he said, "I'll see you tomorrow."

She nodded, but he didn't see it. He was out the door. His boot treads fading as he jogged down the stairs.

Then silence.

The kind that stretched to fill the four corners of a room. A quiet that left little doubt you were utterly and completely alone.

****

Seth climbed into his truck, grateful to reach a sanctuary of sorts. Shit. Shit. Shitfuckshit. He let his head fall back against the seat, gave the steering wheel a solid punch with the heel of his hand. It didn't help. He willed his body to calm down. No way was he kissing her or worse with her father breathing down his neck. No matter how badly he wanted to. And he wanted to pretty damn bad.

Guess he was her type after all.

Worse, he had to walk back in there tomorrow. Pretend like he was *that guy*. One who valued a quick fuck over sharing bagels in bed the next morning.

Futility soured his stomach. He was pretty certain her father didn't want her to know about their little arrangement. Bill Logan wasn't someone you messed with or crossed, no matter how affable on the surface. He'd witnessed it first hand at the Yard.

Damn it, he had to work. His job meant food in his stomach, bills paid on time, and supplies for his studio. It wasn't like Aspen Lake was a hotbed of career opportunities. He caught a glimpse of her silhouette in the window, cellphone to her ear, hand waving around in the air. He was parked a ways down Main Street so it was unlikely she'd spot him stalking her from his truck.

Tangled web woven. Yay for him and his hollow victory. Heartburn corroded his insides. He wasn't cut out for this shit. Make love not war and all that. He rubbed at his chest and tried to ease the ache.

His cellphone rang and he pulled it out. One glance at call display and he groaned. Perfect timing as usual. He was tempted to ignore her but she'd keep phoning until he answered. Or worse, show up on his doorstep.

"Caroline, I told you to quit calling me."

"Seth, where are you? Ashley and I are frantic."

She meant broke. "I'm busy. What do you want?"

"Well," she sputtered in his ear. "You'd think you'd care enough to check in."

He closed his eyes and prayed for patience. "I'm tired, Caroline. Get to the point."

"I'm a little strapped for cash, honey. Can you help me out? The dishwasher quit this week and I had to call a repairman. That was why I was desperate to get a hold of you. If you'd been here, been available…you might have been able to fix it." She coughed, her voice raspy from the menthol cigarettes she'd gone from hiding when his dad was alive to chain-smoking after he died.

He ran a hand through his hair. "I don't have it."

A pause. "Just a couple hundred should do."

"I just gave you four hundred bucks two weeks ago. That's it, I'm tapped out. I don't have any more to give you."

She sniffed into the phone. "If your dad could hear you. It was his dying wish that you take care of Ashley and me. Doesn't that mean anything to you anymore?"

It meant less and less. He hit End without bothering to reply and to avoid the bitter tears, angry accusations, and vicious threats sure to follow. She'd abandoned all sense of responsibility after his dad died, if she'd ever had any. Her constant need for him to be the man of the house. Fix this. Pay for that. Handle this. Was unrelenting.

He shrugged into his coat and settled back. Life was sooo much better now. Cold truck, stupid conscience, sexually frustrated. Friggin' fantastic. He shifted on the seat seeking a comfortable spot to spy from. Her lights were still on. Until they went out he'd sit there sketching. No surprise, a face emerged in the midst of the charcoal strokes. Her mouth parted, eyes at half-mast. Head at a slight angle, neck exposed. The necklace she favored resting against her skin. A great tumble of long, dark hair. He drew his hand cupping her jawline. His thumb rubbing against her bottom lip. The next time he checked her windows were dark.

****

Her reprieve was over. Kate hadn't laid eyes on Seth since she'd tried to kiss him, which was all Grace's fault. Her best friend was going to pay and pay big. Thankfully, her dad called him into the Yard on Saturday, and she'd left late that afternoon for the city and an AA meeting. Sunday everything shut down, including her. Monday she'd spent most of her day out of the boutique and in meetings about the fair, while Seth toiled away at replacing shelving.

"Can I talk to you?" asked Seth.

Today was Tuesday and the one day out of the year guaranteed to suck no matter what. There was nothing to do but put on her big girl panties and survive it. "What can I do for you?"

He signalled for her to follow him. "Back here."

She trailed after him taking in his long legs, the

low slung tool belt, his tight—

"Have you talked to your dad yet?" He turned and caught her staring at his ass. He backed up a little further putting a sawhorse between them.

Just…great.

She sighed. "No. He's dodging my calls."

He braced his hands against the wooden structure, his eyes earnest and a little desperate. "I think you should talk to him. Keep him more in the loop, you know? Especially about this shepherd guy. He's worried about you."

She traded mortification for suspicion. "Did he put you up to this? Because if he did, my father and I are going to have words."

"What? No." He straightened, pushing a hand through his hair loosening the band and letting it fall around his shoulders. "I'm just saying, it would probably keep him off your back."

Nice thought. Not going to happen, but he didn't know her dad like she did. "Like I said, he's dodging my calls so…"

He muttered something she didn't catch. "Pardon me?"

He shoved his hands in his front pockets, rolled his shoulders. God, could things get any more awkward? "Kate, about the other night, I—"

Ask a stupid question. She put up a hand to hold him off. "No need."

Grace poked her head around the corner. "I'm off to Mary's for lunch. You want me to bring you back a Cobb salad?"

Saved, God bless, Grace. She discarded her plans for revenge. "Yes, please. And coffee. I'll watch the front."

"Seth?" prompted Grace.

The little bell over the door rang. Thank goodness. Kate put a hand on Grace's arm. "You go for lunch. I've got it."

"No, nothing for me." He was the picture of male frustration. Too bad. She couldn't face that conversation. Not today. He shrugged. "I'll catch you later."

After lunch, the whine of power tools and the pound of a hammer accompanied the passing of slow minute after minute. No doubt her shelves were coming along. She hadn't gone back there to check. It would disrupt the rather nice pattern of avoidance they'd set. As the end of the workday crept closer, she thought of the bouquet of pink and purple daisies waiting for her. Rose would keep Petals open an extra couple of minutes. Long enough for Kate to pick up her flower order. Then it was off to the cemetery and back home for a good cry.

With half an hour until closing, she saw her only customer out the door. Desperate for a distraction she grabbed her laptop. Matthew Parsons knew things about her past. It was time to level the playing field. The Shepherd was an attention seeker. It wasn't a stretch to assume he'd have an online presence, or left a footprint. She typed in Valley of the Shepherd Church and Matthew Parsons hoping for any kind of scandalous tidbit.

"Anything interesting?" Grace peeked over her shoulder.

"Doing a little look see into Matthew Parsons. And nope. No website." She scrolled down the list of links.

"Nothing relevant. Not that I have time to search through the four million possibilities. Why did I think this would be easy?"

"Have you searched religious cults, people claiming to be shepherds, prophets, that sort of thing?"

"Not yet, but good idea." Kate leaned in and started pecking at keys.

"Here let me give it a try." Kate made way for Grace. Watched the screen while she typed. Grace tapped out an impressive list of search parameters. "They had to come here from some place. And there's what? Fifty of them?

Kate kept her eye on the door for late coming customers. "That we know of."

"Exactly. So, relocation couldn't have been easy. But maybe it was necessary." Grace's fingers flew over the keyboard.

"I never thought of that angle." Kate gave up her vigil and squinted at the screen. "What are you looking for?"

"Religious groups, cults that have been kicked out of places. Likely from one of the neighboring provinces, or even from across the border. Law suits. Newspaper articles. That sort of thing."

"Oh, good idea. Why didn't I think of that?"

"It's probably the only time having a parent who is a conspiracy theorist has come in handy." Grace paused and then smiled. "This sounds promising. Check out this link."

The front door opened. With a welcome smile on her face, Kate lifted her head. A second later she reached out and slowly closed her laptop.

Grace objected, gaze focused on the screen. "Hey, I

was just getting to the good stuff."

"Mr. Parsons. Welcome to Kate's Closet. Can I help you with something?"

Beside her, Grace muttered, "Look what the devil dragged in."

Kate jabbed an elbow in her side. "Be good," she mouthed.

"I thought it was time I dropped by." He searched the boutique, his tall, reed thin body stiff with intensity. Disappointment at finding it empty soured his expression, changed his tone from engaging to sneering. It complimented his outfit of judgmental and dull. The whole group needed a serious makeover. Mentally and wardrobe wise. "About this fair you're hosting?"

He and his narrow ideals were the very last thing she needed today. Kate tacked on a smile. "You flatter me. I'm not single-handedly responsible; the town hosts the fair."

"If you'll excuse me…" Grace slipped away. Kate knew she was heading for Seth.

"Are we to split hairs now? Your name and face are all over it." Parsons barely gave Grace's departure a glance. He focused in on Kate. She felt it like a punch. Thank God, Seth was around. She'd be a fool to want to be alone with this man. And she wasn't a fool, not anymore.

She nodded her head in agreement. "You're right, I am head of the committee. I'm also sponsoring one of the major events, so yes, my name is on several of the promotional materials." She refused to let him intimidate her. If she could survive all the tabloid trash talk, she could survive this conversation.

"Ah yes. Sunday's A Woman's Affair." His eyes were bright, unblinking, fixated on her. "Tea, Cakes, and Couture. Do I have that right?"

"Yes." Kate breathed a small sigh of relief when Seth strode out of the back wiping his hands on a rag, Grace stalking after him. "If you're interested in attending, I'm happy to sell you a ticket?"

"Unlike you, I have morals. Those morals do not include inviting the devil in by dishonoring the Sabbath." He reached into his jacket pocket. A small vial appeared in his hand. "Or any other day of the week."

Kate scrambled off her stool and out of reach. The man really was a lunatic. "Whatever that is you need to put it away. Then you need to leave."

"What's going on here?" Seth stuffed the rag into the back pocket of his jeans and picked up his pace.

"I fail to see how that's any of your business, Mr. Stone." He spared Seth a quick smirk before unstopping the tiny bottle and holding it up. "In my experience, there is nothing that puts the devil to flight better than a little bit of this."

Kate held her breath. Grace tugged her arm. Seth stepped in front of them both blocking their view. "Give it to me or I take it from you. Your choice."

"Every courtesan has her benefactor."

Kate raised a brow as she stepped out from behind the lovely view of Seth's back. "Did you just call me a whore, Mr. Parsons?"

"May His mercy be upon us. Take hold of the old serpent, which is the devil, bind him that he may no longer seduce this woman." He lifted the vial high.

"Save the sermon." Seth grabbed his hand and

pried the bottle out. "No one here cares."

"Scared of a little holy oil, Mr. Stone?"

Seth sniffed at the opening. Spread a drop on his fingertip and rubbed it with his thumb, then sniffed again. "Olive oil and balsam."

"Very good. I may have to adjust my opinion of your intelligence."

Kate held her breath as Seth tensed, his hands clenching into fists. "Like I give a shit what you think."

Kate put a hand on his arm and squeezed in warning and addressed Parsons. "Well, it's been nice but we don't want to keep you."

Seth tossed the vial in the garbage can and crossed his arms.

Matthew Parsons glared at him. "That particular combination is often used in the sacraments of baptism and confirmation. Renewal, fresh starts. Where would we be without the promise of a better tomorrow?"

Kate didn't give a crap about balsam or whatever the heck else the crazy Shepherd stashed in his pockets. Not like she was going to melt upon contact. She was more worried about Seth, who was one muscle spasm away from ripping free and going for Parsons' jugular. "Do you believe in karma, Mr. Parsons? Because I do. We judge others. In turn, we ourselves are judged. That's how it works. Can your ideals withstand that kind of scrutiny?"

At her side, Grace stifled a laugh.

"I'm glad this is a joke to you. But God speaks to me. With his guidance, I gather lost souls. Offer them the gift of redemption." He pointed to the trash bin. "I can help you find your way back to the light."

"I don't need your help finding anything." She had

her own flock. Her own pastor. She didn't join them every Sunday in the family pew but often enough.

Seth's patience ran out. "Get out."

Parsons ignored him. "We all need finding, Ms. Logan. One way or another."

The sanctimonious bastard. "Does that include your flock?"

He puffed out his skinny chest. "Every one of us has been found by the only truth that matters."

Was he responsible for the note ending up in her pocket? Was it mind games? Or a cry for help? "But what if one of you wanted to be lost? Or found somewhere else? Would you let them go?"

His eyes narrowed, but Kate couldn't decide if it was speculation or satisfaction. "The members of my community are here because they choose to be. Each and every one of them committed to a certain way of life."

If Kate had a superpower, it was the power of the blank face. "Are you sure about that?"

His lip curled. "What are you implying?"

She prodded, "Concerned?"

"I'm concerned about a great many things. But not about the commitment of my followers. However, if you are privy to information that I am not aware of, please, by all means, enlighten me."

Kate shrugged. "It was only a question. People are allowed to ask those, aren't they?"

Parsons studied her, his face relaxing into a self-assured smirk. He rubbed his hands together. "Unfortunately, those of questionable morals rarely ask the right ones. For instance, you would be better served inquiring how to save your immoral soul."

Seth interrupted. "And I'm not telling you again. This conversation is over."

"I agree." Grace marched over to the front door and swung it open. "We really do have a 'No Bullies Allowed' policy."

Parsons' glare raked over her. "First warning, stay away from my people."

"Or what?" asked Seth.

"Or judgment day will be upon you." Parsons headed for the door, but turned back at the last second. "I will shut this fair down. One way or another."

He swept past Grace, who swung the door closed behind him.

"Arrogant asshole." Grace started toward her, worry written all over her face.

"Don't. Please." Kate massaged her temples in a bid to buy herself some time to regroup. Where others only hinted, Parsons' came right out and said it. She was a mess. "I'm fine."

"It's okay not to be fine, sweetie. Anybody would have found that upsetting."

She was in desperate need of a hole to hide in with nowhere to go. She didn't dare look at Seth. "But I'm not just anybody. In case you missed it, I'm a whore who's in bed with the devil."

"He does have a way with words." But her attempt at sarcasm contained traces of concerned. It made Kate cringe.

Seth, on the other hand, was like a big cat who found himself caged but still coiled and ready to spring. "You need to let the police know what happened here. He threatened you. The fair. It's nothing to joke about."

"I'm not laughing. And I happen to agree with

you."

Grace reached over and opened the laptop, refreshed the screen. "If this is the same group of people, the police definitely need to be warned."

Kate leaned over to catch a look at the screen. She brought up a hand to cover her mouth. "Oh my God."

Seth came up behind her. His eyes did a fast scan. His hands went to his hips, his face going hard. "Ah, shit."

Kate reached for her cell. The bell over her door chimed again. Her fingers clutched her phone. She couldn't take anymore. She really couldn't. So, why was her father's mistress walking in the door when Sunni Bennett was careful to keep her distance and stay out of Kate's way? With good reason.

Grace gave Kate a quick glance before jumping in to head off the new arrival. "Sunni, can I help you?"

Sunni swallowed, shot a nervous look at Kate before wisely addressing Grace. "I saw that awful man leave. I wanted to make sure everything was all right."

Sunni never crossed the threshold of Kate's Closet. That was Kate's rule, and Sunni loved Kate's dad enough to respect it. So, why did karma have to pick today to bitch slap Kate across the face?

"Seriously?" Everything she wanted to throw at Matthew Parsons but hadn't she turned on Sunni. It boiled up and bubbled out of her along with a nasty laugh she couldn't have controlled even if she wanted to. "That *awful man* walked in here and called me a whore. To my face. In my place of business. Ironic, isn't it? That the next person who walks through the door wrote the book."

Sunni's lip trembled, but she bit it down. She stood

her ground. A person had to admire her gall. But Kate figured that went with the territory. "Here you are. The other woman. Worse than."

"Kate." Grace put a hand on her arm. "Don't."

Kate shook her off and pointed at the door. "Get out."

Sunni twisted her fingers together until her knuckles went white. "No. Not until I know you're okay."

"Do I look okay?"

"Kate…"

"Sunni, please," murmured Grace.

"It's a tad late to be wondering after my welfare, don't you think?" She was making a scene. The awful thing was she couldn't seem to stop. Sunni made everything worse. Fighting with her, hating her, was like kicking a puppy. Hardly enjoyable and a lot sociopathic. She was the bad guy here. Knowing it, seeing it register on Seth's face, only made her think less and speak more. "By all means, bring on the concern. My dad's sure to be impressed. Maybe he'll decide to make an honest woman out of you. Even though it's thirteen years too late for that."

Great big tears welled up in those huge adulterous eyes, but she was still too stupid to move her ass out of Kate's shop. "Kate, please."

It was back to the blank face. "Go. Away."

When she didn't move, Kate did. Seth pushed his way in front of her and blocked her path. "What the hell is wrong with you?"

She looked up into a pair of very confused eyes. He was trying to get a read on her and he was failing, which was good. The last thing she needed was Seth in her head figuring things out. "This doesn't concern you."

"Bullshit. You doing this now, here, makes it my business. You think I'm going to stand here and let you get in her face when you're not thinking straight, forget it."

Sunni picked that unfortunate moment to remind Kate of her presence. "Your dad—"

She dodged Seth and jabbed a finger in Sunni's direction. "I'm not talking about my dad with you."

"Get her out of here." Seth motioned to Grace. He'd clued in. She saw it on his face. Then it got hard with something else she didn't understand.

Grace's voice in the background. "Come on, Sunni. Let's grab a coffee."

Then she had Seth's undivided attention and she didn't like that either. "You don't call the shots here."

He bent his head toward hers. "Rein it in, princess."

Her eyes went wide, right before they blinked in shock. Her mouth fell open. Very attractive she was sure, not that she cared. "She's not welcome here. She knows that."

Seth's head fell back like he was praying to the ceiling. "Yeah, I got that part."

"I don't have to explain why."

"From your use of the words *whore* and *dad,* I think I got an inkling, princess."

"Stop calling me that." She inched a step closer, curled her lip.

"Stop acting like one."

"Maybe you should save all this interest in my personal life for your *art*."

He turned his head to the side, his lips thinned in frustration. His tongue did a slow swipe over his top teeth. It was fascinating to watch. The tortured male forced to deal with the crazy, hysterical female. The minute shake of his head told her his last thread of patience was unraveling. Well, too bad for him. Then his eyes were back on hers. He pressed closer. "You want in my bed, *Kate*? I laid it out. Agree to the terms and I'll put you there."

Oh. My. God. Those words had not come out of his mouth? "You want a quick fuck? Fine. It's not like I'm looking for a deep, meaningful relationship with the hired help."

"Okay, that's it." A muscle worked along his jaw. His palms came up. He backed away. "I'm out of here."

The thud of his boots and the slam of the door echoed around the empty space. Kate spun in a circle, placed her hands on her head trying to hold it all in and failed. The tears spilled over. Her breaths came out in little puffs. She closed her eyes tight.

"Shit."

Calm down.

"Shit."

Not working.

Shit.

What was wrong with her? Damn it, Sunni knew Kate had her reasons. She'd still sprung a surprise visit on her.

Why?

Today of all days. The anniversary of her mom's death.

She concentrated on her breathing. On slowing it down. On regrouping. On going through the steps. Then she locked up before making her way up the stairs and into her apartment. She crossed over to the window overlooking Main Street. Down below a few townspeople hustled along the sidewalk. The nine-to-five crowd heading home.

Saturday the whole town would start decorating for the fair, including Kate's Closet. She rubbed some warmth back into her arms. She concentrated on her To Do list for tomorrow and the rest of the week. Saturday was also a town day for the followers of the Valley Church. She planned on searching for the girl, on getting to bottom of the note-giving campaign.

She picked up her phone and texted Grace a message asking after Sunni. Grace assured her Sunni was fine. She was going to have to apologize. She knew it. But her mental health wasn't up to it tonight. Seth was her priority. She went to dial his number and stopped. She didn't want to give him the opportunity to shut her down before she said what she needed to say.

Instead, she dialed Constable Mike Davenport's number and told him about Parson's visit, and when she was done she texted him the link to the online information. She grabbed up her keys and headed for her car, her flowers, and her mother's grave.

****

Kate stared up at Seth's cabin that wasn't really a cabin at all. It sat two stories high on prime waterfront property amongst a cornucopia of trees and a natural landscaping of rocks, clinging plants, and wheat grass. Definitely, more chalet than shack. She estimated 1500 square feet complete with two huge decks and a mammoth stone chimney.

Instead of being a showstopper, it blended in,

hidden from the front and open to the views at the back. She hadn't known his grandparents very well, but somehow it fit Seth.

Needing the connection, the courage, she ran her fingertips over her grandmother's necklace before climbing the steps to Seth's front door. No answer. No lights on either. She searched for his truck. It sat in the parking area along with a sleek-looking muscle car. Lights were on in one of the outbuildings. She made her way back down the steps and rounded the corner of the cabin. Loud music met her halfway to the door. The big bay door was closed so she knocked on the smaller one next to it.

Her knock was lost amidst the low pounding bass. The knob turned in her hand, and she eased the door open. He was perched on a stool hunched over a piece of wood, a tool in his hand. His hair was pulled back in a messy sort of bun. Despite her resolve, her resistance wavered, the empty spaces inside her aching to be filled. By him.

He caught movement out of the corner of his eye and stilled. After a second, his head bent back to the piece he was working on. It took him another couple of seconds before he pushed back his stool and stood to face her. She mouthed words at him while pointing to her ears. He reached over and shut down the music.

She didn't waste time trying to figure out the best way to say it. "I'm sorry. I was having a bad day. I took it out on you. I shouldn't have."

He shoved his hands into the front pockets of an old pair of faded jeans. "I'm listening."

That was kind of it. All she had. What more did he want? Okay, maybe her apology did require a couple of clarifications. "I didn't mean it. The hired man remark? And then the other night—I made things uncomfortable between us. I embarrassed both us by misreading the situation. I'm sorry about that too."

She tugged down on the sleeves of her blouse, made sure everything was buttoned up. Made sure it was tucked in tight at the waist. Fiddled with her collar. While he watched and waited. Her whole body trembled with the need to make things better. "I need you, Seth. Your skills. As a carpenter. Good ones are hard to find."

He shrugged and picked up his tool. "Apology accepted.

She was getting a little tired of the mixed messages. Care and concern, then nothing. How dare he dismiss her.

She turned back, walked over, and plucked the tool out of his hand. "My mom died when I was sixteen. Complications from dealing with multiple sclerosis. Today's the anniversary of her death, by the way. Anyway, a couple of weeks before she died she was having a really bad day, and I got scared. Dad wasn't home. He wasn't answering the phone. I knew he was at the Yard so I went to get him. It was a Sunday and it was closed, but he'd left the door unlocked. Stupid mistake, that. He and Sunni were in his office. Together. *Very* together."

"Kate." He pushed up to stand in front of her. Not looking exactly sorry for her, but the pity she hated was moving in. The tells were there. The careful set of his mouth, the softening of the muscles along his jawline, and worst of all, the look darkening his eyes.

She held up a hand to ward him off, closed her

eyes against the memories. "I knocked something over on my race out the door. Dad caught up with me before I got through the gate. It all came out. How they'd been together for years. That my mom knew all about it. I was in shock trying to figure out what it all meant. Then my mom died. I spent the next year doing whatever I could to rip my dad to pieces."

"Understandable."

"Now it's understandable?"

"He hurt you. Betrayed your trust. But he loves you."

"Yes, he does. But Sunni? I never quite managed to forgive her. They're still together. I avoid her, and she makes it a point to stay out of my way."

"Not so easy to do in a small town."

"We manage. Until today. She took me by surprise. I reacted badly. What happens next is between Sunni and me."

"It's a long time to hold onto something."

"That's my business and my decision to make."

"And here I thought you were all about second chances?"

"I don't expect you to understand. Or care. I'm pretty sure you've already guessed I've got more than my share of attitude." She wasn't giving it up. Or toning it down. Not for anyone. Some days attitude was the only thing holding her up. Like now. "I should go."

Her hand was twisting the doorknob before he unbent enough to speak to her. "I'll see you tomorrow."

She closed her eyes and addressed the door. "I'm going to be honest and say I need a couple of days. Can we make it Thursday?"

"Thursday, then."

"Thank you." She secured the strap of her purse over her shoulder and turned to face him. She might as well finish it up right. "I hope you know how much I appreciate your helping me out. From now on I promise to keep it professional and not involve you in any more drama."

He nodded then reached over to turn on his music. Dismissed.

On her way down the drive, she changed her mind and decided to get all her apologizing over with so she had at least a chance of sleeping tonight. Even with her almost positive thinking urging her on, it took a lot more effort to lift her knuckles to knock on the next door. A door that had kept the world at bay for the first sixteen years of her life. These days she avoided going through it when Sunni's car was parked out front. But since Sunni was here now so was she.

"Katie." Her dad's smile hurt it was so bright. It meant Sunni hadn't told him what happened. It was also clear he was delighted to see her, especially seeing he knew she knew who was there.

"I need to speak to Sunni."

His smile disappeared. A frown took its place. "Why?"

"Privately."

His eyes narrowed. "What's going on?"

"It's okay." Sunni pushed past him and pressed a kiss to his cheek. Her dad's eyes widened in surprise at her public display. Kate figured after her remark this afternoon the gloves were finally coming off. "Go on inside."

He didn't budge. "I don't think that's a good idea."

"Fine." Kate would make her apologies on the

front porch. "Sunni, I'm sorry I called you a whore this afternoon. It was uncalled for and it's not true."

"Jesus Christ, Katie." Bill Logan rubbed a hand over his short hair. "What the hell is this about then?"

Sunni gave him a look. "Bill, go inside."

"Not on your life." He crossed his arms over his bull-like chest. "I think instead I've got a few things I want to say to my daughter."

Sunni put a hand on his arm. "Please."

"No." He pointed a finger in Kate's direction. "You and me? We're going to sit down and we're going to finally talk this shit through."

"Not today." Sunni got between them. With her hands resting on Bill's mighty arms, she repeated, "Not today, Bill."

"You don't think I know what today is?" Bill set her aside and faced Kate. Wet filled his eyes. Surprise and something a little like guilt made Kate want to reach for him. He gave an angry brush to his eyes. "I lost her too. I know you don't want to hear that, and I've probably got no right to say it. But it's true." Another swipe at spilling tears. "I loved her too, Katie. Not the way you wanted or thought. But she was a good woman. The mother of my child. My best friend. So, don't you for one second think anything differently." His jaw trembled with effort. "On second thought, Sunni's right. I can't do this. Not today. When you're ready for a mature conversation, you know where to find me."

The door banged shut after him. She didn't know what to say, what to do with his words. Except cry and she was so done with tears. She wanted to shrug off Sunni's warm hand on her arm, but everything was getting blurry.

Sunni put a gentle hand on her other arm, left it there in a tentative experiment. Kate didn't have the energy to push her away.

"I'm sorry, too. That I came into Kate's today. It won't happen again."

Kate looked past her to the door. And she knew. "He told you to watch the boutique, didn't he? In case Parsons showed up?"

"He didn't have to ask me to do anything."

Kate blinked back tears, sniffed, waited while Sunni produced a tissue. "I don't need—"

"Oh, Kate. Yes, you do. You need as many people watching your back as you can manage."

"You're making me sound pathetic, and I don't care for that much." Then she blew her nose in the tissue and cancelled out everything she'd just said.

"Never pathetic. In an impossible position. There's a difference."

Kate raised her brows. Granted, she hadn't had many conversations with Sunni, but she'd made assumptions about her. None of them good, not surprising. One of them having to do with her lack of a backbone. "Pardon me?"

"I love your dad. That makes you my business. I know you don't like that idea, but you're just going to have to get over it."

"Excuse me?"

"Matthew Parsons is trouble. He's looking to make more, and he's looking to put you in the center of it."

"How is it you know more about this than me?"

"You're right. That's wrong. Come with me." She opened the door and motioned Kate through. Sunni led her to her dad's office. He was slumped behind his desk, head in hands. "Show her the emails."

He sighed and sat back. "Sunni, this isn't the time. She's upset enough."

Sunni leaned in. "She's upset because she has a right to be. She needs to see them. To know what she's dealing with."

"And I'll show them to her when she's not so upset."

"You'll do it now," insisted Sunni.

He looked between the two women and blew out a frustrated breath. "Fine. Might as well. Things can't get any worse."

"Daddy." She hadn't called him that in thirteen years. The gratitude flooding his eyes made her heart hurt. Three apologies were a charm, right? "I'm sorry for being so miserable to you after Mom died."

"No apology necessary. It was a difficult time." He studied her, not knowing what to do with her proclamations. "It's how we move forward from here that matters.

"I agree." Sunni beamed, proving her nickname wasn't an exaggeration and ran a hand down her partner's arm. "I'll make tea while you show her the emails."

Chapter Four

Kate waited, hands on hips, ensuring the raised banners with the fair's logo and colors were perfectly straight. Tradition dictated the first Saturday of October was set aside for decorating for the fair. All businesses participated and many townspeople chose that day to hang lights and put up yard decorations of their own. Banners and Halloween wreaths swapped out the summer flower baskets on the town's retro-styled street lamps. Planters were cleaned out and replaced with pumpkins of all sizes, sprigs of cedar, and cornhusk decorations.

Mid-morning, Aspen Lake was bustling with activity, and Kate was all kinds of happy. The sun shone and unseasonably warm October temperatures infused energy into the efforts. Everything was going according to plan. Clipboard in hand she marched the length of Main Street and back. The happy mood of the people out and about was infectious. The Valley Church flock weren't in attendance, but she was sure they'd show up. Confidence being her new middle name, she was determined to find the girl responsible for the note in her pocket.

Seth shinnied halfway up a pole to help secure a knot. Kate kept her eyes on her notes and resisted the urge to fan her face with her clipboard. They'd kept it simple and very distant the last couple of days. But close proximity, with him in his soft flannel shirt, faded jeans, and smelling like warm, comfy sunshine, made practicing nonchalance darn near impossible. But she was managing.

Barely.

"Don't you have something, anything else, you'd rather be doing?" she asked. It would be a lot easier to avoid him if he wasn't under foot.

"No." But his tone suggested yes, he did in fact have many, many other things he'd rather be doing.

Whatever his intentions, they caused more than one raised eyebrow and speculative glance. You didn't have to be psychic to hear what they were thinking.

Do you think they're sleeping together?

He's hot.

But she's...Kate.

They can't be sleeping together?

Proof says otherwise.

Did you see that? He smiled. My panties just melted.

Oh wait, those last few thoughts were hers.

Seth was oblivious. Too busy yukking it up with the townsfolk. It was annoying. Willing and more than able bodied, he climbed ladders and toted boxes. He even drew an elaborate picture of some flowers in chalk on a board outside of Petals. It had sported nothing but Rose Flannery's spidery handwriting for the last three decades. Her blushing gratitude earned her a quick peck on the cheek from Seth with an offer to come back next week to draw a new picture for her.

It was a kind thing to do. Which pissed Kate off for no good reason. Which drew Seth's attention, because of course he would notice all things less than flattering when it came to her. "I'm sensing not everything is okay?"

How intuitive. "I'm fine."

He raised his eyebrows.

"What?"

"Taking 'fine' at face value would be a rookie mistake I haven't made since I was sixteen."

"So, yesterday then?"

"You got a problem with my age?"

"No, just your grammar." That sounded old. And prissy.

"Ask me."

Her nose lifted. Better to smell the high ground. "It's none of my business."

"Nose in the air, buttoned up tight, fuck me shoes. It's a challenge I'm getting tired of walking away from."

She gasped, as would any decent prude worth her weight in buttons and hairbands. "Tell me you did not just say that in the middle of Main Stre—"

She stopped on a huff of breath as he brushed passed her. When she realized her eyes were zeroed in on his ass, she did a hasty check to make sure no one was watching her watch him. Then it became official. She was losing her mind. She couldn't afford to lose her mind again, not when the success of the fair and her entire life savings were at stake. She peeked down at her black patent leather, five inch high heeled, red-soled shoes with the two ankle straps. They were her favorites. They gave her some extra height…and confidence. Other than that they were just shoes. You bought those other kind at Hooker Shoes R Us.

God.

Men.

She made her way to Kate's Closet. So sue her. She wasn't dripping in beads and peace signs and going barefoot to the love-in. Which she was sure was more in line with his type. And what would he know about foot apparel? He was wearing a decade old pair of motorcycle boots. And why she found that sexy was a mystery.

Seth disappeared inside, and Kate stole a moment to inspect the window to Kate's Closet, which looked amazing thanks to Grace. A backdrop of black velvet and fairy lights showcased the mannequin in her long, dark coat, left open to reveal dark slacks and a cashmere sweater. Her face was concealed behind a mask, leather gloves hid her hands, boots on her feet. Leaves lay scattered at her feet with a black raven perched on a pile of plump pumpkins.

Then Grace was tugging her through the door. "You've got to see this."

"Okay." Inside the door she stopped dead.

Seth shrugged. "I thought maybe you could use this in your display to give it a little more punch."

Without thinking, Kate reached out to touch the raven in the process of lifting off from its post. Black wings preparing for flight, the bird stood two feet tall on a perch three feet high. Its large beak was open, protesting. A garland of barbed wire circled the fence post, leading down into a metal tangle of tall grass.

"It's beautiful." In awe, she inched closer, ran a fingertip over the life-like feathers of one wing. "Harsh. That's the word that comes to mind."

Along with aggressive. This bird had no pet like qualities. No pretty plumage.

Wide-eyed, Grace circled the raven. "It's incredible."

"Thank you. Both of you." He grinned in uncensored appreciation.

Resistance was futile. But smart. "What do you call it?"

"Unfettered."

She wondered if he knew how much his sculpture and its name said about him. Kate met his look hoping he didn't guess how much she craved those very things for herself.

She cleared her throat. "The attention to detail is amazing. I'd love to put it in the display window, providing you attach your name to it. We get a lot of street traffic going by. A lot of artisans coming in for the fair. Buyers."

"Done."

"Well, then, let's get it out there so it can attract attention," announced Grace.

They ditched the plastic version and, with much adjusting and shifting around, found the exact right feel for the display.

Kate cast a critical eye from street-side. "Suddenly, there came a tapping."

Seth rubbed a hand over his jaw. "Keep the windows closed. You never know."

Grace laughed, even as she hugged her arms. "That bird certainly looks intelligent enough to find its way inside. Very eerie. It's perfect for the fair."

"What the hell is that?" They turned in unison to find Tyler, mouth curled in a sneer, pointing at the window.

"The coat is London Fog. The shirt is cashmere.

And the pants are, well, they're pants."

"Kate, have you lost your mind?"

"That's the sixty-four thousand dollar question, isn't it?" As she'd done so many times in the last year, Kate resisted the urge to smack Tyler. "But if you're referring to Seth's sculpture, I think it's beautiful."

"If you're into having nightmares for the rest of your life, sure." He tugged on her elbow leading her away from the group. "Can I talk to you?"

"No. Sorry. Swamped." She dug in her five-inch heels. "Today is the day we decorate Main Street, and I need to be available."

Seth moved in behind her. Kate shot Grace a pleading look. The last thing they needed was a cockfight in full view of everyone.

Tyler smirked at Seth. "Take a hike, buddy. I'm trying to talk to my girl."

Seth's chest expanded with his intake of air. Kate prayed for patience. "Tyler, we've gone over this. I'm not a girl. Addressing me as such is offensive. I'm not yours. Stop acting like I am. Go away. I'm busy."

"Seth, I need some help in the back. Big boxes. Must weigh a tonne." Grace laced her arm through Seth's. Kate sensed the second he gave up and decided to leave them to it. It was in the shake of his head and the smile he gifted to Grace. Kate rubbed a hand over her heart.

"There, that's better." Tyler caressed her arm in a bid to coax her closer. "How about having supper with me tonight?"

"You know you just made everyone feel awkward, right?" Kate huffed.

"If you mean Stone? I don't really care."

"That was obvious."

"Why are we wasting time discussing that guy?" He tucked a strand of escaped hair behind her ear. "About dinner?"

"I can't."

"You can. Come on, Kate." Tyler grinned, immune to rejection and firm in his belief no one stayed mad at him for long. "We'll head on down to Riley's Grill. Order the biggest steak on the menu. Have us a meal to remember. What do you say?"

"No. I say no. I don't know how many more ways to say no."

"With all the mixed signals you're sending my way you can't expect me to take you seriously." His hand tightened on her arm as she went to brush past. "Come on, Kate. Don't be like that."

She leveled him with a look even Tyler could not fail to understand.

"Take it easy." His grin disappeared. The good-ole-boy act dropped. "You know me, darling. I'm not asking for anything you don't want to give. I didn't help you shovel out this place because I had ulterior motives. I didn't nail, sand, and paint for days for any other reason than helping out a friend. And as a friend, all I'm thinking is you could use a break. For a couple of hours, that's all. As friends."

Her head throbbed. He was right. She couldn't have done it without him. The knowledge made the hammer in her skull strike harder. He had helped get Kate's Closet up and into decent shape. He'd come through at a time when she'd had very few offers of assistance, and a lot of people quietly and politely expecting her to fail.

After one late-night work session, mired in loneliness, tired of self-induced orgasms, and craving a shot of whiskey, she'd kissed him. He tasted familiar and safe. Desolate and frustrated she'd gifted him more than a kiss. When it was over all she'd wanted to do was forget it ever happened. All Tyler wanted was to repeat their big, messy mistake.

He rubbed her arms. "You need to take a break. And someone to remind you to take care of yourself."

While she owed him a debt, she wasn't paying him back with sex, or worse intimacy. "Not tonight. I really have too much work to do with the fair only two weeks away. Maybe after it's over and things have settled down we can grab a quick lunch. As friends. Nothing more."

He stuck his thumbs behind his belt buckle and adjusted its position. It made the shiny buckle jump. His color high, he tipped his head in frustration. "Then promise me after you're done doing what you need to do for the stupid fair, you'll get some rest. You can't fool me. You're not getting enough sleep."

"Tyler, it's not your job to worry about me."

"That's where you're wrong, Kate. It'll always be my job."

And he was gone strutting down the street calling out hellos, offering a wave here and there. She spent a few calming seconds studying her display window. Seth's sculpture was magnificent. A brave, intelligent bird too smart to get caught up in the mess of barbed wire.

It represented everything she wasn't.

"Subtle is not going to work with Tyler. You know this." Grace leaned against the open boutique door, arms crossed. She pushed off and came to stand beside Kate. "If anything, he's becoming more and more of a problem. Don't fool yourself into thinking he's the same guy you dated in high school. He's not. You need to figure out how to cut him loose."

"I know. I'm just trying to do it in a way that guarantees the least collateral damage." Then her debt to him would be paid.

"Just saying, he looks at you like he's got the church booked and he's counting down the hours to the honeymoon. Neither of which can come soon enough for him. He's running out of patience, which on Tyler can be a very bad thing."

Seth's bruised face came to mind. She didn't want them fighting over her. Or for her. Changing the subject was easier than conjuring a solution. "Did you take another look at the link?"

"I did." Grace winced. "I hate to think these are the same people."

"Landslide, Montana, is lucky to be rid of them. I found a personal blog hosted by a local. Once the Wild Rose Prairie Church were done picketing the school, the library, and the local pub, businesses were losing money." She checked for passersby before lowering her voice. "Not to mention the little matter of the church's most vocal opponent turning up dead."

Grace shuddered. "From what I read, other than a different name and a few details they've changed like how they dress, it's the same people."

"Abandoning Landslide, Montana, and turning up here." A sick feeling washed over Kate.

"Yeah, lucky us."

"I phoned and talked to Mike."

Grace made a face. "And what did Constable Do-Right have to say?"

Kate nudged her. "Other than they'd look into it? Not much. Did you know they have some crazy philosophy of adopting secondary families? Apparently, male members have the option of adding an additional wife and her children to their first family."

"Bunch of misogynistic asshats. More like indentured service than anything to do with lending a helping hand and the stability crap they were spouting."

Kate agreed. "I need to find the girl who put the note in my pocket. I think she might be in trouble."

"I don't know..." Grace gave her a worried look. "The less contact you have with them the better. I don't think it's a good thing to seek any of them out. They probably start the brainwashing early on."

"You're probably right. But if I happened to run into her while doing my rounds, then it would be fate, right?" And who was she to argue with that? "I have to stop in at Mary's and finalize a flavor for the petit fours. We're thinking pumpkin sponge cake with caramel butter-cream and coated in chocolate. After that I'm going to take a quick walk around, check on how the decorating is coming along."

"I know I don't need to remind you to stay out of trouble." Grace sent her off with a reluctant wave.

No, she didn't. Besides, she could do subtle. Kate headed across the street to Mary's Café. It served the best comfort food in Aspen Lake along with the latest gossip. The scent of cinnamon and coffee warmed her heart. Mary spotted her and waved her over to the side.

Too late to wonder if Sunni had confided their last conversation to her mother. "Business is booming."

Mary dusted her hands off on the towel that hung from her pristine apron. "And I thank the Lord for it. Come on back."

Mary wasn't only a great cook, she was an efficient organizer. Seated at a table in the back of the kitchen area of the restaurant, they made short work on the menu for Kate's Tea, Cakes, and Couture luncheon.

"It's going to be great. Thank you." Kate shut the file and handed it back to Mary. The same Mary who'd never begrudged her a smile and a hug when she needed it. Even though Kate had never granted the same respect to her daughter.

It was starting to seem a lot...churlish.

Not to mention, a weight she didn't want to carry anymore.

"I owe you another thank you." And an apology, but one step at a time. She put a hand on Mary's arm.

Mary gave her hand a pat. "For what, dear?"

Okay, like ripping off a bandage. Plain words. Honest ones. "For not judging. For your care and support these last couple of years, even though I've continued to be a total bitch to your daughter."

"There is that." Her smile was sad and it broke Kate's heart to see the results of her bad behavior. "And I admit, it hasn't been easy at times, but...well, you had your reasons. Sunni knew that. She didn't want to make things worse for you. I agreed with her."

It had to be said, admitted to, even if it was a roundabout way to say it to the right person. "She makes my dad happy."

Mary nodded and gave her hand a squeeze. "It works both ways."

Kate sniffed. "She's a good person. Like her

mother."

"She'd be happy to hear you say it."

Kate was working up to it, but it was going to take a couple more days. For now, a change in subject was needed. "Can I ask something else?"

"Anything."

"What can you tell me about Matthew Parsons and the Valley church?"

"Heard you had a run-in with him the other day. He's a fool, if you want my opinion." Mary's salt and pepper hair danced in disapproval. "Don't know much. Heard some funny things about how they operate out there."

"He's certainly adamant about stopping the fair."

Mary shook a finger in her face. "You listen to me. Keep your distance. That man's bent on making trouble, for the fair and for you."

"Anything you've heard might help."

"Heard rumors he's got two wives out there." Mary continued, "Also heard he's in charge of everything, including the money. Doles it out about as handily as a miser with his last ten dollars."

"Anything about the children?"

"What children? If you've seen the looks on those kids' faces you know the last thing they're allowed to be is children. Gives a body the shudders."

"Doesn't sound legal."

"Just between you and me, Chase and Mike were out there last week. Matter of a missing girl."

Kate sat up straighter. "A missing girl?"

"Poor thing. I heard they found her. Not the police, but that awful Parsons. What does he call himself? The Shepherd?" Mary rolled her eyes. "Nothing but a pretentious bag of bones.

"What did the girl look like?"

"Not sure. Just know she's back with them."

"Do you know how old she is?"

Mary narrowed her all seeing eyes. "No. Not sure why I would?"

"I was just curious." Kate waved away her questions certain they were talking about her girl. "I need to get going. I want to make the rounds and see how the decorating is going."

"I'll walk you out." Once they were back in the restaurant area, Mary put her hand on her arm. "Wait here a minute. I've got something for you."

Kate stifled a grimace but accepted the bulging grease stained brown paper bag. Fried chicken at its finest. She tried not to inhale the delicious scent of lard and the best fried chicken for miles. She was pretty sure she gained a pound just holding the bag. "Thanks."

"It's nothing. Just a batch of today's special. It'll put some meat on those bones."

Her bones had enough meat, thank you very much. She backtracked to the boutique figuring it might come in handy as a peace offering. She slipped passed Grace and found Seth out back in the alley. She set the bag down on a workbench. "I brought you some lunch."

"You didn't have to do that." Seth opened up the bag and peeked inside. "Man, this smells fantastic."

How did he manage to look sexy sniffing a bag of fried chicken? "No problem."

"You want to share?" He lifted a leg out of the bag.

"No. Thanks." Kate dusted off her hands. "I'm good."

There was an awkward couple of seconds while he

waited, eyebrows raised, chicken leg in hand.

"You sure?" he asked.

When had she forgotten how to take a hint? "Oh, no. I'll leave you to eat. Enjoy."

She didn't move, probably struck immobile by thoughts of sex and Mary's special spices

He lowered the leg. "You gonna stand there and watch me eat?"

Yes. "No. I have things to do."

"Well, then...bye?"

"Right, I'll be going." She and her, if not sensible then certainly fashionable, shoes headed out to the street. She collected her clipboard, fixed her hair, and made sure everything about her screamed professional. That included her shoes. Shoes that did not inspire thoughts of illicit fornication. They were supposed to inspire envy and respect. Why else would a person pay the nose bleeding amount of seven hundred dollars for a pair of shoes?

Sheesh.

****

Guard dog duty was getting old fast, even though Seth had done more avoiding than protecting this past week. And guess what? The world hadn't ended. Seth washed up in the bathroom, splashed a little water on his face before heading for the front of the store. He expected to see Kate. Needed to see her.

Wanted his hands on her. Wanted to pop open buttons, peel off her clothes, pull the pins from her hair. He'd bet everything he owned, which wasn't much, he'd find lace, maybe a bow or two. He wanted to be buried so deep inside her his head spun.

She was making him crazy. Too busy dreaming up

dirty scenarios, he wasn't sleeping. He could swear he'd lost weight. The upside was he was spending lots of time in his studio. Inspiration pummelled him. Ideas flooded his brain. His productivity level was off the charts proving frustration was good for his creative soul.

It took him all of two seconds to realize she wasn't there. He was smart like that. So, where was she? And was her absence cause for concern? He reckoned trouble was the bigger possibility. Shouldn't be his problem. Except it was. Because he was an idiot with a capital I.

Talking to her about her dad had failed. He'd have to try harder. If she agreed to keep her father in the loop, he'd cancel out of this stupid arrangement. The sooner that happened, the sooner he could cajole her into his bed.

Grace paused on her way by with a couple of dresses on hangers. "She's out doing her rounds."

Great. Now he was obvious.

Grace elbowed him in the side. "When you find her tell her I could use some help running her store."

Seth gritted his teeth. "Which direction?"

"She went left." Grace hustled by him toward a group of young women. "Look what I found in the back."

Out on the sidewalk Seth headed in the direction of Cut and Dyed. He stuck his head in the door. There were customers under dryers, in salon chairs, at the sinks but no Kate. Back on the street he sidestepped a miniature cherry picker, one man on the ground, one in the bucket hanging decorations. The sidewalk was congested with all kinds of people. You'd have thought the fair had already started. On any other day he'd have taken the time for some mental snapshots. Immersed himself in the hustle and bustle. Soaked up the inspiration.

But no.

He wasted a precious fifteen minutes dodging in and out of stores. Every shop, bank, or office on Main Street got into the spirit. It was a gothic explosion of ravens, pumpkins, and wheat sheaves with Kate nowhere to be found.

There was a tug on his sleeve. A girl with braided hair in a baggy dress stared up at him doe-eyed. She didn't say anything, just pointed in the opposite direction before scurrying away.

"Wait." Seth lost sight of her when she ducked past a couple who looked like they had antiquing down to an art form.

If she'd been an ordinary kid he would have shrugged it off. But she was from the compound. So...what the hell was she doing seeking him out?

Main Street ran west to east. Seth squinted. Matthew Parsons was setting up shop at the east end of it. The only ones paying him any attention were his flock. But if Parsons wasn't shy about making his presence known Seth wasn't going to care about doing the same. People on the street parted to let him through. A church member thrust a paper at him. Seth crumpled it up and tossed it back.

Then he spotted a flash of black and white. Her timing was impeccable. Kate exited a store across the street from Parsons and stopped at the intersection intending to cross the street. When she saw Parsons, she made an abrupt turn and headed away from him.

Good. She did have some sense of self-preservation.

"JEZEBEL!"

Everyone froze, including Kate.

Seth picked up speed, shouldering his way through a crowd of gaping, snickering teenagers. He willed her to move forward, toward him, his protective instincts on high alert. Instead, she glanced back. It was all the encouragement Matthew Parsons needed.

"That's right." Matthew Parsons lifted a condemning finger and pointed it straight at Kate. His voice carried on the calm, crisp air, bitter and hard. "Take a good look, faithful followers. Do not be deceived. She walks among you. A drunkard. Worshiping at the altar of vanity. Infesting you good people with her loose morals. Do the right thing people of Aspen Lake. Cast. Her. Out."

To the townspeople's credit, they shook their heads or waved his words away in disgust. Kate lifted her chin and started to walk away.

Parsons lifted a black book into the air and raised his voice. "For once you invite Satan over the threshold the welcome lasts a lifetime."

So, Satan and vampires. Good to know. Seth was almost there. Around him people whispered words like cult, crazy, and maniac. His heart pounded with the need to get to her. To spare her. Then Kate moved in his direction and he breathed a sigh of relief. It was all good. Until it wasn't.

Before he could reach her two men blocked her path. She made a show of shrugging her shoulders and, with a quick flick down both sides of the street, she crossed to the other side even though it brought her closer to Parsons. Seth was forced to wait for a pick-up to move by before he followed her. She headed west, away from Parsons. This time a group of four men cut her off. Her only choice was to push through them or go back. She hesitated and they used the opportunity to herd her in the direction of their shepherd.

Seth elbowed his way through the men to get to her. He resisted the mind-warping urge to wrap her up tight with one arm and lash out at the men blocking her exit with the other, like some avenging knight of old. She didn't want a scene so he wouldn't cause one. In a show of solidarity, he put a hand on her arm. "How's it going? Little crowded in town today, don't you think?"

She pressed a hand to her stomach as her eyes darted from one man to the next. "A little."

He willed her to concentrate on him. "We'll find better company at the café. What do you think? Have coffee with me?"

She nodded, but didn't say anything. Didn't move. The men remained a wall in front of them, while Parsons' preached nonsense behind them.

"Come on, princess. Let's go."

There was gratitude mixed in with her shaky shot of laughter. Then she lifted her chin. So sexy. She picked one of the four men to focus on. Her gaze wandered over him, her smile turned a little pouty, a lot flirty, all fake. She winked at him. He looked ready to pass out, or fall at her feet. "So kind of the Valley of the Shepherd Church to help us out by bringing even more attention to our fair." She patted down a corner of his shirt collar, smoothed a hand over it. "Be sure and pass along my thanks to your leader."

He turned white. She had him by the balls. The

shepherd had done too good a sell job on her character. The man was terrified of her. They all were. You could see her confidence come flooding back. Sexy stilettos met ugly black boots. They managed to hold their ground, eyes wide, lips clenched shut. A low purr sounded on the hushed air. She leaned in and ran a finger down his cheek. "Tsk, tsk. Rumor is you can go to Hell for what you're thinking."

Blotches of red painted his cheeks. She blew a kiss to the man on his right. He tripped over his feet backing up. The other two sidestepped before she could get to them. The sea parted, her exit a thing of beauty.

Every man on their side of the street, openly or covertly, had his eyes glued to her ass. She did them all a favor. She took her time walking away. Shoulders back, hips swaying, impossibly graceful on those killer heels of hers. They watched her cross the street, not looking away until the door of Kate's Closet closed behind her. He rubbed a hand over his heart. The man, who'd had the pleasure of her finger brushing his cheek, stood rooted to the spot. Yeah, he was definitely going to Hell.

Seth checked in with Parsons. The man's anger hit Seth from half a block away. He pointed his book at him, shook it, and shouted, "Be careful which side you choose, Mr. Stone."

Seth ignored him and zeroed in on the girl tucked into his side. Even with her head down, he recognized her as the one who'd pointed him in the direction of Parsons. She ducked under Parsons' arm and slipped away.

Her timing was excellent. Next second a cop car pulled up in front of the preacher's temporary sidewalk pulpit. Two officers exited the vehicle. Seth decided it was safe to leave. He passed Mary, who stood sentry on the sidewalk, arms crossed, watching the police talk to Parsons. She nodded her satisfaction at him, put out an arm to stop him, and pulled him into the cafe.

"Wait here." She left him standing at the front of the cafe and proceeded to pour coffee into two to-go cups. She glanced over her shoulder. "Cream? Sugar?"

"Just black, thanks." Everyone's eyes were on him. It wasn't paranoia on his part.

"Kate, too." Mary passed him the cups. "On the house."

Pot in hand, she walked away to take care of refills at the tables and booths full of customers. Seth blinked. Chatter resumed, the tiny bell above the door chimed as a couple entered. Stan Knight clapped a hand on his shoulder and smiled before making his way out the door maneuvering Seth along with him.

Stan looked up and down the street. Seconds passed before the old man decided to say something. "That man's going to cause more trouble before he's done. Bill seems to think he can trust you to run interference. From what I saw, I'm inclined to agree. Keep your eyes open, son."

Seth didn't know what to say, and Stan didn't seem to need a response but moved on down the street. Surprise morphed into guilt. He'd spent considerable time last night plotting how to shed that particular duty. The idea of spying on her was making his skin crawl. And he would fix it. As soon as he figured how to manage it, keep his job, and Kate. But as much as he was starting to like the old guy, Stan Knight didn't need to know that.

Seth stared after him. A customer he recognized from the Yard shuffled past him, lifted his hand in greeting. Seth grinned back. No words needed. And no stopping the warm flood of feeling washing through him. It had nothing to do with fresh coffee. More a sense of belonging. Something he hadn't felt in years.

Under the awning of the local café, across the street from Kate's store, standing in the middle of nowhere, he recognized it. His place. His spot on the planet. He wasn't only falling for his gutsy boss, he was falling for the town, its people, the whole package.

****

Kate pushed an exhausted Grace out the door at 5:00 pm but kept the boutique open for another hour. Very little traffic came through the door leaving her with lots of time to think. It wasn't every day a raving lunatic called her a whore in the middle of Main Street. But she'd survived. What she lost in dignity she gained in sympathy. And sales. She indulged in a quick and dirty happy dance to the sweet, sweet tune of take-that-you-sanctimonious-bastard.

Next on her list, a thank-you to Seth for his help earlier. She flipped the Open sign to Closed. A little high from the volume of sales, a lot smug over her victory in the street, and totally panicked at being alone with Seth, her whole body echoed at the sound of the door clicking shut. Her heart hammered. Her skin bristled. The Venus in her wanted his hands and mouth on her. The mouse in her longed to scramble for its hole.

Sated or safe? She wandered back than stood paralyzed, neither in nor out, of the doorway leading into the storage room. Seth was bent over the plans they'd discussed the night she'd tried to kiss him. The fading afternoon light retreated across the floor while she breathed in the scent of man at work. A door sat off its hinges leaving an empty space leading upstairs to her apartment. And her bed.

Her fingers itched to trace the bold lines of ink and bronzed skin, no matter he had bad idea written all over him. He'd come to her rescue.

Why was it sexy when he did it?

She pushed off from the doorway and picked her way across the room over bits of this, pieces of that, and the odd tool. With the ear buds in his ears, he didn't hear her approach. When she tapped him on the shoulder, he swung around and bumped into her. She tried to dodge but managed to trip instead. He caught her, pulled her up against his chest, her heels lifting out of her shoes.

"Shit. Sorry. Are you all right?" With one hand he pulled the ear buds out. The other hand wrapped around her waist and held on. The warmth of his skin seeped through his shirt and hers. Her buttons, his belt buckle bit into sensitive skin. If they were fruit, you'd have to peel her off to get to him.

"I'm so far from all right I don't know where to begin." She studied his eyes, noted the pores of his skin, the slight parting of his lips. The material of her shirt bunched as his fingers tightened across her back. His other hand smoothed up the back of her neck.

The appeal in his eyes was mesmerizing. His voice pleading. "For both our sakes, tell me to take a hike."

It was the one thing she couldn't do.

In slow motion he dipped his head. His lips brushed hers, warm and firm to her stiff and out of practice. He nipped at her bottom lip, his hand cupping her cheek, his thumb caressing the line of her jaw. He watched and waited until her body purred in response to his petting. "It's your move."

Her body reacted like water called by the moon. Her arms, until then left useless and dangling, lifted to rest on his wide shoulders. Her fingers absorbed his heat through the thin cotton of his shirt. She met his mouth. He tasted like sin. And more.

She had no idea how to deal with anything beyond a kiss, as wonderful as it was. It involved the section of her programming she'd lost, confidence and self-possession. She pulled back but left her eyes closed and savored.

"That was nice." She bit down on her bottom lip. Her eyes opened to find him studying her. Not looking for cracks in her psyche but like a man who wanted to stick his tongue down her throat. It was a good look on him. A bit of self-assurance crept back in. "We should do it again sometime."

He dropped kisses on the corner of her mouth, along her jawline until he hit the sweet spot behind her ear. "Next go around I'll try to do better than nice."

Her resistance packed its bags and hit the road. "Okay."

"Goodnight, princess." He tucked her against him in a warm hug, his chin coming to rest on the top of her head. She melted against him, her knees in danger of buckling. His breath whispered against her hair. "I'll come in tomorrow. With the fair looming, I want to start on the display counter."

"Tomorrow," she repeated, as nothing else came to mind and the swelling silence begged for words to fill it.

"Lock the door behind me." His knuckles scraped across her cheek.

He let himself out the back, and she covered his touch with her fingertips. She hadn't felt anything close to sexual desire in a very long time. All she'd felt in relation to any kind of craving was panic.

Which reminded her, she wasn't in her car on the way to the city and her regular AA meeting. Even though she knew Our Saviour's Lutheran two blocks over hosted one every Saturday night too. So far the courage to walk in and join the circle had evaded her.

But not tonight.

Tonight that changed. She would own it. No apologies for taking up a seat. She would be a woman who wanted to do better. Be better. To be more than a survivor. To be a woman who thrived.

One confident enough to invite a man into her bed. To enjoy him. And herself. And the hell with what anyone thought. Before she could rethink, she grabbed her purse and headed out the door.

Bravado deserted her on the doorstep of the church. Stubbornness got her through the door. Coffee and tenacity gave her what it took to say her name and state why she was there.

She'd done it. Not only that, she stayed and waited. And listened. She made connections. She triumphed. All of her tingled with the high of climbing another section of her personal Mount Everest. Exhausted, she crawled into bed early. She grinned at the ceiling until her eyes closed.

The first call came in at 11:00 pm. Private caller. Silence greeted her. She shrugged it off. Kids being kids.

Three more followed. She was not amused. She was freaking out. Her head full of paranoid thoughts of axe murders coming to finish the job. After the fourth call and another attempt at *69, and still not getting the blocked caller's number, she went into full panic mode. Another call. She disconnected the line-in cord from the wall.

Then her cell rang. By then she'd triple checked the deadbolt on the one door that hadn't yet been replaced.

She switched her phone to silent. It kept flashing, flashing, and flashing until she thought she'd go insane. She didn't dare turn it off completely. What if that was what he wanted? To isolate her? She didn't dare step foot outside her apartment. The only thing out there was a narrow staircase.

She was deciding who to call, the police or the phone company, when the calls stopped. She stared down at her phone expecting it to light up. Or explode. When it stayed silent, she tried not to think the worst. Instead, she switched back to her prank calls theory. She reconnected her landline and waited. Nothing.

She breathed a cautious sigh of relief. No going back to bed for her. Someone was watching, she could feel it. Watching and waiting with his axe for her lights to go out.

Oh God.

She called the police not caring if she was overreacting. They got paid to deal with crazy. Lucky for her, Mike and Chase were on duty. They came bringing their calm sense of authority with them.

"The alley's clear." Mike came to sit down beside

her on her tiny loveseat. There was nothing more reassuring than the creak of leather, the shift of stiff clothing, the sight of a red stripe running down a pressed pair of pants. The badass black boots, the crackling radio soothed her hammering heart. He put a hand over her white knuckled clasp of fingers nesting in her lap. "So is the street. Chase is doing another check of your shop."

She slid one hand out from under his to rub her aching forehead. "I overreacted. It was probably just kids. But with the break-in and everything..."

"Don't be sorry, that's what we're here for." He reached for her mug of tea and coaxed her to have a sip. "Any idea who it could have been? Besides kids playing games."

"Well, let's see...other than an axe wielding maniac, the creepy shepherd from the compound, or any number of his followers, nope no idea." She wrapped her fingers around the mostly cold cup.

"Heard what happened on the street today."

She grimaced. "I'm guessing name calling isn't against the law, and he's still free to roam about and cast stones?"

Mike lifted her chin and stared her down. "It's not a joke, Kate. If you're being harassed by this guy, we need to know."

She wilted with exhaustion. Engaging with Parsons would give him what he craved—attention. "It was nothing. Let's not make it into a big deal. That's what he wants."

Mike dropped his hand. "You should think about getting an unlisted number. If the calls keep happening get your provider to set up a phone trap. They turn the information over to us, and we'll deal with it from there."

"It's just kids." She was almost convinced of it.

"Doesn't matter," insisted Mike. "We'll talk to whoever it is and make it stop."

Constable Chase Porter strolled into the room, settled on the arm of the couch on the other side of her. "Downstairs is clear. Main Street is clear. No one's around. But darlin', you need to get your alarm hooked back up."

"Believe me, it's on my to-do list."

Chase laid a hand on her shoulder. "You okay?"

"I'm fine. Thank you for coming."

"We aim to please, Ms. Logan." Chase winked and gave her shoulder a squeeze.

Mike stood up. "Don't give it another thought. And don't hesitate to call us back. I mean it, Kate. That's what we're here for."

Chase smirked at her. "I could stay for a bit. It's quiet for a Saturday night. You'd be doing me a favor and saving me from listening to this one whine about how his hair *stylist* trimmed off a quarter inch too much of his precious hair." He jerked a thumb in his partner's direction.

"You're never going to let that go, are you? And it was one time." He turned to Kate, all wounded ego and searching for some sympathy. "I mentioned it one time."

"Yeah, well, next time something goes wrong at the spa keep it to yourself."

"It was a barbershop, and for the price you'd expect a little more attention to detail."

"What evs, bestie."

Their banter worked. Kate managed a laugh. "You two make such a cute couple."

"Already married." Chase pointed to the band on his ring finger. "And one wife is enough, thanks."

Mike grinned at Kate. "I'm too good looking for him anyway."

Chase rolled his eyes at Kate. "Yeah, that's it."

"You're both too handsome for your own good."

Chase shook his head at her. "Don't say stuff like that. It goes straight to his head, and then there's no living with him."

"Moving on." Mike held out a hand and pulled her to her feet. "We're here if you need us."

Chase gave her a pat on the shoulder. "We'll make our presence known out front with regular patrols. You're safe. Get some sleep."

"Thanks, guys."

After they left, she slipped between the covers and tried. She really did, but it was never going to work. She didn't manage anything but a light doze. At two thirty in the morning the calls started again. She unplugged her landline and turned her cell on silent. She crawled back into bed. Wrapped up in her grandmother's quilt she stared at the moon out her window. She closed her eyes and imagined Seth was with her, that his arms were wrapped around her holding her close and blocking out the world.

Chapter Five

Seth had given up on sleep. So, he was frustrated? He added a couple of rough strokes to his sketch. What guy didn't know the feeling? But this thing with Kate was taking it to a whole new level. Jerking off had become his favorite pastime. Which reminded him, he needed to get his sheets out of the dryer and back on his bed.

She was inspiration overload. But that was a good thing. A very good thing. The proof was filling up his sketchpad. Kate kneeling on the bare floor, hands clasped and resting at the small of her back, head bowed, wearing only thigh high stockings and high heels. She'd hate it, not that she'd ever see it. He loved the idea of her on her knees before him. A little too much. He'd spent an extra fifteen minutes in the shower because of it.

He flipped the page. This one showed her posed in the street, hands wrapped around the hilt of her sword. The tip of it plunged into the pavement. Clad in a leather corset, short skirt, and thigh high boots she was magnificent. The next picture proved he was becoming a little too obsessed with women's footwear. An almost naked Kate lay curled up on his bed. Shoes on, a hand resting under her cheek, the other between her legs.

Possibly he was on the brink of needing an intervention. He tossed his sketch pad down onto the pile of crap spilling over his coffee table. Instructed himself to think about something else. Anything else. Like how much he needed to do some paperwork. And filing. Which he hated and therefore avoided.

The pages fluttered and flipped back to the face of the mystery girl. Ask and you shall receive. Thoughts of the Shepherd and his plans were enough to kill the most stubborn boner.

What was she? Eight? Ten? Sad eyes. Watchful. Still. No smile. Victim? Or pawn? He flipped the book closed. She wasn't, couldn't, be his concern.

He had the custom cabin beam for the northern fishing lodge to finish. A gallery in the city had offered to take two more of his pieces on consignment but they wanted them by the end of November. One was half finished, the other was in the preliminary stages.

He'd hauled the huge birch burl out of his truck, and it was drying in his studio. Once its weight stabilized, he had big plans for it. He figured two pieces. One large and one small. The concept so clear, the vision so precise, he was able to map his process all the way to completion. Kate might make him crazy, but her kind of crazy inspired his ingenuity. He sat back on the couch. Let his head fall back and stared at the ceiling. Sleeping with her was a given. He was over denying it.

Onto plotting how to make it happen.

A rare knock on his door shattered his quiet. He frowned. No one visited him here. That's the way he liked it. The knock sounded again, and he headed in the direction of the back door. His stepsister grinned at him from across the threshold. "Surprise."

Seth's heart sank. He checked to see if Caroline

was with her. But, no, looked like she was alone. "Ash. What are you doing here?"

She swatted his arm. "Could you pretend to look happy to see me, please?"

"I'm happy to see you." He frowned at her. "Are you alone?"

"You're safe." She stuck out her bottom lip. "She sent me as proxy."

"Still happy to see you." He gave into the urge to gather her in his arms. "Missed you."

She clung to him. "It's been awful since you left."

"Come on in." He eyed the two bright pink suitcases sitting just outside the door. "Planning on staying awhile?"

"If you'll have me? I can't take the crazy anymore."

"No problem." He slipped past her to grab her bags.

"She's totally losing it, Seth."

He swung the door open wider and motioned her past. "How about we get through the front door and we'll talk."

"Thanks, bro." She grinned. "I won't stay long. I'll figure out a plan, and then I'll be gone. I promise."

"Don't worry about it. *Mi casa es su casa.*" He winked at her.

She reached up onto tiptoes and gave him a peck on the cheek. "You're too good to me. I hope you know that."

He opened the door across from the laundry/mudroom. "You can bunk here until you figure shit out."

"Thanks." Ash turned in a slow circle. "Nice

place."

"It's a place to crash."

On light feet she danced over to stand in front of him. "Master of the understatement, as usual. God, I missed you."

After his father died, Caroline had crawled into bed and stayed there, weeping and wailing at the unfairness of it all. Seth and Ash had fended for themselves. It was either that or starve.

Seth grinned. "Come on, I'll show you the rest of the place."

She punched him in the shoulder. "Sounds awesome."

After a tour of the rest of the cabin, they ended up back in the kitchen. Ash picked a discarded t-shirt up off the edge of the couch. "I see you haven't gotten any neater."

Seth put a hand on each of her shoulders and pointed her at the fridge. "I'll be back in an hour. You can start earning your keep and make lunch."

"Where are you going?"

He called back over his shoulder. "Studio."

"Hey, can I see—"

"Off limits." He yelled back and let the door slam shut after him.

He'd give her an hour to snoop and to settle. They'd have lunch, catch up, and then he'd head into town to work at Kate's. He had an apology of his own to make.

****

Kate grabbed her phone and read the latest text.

Lily: *Srsly, get unlisted # stat.*

Her: *Yes, Mommy.*

Lily: *Black with pink polka dots*

Her: *What?*

Lily: *Oops, 2 conversations going at once. Disregard.*

Kate: *OMG Awkward*

Lily: *Gotta keep my man happy...*

Kate: *SFL*

Lily: *?*

Kate: *Scarred. For. Life.*

Lily: *LOL, gotta go dr's finally here*

Kate tapped out a *Give her my best* and slid her phone into her pocket. She went back to work stocking display shelves and checking the hanging racks. She'd abandoned her apartment early this morning. Being fueled by anxiety and caffeine had its advantages. It was amazing how much work she'd gotten done.

She refused to think about their kiss. Chaste as it was. Fantasizing didn't pay the bills. Or settle her nerves. She went back grabbed another box of inventory and carried it through to the front. Someone banged on the door, and she jumped. Seconds later, she heard a tapping on the front window. Tyler motioned for her to open the door.

Kate inhaled and held it for a couple of beats. Then released it still no closer to having the emotional stability to deal with Tyler. He grinned at her through the glass and held up an enormous bouquet of flowers. Hands on hips, she shook her head at him. He spread his arms wide in appeal. In that moment, he looked so much like the boy she'd dated in high school. Silly when she needed. There for her when her mother died. First base. Second. Third. All the way home. He'd wiped her tears and wrapped her in a blanket he'd brought along.

He'd loved the tall, gawky girl before she'd become Kate Logan. When that Kate Logan had slunk home messed up and rung out, he'd been there for her.

Facebook had it right. It was complicated. She knew it was stupid to let him in, but she unlocked the door anyway. Hoping she could make him understand without killing their friendship dead. Sweetheart pink roses and masses of tiny white flowers came through the door first. Hat in hand, he offered them to her.

She sighed, the green florist paper crinkling in the frustrated crush of her grip. "Tyler."

"Your favorites."

When she'd been sixteen. But she smiled. "They're beautiful. Thank you."

"I happened to be in the neighborhood and thought I'd stop by and see how you were doing?" He swiped a knuckle down her cheek. "You look tired, Kate. What happened to getting some sleep last night?"

A wave of suspicion swamped her. She narrowed her eyes searching for the tiniest hint of guilt. Did he know? Had he been behind the hang-ups? "Why wouldn't I have slept?"

He frowned at her. "You had a break-in not that long ago, remember? Anyone would lose sleep." It was his turn to be suspicious. "Why, did something else happen? I hate the thought of you alone up there in that cubbyhole you call an apartment. It isn't safe. Thank God, you weren't home the night of the break-in or who knows what could have happened."

"I'm fine." Maybe she should tattoo it on her forehead. Save herself the trouble of repeating it.

"Think about moving into the empty house on

Birch Street. You'd be doing me a favor by staying there. It's not good for a house to sit empty."

It was an old argument. One they'd had many times. She ignored his prodding. "Where were you last night?"

"What?"

"Last night? Where were you?"

He tilted his head and gave her a funny look. "The Cattlemen's Dinner, remember? It ran late, as usual. Shit, you should have seen Martin Higgins and Edward Mullins arm wrestling. On second thought, be glad you missed it. Two old has-been rodeo riders trying to reclaim their youth. Pitiful. Shoot me when I get to that stage, yeah? By the time we finished up, and got the grandpas home and tucked in, it was the wee hours."

She closed her eyes. The district's Cattlemen Association met the second Saturday of every month. Tyler was the president. She shook her head in apology. "I'm sorry…I'm not thinking straight this morning."

Tyler went on alert. "Something did happen."

She put a restraining hand on his arm. "No. Nothing. I promise. The fair is taking up every waking moment, and I'm feeling the panic of last minute details, that's all."

"It sounds like you could use a break. So…" He set his hat on the counter and rubbed his palms together. "…what say you and I grab a blanket, take a ride, and have a picnic somewhere?"

"I can't."

"Yes. You can." He plucked the flowers out of her hand, laid them down, and grabbed for her hand. "Time for some fun."

"Tyler." She worked to disengage her fingers, but

his grip tightened. "I said, I can't."

"Come on, darlin'. I've only got a couple of hours before I'm meeting the guys and heading to the city to see some Sunday night football." He tugged her up against him. "Let's spend them together."

She slapped a hand against his chest. "Stop it. That's enough, Tyler."

He grabbed her arms and squeezed. "This better not have anything to do with that carpenter of yours?"

"It has to do with you. No does not mean 'convince me,' Tyler." She pushed him back a step. "It means no."

He gave her a shake. The shock of it had her lifting disbelieving eyes to his. Having gained her attention, he did it again. "I don't believe you. I see the way he looks at you, and I don't like it. I thought you were done with that kind of guy. I thought that's what the last year and half was about."

She glared up at him. "You're missing the point. It's not for you to dislike."

He let her go like all of a sudden he couldn't stand the sight of her. His finger stabbed in accusation. "I thought you were finally starting to get it together. To figure out what it is that works in your life. *Who* works in your life."

She rubbed her aching arms. "You need to leave. Get out. Now."

He laughed. "You want to know what I think? I think things are finally settling down and starting to go your way and that scares the crap out of you, so you're determined to find a way to screw things up."

"Leave." She pointed to the door. "I'm not telling you again."

He advanced, brows raised, mouth taut. She retreated, but he caught her and dragged her back. "Get your coat. We're going for a drive."

"Let go of me." She kept the panic in check. Tried to pry his fingers from her arm.

He yanked her closer. His breath came in hard puffs against her face. "I'm sick and tired of waiting for you to come to your senses. Grow up, Kate."

His tough guy cowboy boots were no defense against the four inch, spiked heel of the last pair of Louboutin heels she'd ever be able to afford. He released her, and she walloped him across the face as hard as she could.

He covered the strike mark with a hand. "What the hell is wrong with you?"

"There's nothing wrong with me." And for the first time in a long time, she meant it. "I'm not telling you again. Get out or I'm calling the police."

She picked up her phone. Dialling with one hand she picked up his flowers with the other, then dangled them over the wastebasket and let them drop.

She pushed the speakerphone button.

"Aspen Lake Police Detachment. How can I help you?"

Tyler's chest heaved. "Don't be stupid."

She kept her eyes locked on him. "Hi, Bernice. Any of the guys around? I've got a bit of a problem."

"Hold tight, I'll send someone over."

"Thanks, I appreciate it. Any chance someone can stay on the line with me for a couple of minutes?"

"No problem. Deke's here. I'll put you through."

"Thanks, Bernice."

Tyler jabbed a finger in her direction, his lip

curled, his fists clenched. "You're going to regret this, Kate."

Tyler pushed past Seth, who was coming in the door. "When you figure out it's a real man you need, you know where to find me."

Seth stopped and stared after Tyler, then turned his questioning, very unhappy gaze to her.

Kate held up a finger for silence. "Hey, Kate. Deke here. What's going on? You need me to come to the store?"

"No. Sorry to bother you. False alarm. After last night, I'm a bit edgy."

"No problem. I'll come down and talk to you anyway. Just to make sure. Set my mind at ease. See you in a few minutes." He hung up before she could dissuade him. Once Deke was in motion, he was an unstoppable force.

"What's going on?" Seth was glancing around the boutique searching out evidence of trouble. "What happened last night?"

"I had some hang ups, and I didn't want to take any chances, so I called the police." She hoped she sounded responsible and competent and that the mention of prank phone calls would distract him.

"And this morning? With crazy pants?" He jerked a thumb toward the door.

No such luck. "I needed to make a point. It worked. We can forget about it."

"You felt the need to call the fucking cops, Kate."

"Can we not make a big deal out of it? Please?"

He picked Tyler's flowers out of the trash and threw them back in. "Bullfuckingshit."

"You have to trust me. I've known him my whole

life. I know what I'm doing. How to handle him."

"That makes you the expert then." With that he stomped into the back.

There was a little too much mocking in there to suit Kate's newly awakened confidence. He hadn't meant it as a challenge, but she accepted it as one. She armed herself with a fresh coat of lip gloss and a tug or two at her clothes. She stepped into the storage area in time to see the hammer fly from his hand and embed in the wall across from him. Bits of plaster flew as he paced in the settling dust. Ink rippled over expanding and contracting muscles that resisted nature and the instinct to leap.

"You don't want to be around me right now." His nostrils flared with his air intake. Strands of his tawny hair escaped whatever he'd tied it back with that morning.

"Seth." Because she was pretty sure she did. Want to be around him, that was. Didn't stop her throat from going dry when those amber eyes zeroed in on her.

"Don't." He stalked away from her. Came back. Prowled away.

"I need you to trust me." She put her hand out and caught his arm. A reflex on her part. To keep him close.

He swung around to stare at her. "You don't *handle* guys like Bodnar. Words don't work. You go for his 'nads. You end things in terms they understand."

"You're right." She held up both hands, conciliatory, quieting. "He's a problem. I know that. I'm taking care of it."

In the quietest way possible.

He looked like he was going to say something then he shut his mouth, only to open it again a second later.

"He's not going to stop. Not until he gets what he wants. And what he wants is you."

"Well, he can't have me." Her stare was a little too direct. Her emphasis on the word "he" too pronounced. His pupils dilated. He pressed closer. A muscle jerked along his jawline.

She'd bet everything she owned he wasn't thinking of her as fragile. Or unstable. Or damaged.

"Don't look at me like that," he growled.

She raised an eyebrow and offered a challenge of her own. "Like what?"

He closed in and, how handy, the wall moved in to hold her up. He wrapped a hand around her throat pushing her chin up. "Like you're putting me on the menu."

Her body soaked up his heat. "Too late. I'm ready to order."

His tongue was in her mouth two seconds after the last word escaped her lips. His hair tangled with her fingers. So glorious. His hand slipped under her sweater, calloused, rough, and warm against her skin. She wanted it to go on, and on, and—

"Kate," Deke called. "You back there?"

They froze. Or rather...she froze, and Seth managed a couple of less than complimentary words at Deke's timing, his hands still roaming.

She broke away and smoothed out her clothes. Into the heated, steamy nothingness, she called out, "I'll be right there, Deke."

Seth caught her arm and swiped a thumb over the skin under her bottom lip. It came away smeared with Blushing Sequin lip color. "There, that's better."

Her lips still tingled. Other places too. When he put

his thumb to his mouth and sucked the spot of pink away, she wanted to forget there was a member of the Royal Canadian Mounted Police waiting for an explanation.

"Go. And remember, it's a crime to lie to the police. I'll talk to you later." He stifled a smirk, then gave her a gentle nudge toward the door and reality.

****

See you later turned into not at all. Kate ended up spending most of the day in an emergency meeting with the fair committee. Then it was Sunday supper with her dad, which now, as hell had apparently frozen over, included Sunni. Awkward at first, the meal ended peaceably enough. Less angry and tense on her part and less trying too hard on Sunni's, but exhausting for all the effort given. When she'd gotten back, Seth was on the phone. It didn't sound like a pleasant conversation so she gave him some space.

Instead of a trail of breadcrumbs or lingerie, she left the door leading up to her apartment open. She rubbed her arms, more nervous reaction than a need for warmth. She was plenty warm. Horny, really, if she were in the habit of using crass words. Too bad it fit exactly.

Her one window faced Main Street. Large enough to brighten the space, it also lessened the claustrophobic feel of her small one room apartment. It offered an excellent view of the skyline, which didn't reach higher than three stories. The sun rested on the horizon, orange and reds cloaking the scattering of other apartments above other shops. A Sunday night silence settled in over the empty street.

Seth's truck was parked in the alley. Not that she

was hiding anything. Or ashamed of wanting him. But the whole town didn't need to know she had urges of a sexual nature when she'd put considerable effort, except for one unfortunate night, into giving the exact opposite impression.

She closed her eyes, heart hammering, nerves tightening at the sound of footsteps on the stairs. The warm, smooth scent of cut wood reached out to her. He came to stand beside her, and the weight of his presence steadied her. Taking a cue from her, he shoved his hands in his pockets and stared out the window. "I need to tell you something."

Separate and facing away from each other wasn't what she had in mind for tonight. "That doesn't sound promising."

When she turned, so did he. She took a step closer, and he took a step back.

"Kate."

But it wasn't rejection she heard in his voice. It was a warning. One she chose to ignore. She smiled as she moved in close enough to pick out the coppery hints in his cat eyes. She laid the palms of her hands on his chest and watched his nostrils flare. His heart hammered a beat to match her own. It was a drum call to the old Kate. "Is this the part where you do your best to convince me this shouldn't happen?"

"No, but it is the part where I'm honest and upfront about a couple of things. One thing in particular. And then you can decide if you still want us to happen. For the record I really hope you do, but I'll understand if you don't."

Her hands slipped from his chest to cross in front of her own. She braced. "Fair enough. Let's hear it."

He scrubbed at the back of his neck, a no-win look to his eyes. "Your father asked me to look out for you."

Her stomach fluttered. "He asked you what?"

"There's more."

"Of course, there is." But she didn't want to hear it.

"He wanted me to let him know if you ran into any trouble."

"So, you're spying on me?" She took a step back.

He lifted a hand then let it drop. "Supposed to, yeah."

Another step back. "Supposed to?"

"That ended about fifteen minutes ago." His hand found hers. He threaded his fingers with hers.

Contact. So tenuous. So easily broken. So why didn't she? "The phone call."

He tugged her close and kissed her knuckles. His other hand lifted to cup her cheek. "Don't push me away. Give me a chance to explain."

She put her hand over his regret flushing away the lovely taste of desire. "Seth, if I can't trust you, I can't sleep with you."

"I understand that. I'm trying to prove you can trust me." Under her fingers his thumb brushed across her cheek. "I'm not going to offer up lame excuses. Bottom line? I was a fool for agreeing to do it, but he can be—" His forehead dipped to hers. "I want to make it right."

She bit at her bottom lip. He was asking for a second chance. Denying them to others was no way to earn one for herself. "How'd he take the news?"

"He's not happy with me." His words were heavy with relief. "I'm picturing a lot of grunt work in my future."

"That makes me feel better."

His lips were warm against hers. "Tell me you forgive me."

She kissed him instead. Nothing timid. Or uncertain. She took what she wanted and invited him along. His mouth opened to her assault, to the wondrous fusion of wonder and knowing for certain.

His hands dropped to grasp the band of her sweater as he broke the seal of their lips. "Arms up."

She didn't question his demand, but lifted them and he swept away her sweater.

He skimmed the back of his knuckles over her collarbone, down to the curve of her breast, and over her bra. "That's what I'm talking about."

She put a finger under his chin and lifted his eyes to hers. "Time for me to confess something." He grew wary under her hands. "I'm not…I've haven't…done this in a while. Be patient with me."

"Never doubt it." His hands smoothed over her hair. "And don't doubt this."

His lips traced along her jaw leaving a trail of sweet longing behind. She felt it swirl and swell until it filled the air around them with the needy scents of passion and want. His fist curled into her hair, the other hand tracked the line of her spine to its base. She shivered as the flat of his hand molded to the curve of her behind and brought her in close.

"Need more." He wrapped his arms around her thighs and lifted her up. Of their own free will, her legs wrapped around his waist. She reached down and took his mouth back, pressing closer until they were fused together.

Small spaces did have their blessings. The bed was

close and took no time to get to. She let him lay her down across the soft comforter. He untangled himself and stood up. She came up on her elbows not wanting to miss a second.

Conscious of her eyes on him, he yanked off his work boots, his socks, undid his pants. When he straightened, they slid off. His underwear dropped to the floor. He wasn't shy about being naked. Didn't have that overpowering need to cover up before anyone got a really good look. Then again, he was a feast for the eyes.

"Your turn," he murmured. He grabbed her ankle and yanked her to the end of the bed.

The covers, clenched in her fists, came with her. Two seconds in and the bed was a mess. She sucked in a breath, lowered her voice. "You really are too beautiful for words."

He frowned as he palmed the heel of her shoe and tugged it off. Very carefully he set it to the side. He repeated the act with her other shoe. "I'm putting these back on after the rest of it comes off."

She wheezed a protest, which he ignored. Strong hands slipped over her insoles, up her calves, her thighs, until he reached the top button of her pants. All of a sudden, she was very aware of the lamp she'd left on. The fact the blinds were open. There was entirely too much light, and she wanted to lose the rest of her clothes in the dark.

The ravages of drinking her problems away were documented on her body. Stretch marks, scars from her accident, a tummy she couldn't hide. Her body was a plump ghost of the one that strutted down runways half-naked. In and out of clothes, with only seconds to spare between changes, modesty had been the first of her inhibitions to go and the first one she'd reclaimed.

"Don't get shy on me now." Her stomach quivered under the press of his palms. She held her breath when his fingers went to work on the fastenings holding her insecurities at bay. He bent over and kissed the tiny pink bow peeking out from the opening of her jeans.

"Not shy." Her eyes slammed shut at the sensory overload of warm breath and callused hands. She exhaled on a whisper, when she wanted to sound strong, in control. "Out of practice."

Her jeans made the slow slide over her quivering thighs, down her calves, to land with a thump of clothing on the floor.

"Relax." The bed dipped as he lay down beside her. There was nothing she could do about the jump of her muscles as he started drawing lazy circles over her stomach, played with the edge of her smoky gray panties. "You're not at the dentist."

The challenge in his voice forced her to focus. With his head propped up on a hand, he wasn't watching her face but concentrating on the traveling path of his fingers as they caught up to her bra. She compelled him to look at her. "I know where I am."

To prove it, she rolled over to straddle him, settling down over his hips. Heated lace rubbed over his erection. Once. Twice. Three times. Need, his and hers, dampened her panties. Then she was on her back again, the last scrap of her clothing hit the floor. Fingers cuffing her ankles, he found her shoes and slipped them back on.

"That's better." He kissed his way back up until his mouth found her bra-covered breast. He pulled the straps down her arms and she was caught up in a silky trap. Then her bra joined the rest of her clothes. He dipped his head and blew across the peak of one nipple. "So perfect."

"Yes, you are." Her fingers searched for the elastic that held his hair back and pulled it out. It was thick and glorious and long enough to brush her bare skin. She twisted her fingers into its length and guided his lips back to her aching breast.

She spread her legs, and his hands warm and coaxing widened the distance. His fingers delved. "So wet."

His lips brushed over her breast, one of his fingers slid inside her. Her back bowed off the covers, a moan clogging her throat. A second finger joined the first. She might have whispered don't stop, or please, or a little to the left. Then she lost the ability to speak as his mouth kissed his way down her body. Until he reached the spot swollen with need.

"That's it." He kissed and licked, while she panted and bucked. "Show me what you like. What you need me to do."

She had no idea how to say she liked it all. And do? She was open to suggestions. His fingers moved inside her.

"That. Do that again." She gasped, her nails digging into his scalp.

"This?" His hand pressed down as his fingers curled inside her. "More of this?"

One last, long lick. "Oh, God. Yes…that."

"Come for me, Kate." Her heels dug into the mattress in an effort to push his fingers in further, to get him to suck harder, to clutch at the high that hovered just out of reach. It worked. She came. So hard she forgot to breathe.

"Beautiful." His lips found hers and guided her hands over ridged muscles and lower until they wrapped around his erection. He let go to fill his hands with her breasts. Hesitant, her thumb swiped over the tip, circled the head of his penis.

"Don't worry." His fingers were back on hers, guiding, teaching. "It won't break."

She squeezed and slid her hand down the length of him, responding to his commands even though she could hardly think for the tightening of her nipples, her stomach, her thighs. For the urgency rebuilding between her legs.

Seth groaned. "Jesus, yes. Just like that."

They were the sweetest words she'd ever heard. A flip switched. Her hand gripped tighter, pumped faster, demanding he respond. The sight of him, breathing heavy, teeth grinding, stalled in that moment of needing more, was one of the most beautiful she'd ever witnessed.

Then his hand was on hers pulling it away. He shifted away from her and she reached for him. "Wait. No."

"Condom, princess."

She panicked. What if it all stopped? Went away? All these glorious feelings. The wetness and want between her legs, the delicious fullness of her breasts, it could all disappear. Evaporate like smoke. When there was no need. "Clean bill of health. And on the pill. So, I'm good."

"Me too." He grinned down at her. "So, okay then."

Okay then.

****

Seth could take a hint. Kate wanted oblivion. He was right there with her. So much so he struggled to call up a bit of finesse. He might not be a fighter, but he was definitely a lover. He put time and energy into relationships, even the temporary ones. When she whispered his name he was powerless to do anything but give her more.

He shifted position until he was looming over her. He bent her knees and guided them around his waist. He wanted those heels digging into his ass. Her nails dragging against the skin of his back. He nudged at her opening, and her eyes fluttered shut. He wanted them open.

"Look at me, Kate." He wanted her full attention. To have her eyes on him, as well as her hands.

At the sound of her name, her eyes opened. He waited a heartbeat, then plunged in.

He didn't take it slow. He wanted friction. He wanted urgency. Slapping skin and her coming around his cock.

The need to move faster overtook him. When she cried out and clenched around him, it filled his head and sent the rush of it to fill every part of him. He made one final push and ground against her, held it for a second, and then let it go.

He swore he saw stars.

For sure, he saw Kate. The sight of her watching him, chest heaving, hands clutching at him, made him want to howl.

So he did.

Then he laughed. "That was incredible."

She smiled, the hint of uncertainty slipping away. "I'm glad you enjoyed yourself."

He kept her pinned to the bed. "Like you didn't."

She pushed at him. "I did. Very much."

He didn't want to crush her, but he didn't want to let go of her either. He rolled off pulling her with him until she was sprawled across his chest. His name came out on a squeak of breath. He pushed her hair back, held the mass of it in one hand while the fingers of his other hand ran a path up and down her spine. "Stop squirming."

She rescued her hair and with a few twists and turns it was out of the way. Her hands landed on his chest. "I'm not."

He pulled her down for a quick kiss. "I think I'm developing a shoe thing."

Her calves, ankles, and thank-you-God heels made a brief appearance in the air. "Really?"

He dug around for the covers and pulled them up. "You have no idea."

"Wait." She kicked off her shoes. When he had them tucked in, she huffed out a breath. "Can I ask you a personal question?"

His afterglow took a serious hit. "If you have to."

"How old are you?"

"Twenty-two."

She sighed.

"What?"

"I'm not twenty-two."

"Then what are you?"

"Older."

"I like that about you." He really did. He didn't feel like explaining why, and it seemed like one of those conversations he couldn't win, so he changed the subject. "Can I ask you a question?"

"Okay."

He was done with weighty topics. "Are you going to feed me?"

She narrowed those lovely baby blues. "Feed you? Is that some kind of kinky thing?"

"No. It means I'm starving. And in the interest of keeping my strength up for round two, I need food." He lifted his head to kiss her neck. She smelled so good. Like Red Hots and sex. "It's the least you can do after taking advantage of me."

She frowned. "Didn't you have supper?"

"Nope."

She batted her eyelashes in delicious confusion. "I ate at Dad's. I brought leftovers. I guess you could eat those."

"Great." He rolled out from underneath her and off the bed. He pulled on his pants without bothering to do them up and headed for her kitchen area. "I'll be right back."

"I'll just…slip into the bathroom."

By the time Kate caught up to him he was pulling a plate out of the microwave. He frowned down at her. "How do you manage that?"

She looked down at herself. "What?"

"Looking immaculate when I know for a fact you just got out of bed." He pulled her into his arms. Ran a hand over her tidy hair. "I did things to you. You should look mussed up. Messy. Properly—"

She put a hand over his mouth. "Don't you dare say it."

He nipped at her hand. She pulled it away

squealing in protest. "Entertained."

"I'm not perfect, you know. I have flaws."

Didn't he know it.

"True." He shoveled food into his mouth. He really was starving. "This is delicious."

"What do you mean, true?"

He gestured with his fork, finished chewing. "No one's perfect. I'm not either. That's what makes us interesting."

She harrumphed.

More food went into his mouth. "What is this?"

"I don't know. Sunni made it." She ignored his raised eyebrows and looked down at herself. "How am I not perfect?"

"Perfect is boring, so it's a good thing you come with attitude. Who knew that turns me on?" He laughed at her look of outrage. She pinched his arm and twisted.

"Ow. Shit."

She looked smug, and sexy, and he didn't try to resist.

"You want to play dirty?" He set his plate down and grabbed her up off her feet. She was forced to cling to his shoulders and glare down at him from above. He carried her over to the bed and tossed her down. She came up in a cloud of hair and flailing limbs.

"Much better." While she sat up spitting out strands of hair, he got rid of his pants and climbed into the bed. "You look good messy."

She swiped the final strands of hair away, accusation brightening her eyes. "I thought you were hungry."

"I am." He dropped a kiss on her pouty mouth. "I'm starting on the next course."

"Cocky and insatiable."

"And you have too many clothes on." He leaned down and her mouth opened under his.

His heart took a hit as she guided his hand to the clasp of her jeans. "I trust you're going to do something about that."

Then he forgot about his heart when her hand wrapped around his dick. All he wanted was more of her hand. Her mouth. Her scent. He gathered her up and rubbed up against it all. His breath clogged in his throat. In deep. Lost. Found again. Washed clean in a rush of pleasure.

Chapter Six

Kate pulled open the door, preparing to raid her own refrigerator. She was ravenous. A bowl of berries joined the fried egg and slice of toast already on her plate. More coffee. You could never have too much caffeine. Once it was dripping into the pot, she did a pirouette right there in her tiny kitchen.

She picked up the latest issue of Vogue. She sipped and savored as she thumbed through the pages, concentrating on the clothes, the colors, the shoes. What was it about having multiple orgasms that added a chaotic vibrancy to everything?

She glowed from her freshly blow-dried hair, which she'd allowed to hang loose today, to the tips of her Chick Flick Red toenails. Which matched the color of her thong. And her bra. Men liked red. Seth hadn't paid a lot of attention to her underwear last night, but just in case he was in the mood to change that she donned her very naughtiest pair.

Parts of her still tingled. She liked his hands. Gentle but rough from the work he did. Nicked from carving. Scarred. Large. There wasn't a part of her they hadn't touched. She looked down at her own hands and knew he carried her marks on his back. Crescent moons hidden in the lines of the massive tattoo covering his back from hip to shoulder blade. Strong lines of black and red. His totem he'd informed over his second plate of food.

She smiled into her last cup of coffee. Time to put in some hours downstairs. She had inventory to order. Had to figure out how to pay for it. After which she needed to square up some details regarding the fair. She rinsed out her cup and stashed her dirty dishes in the dishwasher. Once the sheets were in the laundry and last night's clothes and collateral damage were dealt with, she headed downstairs. Seth wasn't due to come in until noon. He had needed to work on a commission and it had been fine by her. She was going to hunt down her dad and they were going to have words.

Downstairs she flicked on the lights, but they failed to brighten the room as expected. They came on. But no natural light was coming in through the front window, leaving Kate's dark and dull. Frowning, she went to investigate and found the windows papered over from the outside.

What the hell?

She stepped out onto the sidewalk to investigate and was rewarded with the sight of her and Seth from the night before, kissing in front of her window. Her bare arms wrapped around his neck. His hands clenched in her hair. With no doubt left as to where it all was leading.

Sheets and sheets of the same photo were plastered to her window, like pixels of the larger picture. She ripped one off and spun in a circle. They were strewn all over the street. Groups of them appeared on most windows up and down this section of Main Street.

Terror gripped her chest. The words hardly mattered, not that they weren't a knife to her heart.

Do not lust in your heart after her beauty or let her

captivate you with her eyes, for the prostitute reduces you to a loaf of bread, and the adulteress preys upon your very life. Proverbs 6:25, 26

The paper in her hand shook. She crumpled it into a ball. Panicked, she grabbed fists full of paper and ripped them clear of the window.

She shuddered. Someone had been watching them. Spying on them. Waiting for the perfect moment to expose them.

God, why?

That awful Shepherd person.

She whirled around at the sound of footsteps, heart hammering, tears waiting to spill. The break-in, the hang-ups, now this?

Sunni raced up to her and grabbed her into a hug. Mary marched along after her, others falling in line as they pulled up in cars and came on foot. She ordered them up and down the street and handed each of them a garbage bag.

"What the hell is all this about?" Mary gestured at the windows.

Her sense of shame was so familiar she wrapped it around her shoulders like a cloak. It smothered her before she had a chance to reject it. "I—Seth…"

"Not the what, but the why?"

"I don't know. I can't think why anyone…"

Mary headed next door and began tearing down sheets of paper. "You got a phone around here. You need to report this to the police."

All her newly found confidence dissolved. She stood there paralyzed by dread. This wasn't happening. The most beautiful moment of her last three years exposed to the whole town.

"Better yet. Sunni, snap some pictures and then take her down to the station. No need to have them pulling up here in front of your door. Shame I didn't catch the son of a bitch who did this. I'm up early. Gotta get things started. But today I slept in, damn it."

Seth had left around three. It was 7:30 am. Between now and then, someone had pinned a big red A on her reputation. The culprit would have needed time to photocopy and distribute. He would have come back, waited in the shadows for Seth to leave.

"Come on now, get your purse. Put your lips on while I finish clearing your windows."

Kate sat through the whole humiliating process of recounting the intimate details of her private life to men she considered friends. It made things worse instead of easier. They promised to look into it. And she believed them. Neither Mike nor Chase were happy.

She walked out into the reception area followed by Sunni only to freeze when she spotted Seth. He wore his usual grunge garb, hair tied back, hands shoved deep into pockets. Strong, competent, she didn't want to need him, to crave the comfort of those arms. The smarter thing was to forget last night had ever happened. Denial, yes, that was the way to survive.

Sunni put a hand on her arm. "I called him. I figured you might not be ready to go home. Besides, he deserves to know what he's landed in."

Seth jerked his head toward the door. "Come on, no one will bother you at the cabin."

It was the last place she wanted to hide. Panic made a liar of her thoughts. The swirl around her pressed in. Sunni hovered, and Mike joined them. She heard his voice but not his words. The phone rang loud and persistently. The smell of over perked coffee burned her nose.

She didn't want to go home. Her vehicle was back at her place. She wasn't ready to face her dad. Or anyone else.

The need for a drink clawed at her. She pushed it back. But there was no space to shove it. It sloshed around her brain in a drunken stupor. So appealing to let it go. To let it take over and give in to the need pulsing through her. Bottle. Glass. Tip it back. The smooth glide of whiskey going down. Padding the razor sharp edges of reality. Making it all manageable.

"Kate." Seth reached for her, urging her forward. He shot the door open hard enough to clang against the detachment's brick façade. "Can we please get the hell out of here?"

Somehow his worry, his anger got her through the door and into the crisp autumn air. Humiliation and the sense of violation still clung with greedy claws, but her craving cooled. The Kate Logan who hadn't touched a drop of alcohol in 743 days put the rest of the world on ice. "Lead the way."

They made it to his truck without saying a word. Again, he opened the door for her. A little more sedate this time. She hoisted herself up onto the bench seat and was faced with a collection of empty to-go cups, scraps of paper, and a large chunk of gnarly wood. She picked up a smelly rag and dropped it on top of the piece of dead tree.

The truck dipped as Seth climbed in and shot her a look. "Sorry about the mess."

Except he didn't sound sorry at all. He sounded pissed off. She raised her eyebrow at the piece of tree trunk. "Yes, well, we all need to keep our hunks of wood somewhere."

A huff of not-so-funny laughter filled the cab. "That hunk of wood is a maple burl. They're a rare find."

She stared out the windshield. "Whatever."

He sat there, no key in the ignition, no escaping to his lair as quickly as possible. "So, you going to show me?"

Kate pulled a crumpled piece of paper out of her purse and stuffed it into his outstretched hand. "This was plastered all over Main Street this morning."

Once he was finished, he balled it back up and threw it at the windshield. "Son of a bitch."

"I know." She dropped her head back, and whispered, "This can't be happening."

Finally, the sound of the key in the ignition, the rev of the engine. "What did the police say? Do they think it's related to the hang-ups? Are they going to talk to Matthew Parsons? My money's on that sick SOB."

She slunk down lower on the seat. "Can we please get moving before anyone sees us? We can dissect the motives of everyone who hates me at your place. In private."

"Little late to be embarrassed to be seen with me." There was an edge to his voice she didn't appreciate.

"I'm not." She wrapped her arms around her purse and hugged it. "Now drive."

"This is what I get for being a nice guy," he muttered. He maneuvered the truck out of the lot, risking a long-suffering look her way. "Look, I'm not giddy with joy over the whole thing either."

She covered her eyes with the palm of her hand

and tried to think. There was no way he could grasp the seriousness of the situation. He didn't live here. Hadn't grown up here. Hadn't slunk back here defeated and broken. "It's not the same for you."

"Yeah? Because I love having my privacy invaded? It's such a turn on to know some freak with a wide angle lens was watching in the dark while we got naked together."

Kate shuddered, not needing the reminder. "Everyone knows me. You're new here. Most people don't even know who you are."

"And that's the way I wanted it to stay." He concentrated on the road, staring straight ahead, death grip at two and ten on the steering wheel. "Now, I'm the guy who's screwing Kate Logan."

Embarrassment shrivelled up and died. She gaped at the side of his head. "Like I dragged you upstairs and into my apartment."

His usual baritone rose an octave. " 'I'm ready to order.' " He cranked the truck around the corner in the direction of the lakeside of town. They all smashed to the left including his ridiculous hunk of wood. His voice settled back into normal range. "Ringing any bells? And let's not forget who tried to kiss who first?"

Setting him on fire with her retinas wasn't working. She sat up straighter. "Correction: screwed Kate Logan. As in past tense. There won't be a repeat performance."

"Hold onto that delusion, princess." He spared her a glance. "You can't keep your hands off me, and you know it."

She choked on her own shock. "Are you for real?"

"After last night? Yeah, I'm feeling pretty darn

confident. Plus you in my truck headed to my place has me reading between the lines."

"I didn't call you." She grabbed up an empty to-go cup and threw it at his head. "Sunni did."

He lifted an elbow to deflect it. "Hey!"

"Stop being an ass."

"Stop being a bitch."

He had some nerve. The old Kate would have rewarded his last comment with eternal silence. Not the new Kate. The new Kate wasn't finished yet. "Fighting over who's being the biggest jerk, which is you by the way, isn't going to get us anywhere."

"Wrong, we're clearing the air. That way when we get to my place we can crawl into bed and work past it."

"I'm not having…We are not crawling…anywhere…" God, she couldn't even say the word. "We're just not."

"That's so cute."

"Stop it."

"You liked it."

"So, what if I did? I've got bigger problems than keeping you satisfied."

"Me satisfied? I'm having trouble walking straight, princess. And in case you need further proof you did your share of demanding?" His voice hardened, got sharper with every word. "I could show you the nail marks on my back."

"Don't you dare raise your voice at me," she sputtered. "That solves nothing."

"So, yell back."

Fine, she'd yell. "Stop insulting me. Stop being infuriating. Stop talking, period."

"Not happening. This is me helping you get over yourself. Something you desperately need to work on."

"Oh my God, you did not just say that to me?"

"Appears I did."

"Why are you being such an asshole?" she demanded. Was it too much to ask for a little compassion?

"Shit happens, princess."

"Stop calling me that. And stop trivializing what's happening. This is serious. Aspen Lake is a small town and *shit* like this has a way of sticking."

His hands twisted around the steering wheel, his words a flat mocking recitation of a beleaguered male. "You're right. I'm sorry. Forgive me. Is that what you want to hear?"

Not sorry. Not remorseful. Not even a little bit. But still pissed. Well, he wasn't the only one. "You don't sound sorry."

"Really?" He glimpsed away from the road to glare at her. "What tipped you off?"

This was a whole new side to him she did not care for at all. "Are you always this charming?"

"I'm trying to clear the air so we can figure out how to deal with this." He tone suggested all of that should have been obvious to anyone with a brain.

She was so sure. "Yelling and insulting me is your idea of resolving things?"

He glared at her. "It's what couples do."

"No, it's not." Because hello, what would he know about it? She was the only one sitting in his stupid truck who been part of a couple. Which they were not. A fact she did not hesitate to point out. "And we are not a couple."

"Yeah, unfortunately we kind of are." He parked the truck and faced her looking as happy as a death row inmate. "Last night proved it. You think that kind of connection happens all the time? It doesn't."

She chose not to dignify his remark with an answer. The whole idea was ludicrous. It definitely wasn't thrilling. Or intoxicating.

Get it together, Kate. She still had to survive the next couple of hours, the next couple of days. Hell, who was she kidding, years. The looks, the gossip, the attention. The productive thing to do was figure out a plan, a way to stop this maniac from ruining her carefully planned life. She needed to concentrate on what was important. And extricate herself from the things that weren't.

****

She was unfuckingbelievable. And he was totally screwed, and not in a good way, if he thought snotty was the new sexy. He wanted to yank her into his lap and continue where they'd left off last night with her grinding down on top of him. Not think about some freak getting his rocks off watching them have the best sex of his life. But Princess was hugging her Arctic cold front of an attitude so close it was all but snowing in the cab of his truck. At least, she'd thawed enough to yell at him. Progress.

Kate hopped out of his truck and met him at the path leading up to the cabin. He hung back to let her go first. She led the way, chokecherry bushes trembling in her wake, wearing a red cape-like thing giving her a Red Riding Hood vibe. In knee high boots with a big assed purse swinging from the crook of her elbow, she stalked over the uneven stones ready to tackle the big, bad wolf. She was also pale as birch wood.

No doubt, he owed her a sincere apology. He'd gotten sidetracked in the truck. Someone was stalking her. Or them. It wasn't funny, and it wasn't something to take lightly. The embarrassment of having his privacy invaded in a very public way was fading. Fear was setting in. For Kate. Promises to her father aside, he'd be damned if he was going to let anybody get to her.

A vee of Canada geese honked their way southbound. The cool air shivered leaves beginning their change. The breeze brought the scent of the lake up from the water's edge. His Eden. Simple and uncomplicated. He'd sworn to keep it that way.

That someone was threatening his newfound sense of paradise wasn't Kate's fault.

He caught her at the door. He tugged her around to face him. "Look, I'm sorry. You're right. This is serious, and we need to figure out how we're going to deal with it."

Her eyes narrowed in suspicion. "Well, I'm going to be dealing with it from one corner, and you're going to be dealing with it from the opposite corner. As in separately."

"You're cute when you're wrong."

To shut her up, he reached behind her and opened up the door. Before she could toss a retort back at him, the unmistakable sound of a female singing distracted them both. Seth looked down the short hallway at the trail of girly stuff leading to the bathroom.

Oh, shit.

Kate froze.

He knew murderous when he saw it. "I can

explain."

She didn't say a word just turned on a booted heel and headed for the stairs. He reached out to keep her in place. "Kate."

She struggled for a bit but gave up when he didn't let go. Her cool eyes met his.

"Steel-toed boots." He backed up a step anyway.

She gave a tug on her arm. He held fast. She leveled her gaze at him again. "Let me go."

"No." Her look had probably frozen other men in their tracks. He'd spent the last six years trying to do right, be a gentleman, and had let two females walk all over him. Too bad for her he was done with all that and, while he might regret his highhandedness, he wasn't going to play nice with her. "I'm going to explain and you're going to listen."

"There is nothing you could possibly say—"

He butted in. "She's my sister."

She gave him her best how-stupid-do-you-think-I-am-look. "You don't have a sister."

"I do, as a matter of fact. A stepsister and her name is Ashley."

"Um hum." Her tone said it all. There was no need to follow it up with the eyebrow of death.

"I do." He rubbed his aching forehead. "Can we continue this discussion in the kitchen?"

Kate didn't budge. A body emerged from the bathroom wrapped in one towel with another turban style around her head. Her shriek of surprise had him wincing and Kate backing up.

One hand clutched a towel that could have used another couple of inches. The other pressed to her heart. Ash shrank back against the hall wall. "You guys scared the shit out of me."

He sighed. "Kate, meet my sister, Ashley."

Ash stuck out a hand. "Stepsister, but why split hairs right?"

"Ashley." Kate gave her hand a brief shake and let go. "Nice to meet you."

"She's staying with me for a while."

"Oh. My. God. You're Kate Logan." Ash's eyes widened in zealous recognition before settling back on Seth. "Do you know who she is?"

Here we go. Seth sighed. "We've met."

Still grasping her towel, Ash took back Kate's hand and latched on. Kate, to her credit, continued to smile. At least, he thought it was a smile. "You are like my fashion icon."

"That's kind of you to say."

Seth let his muscles relax.

She gasped. "No, really. You're an inspiration. Like Sarah Jessica Parker."

"Thank you."

Maybe this was going to go better then he'd thought.

"Because sometimes old school ideas are the best. Especially, when you mix them with younger, newer thoughts. But you can never go wrong with the classics. And you are definitely a classic."

Or not. Because he was pretty sure his sister had just implied Kate was old.

He caught the slight tightening of her jaw and willed Ashley to shut her mouth.

Ash repositioned the towel surrounding her oblivious brain before squinting at her new BFF. "Was rehab awful? I bet it was awful. Were there any other famous celebs in there with you? I bet there was. You can tell me, I swear I won't tell a soul."

Except for her seven hundred and ninety-five Facebook friends.

"Okay." The meet and greet was over. He gave Ashley a push in the direction of her bedroom. "Time to get dressed."

Instead, Ash leaned closer to Kate, face serious, and lowered her voice. "Even with everything that happened, I just want to say how sorry I am." Once again she pressed a hand to her chest, clueless but earnest. "Everything you went through? It broke my heart.

"Again, thank you." Kate faced Seth, and if looks could kill…"Is there somewhere I can freshen up?"

"Sure, follow me." When Ash moved to follow them, he pointed at the floor. "Stay."

He guided Kate down the hall, through the kitchen, and up the stairs into the loft area. There were only two rooms up here, his bedroom and the master bath.

"Wait here for a sec." He beat her into the bathroom scooped up his dirty clothes and stuffed them in the hamper. He had no idea what freshen up meant but he dug out a clean towel and, seeing as she was a girl, added a never used facecloth. Back in his bedroom he signaled an all clear. "I'll leave you to it."

She leaned in to look around the bathroom. It must have passed inspection because she stepped in and closed the door in his face.

Seth toured his room grabbing up clothes and miscellaneous crap. He threw the lot of it into his walk-in closet. He'd deal with it later, or next year. He yanked the covers into place on his bed and straightened the pillows. Then he headed back down the stairs to get Ashley under control.

On her okay, he opened the door to girl central. Jeez. The room was unrecognizable. "Make yourself at home."

Ash patted his cheek on her way to the closet. "Thanks."

There were posters tacked to the walls, beads hung over lamps, and pink shit everywhere. "You do remember this is temporary, right?"

"Of course, but a girl needs to set out a few things." She traveled the path back to her suitcase, pulled out a stack of shirts, and headed for the one and only dresser in the room now covered with a frilly cloth and a bunch of little boxes.

He shook his head to clear the horror. "I need you to leave."

She turned, surprised, and a lot sad. "What? Why?"

"No. No...just for a couple of hours." He held up his hands in apology. "I don't have time to explain, and since it's my place and you're here on probation, I don't have to."

She pulled a bathrobe out of her suitcase and hung it on the hook behind the door. Where the hell had that been ten minutes ago? She wrangled her eyes at him. "Am I interfering with a booty call?"

"Ash."

"But I want to stay and talk to Kate," she whined.

"No. No way."

She pouted in his direction. "I don't want to go. I just got here. I'm settling in."

He repressed the shudder. "I'm not asking you. I'm telling you."

She sighed in resignation. "And what exactly am I supposed to do with this free time I've been given?"

He pulled out his wallet and some cash. "Buy groceries. We need milk and—never mind I'll make you a list."

She pursed her lips and grabbed the cash. "Fine. Two hours."

"Deal."

"I need ten minutes with my hair."

"I'll do the food list."

It was fifteen minutes before she emerged, her short, pink-tipped platinum blonde hair spiked up. He handed her a sheet of paper. "Here's the list. Get everything on it and nothing more. And I want the change back."

She saluted. "Yes, boss."

"Good." He grinned and pushed her toward the door. "Now get out."

"Hey, watch it." She pointed at him. "Remember, two hours. Be decent by the time I get back."

Ash banged out the door and Seth climbed the first couple of stairs to the loft and listened, heard Kate talking on the phone. Did he hide the booze? Not hide the booze? What was the protocol here? And when the hell had he turned into a neurotic old woman? Fuck it, they had to eat. He'd make lunch instead.

He was halfway through heating soup when she came down looking pretty much the same as when she went up. Minus the cape now draped over her arm and the cell phone in her hand. She avoided him and walked over to the windows to study the view of the water.

"Your work?" She ran a hand over the rough planks of a shelving unit next to the massive windows.

He'd carved out a trail of aspen leaves from the wood on the sides of the piece.

"Yeah. It was a gift to my grandparents for their fiftieth wedding anniversary."

Eyes glued to the view, she said, "They're missed around here."

Okay, he could do small talk. "Thanks. I saw them in June. They're happy. Content. This place was turning into a lot of work. Too many stairs. That kind of thing."

She hummed in response as she wandered around the living room area, arranging her outerwear over the back of the couch. He went back into the kitchen area and gave the pot a final stir. "I'm sorry about earlier with Ash."

"Don't apologize." She smirked at him. "She's delightful."

He knew sarcasm when he heard it. "She's got a big mouth, but her heart's in the right place. She hasn't had it easy. Her mother's never been much of a parent, except for the brief time she was married to my dad."

"But she had you."

"We had each other." He set two bowls of soup on the counter along with a plate of crackers. Hunted up some spoons. "Lunch is on. Canned soup. Best I can do on short notice."

She sniffed at the soup. "I'm not really hungry."

"Suit yourself." He pictured the contents of her fridge in his mind. "There's yogurt in the fridge, plus fruit if you'd rather. Water's in there too. Coffee's in the pot."

She headed for the coffee pot before grabbing an apple out of the fridge. She sat down on the stool beside him and must have changed her mind about the soup because she picked up her spoon and sampled. "This doesn't taste like it came from a can."

"I added a couple of things." He held off on the questions while they ate a few mouthfuls. "So, how do you want to deal with this mess?"

She cleared her throat before pushing her plate away. He wished he'd waited until she'd eaten more. Too late now. He pushed back from the counter and grabbed a knife and a plate. He picked up her apple and started to slice it. Handed the plate to her.

"The police said they'd look into it." She reached for her coffee. After a couple of delicate swallows, she set it back down and pushed up her sleeves. "They know the Shepherd has been causing trouble for the fair and for me. They're going to talk to him."

He wasn't listening. He was focused on her arm. At the four narrow bruises that looked a lot like finger marks. He reached out for her arm, brought it closer, found fainter ones circling her wrist. Finished with his silent inspection he looked up at her. It took everything he had to keep his voice even. "Things got pretty intense last night, but I'm pretty sure I didn't put these marks there."

She tugged her arm free and pulled the sleeves of her sweater down over her palms, tucking her fingers over the edges, like women did. "It's nothing."

"Bodnar." He and that son of a bitch were going to have words.

Her bottom lip disappeared, only to pop back out a second later. "And he has marks of his own. We're even."

Not even close. "Bull. Shit. We both know self defense wounds don't fall in the same category as the ones on your arm."

"Can we please not make a big deal of it? We've got more pressing matters to solve." There was no denying the pleading in her voice or in her eyes.

If it killed him, he was going to deal with her request like a reasonable adult. Not a caveman. To put aside the urge to do what would only hurt them both. "But he adds another layer to our predicament. You shut him down. He was angry. What if it was Bodnar behind the lens and not the Shepherd?"

She shook her head. No hesitation. "Tyler would never do that. He's angry, yes. But jealous too. The last thing he'd do is announce to the whole town I'm sleeping with someone else. I'm not saying he's not a problem. But he's a different kind of problem. "

Like she was collecting them or something. "You sure about that?"

"Yes." Complete confidence she was right. "Besides, he was heading into the city to watch football last night."

"That's not to say he went."

"He wouldn't expose me like this." At his skeptical look, she gave an emphatic shook of her head. "He wouldn't. He's worked too hard to create the illusion he and I are together."

"That puts Parsons back at the top of the suspect list."

He might have broken his agreement with her father, but it didn't mean he was done keeping an eye on Kate. It was his problem now too. He was going to find out who was behind the subterfuge. Find out and take care of it.

****

There was a nice big bed upstairs. In a moment of complete and utter weakness Kate had considered climbing in, pulling the covers over her head, and staying there. She'd resisted. Barely. Thanks to her common sense, which was kicking in three years too late, she was forced to endure this awful conversation.

She still couldn't escape the feeling of being caught doing something scandalous. Considering her behavior pre-rehab, that was saying something. But sex wasn't a crime. Someone else had committed the crime. Invaded her privacy. Ruined that glorious euphoric feeling of finally maybe finding the right guy and turned it into something trashy.

Wait? What?

God, no. That couldn't be right.

The right guy.

She was overwrought. Traumatized. And no doubt her brain was dehydrated due to overthinking. She picked up her coffee and took a healthy chug.

"Kate?"

"What?" Right back to business. Her stalker. "You're right, all roads point to the Valley of the Shepherd Church." She toasted in his direction. "Nothing to do but hope gossip is good for business."

His phone vibrated on the counter and after a quick check, Seth said, "A client. I should probably take it."

"No problem." Kate tilted her head and watched as he made his way up to the loft area.

She picked out another slice of apple and nibbled until all the slices had disappeared. To pass the time and say thanks for the meal, Kate gathered up the dishes and stacked them in the dishwasher. Still no Seth.

She glanced around the open floor concept room. The place was cluttered with newspapers, sketch pads, pencils. Opened and unopened mail. Books, mostly nonfiction, and magazines were stacked on the side tables. At least, he was a reader. With nothing else to do, she collected all the dirty coffee cups and plates then located the laundry room and dumped an armload of clothes inside.

Once his mail was sorted and the countertop tidied, she dropped onto the overstuffed couch and picked up a book. Set it down. She wasn't much interested in *Elements of Woodcarving*. Chose a magazine: *Sports Illustrated*. Ugh. Worse.

Then she spotted his sketch pad. No. So wrong. She had more integrity than to snoop through someone's private belongings. She was definitely not going to pick it up and have a quick peek. Absolutely not. Because that would be wrong. Even though the curiosity was killing her.

No. So wrong.

Not to mention, horrifyingly ironic.

Clearly not in her right mind and who could blame her, she leaned over and picked it up off the table. It was heavy in her hands and smelled of temptation. She set it back down. Considered accidently knocking it to the floor so she'd have to pick it up and could she help it if it opened in the process exposing whatever drawings were in there. She nudged it closer to the edge of the short table.

"Go ahead, open it."

She jumped and sure enough knocked the stupid book to the floor. Except now she was too embarrassed to take advantage. Damn his sock feet. Bad enough to contemplate snooping. But to get caught actually attempting it was worse.

Smirking was not a good look on him. Seth picked up the pad and set it in her lap. "Take a look. Tell me what you think."

Face blushing a most unbecoming shade of too-stupid-to-live, she handed it back to him. "Seth, I can't...you don't have to show me. It's none of my business."

"Hold onto that thought."

Why was he looking like the guilty party? She stroked a hand over the cherry red cover. "What's that supposed to mean?"

He perched on the arm of the sofa and crossed his arms. "Open it and find out."

There was no way she wasn't going to look now. Once again she ran a hand over the cover, like she was handling a priceless work of art. God, what if she hated his sketches? She pulled her blank mask into place and flipped open the cover. All pretense fled. "Oh, that's incredible."

It was a sketch of a wolf in a bluff of trees. "Was out hiking and following a hunting hawk. Caught him with my binoculars. I was downwind and far enough away he didn't see me. He obliged me by keeping still. I did a little research. It's pretty rare to spot them. They've always been in the park, but they're pretty shy."

She kept turning pages, fascinated by his skill, how he perceived things. Wanted to watch him create these incredible images in person. There were a lot of bits and parts of things. Lots of things she didn't get but it didn't matter. She pictured him hunched over, skilled hands at work, focused on what he was creating. Then she turned the next page.

Oh, my.

She may or may not have breathed those last words out loud.

It was her. She was almost sure of it. She hesitated then looked up at him for confirmation.

He stared back at her, eyes shadowed by apology but no pretense.

Okay, it was her. But no her she'd ever seen in the mirror, or even a magazine. And she'd seen plenty of pictures, to the point of being nauseated by her own image.

This was different. She felt it in her nipples. Not that she needed the verification. She opened her mouth, shut it.

"I drew it the night I made an ass of myself by implying all I wanted was a one-night stand."

She cocked her head and frowned at him.

"I'm not that guy. Never have been. I'm not going to leave you to face the whole town on your own. I hope you get that."

She licked her lips. "I think I'm starting to."

"Good." He gestured at her lap. "I've sketched my share of women. But none of those women haunted my dreams."

She felt funny. Definitely a little lightheaded. "Can we please just take this one step at a time?"

"Turn the page."

From his tone, she knew it was the last thing she should do. She did it anyway and was struck speechless yet again.

"And here I thought you'd have plenty to say about

that one."

She swallowed, scared to ask, but needing to make sure. "You're not expecting me to—"

"No."

"Good, otherwise this—whatever this is—would be over before it started." Booze had brought her to her knees. She wasn't landing there again. Not for anything. Or anybody.

"Moving on." He signaled for her to turn the page.

Still not knowing what to say, she sought out the next picture. This was more like it. She tapped the page. "This one I like."

She considered the picture again. "I do own a similar pair of boots."

"You're killing me." He reached out, grabbed the sketch pad and tossed it aside. "Good to know."

"Hey, I wasn't done."

"You can finish later." He toppled her over.

"No, I want to see." The last thing she expected to do today was laugh. She tried to grab for the fluttering book.

"If they're going to damn us for being together, let's give them a good reason." His mouth found hers and he tasted so good.

She stretched her neck to give him better access and caught sight of the open sketch page. She pushed him back and reached for it.

"Later," Seth groaned, and pulled the book out of her hands.

"No. Wait." It was the girl from the compound. The one who'd run into her on the sidewalk that day. The one to put the note in her pocket? "This girl?"

Seth frowned, and leaned back to look at the page.

"What about her?"

"Why did you draw a picture of this girl?"

He tucked a stray lock of her hair behind her ear. His lips brushed kisses down her jawline. "Do we have to do this now?"

She twisted and gave him a look. He sighed as he leveraged off her. "The day Parsons challenged you in the street I was looking for you. Couldn't find you. She was the one who pointed me in the right direction."

"This girl bumped into me the day Parsons came to introduce himself. I think she left a note in my pocket. It was a warning about Parsons."

"Kate." His face was full of caution. "Don't look like that. Chances are that's exactly what he wants, and she's just a pawn in his sick game."

"She's just a child."

"She's also one of them."

"Maybe she's being held there against her will? Mary mentioned something about a child running away from the compound. What if it's her? What if she needs asylum or something?"

"Kate, come on."

"What?" She tried to squirm out from under him, but he held her tight. "She can't be more than nine or ten. Hardly old enough to be a criminal mastermind."

"Just a pickpocket. Or the reverse in this case." He kept on talking when she didn't want to hear it. "And while your first instinct is to trust her, remember where she lives and who calls the shots out there."

"I'm not likely to forget."

"Did you talk to the police about this?"

"Yes," she admitted.

"And?" he prompted.

She heaved a sigh. "They're looking into things."

"I get that's not a very satisfactory answer. And just in case you've got any crazy ideas about checking things out yourself, remember she might look innocent but it doesn't mean she is."

She studied him. "So young to be so cynical."

"Not cynical. Concerned." He moved in and captured her lips. She wrapped her arms around his neck and let him lay her back onto the nice soft sofa.

She smoothed his hair back. "Thank you."

"For what?" But he wasn't listening. He was too busy concentrating on her shirt buttons and slipping them through the accompanying holes.

She placed a hand over his. When he lifted his head his eyes were a tawny mixture of sleepy and hot. "For fighting with me, for giving me some space, *a* space, for making me feel beautiful when I all I felt was dirty."

He framed her face with his hands. "Nothing we do together could ever be that kind of dirty."

She bit her lips. That was an intriguing idea. So captivating she needed clarification. "But it could be a different kind of dirty?"

"Princess, I can show you all kinds of dirty." He put his hands to her sides and she held her breath in anticipation. When he fingers curled in and wiggled, she shrieked.

"Stop that." She puffed out a laugh while trying to grab his hands, but he was relentless.

"Say uncle." His tickling fingers kept up the exquisite torture as she twisted under him.

Breathless and desperate she grabbed him and kissed him. Then his hands got a different kind of busy. So did hers. They slid over his back to grasp his superior ass and squeeze.

With her shirt more than halfway open he stilled, ran a finger over the red lace of her demi bra. "Red is my favorite color."

She was saved from responding by the hammering on the door.

Seth dropped his head against hers. "Shit."

"Oh, crap." Dread deadening her fingers, she scrambled to do up her buttons.

He dipped his head to leave her with a quick kiss. "Hang on and leave those buttons be. I'll get rid of whoever it is."

She didn't listen. She scrambled off the couch and was close enough behind him to hear his whispered *fuck* after he'd risked a peek out the tiny window by the door. He turned back and mouthed the worst possible words. *Your father.*

More pounding. "Kate, I know you're in there."

Seth didn't take his eyes off her. She swallowed, squared her shoulders, and nodded that she was ready. He opened the door to her dad's blustering and Sunni's shushing.

"Where is she?" Bill Logan demanded.

"I'm right here, Dad. There's no need to shout."

"I've been telling him that since we left town." Sunni planted her fists on her hips.

He spared her a glance. "Hush, woman."

Sunni stuck a finger in his face. "Don't you hush me, Bill Logan."

Her dad threw up his hands, going from angry to exasperated. "Isn't that what you've been doing to me for the last ten minutes?"

Hands back on hips. "No. I've been trying to save

you from having a heart attack over nothing."

"Nothing?" he roared, his face beet red. He pulled a piece of paper out of his coat pocket and shook it. "This is not nothing."

"She's a grown woman, Bill. She can sleep with whoever she wants."

Kate didn't have time to dissect Sunni's defense act or the unwelcome warm fuzzies it gave her. She was too busy figuring out how to avoid a discussion about her sex life. "Daddy, calm down."

"How about we move into the kitchen?" Seth did his best to guide them forward. Only Sunni cooperated and scooted past giving Kate a face full of apology.

"Come on, Daddy." When her father didn't budge, she grabbed his arm and dragged him.

Under the open beamed ceiling, he zeroed in on Seth. "I trusted you not to be stupid, boy."

"Oh my God, really?" asked Kate. Before Seth could object to being called a boy, or stupid, she spun to face her father. "What about you asking him to spy on me, huh? Maybe we should focus on that for a moment?"

"Bill," gasped Sunni.

"I didn't ask him to spy on you." He stuffed his hands in his pockets, which was good, no more pointing. He enunciated his next words very carefully. "I asked him to watch out for you."

Kate cocked a hip. "Like there's a difference."

"Why don't we all sit down?" Seth held out a chair, which no one sat in. "Okay, standing it is."

"You'll feel differently, Katie, when you have kids and one of them is being threatened."

"Well, I can tell you what I won't do. I won't send

a complete stranger to spy on them."

"He wasn't a stranger to me," Bill sputtered. "I asked him because he was going to be around anyways, fixing the doors and the case. I didn't think you two were going to end up—you know—getting along."

Kate narrowed her eyes. "You had it planned from the minute you sent him to my shop, didn't you?"

Her father was back to yelling. "Because I didn't think he was your type."

"My type?"

"Yeah, slicked up with bastard written all over him." He mumbled in Seth's direction. "Now I'm not so sure about the last part."

"Daddy," gritted out Kate. "You're in no position to judge."

Seth rubbed a hand over his jaw and dropped his head back to stare at the ceiling like he was praying for an intervention. God wasn't in the mood to run interference.

"Jesus H Christ, always with the drama. How is asking the guy who's going to be hanging out at your store if he wouldn't mind keeping an eye out taking things too far?"

"AHHH." She threw up her hands and walked away.

He came after her. "Don't you walk away from me, Katherine Marie. The man has come at you numerous times. Don't tell me you haven't been grateful that Seth's been there to head him off?"

She turned around and pointed at him. "I can look after myself."

"You bloody well cannot, and you shouldn't have to. That's what family is for. None of us can get by without a little help. Except for you, apparently." It came spilling out of him and flooding into her. "Ever since your mother died, you've closed yourself off. Shut me out. And God knows, you had your reasons. But I'll be damned if I'm going to stand back while some judgmental, self-righteous prick comes after my little girl."

How much her withdrawal had hurt him was written in the lines of his face, the grim set of his jaw, and the tears in his eyes. She'd blamed him for so long, punished him for the same length of time, withheld her affection. As awful as it was to admit, those feelings were so familiar, so comfortable it was hard to let them go. But that wasn't the person she wanted to be anymore. "Oh, Daddy."

His arms wrapped around her, and she gave in to the warm comfort of letting go. Of taking a moment and soaking up the way it had been between them before everything had changed.

Chapter Seven

It was Wednesday and Seth worked late, waiting for Kate to leave for one of her endless meetings. He knew it wasn't going to be easy for her to walk into it knowing gossip spread like a bad rash. But she left without a hair out place, dressed to perfection. A little wary around the edges but determined. He'd admired the shit out of her for that.

He was planning a little get-together of his own. He hadn't forgotten about Tyler Bodnar. Or the marks he'd put on Kate. They were going to have words. But he'd learned the value of patience from his dad.

At eight o'clock, he packed up and locked the doors. The rink and winter hub of any small prairie town was four blocks off Main Street. Tonight the parking lot was full of pickup trucks. He parked a couple rows back from Bodnar. With the window cracked and the chill night air filling the cab, he did what he always did to make time go faster.

Charcoal pencil in hand, sketch pad braced against the steering wheel, the scene came to life on paper: a line of vehicles, the bulky shadow of the ice rink in the background. When Bodnar walked out the door with his hockey bag and skates, Seth waited while he yakked with his band of bullies. Hockey practice gave them hardcore jollies judging by the laughing and backslapping. According to the guys at work, a grudge match between the Aspen Lake Mooseheads and their arch-rivals, the Glenville Bloodhounds, was a big ticket part of the fair activities.

Finally, his buddies sauntered off. After a quick glance around Bodnar lowered the tailgate and flipped back the tarp. Seth caught a glimpse of drywall sheets, long wrapped rolls, and a couple of industrial-sized buckets. Proof an asshole's work was never done. He scribbled a note while watching him stuff his hockey bag in amongst the bales of insulation.

When Bodnar pulled out, Seth followed. Kate would have his balls if she knew he was out here stalking her ex-boyfriend. But he wanted him alone. Let's see how tough he was without an audience. A few kilometers down a gravel road leading to the Bodnar family farm Seth increased his speed and flashed his lights. He'd recognize Seth's vehicle. Sure enough his brake lights flared.

Gravel sprayed. Seth left his truck running, headlights glaring. This wasn't going to be a long conversation. The slam of Bodnar's truck door vibrated in the still air. He looked a little less badass in his toque and runners and no plate-sized belt buckle to flash around.

They met in the middle of the spill of light coming from Seth's truck. "What the fuck, Stone?"

"Evening, Bodnar." Seth crossed his arms.

Bodnar copied him. "What's this about?"

Seth nodded toward the other man's truck. "Planning on some renovations?"

Bodnar planted his hands on his hips, a nasty curl to his lips. "You following me around, Stone?"

"Got better things to do," drawled Seth.

Bodnar pretended confusion. "Yet, here we are."

"This won't take long. Just here to give a little reminder on how to treat women."

"Seriously?" Bodnar's sharp laugh set his teeth on edge. "I'm not the one disrespecting her in front of the whole town."

Seth took the verbal hit because he deserved it. He put it behind him and went on the offensive. "Who she sleeps with is none of your business. She made that clear. You need to start paying attention."

"I have nothing but Kate's best interests at heart. Ever since we were sixteen, I've had her back. So, don't you tell me she's none of my business."

"You put marks on her."

Bodnar stuttered, then shook his head. "Bullshit. We had a discussion. That was all."

Didn't Seth just bet. "I saw them."

Bodnar's swallow tracked all the way down his throat. "You're lying."

"First and last warning." Seth took a second, turned it into ten. He wanted him to wonder, to remember. "Stay away from Kate."

"Or you'll do what?" Bodnar advanced, ready to go toe to toe. "Rumor has it you're one of them pacifist types."

Seth stretched his fingers, curled them into a fist. Unfurled them. His muscles coiled against his wishes, waiting to strike. "I might make an exception for you."

Bodnar got in his face. "You go ahead and give it a try, boy."

Seth was petty enough to gloat. "I'm in her bed now. Take it like a man. Go. Away."

Bodnar tilted his head back and howled with

laughter at the stars. "You keep that positive attitude. You're gonna need it." He looked back at Seth and wiped an imaginary tear from his eye. "She's going to eat you alive. I for one can't wait to see it."

"I'm not going anywhere."

"The hell you aren't." He jabbed Seth in the chest. Hard. He did it again. "You're out here accusing me of shit? I didn't embarrass her in front of the whole town. I didn't hand that stupid as shit reverend the opportunity he needed to come after her. That's on you, Stone."

There was enough truth in what he said to stampede over Seth's good intentions. He pushed Bodnar back a full two feet and sent him stumbling over the loose stones, but it didn't stop him from coming up grinning in triumph. "Touched a nerve, did I?"

"Fuck you," ordered Seth. Then he braced as the other man rushed him. Seth grabbed for the front of his jacket.

"If it's all the same to you…" Bodnar pulled back and landed a shot to his gut and another to his ribs. "I'll hold out for Kate."

Seth doubled over trying to suck in air. He brought Bodnar with him. Still keeping his own fists in check. Knowing resistance wasn't futile. Resistance was everything.

Bodnar wasn't all show. He was tough. He was motivated. And Seth was fighting with his hands tied to a promise. Bodnar rammed against him and momentum took them to the ground.

The landing broke them apart, and Seth rolled. On their feet, Bodnar jabbed at his head. Seth dodged. Bodnar took another shot and missed. "Fucking coward."

With gravel dust stirring at their feet, it was his words Seth choked on.

Bodnar's head rebounded with Seth's punch. Blood trickled from his split lip. Something a lot like satisfaction ran through his bloodstream. He took a deep breath and shut the feeling down.

"She'll be bored soon enough." Bodnar spit onto the road. "And need a real man in her bed."

"Which seeing as she ditched your ass…" The guy was friggin' delusional. "Won't be you."

Bodnar's fist nailed his cheekbone. *Shit. Fuck.* Seth stumbled, then lurched forward. In pain and dizzy, he gave into the traitorous instinct to hit back. He was not ending up in the fucking dirt. Not this time. Not with this guy.

He levied a return punch. Another. Another. Bodnar managed one bell ringing punch to his ear. Seth retaliated with an upper cut to the jaw. Bodnar stumbled to the ground. Seth reached down to drag him to his feet, but Bodnar had his hands up in surrender.

The rush of satisfaction receded. Regret crowded in. For a vow broken. He unclenched his fingers, shook out his hand, inspected the damage. All to buy a little time to regroup. But the blood on his knuckles elevated his remorse to shame.

Not that he was going to let Bodnar see it. "If I find out you had anything to do with circulating that photo? I'll make you sorry you were born."

It eased his conscience to hold out his hand to help the other man up.

Bodnar swatted it away and glared up at him like he was crazy. "Get the hell away from me."

"Fine by me." He backed up a step.

Bodnar pushed to his feet and shot Seth a disgusted look as he swiped at the blood leaking from his lip. "Like I want the world to know that she's banging the hired help."

Seth pressed a hand to his aching cheek. "Because it should be you?"

"It was me until you showed up. And it'll be me again when you're gone." Bodnar sensed he hit a nerve. He snorted out a laugh. "Your type don't generally stick around. Me? I'll always be here. Ready to pick up the pieces. And there will always be a need for that service with Kate."

What was the saying? Dumb as a post? "You underestimate her."

Bodnar smirked at him. "Maybe. The real question is: Am I right about you?"

When Seth remained silent, Bodnar continued, "You got the jump on me tonight, and good for you, but it won't be so easy the second time." He started walking backwards to his truck. "You want to protect Kate? Stay away from her. This freak can't take advantage of a situation that's not happening."

He climbed into his truck. Gravel scattered as he sped off. Seth picked up a rock and hurled it into the night. His body ached, but his mind was clear. Bodnar was right. And that hurt worse than any blow to the head.

The need to protect her was instinct. Staying away from her required honor, selflessness. He was no longer in possession of either of those qualities. He'd lost them with his first swing. In the dark with his headlights shining down the road, he shed the promises he'd made.

He was done being a martyr.

He was his father's son. But not his clone. A lone coyote howled into the night. It was time to find his own way. To decide his own limits. To live with the consequences. To defend his ground. However he chose to do it.

****

Kate tuned out the other two committee members and Tessa Morris, manager of the Abbey. They were wrapping up the final details for the Mad Man's Ball. It was all going according to plan. She could picture it in her head. It was going to be spectacular. She dabbed a hand against her aching forehead. Was it hot in here?

She marked items off her list: decorations had arrived from the party rental warehouse in the city, along with shimmering swags of purple and deep gray, the candelabras, the smaller votives, and the candles to fill them. All check.

Definitely hot. She added confirming the final decision on the flower-filled pumpkins with Rose to her list. The cake, complete with gargoyles, had been ordered from a bakery in the city. So...check. The photo booth was on its way. Double check. She glanced over the menu for the midnight lunch proposed by the Abbey and signed off on it.

Tickets had sold out months ago. No one wanted to miss the ball. Locals and visitors loved it. The beer tasting Friday night would set the tone for the weekend. But the ball...the ball was the showcase. The dress code was formal and the profits went to charity. Camp Easter Seal to be exact. So children with disabilities could go to camp.

Kate thought of the endless emails needing

answers. All of a sudden it hit her that there were only two weeks left until the fair. She pressed a hand to her queasy stomach and breathed deep. Just nerves. And too many last minute details to take care of.

Turning away in apology, she lifted her buzzing phone to her ear. One of her readers was away on a family emergency and didn't think she'd be back in time. Kate had been on the phone all morning. She stifled her sigh of disappointment at another regretful refusal.

On to the next name on the list. Then the town's blog needed updating, her least favorite job. The good news was she'd figured out how to block Matthew Parsons from ranting in the comment section. Inspiration struck. She made a note to ask a representative from the charity to do a guest blog spot. She unscrewed the top off her water bottle and took a careful sip. She fanned her heated face.

So hot. Not good.

An Abbey staff member hustled in and pulled Tessa aside. It signaled the end of their meeting, thank goodness. She bid the rest of the group good-bye. Off to the high school to confirm rehearsal dates for Tea, Cakes, and Couture.

The sun blinded her, making the hammer in her head pound harder. Fishing around for her sunglasses, she didn't catch sight of the petite blonde leaning against her Audi until they were almost toe to toe.

Felicity Taylor shoved the phone she'd been staring at into the back pocket of her jeans. "Kate."

Kate squelched the urge to push her out of the way. They hadn't spoken two nice words to each other in thirteen years. Not since Tyler had draped his letterman jacket over Kate's shoulders.

She'd have happily stretched it out to thirteen years plus one day. But here she was leaving fresh butt prints on Kate's car door. Nauseous and running on empty, she sucked it up. Felicity would never know how much it cost her.

"Felicity. So nice to see you." As usual she was dressed head to toe in faded country chic with some rock n' roll attitude thrown in. Problem was it looked good on her.

Felicity crossed her arms. "Oh look, the town's unlucky penny."

"Alas, no time for riddles today, sorry." Kate slid on her sunglasses. So much better. But what she really needed was Tylenol. And a nap. And to not have this conversation. "So why don't you skip all that and get to the point."

Because she really needed to sit down. Before she lost her breakfast. Who better to gloat over her loss of control than an ex-best friend? High on hormones and hair product fumes, Kate, Lily, Grace, and Felicity had fancied themselves the Spice Girls of Aspen Lake. Good times and plenty of righteous teenage rebellion. Until Tyler chose Kate. After that she'd formed an all new cowgirl clique. Kate had left town and that had been the end of their friendship. One more ex left behind. She'd never admit how much Felicity's desertion had hurt.

Felicity shrugged in agreement. "You owe it to Tyler to cut him loose. Once and for all. He can't breathe for all the dust you're kicking his way."

"Excuse me?" This was about Tyler? Again? Make that still. Dust? Kicking *his* way? If she wasn't in danger of losing her morning cereal she would have laughed in her face.

Felicity was all attitude and utter denial. "You heard me."

"Yes, but since you're not making any sense I'm trying my best to ignore you." Enough was enough. She waved her off. "If you don't mind you're blocking my way."

"Not super smart of you." Felicity dug her cowgirl heels into the pavement and her fingers into Kate's arm.

Kate narrowed her eyes at the sweaty hand wrinkling her favorite white silk shirt. "Hands off."

"He's done being your unlucky plus one. Cut him the hell loose. That way when he sees naked pictures of you with another guy plastered all over town it won't be quite so humiliating to be *that guy*."

"Oh. My. God. Seriously?" She yanked her arm back. "Who I sleep with is no one's business but mine. And it certainly isn't Tyler's."

Felicity flipped her hair back. "You can't be that stupid."

She was unbelievable. "At the risk of repeating myself, *excuse me*?"

"That's all you have to say?" Her voice took on an insulting falsetto. "Excuse me?"

Kate chose silence over retribution.

Felicity scoffed. "You used to be a worthy adversary, Kate. Now you're just pathetic."

She turned to walk away, and it was Kate's turn to grab a fistful of shirt. "Was that the point to this impromptu meeting? Throw a few insults and stomp off? I don't think it's me losing my touch."

The look Felicity gave her caused her shoulders to

tense. Pity had that effect on her. "Oh, Kate. Look at you. You have a store full of clothes and dress like a nun. Don't get me started on the hair. A bit too Little House on The Prairie for the 21st century, don't you think? I mean, come on. Did you give up booze and mirrors?"

Kate's hand went to the back of her head and the neat bun she wrapped her hair into, the other went to her heaving stomach.

Felicity stomped off only to hesitate and stomp back. "God, I can't believe you unwound enough to get it on with the new guy. Or maybe I should I say, I can't believe he ignored all of the above and got it on with you."

She fought it. She really did. But along with the stomachache and pounding head, the tears bubbled up and hovered because she wondered all those things too. Which was as humiliating as it was demoralizing. Not to mention plain sad. She scrambled to open her car.

"Ah, don't be like that." Felicity reached out a hand then drew it back without making eye contact. "Crap. Kate."

Her cheeks burned. "Don't."

"Fine." Felicity rubbed the spot between her brows. A deep sigh escaped. "How about I make you a deal."

Kate didn't like where this bizarre conversation was leading. "A deal?"

"Actually, it's a good idea." Her frown disappeared and in its place something far more distressing appeared. Excitement. "I'll help you with your Shepherd problem—"

What was this? Were they making up? Playing nice again? Kate couldn't keep up. Good thing her hand was still on the door handle. "I don't think so."

Felicity bobbed up and down on her worn out and completely charming boots and trampled thirteen years of discord. "And in return you send Tyler my way for a little TLC."

Kate wasn't sending Tyler anywhere. It was a ridiculous notion. "I don't need your help with Matthew Parsons. And as far as Tyler's concerned—"

She wasn't listening. The cogs were turning. Kate could hear them from where she stood. "The compound land borders ours. I can give him plenty of other things to worry about besides you. Or the fair. Without anyone knowing it was us."

"No. No, no, no. There is no us." Kate gestured back and forth between them, the motion making her stomach roll. "We are not teaming up. We are not conspiring together. You just finished insulting me in the worst possible way."

Who was she calling a nun? And her hair did not look that bad.

"Don't be so sensitive. And that wasn't an insult. It was much needed constructive criticism which everyone else is too scared to give you." She waved away Kate's gasp of indignation and her bubbling over, fumbling objections. Kate's head spun at the abrupt three-sixty. More bobbing up and down, more dizzying excitement. "Keep doing what you're doing with the new guy. Tell Tyler it's over, once and for all. He'll finally get the hint. I'll console him. It'll be good."

Kate looked around hoping for an intervention and whispered, "I don't understand what's happening?"

Because really? What *was* happening?

Felicity leaned in, crazy giving her a nice pink

glow. "If you tried loosening up a bit it might help. Try a bit of color, clothes wise. You know, let your hair down. Like, literally. Leave it down." She rolled her eyes and gave a slight shudder. "I'll get the first strike organized."

Strike?

Wait, she wasn't agreeing to anything. Mending fences. Or deals. Or fashion advice. She put a hand on her forehead to gauge her raging temperature.

Unfortunately, Felicity kept on talking. "Relax, it's not going to be like that time in eight grade when we blew up Keely Greg's locker. I'm talking about a few loose fence posts, some cut wire. A few dozen cows wandering around the wrong property. To start. Hand me your phone." She reached into her back pocket.

Kate dropped her hand. "Why?"

"To exchange phone numbers. Sheesh. I wouldn't have had to walk the old Kate through every little detail." The disgust was in her silent pleading skyward.

Kate had no choice but to accept the phone Felicity thrust at her. She was mesmerized by the outline of a pair of silver cowboy boots with the words *Cowgirls Do It With Their Boots On* printed on the cover in cherry popping red.

Felicity tapped her foot. "Well?"

Kate frowned. "Well what?"

She waggled her fingers at Kate. "Give me yours."

She was not exchanging phone numbers with Felicity Taylor for the purposes of conspiring to commit illegal acts. They would not do well locked in a cell together. But how to explain it so it would sink in after what appeared to be too many kicks to the head in the corral? "Felicity—"

"God, Kate." Her fingers tapped against her waist in time to her boot. "Do you want to be pathetic for the rest of your life or what?"

She arched her brow. "Stop calling me pathetic."

Felicity pushed out her chin. "Then stop acting like it."

She countered with a look down her nose. "It's a ridiculous plan."

Felicity raised Kate's glare and leveled an insulting head to toe skim. "I don't see you coming up with any better ideas. All I'm seeing is you handing the Shepherd ammunition by getting naked in clear view of the street. They have these things, you might have heard of them? They're called curtains."

Kate swallowed a gasp. "What I do in the privacy of my own home is my business."

"I couldn't agree more. But Tyler's freaking out. He's pissed. I have to strike while the iron's hot."

Kate bit her tongue. It made a twisted kind of sense.

"Come on, Kate," she urged, getting impatient. "I'm handing you a prime opportunity here."

On a huff she dug into her purse and pulled out her phone. She slapped it in Felicity's outstretched hand. "This remains between us."

"Please, like I want anyone to know I've resorted to this." She started typing.

"Likewise." Kate got busy adding her number to Felicity's contact list.

They handed the other's phone back. "I plan on attending the Mad Man's Ball on the arm of Tyler, so don't screw up."

They deserved each other. They really did.

"You can go with what's-his-name," Felicity offered.

"Seth." Kate shoved her phone back in her purse. "His name is Seth."

"Whatever." Felicity shrugged. Then her outrageously blue eyes widened with a stray thought. "Although you should know Brittany isn't too happy about you hooking up with *Seth*."

She was back to being confused. "Brittany?"

"Apparently, she liked what she saw the other night at the bar. She was kinda counting on getting to know him better. Likened his smile to panty remover, if I recall."

Kate pressed her lips together. Against her will a little something ugly slithered through her subconscious. It wound its way down into the pile of things she tried not to feel. "Brittany?"

"Yes, Kate. Brittany. You didn't think someone who looks like him would go unnoticed, did you?" Felicity shook her head like she couldn't believe anyone could be quite that clueless. "Gotta go. So, we good?"

If by good she meant the exact opposite of smart, then, yes, they were. She nodded because she could not push the word past her lips. Felicity hopped onto the running board of her truck and pointed at Kate. "Talk to Tyler."

Right." Kate gave her a thumbs up. Like she hadn't tried that. On numerous occasions.

She climbed into her car and pointed it in the direction of the high school and her next meeting. Two hours later it was a wrap, and she was an absolute wreck.

Grace looked up from tallying the day's totals. She did a shocked double take. "Oh my God, are you okay?"

"Not really." She felt like not-quite-dead road kill. "I think I might have the flu."

"You think or you do?"

Kate shrugged. "Is Seth still here?"

"He had to go and spend the afternoon at the lumberyard." She glanced at the big silver watch with the black leather strap on her wrist. "Said he'd be back right about now to put in a couple of hours to make up for it."

Just what she didn't need tonight: banging, sawing, drilling. All she wanted was uninterrupted sleep. She set her stuff down. "Do you think you could text him and tell him not to bother. That I'll see him tomorrow?"

"No problem. I'll lock up."

Kate sagged in gratitude. "Thanks for holding down the fort this afternoon. I couldn't do this without you."

When she wobbled Grace frowned at her. "Are you sure you're all right? You didn't get hassled about that stupid photograph, did you?"

"No." And surprisingly enough, not counting Felicity, she hadn't. There was one thing that was bugging her though. "Do you think I dress like a nun?"

"What?" Grace paused, then forced a fake laugh. She picked up a stack of receipts. Put them down. Straightened them. Looked up. "No."

"You hesitated." Grace stuffed everything into a bank bag. Kate was pretty sure they weren't going to appreciate finding a garment tag or the ballpoint pen.

"You always look professional. Not to mention

lovely." Grace cleared her throat. "Are you sure you're going to be okay by yourself because I don't mind staying."

"So you do think I dress like a nun," insisted Kate.

Grace hedged. "Not like a nun. Exactly. More like…like—where is Lily when you need her—like that vice-president wannabe from the States. You know?" She snapped her fingers in triumph. "Sarah Palin."

"What? That's the most ridiculous thing I've ever heard. She ran a hundred years ago. She's like fifty."

"Well…you know…after the makeover."

"I do not look like some Alaskan mayor."

"Vice-presidential candidate. There's a difference." She waved a hand in front of Kate. "You're looking to project an image that you need right now. Rocking the power suit by the way."

"Oh my God." Kate pulled out her phone. "I'm texting Lily."

"Good idea." Grace slumped and blew out a breath. "That's what you should have gone with in the first place."

"Fine," Kate muttered.

"Good." Grace rubbed her arms. "You sure you don't want me to stay?"

Kate gave her a hug then a shove. "You'll just be watching me sleep. Go, I'll be fine."

She trudged up the stairs, mind on her closet. Maybe her wardrobe was a little harsh. She worried her pearls. It wouldn't be giving in to soften things up a bit. Add a scarf. Undo a button or two. And her hair did look great down. But none of it was going to matter if she didn't get some much needed sleep.

In her apartment she made sure the blinds and

curtain were shut tight then she stripped out of her *power suit*. Popping pills she climbed inside her tiny shower. Steam filling the small space, she braced her hands against the wall and let the water wash away her day. Clean and dried off, she crawled into bed. Dreams kept her company. Strong hands tucking the covers in around her, smoothing over her hair, soft kisses against her forehead, whispers of comfort. Even though they were ghostly and intermittent and she knew it was fever induced, she pressed closer into them.

Let them seduce her. Quiet her. Protect her.

Chapter Eight

Kate rose with the dawn of a new day. The contents of her stomach rose with her. The flu forced her to crawl back into her bed, and it kept her there until noon on Saturday. Sunni had sent over homemade chicken noodle soup. Grace arranged for extra help in the boutique. Everyone looking out for her. Again. And Seth? Seth sent flowers with the cutest hand drawn note.

Sigh.

He needed to stop doing things like that. Her heart couldn't take it. Her mind obsessed over it. And him. When she had bigger problems. Responsibilities. And an agenda she couldn't afford to ignore. She ran a hand down her hip and slipped into her boutique. The hush of laughter, low conversation, and muted music calmed her nerves. This was what it was all about. Success. It was a scent she drew into her lungs.

Her cell vibrated from inside her day planner.

Tyler.

Meet me at Mary's at 7?

She frowned. She typed back. *Why?*

Come on, Katie.

Sorry. Busy.

Let me say goodbye in person.

The bell over the door dinged, and Seth stepped over the threshold.

And…just…un-freaking-believable.

Seriously?

Again?

An ugly purple bruise bloomed along his cheekbone. Her sick feeling had nothing to do with the flu. Kate cocked a hip. "Please tell me you and Tyler didn't get into it again?"

He blocked her with a question of his own. "How are you feeling?"

Oh, yeah. She was definitely meeting with Tyler. She typed a hasty confirmation. They had things to discuss. Like how she was getting tired of dealing with little boys instead of adults. She focused on the one in front of her. She tapped a foot. "Answer me."

"Have I told you how much I love it when you order me around?"

Sexual innuendo coupled with sarcasm. Be still her heart. "And I don't need a knight in shining armor. I need a man who knows how to keep his own counsel. One with some restraint."

"Really?" He looked off to the side, feigning deep contemplation. "I don't remember restraint being a requirement the other night."

Unimpressed, she titled her head to the side and waited.

"TMI." Grace hustled passed, coat and purse in hand. "And my cue to leave." At the door she turned back. "Good luck with…whatever this is?"

Then she was gone, and Kate was alone with Seth. Only not in a good way, but in a frustrating, oh-my-god-you-did-not-just-say-that kind of way. "You do understand how juvenile that last comment was, right?"

"You do realize you're talking to a flesh and blood

guy, right?" he mimicked her. "Not a mannequin?"

Their night together seemed like ages ago. Almost like it hadn't happened. She straightened her shoulders. "It's not out of line to want you to stay away from Tyler, especially when this is the result."

Seth crossed his arms. "But he puts bruises on you, and it's out of line for me to want the same thing?"

Touché. But admitting she was wrong wasn't happening. She lifted her chin. "The difference is you went behind my back over something that had to do with me. Not okay."

"I guess this is the point where we agree to disagree." He headed for the back. "I need to put in a couple of hours."

She rubbed a hand over her forehead in an effort to ease the ache.

Damn it.

She'd spent the last two years fighting for control over her life. It was second nature. Her struggles were public knowledge. Fodder for conversation. Solitude had seemed necessary to her recovery. Her sanity.

Seth looked up when she walked in. "You look worn out. Take a break."

He looked better than anyone should in bruises, faded Black Sabbath cotton, and a messy ponytail. Touchable. Kissable. Lovable. And what was any of that without honesty? "I have to step out for a few minutes."

The hiss of the nail gun shot out. He pushed up his safety glasses and leaned on the sawhorse. "Okay. What's up?"

It took effort to squeeze it out. She cleared her throat. Strived for a mirage of calm, cool, and collected.

Seth sensed her hesitation. A low warning growl escaped his throat. "Kate."

When she made a decision she stuck to it. "I'm meeting Tyler."

"You're meeting Tyler," he repeated, in a very quiet, very deadly kind of voice.

She backed up a step. "Yes."

Seth advanced. "Why are you meeting with that asshole? And where?"

"He asked me to meet him at Mary's and I agreed." His body language hardened. Kate put her hands up to stop whatever was going to come out of his mouth. "But I want you to be there too. Even though it's a public place, and I'm sure nothing is going to happen. It might help make my message clearer if he sees you there. Even if it's sitting at a different table, booth, stool-whatever."

His arms boxed her in as his eyes searched her face. "I can do that. Why the about face?"

"This is me compromising." She pressed against him, unable to resist the curve of his lips. How was it possible to ache with missing a guy you barely knew? "Now it's only fair you do the same."

"Kate, he put bruises on you."

"Yes, he did. And it's not going to happen again."

"Damn right."

Those two words shimmied right down to her soul. "I need you to stay away from Tyler."

He rubbed a hand up and down her back. "Does my answer affect where I'll be sleeping tonight? Because I really need to be in your bed kissing every crazy inch and ending up inside you."

She tilted her head back, not sure about the *crazy*

part. "You're not shy about sharing, are you?"

"Unlike you." His lips turned up at the corners, hinting at a smirk.

She was so not a prude. "Please. I've walked down runways just shy of naked."

"As Kate Logan."

"And who else would I be?"

"This Kate Logan. The one who's blushing because we're talking about sex. The one whose voice is a little husky because she's uncomfortable. The one who won't look me in the eye."

With that she squared her shoulders and made direct eye contact, one brow raised. "There, happy?"

"You do that thing with your eyebrow again and it's all over. It's like this sexy challenge."

"Stop saying things like that and answer my question."

"Maybe I'll kiss you instead?"

She ignored the flutter in her belly. Her fingers curled into his hair and tugged his head down. She whispered against his lips. "Agree to stay away from Tyler."

"Fine, I'll do all the work." His lips were soft over hers. They nuzzled and charmed. His palms rested against her neck, thumbs stroking her cheeks. His words were a naughty lie. "It's just a kiss, Kate. Relax."

They had time for one quick kiss. Maybe then she could breathe, and the awful fear of making a mistake that would cost her everything would lift from her chest. Her hands slid to his hips and twisted into the cotton of his t-shirt. It bunched and stretched in her hands pulling away from his warm skin. Warm, tempting skin. And with no need to resist her hand slipped under to caress.

His mouth opened over hers, and she answered his call. The skin of his back warm under her wandering hand. She opened up further, and his tongue was in her mouth. One of his hands pulled her shirt out of the waistband of her skirt. There was the chill of air on her back then the stroke of strong fingers.

A minute, or three, later she pulled back, breathed in deep. Seth did the same with eyes that said he wasn't anywhere close to finished with her. She pushed at his chest. "I have to go."

"We have to go." He didn't look away. Or move back. He shook his head. "What he feels for you...it isn't normal. Or safe. But I get it makes things harder for you if he and I are beating the crap out of each other. Add to that, he's not worth it. So, yes. I'll avoid him. But if he comes at me, or you, all bets are off."

"He won't."

He pressed a quick kiss to her pursed lips and let her go. It was a hollow victory. He didn't understand Aspen Lake dynamics. Heck, she didn't understand them half the time. Kate did know they had to co-exist in the same small town. They all lived and worked here. She and Tyler were heavily involved in community affairs. They had to come to an understanding before the only thing left was legal action. Because she would take those last-resort steps...if Tyler left her with no other choice.

Mary's was crowded with all types of diners enjoying a home cooked dinner. No sooner had she found a deserted booth and Seth settled in at the counter, Tyler slid in across from her.

"Thanks for coming." He didn't look like the man

who'd threatened her. With his smile cautious, he looked more like the boy he'd been. He lifted the cowboy hat off his head and set it down next to him. The swagger was gone. His own bruises purpling under his skin. It didn't mean she was letting her guard down.

"It's a public place, so…" She lifted a shoulder, let it drop.

"Low blow, Kate." He held up a hand to ward her off. "But I deserve it."

Confusion had to wait as the waitress arrived and filled their coffee cups.

It was impossible to know the best approach to take. Her stomach muscles, sore from the flu, clenched. "I—"

"Let me go first." His eyes begged. "Please."

She nodded, without a clue to where this was going. It was a disadvantage she refused to acknowledge.

"I'm sorry about the other day." He reached across the table to take her hand, thought better of it and pulled back. "I didn't mean to hurt you. There's no excuse for it."

She swallowed, not knowing what to say. She didn't believe him. There was no trust there anymore.

Like he read her mind, he nodded. "I know what you're thinking. And you're right. You have no reason to take what I'm saying as the truth."

Silence settled between them.

"I know you don't want to hear this, but I care about you. I always will."

This was more familiar. She sat back on a sigh.

He held up a hand. "But I'm done hitting my head against a brick wall. I wanted you to know I won't bother you anymore. I get it. It's time to move on."

He dug a five dollar bill out of his pocket and dropped it on the table. Hat in hand, he slipped out the booth. "Take care, Katie."

He was gone. Part of her problem solved without her having to say a word.

****

Seth was desperate to pull her into his arms. She trembled, standing with her arms tight across her stomach. It wasn't a very big apartment, but it engulfed her. Her shoulders hunched, her back tight. She was alone in the space even though he was less than three feet away. Offering up a silent prayer, he walked up behind her and put his hands on her shoulders. She flinched. His hands pressed closer, kneaded. "Take it easy."

Her shoulders gave the tiniest bit. "I slept with him. It was wrong...but I was so damn lonely. It was either sex or a drink, and I picked sex. I'm not proud of that fact, by the way."

"You're human. So what?" He pushed his fingers to keep digging into the knots bunched together underneath her skin. "Doesn't give him the right to treat you like you owe him something."

"But it gave him the wrong idea." She unbent enough to let the tiniest moan slip.

"You're sure it's done?"

"He said he was sorry. That he won't bother me anymore. That he was moving on."

It was a repeat of what she'd told him on the way back to her apartment. His surprise hadn't lasted long. Suspicion rolled in and hadn't left. He repeated his question from the street. "And you believe him?"

"You didn't see his face." Kate's head tilted back and fell to the side. Her shoulders rolled under his hands. "That feels so good."

"Give me an hour and it'll be more than your shoulders that are feeling looser."

"I don't think I'm up for anything physical tonight." She turned in his arms and dropped her forehead to his shoulder. "Honest to God, this flu is kicking my butt."

"Time for your beauty sleep." He picked her up and carried her over to the bed. She wasn't a lightweight, thank goodness. All curves and hidden treasure. Nothing beat the feel of her soft and pliant in his arms, her cheek cool under the brush of his lips.

Her arms stayed looped around his neck. "The window."

He laid her on the bed before closing the curtains. "Your tower's locked up tight."

She opened her eyes a slit. "Thank you."

"I need a shower." He rubbed a thumb over her lower lip. "Mind if I use yours?"

"Um…sure." But she didn't look sure at all. Cute confusion wrinkled her nose. "Something wrong with your shower?"

"Nope." He reached back and grabbed a handful of t-shirt and pulled it off over his head. He grinned, as her eyes went from wide and staring to narrowed and accusing when he dropped it on the floor. His socks were next, then his pants. He stripped while she pretended not to enjoy the show. Finally, his underwear hit the pile. She was ill. It was so wrong of him to get off on making her squirm. But she was so adorable, chewing on her bottom lip, hands twisting in her lap.

Better her focus be on him than waste her time feeling guilty over a shit like Tyler Bodnar.

He headed for the bathroom knowing her eyes were on his ass. She wasn't the only one who knew how to strut their stuff. In her tiny shower, he lathered up with body wash promising softer, smoother skin. The hot water and steam, the scent of vanilla, made him think of Kate. He rinsed off before things got out of control. He had no qualms about being naked but flashing his erection, when she was clearly down for the count, was taking things a couple steps too far.

He wrapped a towel around his waist and went out to find Kate sitting up in bed, covers at her waist in what had to be the least sexy nightwear he'd ever had the bad luck to see on a woman. Her eyes were glued to the laptop resting against her bent knees.

"It's safe to look. I'm decent." He'd towel-dried his hair but it was still wet. To get it out of the way, he hooked it behind his ears.

She gave a cautious peek. "I have work to do."

"You need sleep." He dropped his towel, again on the floor, which she didn't seem to approve of, and climbed under the covers. He wrestled with a couple of frilly pillows until he got them just right. With a sigh of contentment, he arranged his arms behind his head.

"Comfortable?" He looked over to find her laptop closed and her arms crossed over her chest.

"Yep." He flashed a smile guaranteed to beguile.

Her lips curved. "Are you sure? No more wiggling? Or adjusting?"

"I thought you were going to work? Don't worry about me. I'll watch TV."

"Do you see a television?"

"Seriously? I was kind of hoping it was hidden behind a secret panel somewhere." She gave him a *really* kind of look, which he ignored in favor of clarification. "What kind of person doesn't own a TV?"

She grabbed a book off her nightstand and slapped it against his chest. "Here."

"Jewel Storm. *One Night With a Duke.*" He studied the half-naked man on the front cover clutching a woman in danger of sliding out of her dress. He flipped it over and skimmed the back. Then he opened it to a random page, skimmed a couple of sentences. "Huh. Interesting."

He started reading: *Her breath snagged in her throat. He rolled them over so she lay on her back. The grass cool against her overheated skin. Against her leg she could feel his hard—*

He paused, put his finger under the next word and nudged Kate, who was studying the ceiling. "What's this word here? I want to make sure I'm pronouncing it right."

She tugged the book out of his hand. "Strange you don't recognize it since you're being a giant one right now."

"Hey, I wasn't done with that."

Her look dared him to keep going. "I don't think this is a good idea."

"And if you think I'm leaving you here alone at the mercy of a brainless preacher or crazy cowboy, you can think again."

She sighed and settled back. "How about you tell me about your tattoos?"

He got his arms around her and tucked her in closer. With her head resting against his shoulder, she traced the lines of his ink.

He sketched the lines with her. "This one's an owl crest. Not pure Northwest Native Indian art but kind of a Pacific fusion blending in some Polynesian style."

"It's beautiful."

"I had it done in honor of my dad." They mapped the lines of the short, hooked beak, the pointed ears. "Owl crests are said to represent the souls of deceased ancestors."

She lifted her head, made eye contact. "You miss him."

"Every day." He twined their fingers together. "Owls were also favored for their wisdom and perception. My dad was both those things, wise and observant."

She dropped her head back to his chest. "I drank to forget her. So I wouldn't have to deal with knowing she wasn't there anymore. Other reasons too, but that was a big one. It took two bouts of rehab for me to figure it out. Or at least admit it was as simple and as complicated as that."

"And since you've been to rehab, you know alcoholism is a disease. It's about figuring out how to manage it. How to avoid the triggers." He squeezed her hand. "It doesn't make you weak. It makes you a survivor."

"You're very good at talking me back from the ledge."

"I'm good at a lot of things." He tucked her in closer as he slipped them further down. "I need you to get better so I can prove it."

"I want to hear about your other tattoos."

"Some other time. Close your eyes."

Exhaustion overtook her, and she was asleep within minutes. Seth crept out of bed to double check the locks and deal with the lights. Back in bed, he stared up into the darkness. His skin was still warm with the memory of her fingers.

Sheets covered in pink flowers didn't make him nervous. Neither did smelling like girly body wash. Cuddling didn't give him hives. But sharing thoughts about his father, listening to hers about her mother? Indulging in that kind of intimacy had the power to keep him awake. In the past, he'd been careful to keep things casual and low maintenance. Lots of sex, lots of laughs, stay friends at the end.

He knew different when he felt it. Knew he more than liked her. More than wanted her. He didn't know if that was a problem or not.

Chapter Nine

Kate slid out of her car. She winced when her feet hit the pavement. Five inch, black patent stilettos did wonders for her ass and her calves, but twelve hours in them was enough to down the toughest shoe diva. The good news was she felt relatively human. She was even starving. The bad news was she'd missed supper, had no food in her fridge, and Mary's had long since closed.

Her phone rang. Seth again. "Hey."

"You home?"

Phone trapped between her ear and her shoulder, she reached back into her car for her files. "Yes."

"I'm almost there."

She grabbed for her purse. "Have you eaten?"

"No, so I picked some stuff up. Don't worry, I intend to feed you first."

His low level purring was doing funny things to her vagina. Worse things to her heart. "I really am starving."

"Princess, I'm counting on it." He disconnected on a laugh.

She was flirting. *Flirting.* It felt so carefree, so…normal. She dropped her phone into her purse. Naughty, dirty thoughts tangled with each other as she chased her keys around the bottom of her bag.

The alley entrance had two accesses: one up the fire escape to her apartment, and the new and improved door leading into Kate's Closet. She rarely used the fire escape entrance, preferring to come and go through the boutique's backdoor. Ah, success. She pulled her keys out. In a hurry to get inside she pulled the edges of her coat together against the chill.

Keys in hand, her foot on the first rickety step, a man stepped out of the shadows. Kate froze. Her heart stuttered like a faulty engine. The dim streetlights worked more like spotlights and lit all the wrong places. There was no way to identify him. Fear ate her insides and spit them back up her throat. Paralysis set in.

He didn't move any closer and for some stupid reason that freaked her out even more. She squinted at him. "Who are you? What are you doing here? My friend is on his way here. He'll be here any second."

The man stepped into a patch of light. Her hand went to her throat. "You? What are you doing here?"

It was the man from the street. The one whose cheek she'd touched. He grunted. Kate lurched back grasping for the railing, desperate for the support. He turned his face fully into the light. Angry red welts slashed his skin. The nausea she'd thought she'd left behind came flooding back.

"Admiring your handiwork?" Another figure emerged out of the dark. The Shepherd put a hand on the other man's shoulder, and he stumbled forward. "It's all right, William. I won't let her hurt you."

"What are you talking about?" Kate refused to succumb to his intimidation tactics. That's all this was. Seth was on his way. She could hold out until he got there and it would no longer be two against one.

"Look how you've marked him. Contaminated him with your touch." Oozing welts covered half of the poor man's face. He lifted shaky hands covered with the same. The Shepherd gave him a pitying look. "He's rotting from the inside out."

"Are you completely insane?" she breathed. He was spewing nonsense but panic rushed in anyway. "He needs a doctor, medical attention."

"Conventional medicine doesn't have any effect on the devil's stain." The man groaned, but Kate kept her attention on Matthew Parsons. The Shepherd once again urged the man closer. Her back hit the door.

"That's far enough." Her hand dropped when the alley swelled with the noise of movement. Men stepped out of the darkness. Six more by her count.

The Shepherd pulled William nearer still. "You see the effect your particular kind of degradation brings?"

"That's far enough." She strove to keep her breathing slow and even. Seth was on his way. There was nothing to do but stall until he got to her. Stay strong. Stay focused. Stay whole. "I don't know what you did to this man, or why you'd want him to suffer such agony, but he needs a hospital."

"Whore." The insult crept out of the half-circle of men. It slunk along the brick walls of the buildings until it was a one word chant echoing in the dark, starless night.

The men swarmed closer. The buzz of their intensity brushed her skin. They wanted her scared. It worked. Staying calm was futile. She lost it. Panic snaked along her spine, swelling as it slithered. She forgot to breathe. Then remembered. Struggled to get enough air, her heart pumping overtime.

Then a couple of the men stumbled to the side and Seth burst into their little circle of horrors, phone in hand.

"Kate." He was at her side gathering her in close. "Don't worry. The cops are on their way."

Panic, relief, and next to nothing to eat made her dizzy. Then nauseous. Seth in their midst confused them. They stopped chanting. But it was too late. She doubled over dry heaves wrecking her body.

"Back the fuck up. Now." His growl pushed them back. Cool hands smoothed back the loosened strands of her hair. "Here, baby. I got you."

"What more proof do you need, brothers? The sickness that infests her soul has been called forth. Brace yourselves. Be strong for Brother William." Further proof he was too stupid to know when to shut his mouth.

Seth's arms wrapped around her. "Back up. Or I swear to God…"

The Shepherd lashed out at Seth. "Watch your mouth, sinner."

The man with the ravaged face fell to his knees and started to sway. His words warbled. He grabbed his throat with one hand and pointed at her with his other. The sound of his choking filled the alley. Kate clutched at Seth desperate for it all to stop.

"She's killing him as surely as if she'd stuck a knife in his soul. Pray, men. Pray hard." Parsons lifted his arms. William toppled still grasping his throat. Shouts of concerns followed, but no one moved. "The devil is in our midst. We need to send him back from where he came."

"You're two seconds away from meeting him there." Seth's warning rumbled out of him. Kate held on tighter, taming the bunching of muscles under her hands.

Parsons reached for her. She jerked. It flipped a switch in Seth. Parsons ended up slammed against the bricks of the wall before Kate could utter a word.

"You do not touch her." Seth's words punched the air one at a time. Kate went from worrying over her own safety to Seth's intentions. She didn't fret for long. A heartbeat later the alley rang with the sound of sirens.

Nothing good was happening between Seth and Parsons. "Seth, please. Let him go."

"Sickness…in…you…too." The Shepherd's words a tortured gurgle. Seth growled another warning but the man offered no resistance.

"Re…pent."

Seth pressed in harder. "Fuck you, you sick shit."

"Seth," Kate pleaded again.

Flashing lights from a police cruiser pivoted around the alley. It galvanized a couple of the men, who leapt to free their leader.

"Seth, stop. Please." Car doors slammed. Her anxiety reached new levels.

"Back up." The order barked out into the night. She recognized Chase's voice and she allowed a small bit of relief to creep in.

"Kate, honey. How are you doing?" Mike's big, blond head dipped into her line of sight, his arms slipped around her. "Do we need an ambulance?"

"Not for me." She struggled to point in the direction of the man with the oozing face.

"I'm not going to say it again. You men need to back up." Chase again. She heard the rustling of men obeying his order. All except one, apparently. "You. Mr. Stone, is it? I need you to plant your ass over there."

"You sure?" Mike asked her.

She squared her shoulders. "I'm sure."

He rested the back of his hand against her cheek then her forehead. "Let's get you inside."

Chase lost his patience. "Mr. Stone, until I figure out what's going on, you will go where I tell you to go. And where I tell you to go is over there."

Seth wasn't in the mood to listen. He appeared in front of her and pulled her into his arms.

"Mike," warned Chase.

But she was too darn glad he was there to do anything but latch onto to him. Her fingers tangled into the material of his hoodie and refused to unclench. Giant, gulping sobs bubbled up her throat, and there was no holding them in.

"Brothers, brace yourselves. Her tears are acid."

"Mr. Parsons," Chase barked. "I don't remember granting you permission to speak."

Seth jerked in her arms and she held on for dear life.

"Something I don't require under the constitution," announced Matthew Parsons. His quivering smugness echoed around the alley.

"And should you continue to speak without first being asked I will not be happy, and you will not like the consequences." Chase did not like to be challenged. Kate locked her eyes shut.

Mike sighed. "Kate, here's what we're going to do. Seth is going to help us out by answering a few questions, and once Chase gives the okay he'll come find you. You and I are going to go inside and go over what happened."

Even though his body vibrated with energy, Seth smoothed a gentle hand over her hair, down her back. His lips brushed her ear. "It's okay. I've got you."

"Seth, it would go a long way if you were to help me out here." It was another warning, this time from Mike.

"I won't be far away," Seth whispered. She nodded. His kissed the top of her head. "I'll come find you when I'm done."

"Okay." She forced her arms to do her bidding, even though it was clear they had a mind of their own and it was the last thing they wanted to do.

"All right." Mike put a gentle hand on her arm and tugged. "Let's go."

She gave her statement wrapped in a blanket Mike draped over her shoulders, sipping ice water he fetched for her. Because as a recovering alcoholic, she wasn't supposed to guzzle booze anymore.

Chase walked in sans Seth and hunkered down in front of her. "How you doing, gorgeous?"

"I've been better." Her eyes went to the empty doorway and her ears noted the silence of the stairway.

Chase patted her knee. "He's taking a couple of minutes before he comes up. The rest of them have gone home. We'll be confirming they made it there after we leave here."

She wanted Seth arms around her. She shivered because they weren't there. "He's insane, you know that right?"

Chase shifted eyes to Mike, back to her. "He's threatening to press charges against Stone."

Unbelievable.

"For what? For breaking up his little séance?

Crimes against Christ?"

"He says Stone attacked him. That when Stone threatened one of his men, he stepped in and Stone went crazy." Proving he might be a friend, but he was still a cop.

She wasn't confirming or denying anything. "He was protecting me."

"Gorgeous, there's a fine line between protecting and slamming someone up against a brick wall and cutting off his air supply."

She tensed. This wasn't happening. "Chase, were you counting bodies down there in the alley? We were outnumbered."

He sat back on his heels and watched her.

"If he hadn't come along…" But she knew what he wanted, and she didn't like being herded in that direction.

"File a complaint against Matthew Parsons," said Chase.

There it was, the place she didn't want to go. The sign, omen, whatever, that she couldn't handle her business. "I don't want to do that. It'll only make things worse."

"We disagree."

"Chase…"

"I appreciate your reasons for wanting to keep a low profile, but our first priority is maintaining law and order. He's fucking with you, Kate. I don't like it. Mike doesn't like it. A lot of people don't like it. But that guy pacing around downstairs *really* doesn't like it. I don't want him doing something stupid and then having to pay the consequences. Neither do you. You know what you have to do. Quit dicking around and do it."

She sighed, her fingers twisting in the blanket.

Mike put his hands on her shoulders and squeezed. "It's the right thing to do."

She nodded her consent. Protecting her was not going to cost Seth everything.

Having gotten his way, Chase was, if not exactly smiling, hinting at one. "Good girl."

"So, we good here?" asked Mike.

"Can I come by the station tomorrow?"

"Mike and I are on the night shift tomorrow too. So, if you want to do it through one of us call and we'll meet you there." He slapped a hand to his knee and pushed up. At the sound of boot trends on the stairs, his gaze went to the doorway before coming back to her. "See you tomorrow."

He was halfway across the room when she called out. "I'm telling Lily you called me a girl."

Walking backwards, Chase put two fingers to his forehead and saluted her. "Great, she can add that to the growing list of shit I'm not supposed to say."

Seth stepped into the room then aside as Chase and Mike strode past him on their way out. None of them said a word.

The air in the room shifted. His hair was wild around his shoulders. Gone was the artist. The easy-going lover. In their place was a man who wanted to break something or someone. When his attention snapped to her, it didn't waver. But his look changed. It pinned her in place, made her panties wet.

"I'm staying." It was a declaration.

"Okay," she agreed. She had no plans to kick him out. Quite the opposite. She let the knowledge mix and mingle with the blood flushing the fear from her veins.

He started to pace, hands clenched at his hips, chest muscles working. Battling demons she couldn't see. "Jesus, Kate."

It wasn't the moment for thank-yous. For gratitude. It was time for honesty. "I'm going to the station tomorrow to press charges. Take out a restraining order."

"Good." No relief. No loosening of muscles. No smile. Just his cat eyes measuring her reaction to his next demand. "Come here."

She swallowed. Adrenaline. She got it. "Seth…"

"Doesn't require a lot of thinking, Kate." Her name was hard off his tongue. His face set, he spread his arms out. A take it or leave it gesture. "Yes or no."

No one had ever spoken to her in that tone of voice. Challenging her. Waiting to see if she had what it took to cross the floor. To surrender her inhibitions. She pushed her legs together. So intoxicating, she wanted to savor the wave of desire a couple seconds longer.

Of course, he noticed. His nostrils flared like he inhaled the scent of her longing on the air. "If you want it, you need to come and get it."

She had no idea how to do that except to take it one wobbly step at a time. On her second step, he reached back and yanked off his hoodie and shirt. He threw it across the room. Feet planted, half-naked, cargos hanging off his hipbones he crooked his finger. Her insides clenched in anticipation. Need rushed up the back of her throat, salted her tongue. She licked her lips.

He growled. She must have stopped because he beckoned her forward again. "No stopping now, princess."

When she was within reaching distance, he snatched her closer. He reached down and yanked the hem of her skirt up and over her hips until it gathered around her waist. No finesse. No gentleness. He was desperate for her. "Tell me you want this."

Even though he didn't phrase it as a question, she knew he'd stop if she said the words. She trusted him. She fumbled with the first button on her blouse.

His hands raced over her, separating her shirt from the waistband of her skirt until his hands landed on her behind. He lifted her up. "Put your hands on me."

She abandoned her buttons and fisted her hands in his hair. Her fingers wrapped and twisted then she yanked. Hard. "Bossy."

His eyes darkened. "Mouth. Now."

Her mouth crashed down on his. If this was a battle, she was determined to win. Teeth and tongues and the taste of consent. She bit his lip. To prove she, above all others, had what it took to take him on.

He hissed and shoved his fingers inside her panties and hoisted her up further, his fingers rushing over her. "So wet."

"For you." She dug a set of nails into his skull and pushed down hard against his hand. "Only you."

Her tongue was halfway down his throat. His fingers all the way inside her. Not a millimeter of sanity separated them. He dropped them both onto the edge of the bed. She scrambled back.

"All mine." He stalked her all the way to the headboard, the covers bunching around her.

"Yours." He reached for her panties and they were gone. He parted her legs. She bit down on her lip. Oh yes, she was all his.

"So beautiful." He pressed a hand against the inside of each thigh and his mouth went down on her.

One long lick later her head fell back, her hands twisted into the covers. More heat. The loss of it. Back again. Her lids slammed shut, and she bit back a moan. His tongue swiped again. She couldn't help it. His name was a prayer on her lips.

"I know, baby." His fingers slid inside her while his mouth suckled. She clamped around him. His tongue soothed. "That's it. Give it up for me."

Aware of everything, knowing nothing, she had no choice. His shoulders pressed her thighs wider apart, his hair trailed over her skin. His breath came in pants and it escalated her own. His fingers were busy sliding in and out. Hers wrapped into the bed covers. Her toes too. The suction, the pull of his mouth, sent her over the edge.

She came all over this tongue. He didn't quit until she stopped shaking. Not that she was satisfied. Not even close. She wanted more than his fingers and some French kissing. She wanted their bodies fused together, clinging to each other. The pump and grind of shared purpose.

The quiet sound of his zipper going down filled the room. She caught her breath. Anticipation swelled like a balloon about to blow apart. From up on her elbows she watched him shed the rest of his clothes, forgetting she still wore most of hers. Then he was over her, pushing into her, wrapping one of her legs around his waist, the other he hooked in the crook of his elbow. He set a brutal pace. She matched it. The slap of skin, the scent of sex, the feast of urgency caused a suspension in time, then dropped them at the finish line.

Their sweat mingled with their gasps for air. A delicious, immobilizing laziness overtook her muscles. Seth rolled off her, settled then gathered her in close. She curled into him, his skin warm and salty under the kiss of her smile.

"What?" His fingers sifted through her hair, spreading the strands, letting them fall.

She thought it important to point out. "I still have all my clothes on."

His hand roamed over her bare behind. "Not all of them."

"I'm going to go clean up." She pushed against him.

He tugged her back down to topple over his chest. "Two minutes. Any longer and I'm coming to get you. Then it's just you crawling back into this bed like you never left."

"Not even a little lip gloss?" Her lips hovered over his, dipping but not quite meeting, teasing.

His hands slid under her shirt and coaxed it over her head. It fluttered to the floor. Two seconds later her bra followed. He smacked a kiss on her lips. "That should save you some time."

"Haha." She punctuated it with a nose wrinkle.

"I thought so." Then he smacked her butt. "Move it, princess. I'm not done with you yet."

"That hurt," she protested. It was a lie. It didn't. It caused a lovely, naughty tingle. Which was not something she wanted to psychoanalyze at the moment.

"Poor princess." He smoothed a hand over the sore spot and beyond. "Want me to kiss it better?"

He reeked of smirking, confident, satisfied male. Because he expected her to answer with the opposite, she lifted a brow. "That's a reward you'll have to earn."

His lips parted, but she was up and off the bed. "Then maybe the next time you'll mind your manners."

She hadn't forgotten about his strut to the bathroom the other night. Had dreamed about it. But he was still an amateur. Unlike her.

She headed for the bathroom her hips swaying as she smoothed them over her hips. The zipper came down along with the skirt. It hit the floor. She didn't miss a step leaving it behind. She glanced back over her shoulder, lifted her hair, and gathered it on top of her head. Turned and gave him a half view of her naked breasts. All sultry slow movements intended to torture.

It worked. He was more out of the bed then in it, ready to pursue her. At the bathroom door she wrapped her hands around the knob from behind and leaned back against it giving him a full frontal view. He thumped at his heart like he was jumpstarting it, then he flopped back on a groan, hands still pressed to his chest.

She laughed. *Laughed.* After a busy twelve hour day. A horrendous evening. Because Seth made it all better. And she wasn't going to psychoanalyze that revelation either.

****

Seth pulled up to his studio in time to see the sun begin to rise. For all the sexual gymnastics they'd indulged in last night he was still wound up. His fingers stayed wrapped around the steering wheel. In a flash, he was back in that alley...that fucking, narrow, dark, should have been deserted, alley. Where he'd lost his shit.

The back of his skull hit the headrest, and he closed his eyes. Scared, sick, and surrounded. The something dark housed in his veins woke with the sun. It slithered and snickered while he replayed his call to the cops. Swam in his bloodstream as he remembered the word *whore* echoing around the alley. He'd only wanted to get to Kate. Then she'd fallen, and Parsons had opened his mouth, and that swirl of darkness flooded his body with the need to act. To strike. To shut the man up. To protect what was his.

Except Kate wasn't his. He didn't own her like some medieval lord of old because they had sex. He didn't want that kind of obligation. Nothing good came from being the puppet attached to those smothering, knotted strings of responsibility.

The main cabin up ahead remained silent in the shimmering dawn. Ashley would be sound asleep and he was in the mood for noise. He changed direction and headed for his studio. He needed to cage the beast and bring back the artist. The part of him that turned those dark needs into art.

He tugged off his shirt, tossed it. The shabby three-legged stool wobbled but held when he planted his ass on it. Boots and socks shed he reached for the hand wraps and started the process of protecting his hands. The preparation did its bit to calm him. Then he reached for his gloves. When he was ready he walked over to the heavy punching bag hanging from the rafters. He braced his feet into the mat.

He didn't focus on one spot, but the entire bag. It became his opponent. Becoming his own man still meant keeping his shit together. Not turning into a monster to battle one. Exorcising Matthew Parsons from his mind's eye, he forced his body to relax. Surrounded by the scent of wood shavings and linseed oil he shut his eyes.

With a shot of breath he whipped out his arm. Connection made he retreated, strived for a sense of relaxation. Another throw of his arm. Smack. More of a shock than a push. Quick recovery. And again. He didn't aim. This was about speed. It was about clearing his head.

The moment he stopped punching his thoughts punched back. He concentrated on his breathing, on his heartbeat. No way did he want his body to tire out before his brain.

He kept his right up when he threw a jab. Delivered a perfect left hook. Even though he wasn't in the ring he kept his elbows down to protect his body, perfected his footwork. He relished the intensity of the workout. Embraced the emotional oblivion. He punished the bag until the bad soaked his clothes straight through to his underwear. Until exhausted he grabbed onto the bag for support.

"Bad night?"

He dropped his forehead to the beaten bag. "Ash, private space. Off limits. Get out."

She listened as well as she ever listened, which was to say not at all. "Definitely, bad."

"Ash," he warned.

Instead of running for the door like an obedient sister, she shoved things aside on a nearby table and hoisted herself up. "Want to talk about it?"

He lifted his head to glare.

"Right." He hurt her by not confiding but she shook it off and smiled. "Okay, change of subject. It's kind of a crazy little town, isn't it?"

Sighing he pulled off his gloves. "Why do you say

that?"

"Spent some time yesterday talking to the goth chick who works at Kate's Closet."

"Goth chick? You mean Grace?" Seth crossed to an old fridge and pulled out a bottle of water. He held one out to her. She put out her hands. He tossed it and pulled out another one for himself.

She caught it on a grunt. "Anyways, she says there's this big fair coming up."

"Yeah, so?"

She clapped her hands. "They set up tarot booths and everything. There's a ball. I am not shitting you. I have to go."

"No." He brought the bottle to his lips and chugged.

"Not the ball, can't afford that, but the rest of it. Let me stay. Please." Her dangling legs started to swing. "I'll be your slave. And you know you need one. Badly. There's like a month's worth of laundry scattered across the floor of your room. How do you even get to your bed?"

"You went into my room?"

"I wasn't snooping," she denied in a rush. "I was familiarizing myself with the surroundings."

"Uh…huh." He let it pass. For now. She picked at the label on her bottle, pulling it off in little pieces and letting them drift to the floor. "Something on your mind, Ash?"

"There's something you need to know. You're not going to like it." She sighed and set her water down. "This is a great spot, prime location. Don't think she doesn't know that, hasn't figured out how much it's worth down to the last cent. She's got dollar signs in her eyes, and she needs the money. Big time. I don't know what kind of trouble she's in, but she's in big."

His eyes narrowed and he got a very bad feeling in the pit of his stomach. The look in her eyes confirmed it. He rubbed a hand over his mouth. "Jesus."

"She spends a lot of time at the casino these days. And this Lenny guy's been hanging around the house, even when she's not there. Bad vibes. Very bad vibes, bro. I had to get out of there." Ash shivered in revulsion.

It was exactly what he didn't need right now. More shit to take care of. Especially, coming from the direction of his stepmother. She couldn't even get it together enough to give a shit about her own flesh and blood. The only person on the planet who cared about her.

But more than revulsion, he saw fear. Real fear. He threw the quarter full bottle of water across the room, put both hands to his head and started to pace. "God damn it."

"I'm sorry."

"*You* don't have anything to be sorry for." Striving for the calm they both needed him to show, he grabbed up a towel and rubbed at the back of his neck. "Did you talk to her about it?"

"I tried. She wasn't in the mood to listen. Or she doesn't have a choice about letting him stay there." The hint of tears but no stunned betrayal. Resignation, but no excuses. Just sadness.

He didn't want that for her but he wasn't giving Caroline another cent to make it better. "I'm not bailing her out. I can't."

"I know. And you shouldn't, but that doesn't mean

she's not going to make you sell this place to make her problems go away. I'm sorry."

"She can't make me do anything. Sell, give her money, come back. She's not getting any of those things." But she had and she would try again.

"Yes, Seth, she can. Because you love me. She's going to give you some bullshit story about needing money to send me to university. Don't believe her. When I go, I'll get there on my own."

He braced his hands on his hips and hung his head. Stared at his feet, while the sweat cooled on his skin. Maybe they were stronger together against her. He lifted his head. "You sound awfully mature all of a sudden."

"Newsflash, I've always been mature. You've just been too busy taking care of us to notice." She hopped off the table and crossed over to give him a hug. "I missed you, bro."

He hugged her back. "You have three days to get a job and you'll have a list of chores."

She pulled away and stuck out her tongue. "Already done and no problem to the second."

He should have known. Out of necessity she'd had a job since she'd turned fifteen. "Where?"

"I start at Mary's tomorrow, waitressing." She smacked a kiss on his cheek. "She's a real fan of yours. Wanted to give your little sister a hand up."

She turned to leave. "Ash? You are going to college, we'll find a way."

"Course we will. You and I together? Invincible." She skipped out the door.

Looking out for each other. He'd never seen it as an advantage before, but now? Maybe it could work.

With Ash here, Caroline couldn't use her against him.

****

Kate skipped out mid-morning to spend an agonizing hour at the police station. Then it was lunch with the fair committee and back to spend the rest of the afternoon in her boutique. No skirt or stilettos today. She'd mixed it up with a very cool pair of black boots, dark jeans, and a dark gray, over-sized knit sweater with her Grandmother's pearls. So far the world hadn't ended.

She entered Kate's Closet to see half the town. The female half. The fair was next weekend. New outfits and accessories were needed, and no one wanted to be wearing the same dress, pair of pants, or blouse. But still it was strange to have such a crowd, not that she was complaining.

Some unexpected shoppers caught her eye. Felicity was there, pawing through a display of graphic tees. Brittany was with her. Felicity saw Kate and shot her a thumbs up and a wink. Whatever the heck that meant. She did not want to deal with a big heaping pile of cowgirl crazy right this minute.

Grace noticed the silent communication and frowned. Great. Grace knew their last civil conversation had taken place a decade ago. Come to think of it that one hadn't been all that civilized either.

Fortunately, a customer grabbed Grace's attention. Unfortunately, Brittany also noticed Kate and hustled over.

"Hey, Kate. Is Seth around?"

It was on the tip of her tongue to say no when she remembered she didn't have to lie because she really didn't know.

"I'm not sure." Kate smiled. Or tried. "If I see him can I give him a message?"

"Kate, there you are." There was no mistaking Seth's deep voice coming in from behind her.

Or Brittany's delighted one. "Seth, I was just looking for you."

Right on cue Felicity sauntered on over looking like the only thing she was missing was spurs.

And this was the woman giving her fashion advice.

Felicity tugged her aside. "I need to talk to you."

Then Grace wasn't simply frowning, she was gaping with shock. And who could blame her. First Sunni, who she couldn't help noticing was also in doing some shopping, and now Felicity.

None of which stopped Kate from noticing Brittany slip an arm through one of Seth's. "Is there a place we can talk? Or maybe you could take a break and we could grab a coffee?"

Really? Had she missed the grainy, sleazy photo suggesting Seth was hers so hands off?

Seth raised his brows in Kate's direction. "Um…I'm not sure…"

He'd saved her the other night. It was time to return the favor.

"Actually, I need Seth for the next little while." She was a lot more successful with her smile this time.

Felicity pulled her back in. "Kate, I really need to talk to you."

She ground her teeth. "Not now, Felicity."

Felicity leaned in for a loud whisper. "It'sway importantway andway an'tcay aitway."

Kate wasn't the only one to turn and stare at her.

Then Felicity opened her eyes really, really wide

and bobbed her head in the direction of the back of the shop.

"Great, then Seth has time for coffee." Brittany bounced up onto her tip toes and back down, her long, loose hair swaying over her spaghetti strapped shoulders which went with her shredded denim mini skirt and high heeled flip flops, because apparently she hadn't gotten the memo that summer was so last month. She was also oblivious, or make that impervious, to the awkwardness radiating off Seth.

"Kate?" asked Seth, like he was still hoping for a rescue but was now distracted into asking, "Why is she speaking Pig Latin?"

Was that what that was? Because that wasn't exhausting at all.

The three ring circus act was too much for Grace to ignore. She hustled over, her BFF face in place. "What's going on?"

She put a hand on Grace's arm. "Nothing, we were just—"

"Kate, honey, do you have this in a medium?" Sunni waved a chocolate brown tee with satin trim in her face. Then she reached over and pulled her out of Felicity's grasp and away from everyone toward the door leading to the back of the shop.

She had some serious muscle power for someone who stood five feet, two inches tall. Kate checked the tag and frowned. "This is a medium."

Sunni looked back over her shoulder. "Right. Sorry."

Except she didn't sound sorry at all. Just intent on pushing Kate along in front of her. She did not have time for any of this. "What is going on?"

Sunni leaned forward and whispered, "That Parsons person is on his way here."

"What?" Then they were both craning their necks to the front of the shop and hoping to get a glimpse of the street through the window. "How do you know this?"

And then Seth was there pushing her the rest of the way through the door.

Which was not okay with her. "Just...wait a minute."

Felicity crowded in behind them. "I tried to tell her."

Grace slipped in beside her. "Good. I have a few things I want to say to that asshole."

Kate was feeling a little overwhelmed. And a bit faint. So, she did what came naturally and turned to burrow into the warmest, most solid surface available. Seth. Because she absolutely could not deal with Matthew Parsons today.

"It's okay." His hand spanned the back of her head, his fingers smoothing over the strands before taking hold of a bunch. "Don't worry. I've got this. I'll be right back."

"No." She held on tighter. No way was she letting him go.

Under her hands the coiling of his muscles matched the tremor in his voice. "Princess, it's going to be okay."

"Way to feed her ego, big guy."

"Hush, Felicity." Sunni's voice had a hands to hips sound to it. "He's looking to make a scene. I'm guessing he doesn't much care if it involves one of you or both of you. What he's not anticipating is half the female population of Aspen Lake."

She didn't like the sound of that either. Her customers didn't need to be subjected to a scene. Someone needed to take charge. That someone had to be her.

"It's my boutique. I'll talk to him." Then Kate made the mistake of letting go of Seth.

Brittany moved to block his way. Gone were the fluttering eyelashes, her wide flirty smile. "How about we go for that coffee?"

Grace frowned at her. "Kate, what's going on?"

Felicity slapped him on the shoulder as she tried and failed to push past. "We got this, big guy. You can stand down."

But you didn't trap a wild cat. Not unless you had a cage to lock him in. And they didn't.

Kate heard the tingle of the tiny bell above her door, the shuffle of feet, the murmurs. And then quiet. Through the silence Seth scented his prey. It was in the tight line of his back. The squaring of his shoulders. In the coiling of his springs. He picked Brittany up and set her aside.

"The tough ones never go down easy. Close formations, girls," ordered Felicity.

"Felicity, heel." Sheesh, you made one little deal with the devil and this was the result. Insanity. "No one is going down."

Kate pushed her way through the door and stopped cold beside Seth who hadn't made it very far either. Grace joined them. Sunni too. The path to Matthew Parsons blocked by women of all shapes and sizes. They did, however, have one thing in common. They were *pissed*. The magnet for their ire was swelling with importance at the front of her precious boutique.

Mary stepped forward from the front of the crowd. "You're not welcome here."

The Shepherd spread his hands. "It's a free country. I believe it's my right to come and go as I please."

"I can understand you believing that seeing as how you're operating under a huge misconception."

Parsons looked down his nose at her. The crowd held its collective breath. "And what pray tell would that be?"

Mary was as round as she was tall, but she didn't need height. She had the voice of authority. She used it at council meetings, in church, to boss her employees and customers. "That somehow this became your town the minute you moved in next door. It didn't."

Sunni slipped through the throng of women to stand beside her mother. "Praise God it never will. Your type of business is not welcome in Aspen Lake." She stabbed her finger into Parsons' face. "And if you ever corner my girl in an alley, or anywhere, ever again you'll regret it."

Mary brought it home. "That's a promise."

And then the rest of them started with the woots and the right-ons, the fist pumping, and the clapping. Parsons didn't bother to try and speak over all the noise. He did however find Kate at the back of the room. She caught his tight smile right before Seth stepped in front of her blocking his view. Then her little welcoming bell signaled his retreat.

Seth's warm fingers twined with hers. "You okay?"

She squeezed back. "What just happened?"

He let out a laugh. "I think this group of ladies just handed Parsons his ass."

She looked up at him, gave him a stunned smile of her own. "Yeah, they did."

From the front of the room, Mary announced, "Come on, ladies, there's shopping to be done, then coffee is on the house across the street."

"We'll rehash what happened later." Grace left to deal with the cash register.

Seth dropped a kiss on her cheek. "I need to get back to work."

It was nice. Sweet. She liked that. "I'll see you before you leave?"

He nodded. "Go, make money."

Oh, she planned on it. But first she had something she needed to do. Kate turned to Felicity. "You arranged this."

"Just keeping the endgame in sight."

"I don't know how to thank you."

"Had a very promising conversation over dinner with Tyler the other night. This is just my way of saying thanks."

"Still, thank you."

"In lieu, I'll take that dress. The red one. With the sequins. We'll call it even."

She smiled before leaning in and whispering, "I'm not that thankful."

Felicity gave her a once over kind of look. A hint of admiration crept in. "Welcome back, Kate."

Felicity headed for the dress rack, her hips swaying in her faded jeans and Kate had to admit she had a first class behind. She called out, "Forget the red. Try the blue one with the straps and the silver belt."

"Gotcha."

The afternoon passed in a blur of sales and receipts. She couldn't wait to tally the numbers. The financial noose loosened a smidge. If things were brisk until after the fair and it carried on through the holiday season, she might manage to keep the doors open.

"How are you feeling?" asked Seth.

She turned back from locking up the front door. "Jazzed…with a lot of I'm not sure thrown in."

"You talk to the alarm people yet? Make arrangements for them to come in?"

"No. Not yet." She sighed and held up her hands. "It's on my list for Monday morning."

He cupped her face in his hands, his face dipping closer, his mouth settling into stern. "I don't want you staying here alone until it's fixed."

Those eyes. All tawny seriousness. They were going to be her undoing, which was why she was thankful Grace had cornered her earlier over the same security issues. She wasn't ready to give in to all the feelings swirling around inside of her. Not tonight anyway. "I'm staying at Grace's tonight."

"Good. I've got a commission I need to finish up." His thumbs swiped along the sides of her jaw and she didn't miss the hint of relief in his voice. "Girls' night, huh?"

"Yeah, something like that." A little distance was never a bad thing.

His lips curved. His tongue did a quick lick of his bottom lip. The lushness of it catching on his teeth like he was imagining all the dirty possibilities.

"Stop it." She slapped at his arm.

"What?" Then he was all wide-eyed innocence.

"Get your mind out of the gutter."

"Princess." He leaned in to tug on her bottom lip with his teeth, then smooth the spot with his tongue. "What I'm thinking? The gutter's a step up."

"What am I going to do with you?" Because the last thing he needed was encouragement, and she didn't need the frustration of hearing what was sure to be an exact accounting, she put a finger over his lips. "Don't answer that."

"Oh, I'm going to give you an answer, but I'll save it for when we're full on skin naked. Possibly horizontal but maybe not. With my tongue inside you."

That was why she didn't require an answer. There was no way to stop the flush of heat under her skin. He enjoyed shocking her. But she was learning. She slipped her hand between them and down until it cupped his balls and squeezed. Not hard, but enough to leave him with his mouth open.

"Easy." He grabbed onto her hand. Not to pull it away but shift it so it was rubbing against his fly. She watched as his eyes drifted shut. His fingers tightened around her hand. His breath puffed out. His other hand wrapped around the back of her neck, and he tugged her face closer, his eyes opening, zeroing in on hers. "Kiss me goodnight."

That she wanted to feel the floorboards under her knees, hear the zip of his fly go down, inhale the scent of him, taste him shook her. He coaxed her mouth open under his, hungry and taking.

"Oh my God, get a room." The click of heels, the sound of them stopping and then retreating had them pulling apart.

Kate opened her eyes, but they were a little

unfocused. His face ducked into her field of vision. "Text when you get to Grace's. Okay?"

She blinked. "Okay."

Yep, she definitely needed a time out. Things were getting a little too intense a little too fast. She wanted to go home with him. Eat with him. Discuss the day. Climb into bed with him. Not good. It wasn't the kind of thinking needed for keeping a clear head. For maintaining control. If she wasn't careful, he'd become another addiction. One that could break her heart. And there was no rehab for romantic fools. And how she'd deal with losing love was a crapshoot she wasn't gambling on. Therefore, guarding against it became her primary objective.

Chapter Ten

Early morning light spilled in the big windows inching its way across the floor to his bed. Seth rubbed his hands over his face and fought to wake up. Kate stirred beside him, nudging closer bringing the warmth of sleepy woman with her. He'd picked her up around 10:30 last night from Grace's. No details given on Grace's latest family emergency, and he didn't want to know. None of his business.

Dragging the covers tighter in against the chill, he settled back to watch her sleep. Strands of her hair clung to his chest. He gave into the temptation to separate them, smooth them out. That he was thinking about how soft her hair was, that it matched her skin, should have freaked him out. Too cozy. Too distracting. Too everything he'd planned against. But it didn't.

Last night he'd left her to lounge in front of the television while he went to his studio. He'd had no choice. The northern hunting lodge who'd commissioned the carved log beam wanted it sooner rather than later. He'd come back in around one in the morning to find Kate asleep on the couch, an old episode of *Sex in the City* playing in the background. Wanting her in his bed, wanting her close, he'd carried her to bed. She let him, which proved how exhausted she was. Necessity had him tucking her in and kissing her goodnight. Longing had him lying awake beside her.

Yeah…he had it bad. But he'd had it bad in the past and gotten over it quick enough with no scars to show for having loved. His fingers skimmed over the bare skin of her arm. She shivered against him. Except this didn't feel like any of those other times.

He tucked the blankets in around her. Even in the half-light dark circles shadowed her eyes. She needed sleep. He needed a distraction. He reached for his phone and checked his messages. An email from his client showed in his inbox detailing delivery instructions. Payment of the invoice was going to make his life a lot easier.

He was tallying numbers in his head when Kate opened her eyes. One drowsy blink and his dick took notice. All thoughts of checks and balances evaporated along with his brain cells. "Morning, princess."

Eyes slipping shut, her lips curved. Her teeth did a quick catch and release of her bottom lip. "Is it? Morning, I mean?"

He couldn't stop the grin. "Barely."

Her eyes drifted open. "Hum."

He didn't try to resist the urge to run a knuckle over her jawline. "How are you feeling?"

"I'm fine." She rolled her eyes. "I keep telling you—"

He didn't give her a chance to finish. He closed in and brought his mouth down on hers. A second later she lifted her arms and wrapped them around his shoulders.

He slept naked. No muss no fuss. Drop it all and climb in. Kate, being Kate, had brought luggage. Not that he didn't appreciate the pink and black polka dots covering her very short shorts and top but they were in his way. He looped a finger around a strap and tugged. His lips followed it down.

"Good to know." He brought his lips back to hers. "Want to get naked with me?"

Her hands slipped from around his shoulders to cup his face. "Yes."

Flexing fingers, shy eyes, he didn't think he was ever going to get enough of her. "Here or in the shower? Your choice."

She blushed. "Here's fine."

"Fine?" He lifted his head a couple of inches and tried to look wounded. "How about a little more enthusiasm?"

"I'm sure you and your ego will survive."

"Me and my wounded dick might slink off and sulk." He reached up to lace his fingers between hers and pulled her hand down. "You hurt his feelings. You're gonna have to make it up to him."

"Oh, please." He was hard under her hand and the gentle clench of her fingers was too enticing to ignore.

"You took the words right out of my mouth." His hand moved over hers, pressing, squeezing, guiding. "That feels amazing. You're amazing."

She shook her head, didn't say a word. But her hand said it for her.

"Other arm over your head." He wrapped her fingers around one of the wooden slats on his headboard.

"You're very bossy when it comes to this." But she said it on a sigh as she shuddered under him.

The combination of her sassy mouth and her hand on his cock had jungle music singing in his blood. It made him growl and nip at the vein pulsing in her neck. "Boss me back."

She stilled, tugging her hand out from under his. "I'll leave the sex talk to you."

"That's disappointing." Her words and the loss of her hand. "Cuz, it turns me way the hell on."

Beautiful confusion gathered between her brows. She swallowed. "So, I should lay it out?"

"Absolutely." He brushed a kiss against her collarbone, felt her quiver. "Anything you want, I'll do it."

"Anything?" she echoed.

He groaned. A million bucks said she was imagining some pretty dirty scenarios. "I draw the line at the super kinky shit, but yeah. Pretty much anything."

"What if one of us doesn't like what the other is proposing?"

"That's why they invented the words *no* and *stop*." He dipped his forehead to hers and whispered against her lips. "At least, that's the rumor."

Even though her fingertips trailed over his cheekbones, she didn't meet his eye. "Laugh at me if you want, but I've never had this kind of discussion before."

Somehow that didn't surprise him. "You and your ex never talked about it?"

She shook her head. "We just…" She shrugged her shoulders. "Did it. Usually one of two ways."

Didn't sound very appealing. Or satisfying. "I'm not shy about voicing my opinion, telling you what I like or what I want you to do. I expect the same from you. You okay with that?"

"I'm going to try to be." But she didn't look all that convinced.

"No rush. We'll take it one step at a time." He coaxed some of her hair back behind her ear. "Give it a try."

"Like right this second?"

"Yeah, now would be good."

"It's kind of bright in here. Maybe we should lower the blinds or something."

"All the better to see you with."

"I know. That's why I'm hinting you should do something about it."

His hand went to her breast, slid down her stomach. "I like looking at you."

"What I don't get is why?"

"Kate." So not going there. Maybe later. Or never if he could help it.

"What?" she huffed.

"Either give me some instruction and a place to put my hands, then my mouth, or I'll give you some."

Half an hour later, sated, satisfied, and showered, he left her dozing. The place was clean. Ash keeping her word. There was food in the fridge. Today was Sunday, a rare day off, and his head was full of plans. Ash was working the morning shift. That meant time alone with Kate. At least, until mid-afternoon.

He loved Sundays, especially as a kid. Sunday mornings his mom had made flapjacks as she called them. It was one of the few things he remembered about her. His father had kept up the tradition calling them the breakfast of champions.

And since he was feeling like a champ, pancakes it was, stacks and stacks of pancakes. In between gathering ingredients, he shadowboxed: fancy footwork, left hooks, right jabs. He heard the water of the shower as he gave the batter a final whisk. Knowing he had plenty of time, he left it to cut up fruit. He was tossing berries into his mouth when someone knocked on his front door.

"Morning." Stan Knight stood there shuffling his feet, hands shoved into the pockets of his coat.

"Morning." Seth didn't get many visitors. Hadn't planned on fielding them off today. "Something I can help you with?"

"Bill here?" he asked.

"No." Seth couldn't resist a look behind him as he frowned. The older man had the ability to make you do a double check even when it wasn't needed. "Am I forgetting something?"

Stan ignored his question. "Something smells good."

"Yeah." Seth pointed over his shoulder. "I'm making breakfast…What's going on?"

"Just in time then." He slapped a heavy hand on Seth's shoulder and pushed passed him into the hallway. "We need to chat."

"Now's not really a good time." Not that it mattered to Stan, who headed for the kitchen area. Seth trailed after him wondering what they could possibly have to chat about and trying to figure out a polite way to get rid of him when there was another knock.

"That'll be Bill," announced Stan.

Not welcome news. Not welcome at all. His daughter was upstairs naked in his shower. They'd already had one scene over their hooking up. Seth wasn't in a hurry to have another one.

The front door opened before he got to it. Bill Logan strolled in looking cheerful and hearty. "Hey there, Seth."

"Hey." Seth rubbed a hand over his jaw. It wasn't like his boss didn't know he was sleeping with his daughter. Bad form to rub it in his face. And who knew with these two? They looked capable of burying a body undetected.

"Hope you don't mind that we stopped in to see how things are going." He sniffed the air. "Smells good in here."

"Usually, anytime is good. Just not this morning. I've actually got something I need to take care of." Or someone. But that was too much information.

"Anything I should know about?"

"No." But it was a little too quick and adamant. Bill cocked his head at him. Sweat pooled under his armpits. "Kind of busy…with stuff."

But somehow they were in the kitchen and his visitor's coat was coming off. Bill lifted his chin at Stan. "Morning."

"Bill."

"Seth's making pancakes." Stan hitched himself up onto a barstool.

Bill patted his stomach. "I never say no to pancakes as long as there's some of your Grandma's chokecherry syrup to go with them."

"Her syrup's the best," agreed Stan. "Made from berries picked right out her back door. Nothing like it."

"So, I guess we'll eat first and talk after." They both looked at Seth.

"Talk about what?" Seth hoped his swallow was quieter than it felt going down.

When he didn't move, Bill slapped him on the shoulder. "Come on, son. Get the lead out, I don't have all day."

"I won't say no to a cup of coffee." Stan settled in, arm resting along the granite countertop.

"I think the better plan would be for one of you to explain what you're doing here." So they could get the hell out before breakfast was served.

Bill commandeered the stool next to his friend. "Now, don't get pissy. I'm sure you can guess if you put your mind to it."

Seth flinched.

Bill rolled on. "It's getting down to the nitty gritty. Fair's coming up and we need to keep Kate safe, at least out of trouble."

Seth barely contained the urge to shush them both up. He avoided rolling his eyes to the ceiling and picturing what was going on above them. The last thing any of them needed was Kate interrupting them planning behind her back. Another knock on the door broke up those nasty thoughts. Jesus, how many people had they invited to their secret meeting? When Bill and Stan gave each other a look Seth went on full alert.

"What's going on?" he demanded.

"You'd better answer that." Stan sat up straighter, squared his shoulders.

Seth didn't budge. "Answer the question."

"Get the door, son," instructed Bill, offering up a nod Seth assumed was reassuring.

At the door he found Constables Porter and Davenport, all businesslike in their uniforms and unsmiling faces. "Can we come in?"

What the fuck?

"Why not." Everyone else was there. His words were causal but his gut clenched. "What's going on?"

They stepped over his threshold, filled the hallway with no hint of apology. "There was an attack out at the compound last night. We need to ask you a few questions."

"Me? Why me?" But he was getting a very bad feeling.

A hand landed on his shoulder, Bill's voice behind him. "Well, well, if it isn't two of Aspen Lake's finest. Constable Porter. Constable Davenport. Fancy seeing you here."

Chase glared at Bill. He was not happy. Not happy at all. "Funny. I was just thinking the same thing."

Mike's radio crackled and he stepped back out the door to respond. Chase dropped all his attention onto Seth. "Maybe we should move this discussion somewhere private."

"No need for that." Bill led the way, Seth following with no choice, Chase in step behind him. The door opened and Mike was back and joining the queue.

Was it getting a little claustrophobic in here, or was it just him? In the kitchen Chase stopped in front of Stan. "Figured that was your truck outside."

Stan shrugged, not intimidated. "No law against stopping by for a visit with a neighbor."

Chase crossed his arms. "I'll bet."

"Someone want to let me in on what's going on?" Seth was done with the pleasantries.

Mike stepped up. "Last night a man walking down Tower Road by the Valley Church compound was attacked. He ended up with a broken nose and two broken ribs."

"What's all this got to do with me?" The anger built, he pushed it aside in favor of a clear head.

"He gave a fairly detailed description of his attacker. Kind of fits you to a tee. So I need to ask, where were you last night?"

"That's insane."

"Answer the question."

"I was here working in my studio. I left for about half an hour on an errand, came back, more time in my studio, and then I went to bed. I've been here all night and this morning." Which was true. He wasn't involving Kate unless he absolutely had to.

"Did anyone see you? Can anyone vouch for your whereabouts?"

He swallowed and didn't answer.

Chase took his silence as a no. "Then we have a problem."

"Come on, do I look like I beat the shit out of someone last night?" He held up his hands, free of scrapes and bruises.

"He claimed his attacker wore bandages wrapped around his hands. Like the kind boxers use to train."

Seth's bad feeling turned into a sick one.

"You own anything like those wraps, Seth?"

"I didn't attack anyone."

"We're going to need more proof than your word for it."

Seth shook his head, not believing his ears. He thought of Kate upstairs. How this was the very last thing she needed. "I'm not your guy. I swear."

"Yeah, we get that a lot. Unfortunately, we still have to conduct an investigation."

Bill moved to stand in front of him, silencing him.

Seth didn't know what to do with that. No one had stood between him and anything in the six years since his dad had died. He pushed past Bill. This was his life. His problem. And his damn house. "I texted a client a picture from my studio. That had to be around 10:30. You can check my phone if you want. I came in around one in the morning and went to sleep."

Chase waited.

Seth caved. "Why would I attack some random guy? What purpose would it serve except to land me in jail? A place I can assure you I have no desire to be."

"Not so random. The man's name is William Killborne. He was in the alley the other night."

There it was. The pound of another nail in the roof of his coffin. "And I happened to be driving by when he was out walking? How convenient."

"He walks that road every night. It's his job to patrol it. Not uncommon knowledge."

Seth worked up a sneer, anything but reveal the sick, scared feeling inside. "I don't give a shit what happens inside the compound."

"How about what happens outside it?"

Bill broke into the conversation. "If Seth lands in jail, it hurts Kate. It's bad publicity. This is petty revenge for making the Shepherd look bad at Kate's store."

Stan's voice was quiet, but no less effective. "The fair starts in less than two weeks. He's stepping up his game. The question is how far is he willing to go to shut it down?"

How were any of them going to defend against madness? Predict the direction it would take? How did he deal with his own bout of insanity and keep Kate safe at the same time?

Those were questions he couldn't answer, and it made him stupid, angry. Terrified. "My guess? Parsons beat the shit out of one of his own. Same way he ruined his face. He's out for Kate's blood. And I guarantee you he's not going to get it."

"Sounds like motive to me. What do you think, Chase?"

"I think we're looking at a problem."

"Fuck you." Seth forgot about careful. About uncomplicated. When the words came they were rough, loud, and damning. "It's not you he's targeting. It's not you facing charges. And it's not the woman you're sleeping with he's threatening."

Chase was in his face before he got the last word out. "Listen up. I've known Kate more years then you've been alive. The woman I sleep with has been her best friend for those same amount of years. I give a shit what happens to her."

"Then why are you standing in my kitchen accusing me of something I didn't do?" His words ricocheted around the room, landing nowhere, and echoing in the sudden silence.

"Seth." A hand on his shoulder, a squeeze, a warning.

Mike shouldered past Chase and gave his partner a warning look. He raised his eyebrows at Seth. "We're having this conversation here, aren't we? Instead of at the station?"

"Good to know you're not here to arrest me." But there was too much relief mixed in with his sarcasm to fool anyone.

"We prefer to gather the evidence first." Mike

sighed. "Help us out here, Seth. Give us an alibi."

"I shouldn't need an alibi. I've only ever seen him twice, once on the street and that night in the alley. We've never had a conversation, never exchanged so much as a word. But since it seems I do, my sister was here last night too. She can vouch for my whereabouts." Except for the time taken to collect Kate from Grace's.

"Is she here now?"

"She's at work. At Mary's."

Stan stepped in. "He's playing all of us to look like fools. That doesn't sit well with me."

Bill agreed. "Any time Parsons has tried to get at Kate, Seth's been there to shut it down. If they were to target anyone, it would be him. If they want to get to her, they have to get rid of him first."

Seth agreed. "I underestimated him. It won't happen again."

Footsteps sounded on the stairwell behind them and Seth's luck ran out.

Kate stepped off the last stair. So beautiful it hurt. "I didn't realize it was a party."

Seth kept his eyes on Chase. "Leave her out of this."

"I can't do that," Chase bit out, then he muttered something under his breath Seth didn't catch. "Kate."

"Looks like he has an alibi after all. That's assuming you've been here all night?" asked Mike.

She did a great job of avoiding her father's glare. Seth didn't fare so well. "I was. Seth picked me up from Grace's. My memory's a bit fuzzy on the exact time. When was it you said the attack happened?"

"I didn't," Mike countered.

"Well, maybe my memory will improve when

yours does."

"Careful, darlin'," warned Chase.

"And he didn't show up looking like he'd come from beating someone senseless." She laced her fingers through the ones Seth slipped around her waist as he closed in against her back. "If you'll excuse me, I have to phone a friend. She's very upset."

Judging by Mike's stiff jaw he didn't appreciate the insinuation. There was a three second delay before his easy-going act settled back into place. "Be sure to tell her I asked after her and that I hope everything works out."

Seth hugged her closer, a warning to stop while she was ahead. Chase pointed a finger at each one of them but he concentrated on Seth. "This is a police investigation. Stay out of it. That's a warning all of you need to take seriously."

Stan didn't take offence, but spread his hands. "Just being a good neighbor is all."

Bill shrugged. "Nothing but coincidence us being here at the same time."

The way he said it lifted the hairs off the back of Seth's neck. Stan and Bill stood together, both the picture of innocence. No one was buying it. Seth kept his mouth shut. It had been a long time since someone had looked out for him. Kate squeezed his fingers. A very long time.

Chase closed his eyes and pinched the bridge of his nose. "That better be the truth."

Mike scowled. He pointed a finger at Stan. "You were the detachment boss for a lot of years, still have loyal friends there, including the two of us. But if I find out someone is tipping you off and giving you information regarding investigations, I'm going to get pissed off. Then I'm going to find out who it is and that person will no longer be employed. Do we understand each other?"

"Perfectly," said Stan, but his tone suggested he made his own decisions.

Bill's was one of dismissal. "You boys have a good day."

Chase looked like he was chewing glass. "Stay away from the members of the Valley Church, especially Killborne and Parsons. We'll confirm Kate's story with Grace. Talk to your sister." He pointed at Seth. "I'd hate to have to lock you up, but I will."

"Got it." He'd still do whatever it took to protect Kate.

"Our meeting still on for tomorrow at three o'clock to talk about security for the fair?" asked Mike.

Kate nodded and Mike and Chase headed for the door. Stan slapped Seth's shoulder. "I think I'll pass on the pancakes."

The door shut behind the three of them. Bill went to follow. Seth wasn't quite ready to let him go. "How did you know they were going to be here?"

"Not much happens in this town I don't know about." Bill pulled his coat on. "We stand by our own around here. At the very least, we learn from our mistakes. If what happened here a year ago taught us anything, it taught us that. Enjoy your breakfast."

Seth chanced a look at Kate who called after her father. "I love you too, Dad."

He stopped at the door. "Come here. Give your old man a hug."

She wrapped her arms around him. "It's going to

be okay, I promise."

He kissed her cheek. "Mind you keep that promise. Both of you."

She sauntered back to Seth and draped her arms around his neck. "My knight in shining armor, doing his best to save the fair maiden's reputation."

His arms slipped around her to pull her close. "It seemed like a good idea at the time."

"You should know you don't need to bother. My reputation was damaged beyond repair a long time ago."

"Job goes with the chromosomes." He kissed the tip of her nose. "Get over it."

"I don't want you to get in trouble because of me. And I don't like to think people are pushing you in that direction either."

"I make my own decisions." He decided to change the subject. Something guaranteed to refocus her thoughts. "God, you smell good. I gotta say, I'm gaining a new appreciation for girly and everything that travels along with it."

Her bottom lipped pouted out, she added a dash of huffy to it. "Is that a nice way of calling me high maintenance?"

"Like it's a secret." He grinned at her, put a little jungle into it. "You might as well own up to it. Anyway, it works on you."

"Is this part of your dating technique? Insults?"

"Princess, you smell good, you look good, and you put the effort into making it happen. I'm not insulting you by pointing out that it doesn't happen with a flick of your fingers."

"Your complimenting skills are sadly lacking."

"You get plenty of those. But I'm happy to work on my other, far more entertaining, skills."

"We need to talk about Matthew Parsons, the attack, the scene at my store."

"Later. First breakfast. Then kitchen sex. Followed by a tour of my studio. Sex in my studio. If I have any strength left, then we'll talk about that sicko."

"Glad to hear you're planning on feeding me. Your schedule sounds exhausting. And we will be having a discussion about Parsons."

Not if he could help it. They needed a day to themselves. Shit was going down. They wouldn't be free from it. But maybe they could steal an afternoon. It wasn't too much to ask.

****

Seth scooped up his vibrating phone before it woke Kate. Noted the caller and braced. Her head in his lap, the rest of her wrapped in a blanket, there was no way to have this conversation without disturbing her. But since her crazy was no secret it was time he showed her his.

"Caroline." Her name tasted foul on his tongue like eye of newt, or wing of bat.

"Oh my God, Seth. Is that you?" She hacked out a cough.

"Yeah." He rubbed at the back of his neck. "Who else would it be?"

"Is that any way to talk to me? Your mother," she sniffed. When she really wanted to dig under his skin she pulled the mother card. And like every other time it sent a shudder through him.

"What do you want?" He smoothed a hand over Kate's hair as she pulled out of sleep and twisted to look up at him.

"I'm worried about Ashley." Yeah, bullshit she was. She never worried over her daughter. Having no time to fret over anyone but herself she left that to Seth. "Is she there with you?"

Kate struggled to sit up and Seth didn't stop her. He pulled his feet off the coffee table and dropped them on the floor. Pacing, movement, helped him deal with what he had to say.

"What's wrong?" mouthed Kate.

He shook his head at her. "Yes, Ash is here."

"I need you to send her home. I don't think it's a good idea, her staying there with you." Her voice settled into a whine. "She needs her mother. Her things. Her friends. She has her future to plan. And…what will people think if she's living there with you?"

"They aren't going to think anything." His neighbors didn't have her twisted sense of ethics. He glanced sideways at Kate, noted her wide eyes and confused expression. "Ash asked if she could stay here for a while and I agreed."

"What?" The whine was gone replaced with shock. "Ash, would never—"

"She did." He almost felt sorry for her.

Disbelief morphed into hostility. "You're lying."

Almost. "I'm not. Deal with it."

Pleading again. "I'm all alone here. She left me all alone."

Not going to work. Not this time. "Who the hell is this Lenny guy she's talking about?"

There was a pause as she regrouped and inhaled a puff of cigarette smoke, blew it out. As she plotted how to play him. "I don't know what Ashley has been telling you, but it's obviously not the truth."

God, she was vile. So lacking in decency. And he was done. "Don't call here again."

He tossed the phone onto the dining room table. It rang immediately. It kept ringing. He ignored it and retreated to the bank of windows at the back of the cabin. To soak in the view of the water over nature's tangle of shrub brush. To relish the calm.

What, he wondered, had his dad saw in a woman like Caroline? Had he known what lurked under her shallow exterior? The idea his dad had been charmed by her bleached hair, tight clothes, and simpering inability to complete simple tasks made him sick.

Made him doubt if the dad he remembered was real or someone his imagination had dreamed up to survive. Guilt rushed in. He knew his father was a good man. A decent one. And he hated that Caroline made him doubt it.

Soft hands came around his middle and Kate's cheek rubbed against his back. "Want to talk about it?"

"Not really." Why dump more problems in her lap?

"Talk to me." She pressed closer, her breath warm against his neck. "Please."

He wanted to. So bad he ached with it. She'd already heard half the story. He soaked in her comfort, her warmth. "My stepmother."

"Ashley's mom."

"Short story—she's a mess." He nodded an affirmative "Long story—she wasn't always. Not when my dad was alive anyway. When he died, she fell apart. Just…totally checked out. I loved my dad, he was a great guy, but he didn't leave much in the way of financial security. My grandparents wanted me to come and live with them. But I figured she'd get her shit together sooner or later. She never did. And then it was too late to bail. I couldn't leave Ash there with her."

His shoulders, the knots of tension, eased under her hands. "Ashley's lucky she had you."

Her fingers dug deeper, encouraging him to keep going. "She, Ash, I mean, followed me everywhere. I think she was terrified I was going to disappear too."

"I know how rough it can be, but at least I had my dad. Even though I blamed him for everything, I knew he loved me, was there for me." She kept working and kneading.

He lowered his head to give her better access to his neck. "That feels so good."

"You're too tall." She took his hand and led him back to the couch. The cushions shifted as she settled in behind him. "So you stayed and took care of things. Of Ashley."

"Not much choice." One of her knuckles carved a line down his back. "Oh, shit. Do that again."

She added another knuckle. "There's always a choice. Some less noble than others. I partied and acted like none of it mattered. A couple of drinks too many each time. No big deal. I wasn't the only one. But I also had a bottle stashed in my room no one knew about. A drink helped me get to sleep."

He bent his head to let her at his neck. "Not as noble as you might think. There was this girl and if I wasn't at work or at the gym, we were screwing each other's brains out. I wasn't in a hurry to leave her behind either."

She smoothed her hands over his neck and shoulder muscles. "There was a boy in my life too. He brought me wildflowers, took heat from my dad, and cuddled me after."

The tension rushed back in. "Oh please, I think I'm gonna be sick."

She tugged his face to the side and ducked to meet him eyes. "Did I make inappropriate comments about your sexual escapades?"

"Gabby Morrison, who is happily married and currently pregnant, is no longer in my life unless you count Facebook. Tyler Bodnar is fucking nuts and too close for comfort."

His cell phone rang again. Seth ignored it but Kate retrieved it before he could stop her. She looked at the screen then held it out. "Ashley."

Seth put the phone to his ear. "Hey."

He listened and nodded. "We're on our way in. We'll pick you up."

Kate raised her brows. Seth hung up. Sharing time was over. And since it had taken a turn in the wrong direction he couldn't say he was sorry. "Ash. Flat tire. I need to go check it out. Change it for the spare if needed."

She pushed off the couch. "Okay, let's go."

One thing still irked. "And just so you know, I'm a great cuddler."

Kate sauntered over. He was pretty sure he'd never get tired of watching her strut her stuff. Her tongue poked out and slid over her lower lip. "Good at other things too. That area of my life has definitely improved."

He ran his thumbs along her jawline. He leaned down to whisper against her lips. "We're just getting started. A lot more territory to cover and rest assured, princess, I'm not scared to get dirty."

"When you say those things, I swear I can smell my inhibitions going up in smoke."

"There are worse things."

She faked a beaming smile. "Like my being so high maintenance."

"Remember, I said you smell good too."

"Uh huh."

He bit back a smile. "And look good."

She raised a brow. "Be still my beating heart."

Why her snotty look turned him on even more he did not know. And did not care. "And when you get going, you get loud. And I freakin' love that."

When he got the gasp he was looking for, he locked his mouth onto hers. His tongue was in her mouth, and like every other time he'd kissed her, it was fire and ice. He slid one hand around to grip her hair. The other slow tracked its way to the base of her spine. He wanted his hand in her panties. She wore the best underwear, soft and skimpy with lacy bits.

Her hand moved in to yank on his ear.

"Ow. Shit."

"Take that back."

"I know the truth hurts, but you're just going to have to suck it up."

"Don't you have a flat tire to fix?" she asked, fingers still tugging on his ear.

"Come on, loud is good." He was doing his best not to laugh, but it wasn't working.

She let go with a final tug. "That's enough accolades for one day, thank you."

He braced one hand at the back of her neck and one over her heart. "Just one more then. No one else but you could pull this fair off in spite of what Matthew Parsons is doing to stop it. He doesn't know what he's up against. He hasn't figured out yet that you're a survivor. That you're smarter than him. Remember that when he pulls whatever he's going to pull next."

Her lips parted, her eyes got soft. They lowered to stare at his mouth before lifting to meet his again and she whispered, "Thank you."

"You're welcome."

This time the kiss was slow. Almost, but not quite, chaste. Sweet, flavored by respect. A taste to be savored. It didn't heat the blood. It widened all those intricate pathways and made it easier to breathe. For once the weight of having someone to care for and look out for didn't feel like a chore. It felt right.

****

Kate twisted and tried to get a better grip on the stubborn zipper of her skirt. "You could help."

Seth was stretched out on her bed, covers at his waist, head resting on a mound of pillows, and his ink on display. "I'm better at getting your clothes off."

"Because it's so much harder to pull a zipper up than down." God, he really was beautiful. Her nipples tightened against the padding of her bra. All lounging satisfaction, cataloguing her every move he smirked at her. No doubt, because they'd made love that morning, after which he'd gone back to sleep while she had gotten up to take a shower. Then he gotten a show while she'd put on her underwear.

"Come here." He crooked a finger, daring her.

"No. I'm not getting near the bed while you're in it. I'll end up mussed."

"Fine." He swept the covers away and crawled out

of her warm bed, the totems on his skin shifting, moving in time with his muscles.

He'd been a sight lying in her bed. Him standing there all sleek muscle wearing only leather cuffs, silver bracelets and bands of woven threads at his wrists was enough to make her tremble. But while she enjoyed the view she had a full day ahead of her. She picked up his discarded jeans and tossed them at him. He caught them with a grin. She kicked his underwear in his direction.

"Gee, thanks." He picked them up and stuffed them in her laundry basket. *Her* laundry. And stepped into his jeans.

His long legs disappeared into faded and ripped denim. To disguise the fact she couldn't tear her eyes away she crossed her arms. "Do I look like your laundress?"

"Do I look like the guy who made breakfast, lunch, and dinner yesterday?" He paced in her direction and signaled for her to turn around. His fingers brushed against her spine and she shivered.

Warm lips kissed her neck. He added a flick of his tongue. "So tasty. Hold still."

To distract from thoughts of crawling back into bed, she asked, "Do you think you'll get the display case done today?"

"I'll start assembling it, but it'll be done Wednesday for sure." He swatted her butt. "There. Ready to go."

She unbent enough to grab up his shirt and hand it to him. Miracle of miracles this one had actual buttons. He slipped it on, left it hanging open. Hair in hand, he slipped an elastic from his wrist and twisted his hair back and wrapped it up. It should have looked ridiculous. It didn't.

How was she going to get through the day knowing he was going commando? He caught her staring. She blinked back into their conversation. Or tried. He raised his brows in question.

"What?" she asked.

"Coffee? Do you want some?"

"Yes, please." Five minutes. It took him five minutes to get ready. Incredible.

A tall dresser stood across from her bed. Strictly configured and containing only items she used and loved. It housed clothes, accessories, and other necessities. She pulled open the narrow top drawer holding her jewelry. Small spaces only worked with extreme organization. Therefore her grandmother's pearl necklace, the one she wore every day for work sat on top of a velvet pouch, front and center. Or it should have. She frowned and started shifting things around.

She bent down to search the floor. Nothing. She did a short search of the room.

"Lost something?" The delicious smell of coffee filled the apartment.

"Yes. My pearls." She straightened. Snapped her fingers. "The bathroom."

No luck. Nothing on the counter or on the tray holding other spare jewelry. She yanked open a drawer. No necklace. She went to shut the drawer but a little pink case caught her eye.

"Oh no," she breathed.

Panic was immediate, crushing, overwhelming.

She could have sworn she'd packed it in her purse. Her heartbeat slammed into her chest as she flipped it open. Three days behind in taking her birth control pills. She squeezed her eyes shut tight. Braced a hand against the sink.

Oh, God.

Please, no. No, no. Don't let it be possible.

"Did you find it?"

She twirled around, hiding the case behind her back. "No. No. I didn't."

Seth frowned and stepped into the bathroom. "Hey, are you okay?"

She needed a minute to think. To do the math any ovulating female could do in a soul sucking second. How could she be so careless? Being celibate she'd gotten sloppy, that's how. In the nasty habit of doubling up after missed days, knowing there wouldn't be an issue. With the flu and going to Grace's and then Seth's, she hadn't given taking them a thought.

"Kate?" His worried tone woke her up.

She shoved past him. One thing at a time. Finding her necklace took priority over worrying over unlikely baby issues. She blew out a breath and went back to her chest of drawers. She tucked the pills under the velvet pouch. Her stomach heaved. God, she was going to be sick. Again.

Breathe.

His hands landed on her shoulders, massaging her muscles. It didn't help. He pressed closer, and she had to resist yanking away. He pulled her around to face him. His brows drew together as he searched her face. "Breathe, princess."

She was trying. Couldn't he see she was trying?

"This necklace? It's important to you?"

She shivered, in a bad way. To avoid his, her gaze drifted to the floor. One crisis at a time. She twined her fingers together and squeezed, invited the bite of her fingernails into her skin. Let the pain sharpen her focus. Don't borrow trouble. "Yes. It was my grandmother's. When I was in…" She paused, swallowed. Closed her eyes. "…in rehab…for the second time." She needed to get it together. "She came to see me and she brought it with her."

"She said it was a symbol of integrity." She brushed her fingertips over her cheeks. They came away wet. The words rushed out of her. A mocking damnation of her continued stupidity. "That I shouldn't feel like I'd lost mine. That I'd only lost my way, and it was time to find it again."

"It'll show up." He pulled her close and fitted her head into the curve of his shoulder. His hand smoothed out strands of her hair. "I promise."

She turned her face further into his neck and she couldn't help it, the tears came. There was nothing to do but loop her arms around his neck and hang on. Crying was ridiculous. But she had no idea how to make the tears stop.

His whispers soothed her. His strong hands comforted her. His warmth consoled her. The fear all those lovely things would be torn from her because she was a walking, talking, breathing disaster terrified her. He thought she was high maintenance now? Hysteria bubbled up like bitch's brew.

Before she blurted out possible pregnancy scares she pushed him away. The chances were slim. Weren't they? She swiped her fingers across her cheeks. "Okay. You're right. It's got to be here somewhere."

They moved things and searched her whole apartment. Nothing. She didn't know what she was going to do without her good luck talisman. Without the weight of it around her neck grounding her. Time ran out. They stopped the search to deal with the alarm person. The whole time they walked through her apartment and the boutique space, deciding how to best set up the new system, she battled premonitions involving increasing waistlines, screaming babies, and no money to deal with either.

Halfway through the morning Seth left for a meeting in the city. It was a relief to see him go. She embraced the separation, telling herself she didn't need him around twenty-four seven. She was fine without him. That things were moving too fast, were too intense.

But there was no time to think despite his leaving, customers keep her busy until it was time to sit down with Chase and Mike. And her dad. *God, her dad.* Half the town council. The organizing committee. With more than one person asking if she was okay, she fought to concentrate. In the end they came up with a sensible plan to keep the fair running smoothly.

She slipped over to Mary's to wait for the takeout she'd ordered, ignoring the buzz of conversation. Until she heard whispers of trouble out at the compound. Something about wandering Taylor cattle, fences needing mending, an injured animal, and old man Taylor threatening vengeance if it turned out he had to put down his horse. Kate added checking in with Felicity to her mental to-do list.

Then Tyler walked in with a couple of other guys and they got in line for a table. Her shoulders ached with exhaustion. The more times she told herself not to worry or borrow trouble, the more she freaked out. She prepared for Tyler's onslaught and got nothing. A nod in her direction but otherwise he ignored her.

Her phone buzzed. She rolled her eyes and knew without even looking.

"Hello," she sighed. It was his third unwelcome call of the day.

"Hey, princess. How's it going?"

She eyed Tyler. "Fine."

"Alarm up and running?"

"No." A pause while he waited for her to elaborate. She turned away from the group waiting for a table. "Tomorrow."

"Shit." Laughter and the clink of glasses rattled in the background. "Just a sec...No thanks, man. I'm good...Sorry about that."

"One more day won't make a difference to anything here." Was he in a bar? The whole idea of it made her mouth water. It moved her past annoyed to pissed off. "Having a good time?"

"Yeah, it's going well." More hilarity ensued in the background, another bout of very female giggling. "Listen, I won't be back until late. Maybe you could stay at Grace's tonight? Or your dad's?"

"Seth, I'll be fine." Teeth clenched, she gripped her phone. Ice froze her next words solid. "Stay in the city tonight. This is a big deal for you. Give it your full attention."

"I don't like leaving you alone."

"I'll be fine," she insisted. Was all the fun and frivolity rendering him clueless? "I appreciate your concern, but I can take care of myself."

He said something away from his phone to someone she obviously couldn't see. Back again, he said, "Don't forget to eat something."

Embarrassment swept all the fear and uncertainty flooding her system out the door. "Stop it. I'm not a helpless child. Or your responsibility."

"Okay, you're right." Awkward silence punctuated with a sigh. "I'll see you later."

"No, you won't. Either stay there or go home." She and her probably pregnant overreacting hormones wanted some alone time.

"Kate—"

"Goodbye, Seth." She hit end with a little more force than necessary.

Tyler walked by on his way to a newly vacated table, hat circling in his hands. Not a word. He'd gotten the message and then some. She watched him laughing with his buddies, as he patted one on the shoulder. Acting like nothing had happened, like she hadn't had to call the police to wake him up. Then he glanced back over his shoulder.

"Kate, food's up."

Appetite gone, she turned and left the past in the past. Time to get a handle on the present. "Great, how much do I owe you?"

Chapter Eleven

Seth parked Veronica in a spot behind Kate's Closet. Right next to a familiar looking pick-up truck. He was tired. He wanted Kate. What he didn't want was any more shit to deal with. Seth jumped out and slammed his door shut with enough force to rock the shadows circling the dark alley. The wisest thing to do was ignore Bodnar. But he'd given up on wise the second he decided to leave the city and come home. He thumped a fist against his driver's side window.

Staring straight ahead Bodnar lowered the window. "Stone."

Overconfidence was one thing. Arrogant condescension was another. The urge to haul him out of his truck and punch the smirk off his face goaded him on. "What the fuck are you doing out here?"

He lifted a thermos cup and toasted in Seth's direction. "Good evening to you too."

Seth grabbed fistfuls of Tyler's denim jacket and yanked. "Answer the question."

"Holy shit! Are you insane?" Tyler jerked back, hot steamy coffee splashing everywhere.

Possibly. "Get out."

"Jesus Christ, Stone." Bodnar shoved his truck door open, knocking Seth back. He shook off the spilled coffee. "Rumor had it you'd taken off so I thought I'd watch the alley for a bit in case that crazy reverend realized it too."

Seth had no choice but to let go. But he did it on a shove. "I told you to stay away from her."

Tyler jerked his jacket straight. "Since I don't take orders from you, I don't really pay attention to a lot of what you say."

He heard his dad's voice in his head telling him to think first, act second. His hands clenched at his sides. Tyler wanted him to take a swing. He knew it like he knew his own name. He wanted Kate to step out her door and find them wrestling in the dirt. Knowing Kate, she'd send both of them away.

"What's that?" Bodnar scooped a hand around his ear and leaned in a fraction of an inch. "Nothing to say?"

He gestured at Kate's backdoor. "The fact I'm going to unlock that door with my key and climb into the bed of the woman I'm sleeping with is enough of a fuck you for now."

But he spoke too soon. Light flooded the loading dock right before the door opened. Kate edged out, phone in hand, murderous glare in place. "What's going on? What are you two doing out here?"

Tyler was back to smirking. He slapped a hand on Seth's shoulder before getting back in his truck. "Yeah. Good luck with that."

Engine noises drowned out Seth's reply. To avoid dealing with Kate he waited until Bodnar's taillights turned the corner.

"I'm pretty sure I told you to go home." Kate huffed at him from her dais at the top of the stairs.

Seth swiped a hand over his jaw. "It's two in the morning. We both need sleep. Can we fight about whatever is bugging you tomorrow?"

"We can talk tomorrow," she agreed. "When you arrive for work."

The ice princess was back. He approached the steps not in the mood to beg for a royal pardon. He changed the subject hoping to distract her. "I got the commission."

Not so confident anymore, she backed up until her back hit the door. "Good, I'm glad."

He braced his hands on the door, one either side of her head. The banked need in his blood to locate, subdue, and consume, not her body but anyone who dared hurt her, had led him here. To her door. Here he stood, in the middle of the night with nothing to woo her closer but his offer of protection, which she didn't want.

She wasn't wearing heels and it was an interesting change to lean down, to have to dip his head to get to her. "Invite me in."

"If this is about some misguided sense of responsibility, I'm not interested." Her chest rose and fell out of tempo, brushing his. He caught her scent on the cool night air. His mouth watered for a taste.

He focused in on the pulse beating at her throat, put his lips against it. "God, Kate. I'm not in the mood for mind games. I just signed a contract for the biggest commission yet. I don't want to fight. Not tonight."

She pushed at his chest and managed to hold up four fingers. She counted off. "Four calls today. Tell the alarm person this. Tell Chase that. Reminding me to eat? To lock my doors? I'm not your pet project."

He backed up a fraction. The taste of her was sugar on his tongue. If only her words sounded as sweet. Or made sense. "Pet project? Do I even want to know?"

"You're in the habit of saving people, Seth." Her chin went up, but her stare wavered. She gestured down the alley. "I've got enough people looking to fill that role."

Seth pushed back from the door. Leftover adrenaline from his meeting, anger from finding Bodnar in the alley made a dangerous cocktail. Add in frustration and the potency level doubled. "You're comparing me to him?"

She wrapped her arms around her middle again. In the harsh glare of the overhead light, she sagged against the door like it was the only thing holding her up. "Why are you here? The truth."

"Not because I have some kind of saviour complex."

"You sure about that?"

"Yes. This commission is a big deal for me. All I could think about was getting back here. To you. To tell you about it. To celebrate. With you." The words spilled out of him as he surrounded her trapping her against the door. He ran his nose up her throat and inhaled, crouched, and whispered. "More than getting my hand in your panties, which is going to happen in a second, I wanted to celebrate with someone who matters to me. You."

Her swallow slid down her neck and nudged against his lips. "I don't know what to do with that."

"Yes, you do." His hand trembled against the warm skin of her side, across her quivering stomach, the waistband of her underwear tight over his traveling fingers.

She put a hand over his, not quite stopping him but

slowing him down. "I'm not going to break. No matter what happens. I need you to believe that, truly believe it."

"I don't know what I believe." He was the one who was going to break in half if she didn't let go of his hand. He linked his fingers with hers and slid their hands between her legs. Her temple was cool against his lips. "Not when we're together like this. When we're touching all I want is more. Of you. Of us. Fucking. Loving. Everything. Are you going to give it to me, Kate? Or are you going to go to bed empty. And send me home the same way?"

Her fingers slipped from his, her arms wrapping around his neck. Their lips fused together. Open, wet, taking. It was all the answer he needed. He fumbled for the door handle until it fell open. His hands full of her gorgeous ass he pushed them through it and kicked it shut.

"Not give it. Take it." Her nails bit into his scalp. Her teeth butted against his.

He dropped her feet to the ground and pushed her yoga pants down. She tripped against him in her hurry to shed her clothes and grab for his belt. The sound of metal and leather coming undone, his zipper going down, the harsh inhale and exhale of lust egged him on. Pants dropped to his ankles, no time to lose his boots, he lifted her thrusting hips. Pleasure rattled his spine as her ankles kicked at the back of his thighs. Her fingers raked down his chest and she ground down on him.

"Holy…shit…yes…harder." He worked for it, hips pumping, hands gripping, desperate to have it all. Desperate to show her what she meant to him. She bit his lip. He tasted blood. And that was it. Her hands pulled at his hair, he pinned her in place. He timed the thrust of his tongue with the piston of his hips. Her moan ravaged her throat, filled the air, and tightened his balls in warning. "*Fuck*. I think I could die like this."

She stiffened around him, squeezing her orgasm out. He went with her. Kept them there. Until his knees buckled, and he slid them to the floor.

"Shit, Kate." Tucked into his lap, he swiped sweaty hair away from her face. "You okay?"

"I don't know." She glanced at the stairs leading up to her apartment then back at him. "Do you expect me to walk up the stairs?"

"Since you're all about taking care of yourself, yeah," he wheezed out. She didn't return his grin, but she studied him like she was solving a math problem with no answer.

She traced the outline of his lips. "We still need to talk."

He didn't like her tone or how her eyes didn't quite meet his, but he was too exhausted to figure it out. "Not tonight. If we manage to drag our butts upstairs, we're going to sleep. The morning will come soon enough."

****

Seth stuffed the rag into his back pocket and stood back to admire. He wasn't nervous about Kate's reaction to her display counter. She'd helped in pulling it together, approving bits and pieces of the various stages along the way. So had Grace. But ever since she'd lost her necklace, she'd been distant. Off. And sure anyone would be. But this was different, and he couldn't help feeling this was about him. Not that she didn't want him around or that she was avoiding him, but that she was working hard at keeping him at arm's length. A coolness was seeping back in.

"It's a work of art." Kate ran her hands along the grain of the wood and gave him a small smile. A sad one. Then it widened, and maybe the sun didn't come out, but a hint of reserve slipped away. She slid open a drawer and dreamy replaced the sad.

Grace slipped her arms around him and squeezed her approval. He tilted his head. Tiredness clung to her like food wrap. Circles framed Grace's incredible eyes. He tucked her in and held on.

"It's beautiful." Her cheek pressed against his chest.

"Thanks."

Between the three of them they'd known exactly what was needed for the space: a piece that would unite the exposed, original brick wall with the stark white of the clothing shelves. An anchor to blend with the modern pot lighting, the hanging racks suspended by steel cables, and the dark wood flooring. The smoky gray stain, the carved loop of pearls and Kate's logo, the dark cherry butcher-block top all spelled understated class.

It was also functional. Sturdy. You could do anything you wanted on the top of it. *Anything*. Seeing his work out in the world always ramped him up. Giving beauty to the useful and the practical took nothing away from his wilder, darker projects. They represented the two sides of him like the ink on his back. There was only one thing to do with the excess. Yep, tonight was going to get dirty. It was tradition.

"No." Like she read his mind, Kate lifted a finger and shook it at him. The warning was in the tilt of her head and the stern look in her eyes.

He flashed a smile, leaving that discussion for later. He gathered her in against him, Grace still tucked close to his other side. "I'm glad you both like it."

The little bell over the door rang and a stern-faced, grim looking Constable Davenport strutted in. Seth didn't know the man but even he could tell something was off. Mike's gaze skimmed over Kate to zero in on Grace and the arm he had wrapped around her. The sight of them all tangled together didn't make him happy. Not one bit. He didn't try to hide it either. Grace's arm tightened across his back.

Kate stepped away after a swift glance at Grace. "Did something happen? Is everything okay?"

At the same time, Grace asked, "Is this about Hope?"

"No news, I'm sorry. This is fair business." For a cop and a smart guy he sure made some stupid moves. He dismissed Grace and concentrated on Kate. "We're going to be checking in frequently for the rest of the week. I talked to Tessa at the Abbey and she suggested reinforcements. Her brother's company handles security for a concert venue in the city, and they're lending her a few of their guys for the night. So we'll have extra eyes."

The more Mike ignored Grace, the tighter she pressed in. Then he was done with Kate, and it was Seth's turn. Constable Clueless crossed his arms. "Stone."

"Right here."

"If you can pry yourself away, maybe I can have a minute of your time?"

Scratch clueless, make that Constable Dickhead. Grace expanded next to him. He wasn't looking to do the guy any favours, but he figured he could spare Grace his continued presence. "Out back."

"After you. Ladies." Mike headed for the storeroom and Seth shut the door behind them.

"What's up?" asked Seth, wanting to get the conversation over with.

"Surveillance suggests something is happening at the compound. A lot of movement. A lot of the men getting together when they'd usually be working. You need to be prepared for trouble."

"Why tell me?" His face was impossible to read and Seth didn't have time to wring the information out of him. "This is information Kate needs to know."

"And I'll tell her when I'm done with you. Word of warning first and that's the part she doesn't need to hear."

Seth crossed his arms and didn't say a word. He was getting damn tired of Constable Davenport's superior attitude.

"We're also keeping an eye on you. I will lock you up before I let you do anything stupid. Kate's safety, and those in her vicinity, are in our hands. Do not let Matthew Parsons provoke you into doing something stupid."

If you couldn't say anything nice...

"The correct answer is: Yes, sir." Mike rested his hands on his belt. "Look, I get it. The woman you're sleeping with is being threatened, and that does a number on any man. But it's important to keep a clear head. Those two women in there are counting on you to keep it together. You hearing me, Seth?"

Yeah, he was *hearing* him, and it didn't take a math whiz to add two plus two. "Is this the part where

I'm supposed to pretend this has nothing to do with Grace and whatever the hell is going on, or not going on, between the two of you?"

It was Mike's turn for silence. Only he was better at waiting it out then Seth.

"I'll take that as a yes," murmured Seth. "I'm pretty sure I don't have to tell you that I will stand between Kate and whatever is coming. Grace too if it comes to that. You don't like it? Too bad. You do whatever you have to do after the fact. That said I'm not going to go looking to bring the bad to their doorstep either. But thanks for the vote of confidence. *Sir*."

Mike stepped closer, the press of his boots to the floor and the rustle of his uniform a warning all its own. "Don't get snotty with me, young one. Keep your head on straight and stay out of trouble, and there won't be anything to sort out."

"We done here?"

"You won't do either of them any good if you're stuck in a cell. We don't need your help. I'm going to go brief Kate on what's happening. Take a moment to think about what I've said." Mike bared his teeth. "If you screw up and either one of them ends up hurt, I'll make sure you pay for that mistake the rest of your life."

Mike closed the door behind him with a click and Seth rubbed at the back of his neck. He didn't much care for being treated like he was five years old. A couple of empty boxes sat on a small workspace. With a sweep of his arm he sent them flying. Not nearly satisfying enough. To cool off, he stepped out onto the tiny loading dock.

A month, give or take, since he'd walked into Kate's Closet thinking he was going to fix a door. He looked up at the crunch of gravel and caught Chase studying the alley.

"Seriously?" Seth turned to leave.

Chase held up his hands, palms out. "Just patrolling the alley."

"Fine." His hand on the doorknob, he figured he'd get the heck out of there before he lost his shit altogether. "I'll leave you to it."

"A couple of things have me confused."

Seth let his head drop and closed his eyes. What was with the head games? He lifted his shoulders in surrender.

"The break-ins. Middle of the night. No audience. No glory. Not Matthew Parsons' usual MO." Chase scanned the alley, his words casual enough, so was his stance. But when he looked back at Seth his face was set, and there was a question in the furrowed lines of his forehead. "They don't fit."

Chase studied him, like his partner he was good at waiting it out. Seth frowned, his mind racing, thoughts fighting to take shape. "It's all bad publicity for the town. For the fair. For Kate."

"There was another break-in two nights ago. Another local business. Hacked into the place with an axe. Lots of damage. No suspects. No leads."

Seth finished for him. "But not likely some fumbling in the night cult member. The kind great at quoting bible verses and addicted to hearing the sound of his own voice." But did it mean they were underestimating or overestimating those same cult members? "The night in the alley? How far would they have gone if I hadn't shown up?"

"We'll never know, thank God. And it's our job to make sure he doesn't try to pull the same shit again."

"Why are you telling me all this?"

"For all Mike was in there giving you shit, he's worried. We both are. About all of you. Something doesn't feel right. Puzzle pieces that don't fit. And we've got civilians taking stands that could get them hurt. Possibly exposing themselves and their loved ones to more danger. We don't know what this guy is capable of yet. Neither do you." With another scan of the alley and a chin lift, he turned and strolled away.

Seth scanned the other loading docks, fire escapes, Dumpsters. So they'd tag teamed him? So what? He wasn't going to let them intimidate him. But he was also done being stupid. He could, and would, keep Kate safe. Whatever the Valley of the Shepherd Church had planned.

****

Kate was so bone tired she could hardly put one foot in front of the other. For the last three days Matthew Parsons and his band of merry maniacs had picketed Main Street and various other parts of town waving placards and foisting flyers on the unsuspecting. They marched behind banners and mastered the righteous art of straddling the line between harassment and freedom of speech.

Unfortunately, word of their insanity was spreading and Aspen Lake was hitting more than the local news. Radio and television reporters far and wide were harvesting the bounty of the Shepherd's ripening rhetoric. Which meant Kate was doing everything in her power to offset it. Twice as many interviews, twice as many blog posts, status updates, and tweets. It was beyond exhausting.

Grace hovered, Seth growled, and her period never showed. Four days late. But it wasn't like she could walk into Davies Variety and Pharmacy, perched smack in the middle of Main Street, and waltz up to the counter pregnancy test in hand. Before the automatic doors closed behind her, the whole town would know why she'd been there and what she'd bought.

It was Sunday, less than a week to go before the opening of the fair, and she was in her car on her way into the city to pick up a few last minute things. When all she needed was a stick to pee on. She was going under the guise of needing a meeting. She'd attended one last night at the church, but nobody needed to know it. Afterwards, she'd hosted an emergency last minute fair meeting, which had included the mayor, the town council, and half a dozen others. Seth spent the night in his studio. Thank God.

She was supposed to be alone, in her car, and on the road. But apparently at twenty-nine years old she needed a sitter. Ergo, Seth, Grace, and her doting daddy had conspired to send Sunni to the city with her. Kate had refused using colorful language and threats of retribution.

She was losing her touch. Sunni was tucked in beside her and valiantly humming along to the song on the radio looking nothing like she been offered up for the common good. When Kate got back, heads were going to roll.

"Comfortable? Temperature okay?" asked Kate, keeping her voice at a carefully controlled and hypnotic level. "Feel free to relax, put in headphones, sleep."

So much easier to worry excessively over the future when your car mate was napping.

"I'm fine." Sunni smoothed a hand over the scarf tied around her throat, rather like a noose but prettier. "We needed a day together. Just the two of us and this was the perfect opportunity."

Kate couldn't imagine why so she fiddled with the radio station to save herself a reply. Or to keep from making any kind of conversation.

Sunni squirmed in the silence determined to be chipper. "That's a pretty blouse. I love the color. It's nice to see you in something other than black and white."

"Um, thanks." She wasn't really listening. She was busy plotting revenge.

Sunni's hands fluttered. "Not that there's anything wrong with black and white. It's a lovely combination and it looks beautiful on you. Everything does. Absolutely everything."

"Sunni, it's fine. You can like my shirt. I don't mind. I even know where you can get one similar to it." Could things get anymore awkward?

Sunni laughed. A bit too long and a bit too high.

Yes. Yes, they could.

Stumped for conversational topics, they left behind their island of aspen and birch in silence. They drove past harvested wheat fields and grazing cattle. Autumn sunshine warmed the interior. CBC Radio One discussed the riveting notion of why cupcakes were in and fondue was out. All of it should have been conducive to passenger dozing.

Unless you were Sunni, who grabbed onto the discussion of food trends in a starving attempt to cook up some conversation. "You know, maybe we should add fish tacos to the menu?"

Kate pretended to care and considered it. "The tourists will love it. The meat and potato crowd not so much."

"You're probably right. I can't see your dad or Stan Knight embracing haute cuisine. It's so hard to know what will work and what won't. And so costly when it fails."

Which was kind of like predicting fashion trends when you thought about it.

Huh.

Maybe they did have something in common.

And you ever corner my girl in an alley again you'll regret it.

Kate concentrated on the road and keeping between the lines. Shame blurring her vision. The surest way to punish someone was to withhold affection. Hadn't she thrown that emotional fireball at her ex-husband more than once? How he was closed off, inattentive, vindictive?

Oh no, she hadn't liked it when it had happened to her. Hadn't stopped her from doing the same to Sunni. Or worse, her dad.

She was such a bitch.

Two years of AA meetings and she was finally getting to the heart of step number four. On to step number five.

"I think I might be pregnant," she blurted, staring straight ahead, fingers clutched at ten and two. And okay, it wasn't exactly owning up to her vast moral shortcomings, but it was a baby step. No pun intended.

Sunni opened her mouth. Shut her mouth. Opened

it again. Shut it again. Another tug of her scarf into place before clearing her throat. "Do you want to talk about it?"

"I think I do." And was surprised to find she meant it.

Sunni blew out a breath and pressed her hands to her chest. "Symptoms?"

Kate ticked them off. "Morning sickness, although I don't know why they call it that. I'm late. And so tired I could nap six times a day."

Sunni hummed in sympathy. "Have you mentioned anything to Seth?"

"Not exactly."

Sunni nodded. "So. No."

"I don't want to say anything until I'm sure."

"Well then." Sunni pointed to the side of the road. "Here's what we're going to do. You're going to pull over, and I'm going to drive while you nap. Then you go to your AA meeting. I'll run your errands for you. We'll pick up a test, go for a late lunch, and we'll talk."

After all that they'd gotten back late, and Sunni had insisted on Kate spending the night in her old bedroom. Embracing the concept of putting off till tomorrow what she couldn't possibly deal with that night, she'd slept a solid eight hours. With the sunlight streaming in through her window, her dad off to work, she worked up the nerve to take the test.

In the bathroom business done, she waited for the appearance of one or two lines in the little window. Impatient she willed it to tell her the future. Unlike a magic eight ball when she shook it a second time it didn't give her a different, or better, answer.

Damn.

Sunni knocked on the door.

"It's open," whispered Kate still staring at the test stick. Whether Sunni heard her or she sensed a potential meltdown, the door creaked open.

"Thought I'd let you know breakfast was ready." Sunni nodded at the stick in her hand. "Well?"

Kate slumped to sit down on the closed toilet. "I guess I need a doctor's appointment."

"Oh, sweetie." Sunni sat down on the edge of the tub and rubbed her back. "It's going to be all right."

"No, it's not." She dropped her head into her hands. "It's really, really not."

Sunni rescued the test from her hand and tossed it in the garbage. "Kate, honey, I know the timing's not great—"

"It's all my fault." Sunni, Kate had discovered, made an excellent confessional. God knew she was contrite and desperate to make amends. The warmth created from Sunni's slow circles on her back did their job. "I told him I was on the pill, which I am, but with the flu and…everything I missed a couple of days at the exact wrong time. So, you see, it is my fault. And I like him. Really like him." She hung her head. "And now this? What's he going think?"

She wasn't making any sense. She tried again. "He deserves better than a knocked up girlfriend who makes Christian Grey look like he's got his head on straight."

"Okay, beginning to see why your dad thinks you're a tad dramatic." Sunni patted her knee. "You have options."

"I know." She did. She was all too aware of them. "I just…you know…wanted to be less of a mess, not to mentioned married, when I did this."

"Now you listen to me, you are not a mess. You have risen from the ashes and are making something of your life. You are responsible, organized, loyal, and intuitive. Look at your father. He built something from nothing too. You've got more of him in you than you know."

It had to be said. "I live in a one room apartment over my shop because it's free and that's all I can afford."

"So, you'll move in here."

"Oh, God." Kate doubled over again.

"Now, now." Sunni wrapped an arm around her shoulder. "The good news is you don't have to figure out the details today."

Kate straightened and huffed out a breath. "I'm sorry I was such a bitch about everything. For so long. I should have let it all go a long time ago."

"Ah well. There was a lot to let go. I betrayed your mother and you in the worst way. I think the reason I let you have your way was because it was easier than facing you and letting you have your say."

She bumped her shoulder against Sunni's. "Thank you. For everything. For not giving up on me. Or my dad. For sticking with him even though he's been reluctant to commit. Another thing that's probably my fault."

"Definitely dramatic." Sunni's hands landed in her lap, twisting and turning. "To date your father has asked me to marry him thirteen times. Once a year he goes all out and proposes and the other eleven months of the year he hints at it. No, no. For a long time being a mistress suited me fine. No offence, sweetie."

"None taken. I don't think." She wasn't really

capable of processing much more at the moment.

"Next time he asks, I'm going to put the stubborn man out of his misery. It's time." She clasped Kate's hand in hers. "I do love him. And I think being a grandma might agree with me."

Kate squeezed. "Here's hoping being a mom agrees with me."

God only knew how being a baby daddy was going to sit with Seth.

****

Kate ran her hand over her stomach for the ten thousandth time. There was a baby in there. She didn't look any different. But everything had changed. She needed to see a doctor, of course, but she knew. After two years of hyper-vigilance, of cataloguing her body's responses to all types of stimuli, she knew when something was up. It was also obvious Seth was picking up on the change in her. One she couldn't help. The more she wanted to hang on the more she prepared to let him go.

The front door of Kate's Closet unlocked and Grace poked her head in. "Look who I found."

A petite strawberry blonde burst into Kate's Closet, and Kate gasped, "Lily."

"Surprise!"

"You're back!" Kate wrapped her arms around Lily and squeezed. "I missed you."

Lily bounced up and down on her tiptoes and squeezed back. "Mom's doing better so they kicked me back home."

"I'm glad to hear it. I bet one of Aspen Lake's finest is more than happy to see you home."

She nodded, her eyes twinkling. "Mike's very

happy I'm back."

"Oh you."

"Seriously, he was sending me rather desperate emails begging for my return."

"That's Michael for you." Grace snorted. "Dedicated humanitarian. Always putting others interests before his own."

Kate hushed her and Grace stuck out her tongue in response. She rubbed Lily's arm. "Chase missed you. We all missed you."

"Seeing as I barely had my foot in the door before he carted me off to bed, I'd say...yeah, he missed me."

For the first time Kate understood the dreamy look in Lily's eyes. Recognized the flush of amazement that still lingered even though they'd exchanged vows and rings. Knew it was the essential ingredient missing from her first marriage. When she'd mistaken a lifestyle for the love of her life.

"Well, since I'm not having incredible sex with two of the hottest guys on the planet...wait that came out wrong...I'm in desperate need of a substitute. Caffeine? Coffee. Lily?" Grace grinned at Kate. "I know I don't have to ask you."

"Yes, please." More bouncing. "Then I want all the deets on the new guy."

"Actually, not for me. I'm off coffee." Two sets of stunned eyes swung her way. But before she confided in her two closest friends, she needed to talk to Seth. He deserved that from her. Kate backtracked. "With all the stuff going on I'm not sleeping very well. I figured I'd cut back on the caffeine."

Grace gave her a funny look. "Okay."

Lily mirrored it. "Understandable."

Kate rolled her eyes. "Come on. It's not like I announced I'm shaving off my hair and moving to a commune."

"You're right." Grace gave her head a shake, but the worried look remained. "Sorry, what would you like instead?"

Good question. "What's that thing British people drink?"

"Lattes?"

"Ha ha, tea I think it's called. With sugar." Kate shuddered on the inside. "Lots and lots of sugar."

"What the heck. I'll try some too," Lily announced.

"You don't have to do that."

"Thank God, because I need coffee." Lily sagged even as she winked. "Did I mention I didn't get much sleep last night?"

"Leaded. Got it. Are we feeling adventurous? Muffins?"

Grace left for Mary's, and Kate locked the door behind her.

Lily raised her eyebrows. "He's that much of a problem?"

"These days I'm operating under a better safe than sorry philosophy." Her hand went to her stomach. Funny how pregnancy blurred some lines and sharpened others.

Lily's brow furrowed. "I can see you've all been light on the details."

Kate put a hand on her arm. "You had enough to worry about."

Lily winced. Then she shrugged. "So, what's our crazy preacher been up to in the last forty-eight hours?"

"The usual. Organizing his version of Occupy

Aspen Lake. Flocking and swooping up and down Main Street, talking at anyone who'll listen. Hanging banners on public property, protesting just outside the town limits. Threatening to occupy Town Hall. It's like a murder of crows have descended on our quaint little town. Generally, he's being as big a pain in the ass as he can without getting arrested."

Loyal friend, but also loyal lover. "The police really are doing all they can."

"I know." She smiled and set aside her frustrations. "Don't mind me. On to happier things. Come on, I'll take you on a tour."

They walked back into the front of the boutique as Grace banged on the door.

"What did I miss?" Grace walked in juggling cups and a brown bag.

"That was fast." Kate locked up after her.

"Not super busy this morning."

"I was marveling at the changes." Lily sighed in gratitude when Grace handed her a muffin.

Kate offered her a napkin. "It's almost done. Only a couple of little things in the back left to do."

"Seth's very talented." Grace passed out to-go cups. They pulled stools in from the back up to the counter and settled in to nibble. "And hot. Ask any number of female customers who've wandered over the threshold hoping for a glimpse. Rose Flannery is completely gone over him, the old biddy. He stops in every second day to draw pretty pictures on her chalkboard. Mary gives him free coffee. Pretty soon they'll be throwing their granny panties at him on the street."

Kate rolled her eyes. Grace's eyes narrowed.

"Deny it. I dare you."

"Really?" Lily slipped off the lid of her cup and blew the steam away before lifting it to her lips. "Do tell."

Grace wiggled her brows. "But he only has big moon eyes for Kate."

They'd see how long that lasted. Kate picked up her cup and sipped. Ugh. Set it back down.

Lily skimmed a hand over the new display counter and teased, "Obviously, he's very talented...with his hands."

"I'll let Kate explain just how good he is." Grace popped a chunk of blueberry muffin into her grinning mouth.

Kate risked another sip. Coffee it was not. "You're enjoying this way too much."

"It's payback for all the pheromones and testosterone the two of you have been flinging back and forth." She fake dodged to the right then the left. "I live in terror of being hit by stray lust bubbles."

"Stop exaggerating." Another sip. Nope, it hadn't gotten better. "How do people drink this stuff?"

"Oh please, it's like spring break in here minus the bikinis and naked abs." Grace sipped at her piping hot, no doubt delicious, coffee and sighed in bliss.

So. Not. Fair.

"Oh, oh, oh." Grace hopped up to answer the door knock. "You're about to see firsthand."

Sure enough, Seth strolled in after dropping a kiss on top of Grace's head. A mess of gorgeousness in a black leather jacket worn gray in spots, bed head, and aviator sunglasses.

"Oh my," whispered Lily.

Grace fanned herself from her spot behind Seth.

"Ladies." He pushed his glasses up into his hair.

Kate nudged Lily, who closed her mouth. "Seth, this is Lily Porter. Lily, meet Seth Stone."

Her baby daddy.

Best not to go there.

Still staring, Lily put her hand in Seth's outstretched one. "Nice to meet you."

"Likewise." Done with introductions, Seth shifted his attention to Kate. "Hey, princess. Missed you last night."

His palm landed warm against the back of her neck. His other hand caressed her hair, brushing it away from her neck. Then he bent his head and kissed her. It was possessive, protective, and sent her already messed up hormones into overdrive. When he backed up, Lily had her hands pressed to her heart and Grace was sticking her finger down her throat making gagging noises.

Lily cleared her throat. "Actually, I think you've met my husband. Chase Porter? Constable Chase Porter."

Seth grimaced, clearly not seeing that as a plus. "I won't hold it against you."

"Thanks." Lily nodded like she totally understood. "Appreciate it."

"I've got a couple of things to finish up in the back." His hand grazed the base of her spine and his lips were back on hers. "Later."

"Later," Kate echoed.

All three of them watched him prowl his way to the back.

"I told you." Grace gulped back some coffee.

"Hot."

Lily sighed. "Mercy."

They didn't know the half of it. He glanced back and caught them all ogling his behind. Lily stifled a laugh. Grace blew him a kiss. Seth hustled his ass out of view.

"See you, handsome," called Grace, her low laughter encouraging snorts and giggles.

"We're evil." Kate's smile widened, and it was such a relief to have it come naturally after days of faking it.

Lily gathered them both in. "I've missed you two so much."

"Likewise." Nothing soothed the soul like a best friend group hug.

"Girls' night. First opportunity," announced Grace.

"After the fair's over I'm going to need one." She tried not to think of how much.

They settled in to finish their muffins and hot drinks. Seth hid in the back. She'd have to apologize for embarrassing him later. Until then she was going to bask in the glow of actually having managed to make him self-conscious.

The morning slid into the afternoon. Since it was the Monday before the fair she opened the door to Kate's Closet. To her surprise a steady stream of people took advantage. On cue the followers of the Shepherd of the Valley Church showed up with their picket signs. Kate watched from her window as Mike and Chase warned members away from private property. The Shepherd made a show of counting out the exact number of paces required to keep his distance.

By three o'clock in the afternoon the ebb slowed,

and Kate perched on a stool to catch her breath. Outside the window, the street was still busy. An air of excitement was building for the weekend activities. Earlier out of earshot she'd made a doctor's appointment for Monday. Until then she was concentrating on her professional duties, not baby booties or tender breasts.

A girl pressed her hands then her nose to the glass and peered in. Kate smiled and waved. The girl jerked back. That's when Kate realized it wasn't any girl but the girl from the compound.

"Be right back," she called to Grace when the girl bolted.

The girl was fast. She looked down both ends of the street and didn't see her. She did see Matthew Parsons leaning down to talk to someone. Someone short. Kate headed in his direction.

He turned, hand on a small shoulder. The girl struggled to get away. He pointed down the street and the girl nodded keeping her head down. He raised her chin with a finger and spoke again.

They were so intent on each other, neither of them were aware of Kate's approach.

"Is there a problem here?" she asked.

Matthew Parsons straightened keeping his hand on the girl's shoulder, pulling her in close. "Miss Logan, how nice to see you out and about. I can't help but notice you've been rather absent from sight lately."

"Mr. Parsons." The girl shrugged out from under his hand. "I assure you nothing could be further from the truth. I've been busy promoting our fair."

"Yes, the fair." He was distracted. Focused on the street and the comings and goings.

Kate decided to ignore him. She crouched down in front of the girl. "I'm Kate."

She answered with a whisper, "Trinity."

"Run along now." Parsons gave her a nudge and after a hesitant smile she scampered off. "Stay away from my followers, Miss Logan. She's none of your business. And you've done enough damage."

"Just being polite." She couldn't help but notice his words lacked the usual pious righteousness. "What interest would I have in a young follower of yours?"

He kept busy scanning the street. "That's rather the point. None."

"Maybe I'm attempting to be friendly, extend an olive branch?"

He finally looked at her. "Spreading your poison, you mean."

Ah, there was the familiar hissing commendation. Kate stepped back from him. "Good day, Mr. Parsons."

"William."

Kate shuddered at the mention of the man with the ravaged face and hands. "I didn't have anything to do with what happened to that man and you know it."

"I know no such thing."

"Are you so determined to undermine our little fair you'll harm your own people?" It was unbelievable. He was unbelievable. She turned to walk away.

"He's missing."

When she turned back to stare at him what she saw in his face chilled her blood. He was worried. Worse, he was scared. "What?"

He covered his reaction with a warning. "Watch your step, Miss Logan."

And he was gone. People shuffled past. Some she

knew, some she didn't. What did he mean? Missing? Watch her step? She wrapped her arms around her middle and studied the crowd. A neighbor of her dad's stopped to ask a question. She gave the best answer she could. Then it was back to searching the street for the wounded Valley church member.

A hand on her arm. She jerked. Mike's voice in her ear. "You okay?"

"I don't know."

Mike didn't waste any time or ask another question. He escorted her back to Kate's Closet. When they were inside he crossed his arms. "Explain."

Kate scanned for customers and found no one except Grace who headed in their direction posthaste. There was no reason for her to whisper, but she did. "Parsons told me William is missing."

"What's wrong?" asked Grace.

Mike held up a hand. "Grace, give us a minute."

"No." She looked at Kate. "What's happened now?"

Mike flushed even as his face hardened. Kate put a hand on his arm. "That's all I know."

They all turned at the sound of footsteps coming from the back. Seth took one look at the group then only had eyes for her, assessing for damage. "What's wrong?"

"Okay, you and you. Out." Neither Grace nor Seth budged. He put a hand on Kate's arm. "Fine. We'll talk in your apartment."

"Not without me." Seth looked to her for confirmation. When she didn't answer immediately, he warned, "Kate."

Grace huffed. "We'll do this here with all of us."

Mike gave up, grabbed a chair and motioned for her to sit. "Tell me everything he said."

"One of the girls from the compound has...shown an interest in me. She peeked in the window today and I followed her. Parsons had caught her, was talking to her. I wanted to make sure she was all right. He told me to stay away. That I'd done enough damage. I disagreed. I went to leave, and he told me William was missing. But it was weird. Like he didn't want to tell me but had to. Then he told me to watch my step."

"Unbelievable. He threatened you in the street?" Seth started to pace even though there was nowhere to go.

"No. It wasn't like that." She looked between Mike and Seth. "It was a warning, yes. But against his will almost. I don't know how to explain it. It was a complete three-sixty. Like he was warning me about William. To keep me safe."

"Okay, we'll find Parsons and talk to him. We'll also be on the lookout for William."

"He knows this asshole is dangerous, unstable. Has known it all along," urged Seth.

"Until we know more, we're not jumping to any conclusions." He put his hand out to stop whatever Seth was about to say next. "Doesn't mean we're not going to look for him."

So...add AWOL Valley parishioner with obvious mental health issues to her list of things to worry about. Great.

Chapter Twelve

Fair weekend was upon them, and Seth couldn't lose the sick feeling in his gut. They managed to survive the first night without any major mishaps. He lifted a hand to block the sun and searched the masses gathering under blue skies and turning leaves. Booths boasting tarot card and palm readers dotted the wider sections of the sidewalk while clowns and face painters mingled and entertained. Noisy squealing delight, laughter, and crying babies all added to the ambience of making Aspen Lake a contender for happiest place on earth.

It was contagious, crazy fun. Seth couldn't wait for it to be over and done. Through the throng he found Kate. Not his Kate, but Kate Logan, looking prim and proper from the top of her head to the tip of her pointed stilettos. She was holding court at the top of the library steps granting practiced smiles to the television cameraman and fair goers far and wide.

From among the multitudes the Shepherd preached from his street pulpit. His followers worked the crowd. The town council and the fair committee had brought in speakers to blast music and drown him out.

If Matthew Parsons was on the street, so was Seth. The revised security measures they'd hashed out late yesterday afternoon satisfied one part of him. But not the other part. The part that wanted to rip out Parsons' throat and drag him back to Kate.

Proof of manhood.

Yeah.

So romantic.

Not to mention wrong.

Probably.

Finished with her interview, Kate smiled and chatted to people filing in for the first reading of the day. Looking for the world like everything was normal, except for the constant smoothing of her hands over her hips and the tucking in of hair at the back of her neck.

It didn't take a mind reader to know something was up with Kate, and it wasn't the obvious. She was back to freezing him out. Spending all her time finalizing fair details, or with Grace and Lily, even Sunni. Fine. He didn't require her attention twenty-four seven. He had responsibilities and the adult ability to amuse himself.

It was more than that. His boss was on a tear. Gone was the father figure and co-conspirator. He'd been busted down to peasant status at work. Sweeping floors, scrubbing the company vehicles, any dirty job Bill Logan could dream up. Whatever. He couldn't do shit about it if he didn't have the details. And no one was sharing.

Across the street his sister dashed out of Mary's Café. Caught up in the fun, she twirled and waved at a familiar face. She spotted him and flashed a smile. He lifted a hand in reply, then carried on dodging a family laughing at a clown's antics, slipped by little kids circling the cotton candy machine.

Ash stopped to help a kid juggling a couple of pumpkins intended, he knew, for the carving contest later in the day. That was Ash. She didn't let being a stranger stand in her way of getting to know someone. Still, it was habit to keep an eye on her. No, he amended. She was family. His family. They looked out for each other. A partnership he hadn't thought possible. Guess he'd underestimated her.

He was back to hunting the sea of faces for potential threats. He caught a glimpse of a man further down the street. Head down he ducked into a doorway to avoid a group headed in the opposite direction. Seth squinted against the glare of the sun. His blood froze when recognition hit. William headed for the library. And he wasn't the only one. Seth pulled out his phone and sent the programmed text to the prearranged number.

Seth kept his eyes glued on Kate. Heart hammering, apologies tumbling out, he did everything but shove people out of his way. Kate paused at the top of the steps. Alerted, the RCMP officer stood guard at the bottom.

Parsons got to William first grabbing his arm and pulling him back. The officer ordered Kate into the library. More of Parsons' followers pushed in behind him. She stumbled, her hand missing the railing behind her.

When Kate fell he focused on one thing. He saw William raise his arm. Saw Parsons pull it down. Heard the gasps of fair goers. Knew the other church followers were circling to protect both men. But he didn't care. All he wanted was Kate in his arms and out of danger.

Seth scrambled up the steps. Behind him the officer ordered people back. Kate staggered to her feet, hands clenched to her stomach, looking pale and scared.

"I'm fine." She put out a trembling hand to ward

him off.

"Nothing about this is fine." But he hesitated at her pleading look.

"Not here. Not now," she whispered.

He put it aside. The panic at seeing her fall. The frenzied need to hold her. The sting of her rejection. All of it. But not before he let her see it. What it cost him to give it to her. Until the scuffling behind them drew both their attention.

William burst out of the circle and headed for the nearest intersection. The sea of people parted to let it happen. Twenty feet. Around the corner. And he was gone from sight. People stopped to stare, gesturing, hugging their kids close. The air crackled with the information given by police radio. With the reality of a real life drama playing out in front of them.

A captive audience.

Parsons didn't miss the opportunity. He jabbed a finger in Kate's direction, his orator's gaze sweeping the crowd before landing on Kate. "See what you've wrought. A good man is losing his mind. All because you invited the devil into the midst of these undeserving people."

Seth cursed under his breath. Kate tensed beside him.

"Oh, please," scoffed Kate, her hands intent on pushing Seth away. "You wouldn't recognize godliness if it bit you on the ass."

Parsons pressed forward his face purple with outrage. "How dare you?"

"Oh, I dare," challenged Kate. Seth guessed she was done being the sacrificial lamb.

"Step back." Arm straight out, the officer ordered

Parsons and his followers away. "Kate, inside the library. Now."

Seth tugged at Kate but she wasn't budging. Parsons was back to spewing his rhetoric. Gone was the polished speaking voice, for the first time there was temper in his words. "Evil is devouring him from the inside out. You're to blame. You."

"Sir, you need to come with me."

At his angry words Kate straightened her clothes, pressed hands down her hips. She retrieved her dropped clipboard from the steps. If she'd played the ice princess the last few days, in this moment she was queen of the whole berg. She picked her way down the steps in rigid royal disapproval. Even Parsons backed up a step.

But her control was an illusion.

"Take your lies and leave me alone. Leave my town alone." Her words were loud and carrying. "The only one causing damage here is you." She tossed the words in his face right before she threw the clipboard straight at his head. "You pious, wheezing windbag."

One undignified lunge later, the preacher's shock was glorious to behold. Too bad it morphed into smug triumph at the collective gasp of the crowd. He made a show out of clutching at his heart and whispered the words sure to ignite her wrath. "You. Dirty. Filthy. Whore."

Kate leapt. Seth snagged her around the waist and held on tight. Lips to her ear, he whispered, "Do not give him this, Kate. It's what he wants. All he's ever wanted. To get a reaction."

Her nails bit into his arms, her body vibrating with the urge to go down swinging. "Let me go."

His heart contracted with the need to do the opposite. "As much as I'd like to see you go all fight club on his ass, princess, I can't do that."

He knew he had her attention when she snorted then tried to stab his foot with her heel.

He squeezed tighter. "Don't give this to him, Kate. And especially don't hand it to him on a silver fucking platter."

The cop was busy helping a suddenly feeble Parsons to his feet. "Did you see that? Do you all finally see what she is capable of?"

"You have no idea what I'm capable of, but if you come near me or my—" She went soft in his arms and whether it was a trick or reason sinking in Seth risked letting her go. "You'd just better stay the hell away from me."

"I don't take orders from you." Parsons raised his hands into the air and shook them. "I don't take orders from anyone but the Lord."

"And I'm sure the Lord God Almighty is as sick of you as the rest of us." Kate ran a hand over her hair. Seth took it as a good sign. She was coming down off the high of retaliation and thinking straight again. She lowered her voice. "You sent that man here to hurt me. Like you sent him out to do your dirty work in Montana. This is about what you're capable of, Mr. Parsons. And how far you're willing to go."

Two other police officers joined them. The Shepherd puffed out his chest but the effort was too much. His shoulders slumped with the effort of maintaining the pious weight of keeping the upper hand. "How dare you accuse me of such a thing? Besides William would never—he's a peace loving man—he would never—"

"You're lying and we both know it." She rescued her clipboard and clutched it to her chest.

They led Parsons away chin wobbling and sputtering a protest.

An officer took Kate by the arm. "I need to take your statement. Is there a room in the library we could use?"

Without a glance at Seth, she nodded. "Of course. Come with me."

Guess that showed him. Seth dropped to the steps. Show over, people went on their way murmuring and glancing back. Until only one spectator was left. He brought his hands together and clapped. "Well done."

"Shut it, Bodnar."

He hooked his thumbs in his front pockets. "Lookin' a little stressed there, Stone."

Fuck you was on the tip of his tongue, but he resisted. "What do you want?"

"Just stopping by to say how relieved I am that you have everything under control."

Seth sighed. "Yeah."

With a smirk, Bodnar walked away. For the first time in a while, Seth wondered why he didn't get up and go with him.

The click of heels behind him meant Kate was exiting the building. She paused at the bottom of the steps while the police officer moved to the side to wait for her.

Seth pushed to his feet. "You ready to go?"

"Can I talk to you for a minute?" She squared her shoulders. "About tonight?"

Two feet of pavement between them and neither of

them closed the gap. "What about it?" he asked.

"Can you meet me at the Abbey?"

"I don't get to give my date a ride?"

"Grace, Lily, and I are going over early. They've given us an upstairs room. We'll get ready there." Her eyes were guarded. Her teeth worried at her bottom lip.

"No problem," he lied. "I'll meet you there."

She unclipped an envelope from her board, handed it to him. "Here, you'll need this. You won't get in without it. Did the tux I rented fit okay?"

"Relax, it's covered."

"Good." That's when he lost her. "I've got things to do, so…"

The officer came to stand beside Kate. "Ready when you are, Kate."

She put a hand on his arm. "I'll see you later?"

"Count on it." The last thing he wanted was to be the third in an awkward afternoon threesome. "I'll be around if you need me."

Kate was running a finger down the page on her clipboard and nodding her dismissal.

The officer beside her gave him a smirk. "I'll take good care of her."

"Funny guy." But they were off, and he was talking to himself.

Only thirty-six more hours until it was done. Seth wasn't thinking good thoughts about how the rest of it was going to go. Or the direction their relationship was going to take when the fair ended. Not that he was giving up. Not by a long shot. What better place to romance someone than a ball?

****

Seth loosened the tie at his neck and shoved it in

his pocket. He couldn't wear it, not even for Kate. A woman in a tux accepted the black and white invitation with its outline of a crumbling castle and circling ravens. What a name—The Mad Man's Ball. He hoped not. Hoped the man out to hurt her wouldn't succeed in breeching the Abbey's walls. If they pulled off a miracle they'd have to get through Seth, who was not in the mood to have anyone mess with his night.

But he'd lost some of his accumulating resentment when he'd sold his sculpture. The one on display in Kate's window. A collector from the city had insisted on purchasing it. After her trip to the bank she'd slipped a certified cheque into his pocket along with her phone number and a whispered invitation.

It wasn't going to happen. But she'd been cool about it. Tacking on the usual if you change your mind…

He wasn't. His mission was to find out what was on Kate's. He crossed the massive summertime patio surrounding the front of the Abbey. The main floor housed a four star pizza joint, the second floor a cavernous cabaret hall. Tonight the patio and above deck were lit with thousands of white fairy lights. Candles burned in hurricane lamps. Piles of pumpkins and urns of fall flowers sat stacked in corners along with bundles of wheat sheaves.

A little glitz and glam under prairie skies. She'd pulled it off. In spades. He waited in line to climb the stairs. Women in long dresses and men in suits pressed in ahead of him. They crowded in behind him. Laughter and excitement perfumed the clear, crisp air. Too bad he'd never felt less like a party.

More lights, more candles, more pumpkins

decorated the impromptu ballroom. Tables covered in white linen with bronze runners held vases bursting with fall flowers. Swags of purple hung down from the roof. It should have looked cheesy, but somehow it all came together with enough shadow to be mysterious and enough light to cast a spell. Seth focused on the nooks and crannies and the plenty of places to hide and countless ways to make trouble.

No sign of Kate in the groups of people mingling and chatting over drinks. He was avoiding alcohol tonight, but that didn't mean he didn't need something to do with his hands. Britt manned the long wood and leather-studded bar. Grateful to see a familiar face he leaned in and grinned at her. "How come you get stuck bartending instead of dancing?"

Smiling she set a glass of wine and a bottle of beer down in front of the man beside Seth and accepted two tickets in return. "Because unless it involves a pole, dancing doesn't pay very well and some of us need money for school next year. McGill and Montreal don't come cheap."

He whistled. "Impressive."

She shrugged in a small town no big deal kind of way. "What can I get you?"

"Soda. Please." He reached up to loosen his phantom tie.

Britt filled a glass and held it out. "Heard about the dust up on the library steps this afternoon."

"Yeah." He tore off a ticket and handed it to her. "Have you seen Kate?"

"No charge." Hands busy she lifted her chin in the direction of the back of the room. "Out there somewhere."

"Thanks." He spared a second for a mouthful of pop. A body slid up next to him. Felicity nudged his shoulder. "Hey, handsome. Buy me a drink?"

"Sure." He tore off another ticket and waited while she gave her order to Britt.

"White wine, please." She crossed her arms and gave him a once over. "So…you clean up nice."

He shot her a look, took in the teasing lines fanning out from her eyes. "You too."

"We know how to do it up right around here." She lifted up her long skirt to do a quick two-step in her studded pink cowboy boots. "Kudos to your girlfriend. She's done an excellent job."

Whatever floated your boat. He was partial to heels. Very high heels. Seth gulped down another mouthful. "I'll be sure to let her know."

"How is she?" She stole a sip of wine. "After the thing at the library?"

Seth wasn't in a sharing mood. "Good, as far as I know."

Felicity raised her brows. "You haven't seen her yet?"

Seth went on alert. "No."

She smiled at Britt, biting down on her bottom lip before sharing what they all knew. "He hasn't seen his woman yet."

Britt snickered. "Hope he's sitting down when he does."

Felicity's gleeful eyes were back on Seth. "Ever seen her all dolled up?"

"Uh…" Seth swallowed. "…no."

She laughed, Britt's low chuckle joined in. She patted him on the shoulder. "Don't drool on her. It pisses her off."

She raised her glass to him, then drifted off into the crowd. Britt moved off to serve a couple of women. He went back to scanning the crowd his heart hammering in anticipation. He spotted Tyler with a group of buddies. One of them lifted a glass, and everyone else tapped theirs against his. Laughing followed. Some backslapping. Seth looked away. He saw Mike and Chase off to the side. Spotted Bill and Sunni, along with Stan and his wife and another couple. Mary from the cafe. Others he recognized from around town and many he didn't.

He headed in the direction of Mike and Chase. They paused their conversation when they saw him coming.

"Hey, how's it going?" asked Seth.

"I'm in a suit," said Chase. Seth could relate.

"Quit whining." Mike punched his partner in the shoulder. "I'm sure you'll be compensated for your efforts later."

"It's the only reason this tie is still cutting off my air supply." He glared at Mike, who looked smug and right at home in what had to be a custom tailored tux. "Speaking of which, where's your date?"

He lifted his drink. Also soda. "I'm flying solo these days."

"Couldn't find a woman desperate enough to go out with you, huh?"

"They don't know what they're missing."

This was nice and all but…"Is there any news on William?"

Chase tipped his head at Mike. "Nosy bastard, isn't he?"

Mike laid a hand on Seth's shoulder. "We should cut him some slack. Poor sap's got it bad. Wish we could say different, but no. We haven't found him."

"There you are." Lily wound her arm through Chase's and beamed up at him. "Don't you look dashing?"

"Was there ever any doubt?"

She went up on her tiptoes and kissed his cheek. "Plenty."

Chase grinned and wrapped an arm around her keeping her pressed against him. "If you'll excuse me gentlemen, I'm stealing my wife and finding a dark corner to neck in."

"Stop it." She slapped his arm. "You are not allowed to muss me up."

Off they went arm in arm in the direction of the back of the room. Mike sighed. "Lucky bastard."

"No kidding. Not sure he deserves her."

"Long story." Mike gave him a look. "The telling of which would involve sharing and shit, so...not happening."

"Thanks for sparing me."

And then the crowd parted like that long ago sea and there stood Kate. His heart stuttered, then pounded, then sputtered to a stop. His words disintegrated into a desperate cough. He couldn't stop staring any more than the dozens of other men with their eyes pinned on her. Warned against the drooling thing, Seth swiped a hand over his mouth to make sure he wasn't.

She was magnificent.

There was no other to describe Kate in unrelenting black. Her hair gathered into a tousled, exquisite mess with naughty strands escaping to trail over her shoulders. Even from this distance he noticed her long, dark lashes, eyes rimmed in smoke, soft pink lips. Her sleeves were long and tight. The dress scooped at the front exposing her collarbones. She turned to speak to someone on her way past.

Heart attack. At twenty-two. How embarrassing.

Her back was bare, the fabric forced to cling to her breasts and ribcage by a miracle. The skirt involved yards and yards of black gauzy material that brushed the floor. No jewelry. Only her perfect bone structure and creamy skin on display.

He yearned for his sketch pad. Tried to embed the memory of her on his brain.

When she moved he noticed the slit. High on her thigh it exposed one very long leg and a shoe. God, the shoes. Were those ribbons?

"Annnnd...another man down." Mike punched his shoulder. "I'm off to get another drink. Talk to you later."

She was the most beautiful woman in the room. Probably for miles. Possibly in the whole entire province. Country. She spotted him and her mouth curved with a gentle lift of her lips. He rubbed a hand over his faltering heart. Then she was heading for him with graceful steps, the skirt of her dress swirling to reveal peeks of long leg with every second step. He was going to enjoy peeling that dress off her. The shoes could stay.

"Well, look at you." The simmer of appreciation in her eyes did wonders for his ego.

"No one's looking at me, princess." Tonight, under a purple canopy, she was the fairy tale. The rest of the world forgotten, he captured her hand and brought it to his lips. The only thing left to do was sweep her off her feet. "You look beautiful."

"Thank you." She leaned in close. Her body pulsed in excitement, her eyes gleaming with it. "It's going well, don't you think?"

Her eagerness and her scent went straight to his head. He fought to focus. "The place looks great. People keep piling in. The ones already here are having a good time. I'd say it's a success. Thanks to you."

She brushed a hand down his lapel, her eyes not quite meeting his. When there was nowhere else for her to look but at him, the hint of vulnerability in them captured his heart. Her lips curved. "Make the rounds with me?"

There was so much more he wanted to give her, but for now he offered his elbow and a wink. "My pleasure."

She looped her arm through his with a smile that shot straight to his groin. He leaned in to whisper in her ear. "You may be in charge of the party, but fair warning, I'm in control of what happens after."

She didn't miss a step but kept staring straight ahead smiling at a couple slipping past them. Her hand tensed on his arm, an innocent blush of pink staining her cheeks. But it was her voice, sexy and low, that tied him in knots. "I'm okay with that arrangement."

They circled the room stopping every few feet. People snapped their picture. Shook their hands. Congratulated, complimented, and fussed over them. He lapped it up, his hand at her back, taking advantage of her close proximity to caress and touch. He liked her there, not yielding but relaxed. It was a connection. A couple thing and he liked that too. The two of them together. Working the crowd. Each donating a bit of themselves to ease the way for others.

"You two are stealing the show." An arm slid around his waist and someone pushed their way between them. Grace giggled and held up her almost empty wine glass. "If we were voting on the Mad Man's King and Queen, you guys would take the crowns."

"Thanks." Seth nodded taking in her loose grin and over bright eyes. "I think."

"You should dance." Hand at his back, she pushed them toward the dance floor.

"She's right. We really should," he agreed. Before Kate could say anything Seth plucked Grace's drink out of her hand and set it on the nearest table. He winked at Kate hoping to ease her concern, her eyes searching her friend's face. He grabbed Grace's hand. "But first I'm going to dance with her best friend."

Kate smiled in relief. "Go on. I need to check on a few things."

Seth offered Grace his arm. "Shall we?"

She hugged his elbow. "Lead the way. I'm in need of a distraction, and you'll do quite nicely."

The band played mostly country and pop, not Seth's type of thing but he enjoyed dancing. Grace did too. And she was inebriated enough to make it laugh out loud fun.

The music switched to a slow one. She turned those killer violet eyes on him. "One more?"

"I never say no when a beautiful woman asks me to dance." He pulled her in close. "Even if she's using me to dodge someone else."

"That obvious, huh?" She put one hand in his, the

other on his shoulder. "Although, it's not just him. It's everything. Which I don't want to get into tonight."

"Fair enough. Been there, didn't want to talk about it either." He matched her rhythm and got them going in the right direction. "So, nice weather we're having."

She laughed. "Isn't it just?"

He steered her out of the path of another couple. "Kate seems okay after what happened this afternoon."

"She's trying very hard not to let it get to her." Grace tightened her grip on his hand. "Any news about the guy on the street or Parsons?"

He concentrated on his step and glide. "None. At least, that's what the guys in blue are saying."

"Shoot, I was hoping…well, we're all hoping this ends soon. She's a rock, but I don't how much more she can take. How much more anyone could take."

"Maybe with the fair over it'll be easier to find him. Or to stop Parsons."

They'd all but halted in the middle of the dance floor, couples forced to waltz around them. Grace's grip tightened as she squinted up at him. "Have you noticed she's been…extra distracted the last couple of days?"

Good to know he wasn't the only one. "Any idea what's going on?"

"None." Grace pulled him back into the dance. "Ignore me. She'd be furious with me for bringing it up. And this is a party. Her party. But I want you to know you make her happy. In case she's…being Kate. And you're wondering. Understand?"

"I think so," he lied, because she was kind of drunk and also kind of incapable of explaining further.

She blew out a breath. "Thank God."

And she was right about one thing. It was a party.

So he let it go and changed the subject. "Just so you know, he's trying really hard to act like he's not watching you. But he is."

She rolled her eyes. "He'll get over it. Apparently, I'm not his type."

"Which is?" Not that he wanted to know or have a picture of who was in his brain.

"Who the hell knows? And it's too lovely an evening to worry about it."

At the end of their dance someone else claimed her attention, and he made his way back to the bar. He leaned back against it surveying the crowd. He ordered another soda. He caught a flash of leg and the ribbons around her ankle. Yep. Big plans. He checked his watch. Another couple hours of socializing, then he was dragging his woman out of there.

****

Kate resisted the urge to put a hand to her belly. It was flat, relatively speaking. No need to give people cause to wonder. She walked up to her dad and Sunni. They were the only ones who knew what was up. Sunni had insisted she tell her dad. No more secrets, she'd said. And she was right. He'd remained surprisingly composed, reassuring her everything was going to be all right. Like always.

"There she is." Bill Logan gathered her up in a big hug. She was back to feeling warm and safe. "The belle of the ball."

Sunni grabbed her hand, squeezed, let go. "You look lovely, as usual."

"You too." The aubergine dress with its wide bands of black trim and its square neckline fit the curvy petite woman perfectly, just as Kate predicted.

"And you." She ran a hand over the lapel of her father's suit jacket. "Very dashing."

She turned to the couple standing with them. "Stan. Doris. I hope you're having a good time."

Doris beamed at her. "You've outdone yourself, Kate. The whole place is stunning."

"Thank you, but the decorating committee deserves all the credit."

One of the wait staff hovered and Kate stepped away. "Hey, Gwen."

Gwen smiled an apology. "Wally wants to see you. Something about the photo booth. He had his hands full so he sent me over."

"No problem. I'll be right there." She kissed her dad's cheek. "Dance. Show them how it's done."

It was all going better than she'd hoped. Little glitches were expected she reminded herself as she made her way to the corner housing the photo booth. No need to panic. And no need for the constant prickle of apprehension that had dogged her all evening. Except with Seth.

"Hey, Kate."

"Wally, what's the problem?"

He wiped his hands on a rag. "Don't know, but it's working again whatever it was. Sorry to pull you away."

"You could never be a bother." There it was again. Stronger than ever. She scanned the ballroom and saw nothing to make her nervous. "Glad you fixed it."

Someone tapped her shoulder, and she jumped. "Sorry, Kate. But Jordan wants to see you in the back room downstairs. Something about the wine?"

She frowned at Sarah, a pretty blonde who was

also a single mother with two little kids to support. She worked at Kate's Closet whenever she needed an extra hand during the summer tourist months. "Downstairs?"

Sarah managed a shrug despite the loaded tray. "Apparently. I said I'd let you know if I saw you. Don't know any more than that, sorry."

Kate shook her head. "That's okay. I'll go check it out."

The back stairs were in the same corner. She opened the door, grabbed up handfuls of dress and picked her way down the steps. It was dark at the bottom, but she managed to search out the light switch by feel. When she flicked it up, nothing happened.

"Great." She gathered up her skirts again. A light was on up ahead. "Jordan. Are you there?"

It always freaked her out down here. The Abbey hosted its share of after-hour summertime parties for locals only. Kate, Lily, and Grace weren't regulars, but they'd attended a few. It was always the same. They took turns drawing for the short straw to raid the kitchen. According to local lore, the place was haunted. Anyone who'd spent time down here believed it. Lights flickered, doors slammed, and pots banged for no reason.

They'd all experienced a little something strange while down here, which was why they usually went in pairs. She suppressed a shudder and called out, "Jordan."

Footsteps sounded behind her.

She went to turn around. "Hey, I was just about to give—"

An arm circled her throat. Another hand pressed at the back of her skull and started to squeeze. She grabbed onto the black suited forearm and yanked. It gripped tighter. She clawed at the arm. Nothing worked. Too late to scream. No air. Couldn't take a breath. Her knees buckled. She twisted away but her shoes slipped on the tiled floor. He dragged her backwards. Her dress caught on something. The sound of rending fabric echoed in her head. Panic blinded her. Colors faded. Blurs of gray, black and white. Then nothing.

The next thing she knew arms held her and they were moving. It was pitch black. She tried to scream. Tape pulled at her cheeks. Total darkness. A hood of some kind. She wanted to rip it off, but her arms weren't working right. Pain cut into her wrists. Bound.

Panic. Complete and irreversible.

Her feet jerked. Bound too. They turned sideways. Cool air hit her skin. The crunch of gravel sounded underfoot. She struggled. He tightened his grip.

Defenseless. At his mercy. Her cheeks puffed in and out. She struggled to get enough air in through her nose. It wasn't working.

He propped her up against a solid surface. A vehicle? She twisted away. She hit the ground and pain shuddered through her. He said nothing. A gentle hand on her arm. The clunk of a door opening. He picked her up again and laid her inside. Then they were on the move.

She tried to calm down. To breathe. To think. But it was hard to do in the suffocating dark. Not enough air. There couldn't be. Tears stung her eyes. The tape sucked in and out with every breath she tried and failed to take.

They drove. An SUV, she thought. They picked up

speed. Turned corners. She fought not to roll around the bench seat. Small stones pinged against the undercarriage. Gravel roads now.

Minutes later they turned one last time and came to a stop. No stemming the terror. Bile rose in her throat with nowhere to go. Every sound registered. The turn of the key. The opening of the door. Closing. Her screams were muffled by her gag. The dark caved in on her. The backdoor opened. She kicked with her bound legs. Heard a stifled oath.

He captured her legs and pulled her out. She dropped to the ground, hitting hard enough to knock the air from her lungs. He picked her up with no effort at all.

She worked to catch her breath.

Oh God. God.

She struggled to breathe. To pray. Then they were inside and going down stairs. The jangle of keys and the turn of a lock. Another door opened and he dumped her on a soft surface. There was a snick of sound and the cuff around her ankles popped off. Free she started to kick and flail. Her attacker sat on her legs. She batted at his back. Got in a couple of good whacks.

Not that it made a difference. Cool fingers circled her ankle and yanked. She heard the crushing weight of dragging chain crossing a hard floor. Cool metal locked around her skin. He pushed off and grabbed for her hands, freed her wrists.

She ripped off the hood as the door shut. She blinked against the harsh light. Next she picked at the tape on her cheek and ripped it off on a scream. She scrambled for the door chain snaking along behind her. Locked, of course. She battered against it until her throat was raw and her hands were numb.

She slumped down to the floor and surveyed the small space. It didn't take long. Blinking the room into focus she zeroed in on a picture perched on a dresser. The revolting truth was too much to take in. Ignoring the terrifying drag of chain behind her, she scrambled to the dresser on her hands and knees and heaved herself up. A picture of her from her high school graduation. With Tyler. *Oh, God.* Another of them at a long ago gravel pit party. The book she'd been reading and lost track of days ago rested beside them.

No. No, no, no, no.

Her fingers trembled as she reached for the small jewelry box sitting next to a bottle of her favorite perfume. She lifted the lid. The sight of her grandmother's necklace brought fresh tears to her eyes. She lifted it out and clutched it to her chest.

Tyler. What have you done?

She pulled open drawers and found clothes in her size. She moved to the small wardrobe. Found more. The missing inventory from her store. She closed her eyes. It didn't help. When she opened them, it was all still happening.

She spun in a circle, pushing back the mess of hair escaping its knot. A man she'd known since childhood had abducted her and chained her to a wall like property. Her fingers clenched around the necklace in her hand. She worried over the hard balls like they were steps in a prayer for deliverance.

He planned to keep her here. Against her will. Bile rose in her throat, and she swallowed it back. She put a protective hand over her stomach. Not happening. She would find a way out. She had too. Before he discovered her secret.

She evaluated. Or tried. All she managed to do was blink back tears. So, okay. No windows but another door. She pulled it open. A tiny bathroom with a shower stall and toilet. The small vanity hosted all her usual creams and lotions, her favorite shampoo, conditioner, body wash. How long had he plotted and planned? Had he sat across from her, repentant and malleable, knowing the endgame?

Seth?

Did he have a plan for him too? It was too much. Her legs refused to do their job. She slid to the floor in a mess of black organza and a clank of chain. Her arms wrapped around her middle to protect the life hidden there. Or draw comfort from it. She prayed for Seth. That he was all right. That Tyler's craziness wouldn't touch him.

Minutes ticked by. Under the bare bulb of light, her fear dwindled until bits of it were replaced with bouts of anger.

How dare he?

****

Seth was on his second circle of the cavernous hall. No sign of Kate. Dread, cold and nagging, spoon-fed his paranoia. One hour since he'd led Grace onto the dance floor. He spotted Grace and Lily in a small group that included Chase. He put a hand on Grace's arm. "Have you seen Kate?"

"No." Grace frowned. Her gaze drifted as she rewound the last few minutes. "I haven't."

Lily immediately scanned the hall. "You can't find her?"

Chase didn't dick around. He pulled out his phone.

Seth scrubbed a hand over his face. This was not happening. "No. The last time I saw her she was off to check on a few things. That was an hour ago."

"I'm sure she's fine." Chase pulled Lily in close and kissed the top of her head. "It's likely nothing but we'll check it out. I'll talk to our man in charge of security, the officers outside patrolling. We'll find her."

Grace rubbed her arms. "We'll check the rooms upstairs to see if she's up there."

"No, you won't. You'll stay here and wait for word from us. Clear?" demanded Chase.

Lily didn't answer.

Chase lifted her chin and stared her down. "Are we clear?"

Lily gave in. "Fine. Just find her."

Mike came up behind him. "What's going on?"

Seth fought back the panic. "I can't find Kate."

All of a sudden Bodnar was there. "What's going on?"

Seth put aside his misgivings. As far as he was concerned it was all hands on deck. "Kate's missing."

"Jesus, what?" Bodnar scrubbed a hand over his mouth. "Since when?"

Mike intervened. "We don't know she's missing. Let's not jump to conclusions."

Bodnar stared past Seth to the crowd beyond, shifting his feet, eyes moving. Seth got in his face. "Have you seen her? Talked to her?"

"No." He stood his ground. "Thanks to you she's not exactly keeping me in the loop these days."

Seth was getting a very bad feeling. Mike's hand on his shoulder did nothing to reassure him. "Don't worry. I'm sure she's here." He pointed at Grace and

Lily. "You all stay put."

"Like hell," Seth muttered.

Bodnar was busy taking inventory of the room. "So, what now?"

There was no other option. "We split up. We search. We find her."

On a nod, Bodnar took off. More minutes ticked by with no word on Kate. Lily and Grace took to searching the crowd too. Mike came back with the news Kate's things were still in their room upstairs. Purse, phone, street clothes, all of it.

Then the worst happened. Mike and Chase were called downstairs. They stayed down there. But they weren't letting anyone else near the area.

Not good. Not good at all. Likely very, very bad.

He needed air. Fast. Before he lost it. A rush of cool breeze met him as he stepped out onto the deck. Because of the Indian summer with its unseasonably warm temperatures, people spilled out of the ballroom to cool off and chat. Seth headed for the railing. He braced his hands against it and lowered his head.

Where is she?

Shouts came from down below, and Seth lifted his head. Chase and Mike sprinted toward a vehicle. More shouts. People running. Seth's eyes met the skyline. In the distance, flames licked it. The cold nagging dread of earlier morphed into a terrifying certainty.

Shit.

He didn't have to be told what was going up in flames. It was Kate's. He hit the stairs running. People jerked out of his way. Tunnel vision got him to Main Street. Blocked off at the entrance, he parked on a side street and ran the rest of the way. His dress shoes skidded over pavement in the damp night air. Dopamine flooded his system with the need to act.

Save Kate.

Like those two words, that collection of eight letters, were encoded into his genetic map. Into every cell of his entire being.

A line of emergency personnel in the form of cops and volunteer firemen created a first response barrier. He shoved his way into the hub. The sign for Kate's Closet let go of the building and crashed to the ground in a shattering of sparks.

Fuck.

Kate.

Where are you?

"Seth, that's far enough." Mike stepped in front of him. "Seth."

"Fuck you." He pushed at the hands clamping down on his shoulders.

"Seth." His hands squeezed tighter. Mike shook his head, and Seth's panic reached a new level. "No one is allowed any closer."

"Kate," he demanded, willing to listen but still pushing forward.

Someone caught him from behind. "Seth. Come on, buddy. We need to stay calm."

Those soft words. Kind ones. From a man who was neither of those things scared him to death.

"It's too far gone." Chase's words in his ear. Mike still held him by the shoulders. The worry there, the fear, mirrored his own.

"Kate?" He was desperate. So desperate to hear news that would keep his hope alive.

Mike's lips thinned. For the first time since they'd

328

met the big blond man struggled with his words. "Seth, we just…We don't know. By the time we got here, there was no way in."

"So, we just wait?" Seth jerked away from Chase. Tried to think. "Stand here? Not knowing?"

The intense heat registered. The noise. The rush of water. Mike rubbed his hands over his face. "We don't know she's in there."

"Where is she then?" It was a demand no one had the answer for.

"We're looking for her." Mike's eyes caught and held his. A promise. Man to man. "We'll find her."

Seth looked to Chase who didn't seem to be faring any better than him. And that's when he knew. He grabbed at Chase. "What are you not telling me?"

Chase swore and closed his eyes. The one thing he didn't do was answer.

Seth gave him a shake. Another one. "Tell me."

Chase stared at him but didn't see him. Mike broke in, his tone careful, "We found evidence of a struggle downstairs at the Abbey."

Seth released his grip. "A struggle? Like, what? Like bad? Was there blood? What? I need to know." Because not knowing was killing him.

Mike sighed. "Like she went downstairs or was lured there and then…" He hesitated, and when cops hesitated, it was bad. "…taken somewhere."

"Oh, *Jesus*." He was right. It was bad. So bad. He grabbed onto his head as his eyes went to the raging inferno of a building. "*No*."

"We don't know she's in there, and until we do, we're going to assume she's not. You got me?" Chase grabbed him, brought him back into focus, and didn't let go.

Mike's words echoed firm, steadfast, and hollow. "We're searching the Abbey, the grounds, what we can of the brush behind it. It's going to be difficult going until it starts to get light." He jerked a thumb over his shoulder in the direction of the fire. "They're working to save the connecting stores and buildings now. Once things have cooled off they'll go in and assess, but that's going to be awhile. If arson is suspected, they'll hand the investigation over to us."

"In the meantime?"

"We conduct an investigation. And we do it the usual way. By the book."

"With no room for error, right?" God, if he wanted clichés he'd turn on his fucking TV.

"There never is."

They all turned at the shout of voices. "Damn it. Here they come."

Chase opened his arms and Lily ran into them. "Is Kate here? Is she in there?"

Chase wrapped her up and tucked her under his chin. He gave Seth a warning look over her head. "Not as far as we know."

Grace clutched at Mike's arm. "Her stuff is still at the Abbey. Her car is in the lot. But there's no sign of her. If she's there, she'd have heard about the fire. She'd be here." Her voice broke on the last part. She put her hands over her mouth.

On a sigh, Mike gathered her in, put a hand to the back of her head and pressed her close. "Shush. We'll find her. I promise."

Seth's heart twisted looking at them. He put a couple of steps between him and their closeness.

Someone yelled Kate's name. Tyler Bodnar slid to a stop beside him. "What the hell is going on? Where's Kate?"

Grace took Tyler's arm and tried pulling him away. Tyler was having none of it. He shoved at Grace. Chase blocked Seth's move, but Mike was the real threat.

He had Bodnar by the throat in a heartbeat. "Do not make me throw your ass in jail. Calm down. Got me?"

Tyler yanked on Mike's arm.

Chase growled. "Mike."

Bodnar pushed back, daring him, daring anybody, to take him on. "Fuck you, Davenport. If you were anywhere half decent at your job, this wouldn't be happening in the first place."

Mike's lip curled, but he let go and ordered, "Go home, Bodnar."

"She's been robbed, assaulted, and now she's gone. And what are you doing about it? You're standing here holding your women, doing nothing while another one is missing."

Seth never expected to side with Bodnar. He grabbed onto the anger. Let it build. Unleashed it. "That bastard from the church and that crazy preacher are responsible for this and we all know it."

Tyler's head bobbed in agreement. "The question is what are you going to do about it?"

Cop façades fell into place. Gone were the two men who counted Kate as a friend. "We'll be sure to keep you informed."

Tyler gave Seth a raised eyebrow look. "There's your tax dollars at work."

Anger was comforting, manageable. Until it wasn't. "We need to check the compound. Make sure she's not there."

Mike shook his head in warning. "You need to go home. Both of you. If we haven't found her by first light, we'll organize a search. I'll let you know the details."

"You damn well better." With that warning ringing in the air, Bodnar stomped away.

All of a sudden, Seth was flanked by Lily and Grace. They put hands on him trying to placate him, offered whispers of support. It was the last thing he needed, or wanted. He brushed their hands away, and he headed for his vehicle.

"Stone."

He stopped, waited. Mike came to stand in front of him. Seth could tell he was trying to get a bead on his intentions. "We will find her."

Seth held up his hands to block his words. He moved to go around him. "Save it."

Mike grabbed his arm to pull him back. Seth stared straight passed him into nothingness. "Do not screw this investigation up by doing anything stupid. You stay away from the compound. You hear me?"

He made one last desperate plea. "There's a girl out there. She knows something. She always appears when there's going to be trouble pointing me in the right direction. I need to talk to her."

"Wrong. I'll talk to her." Mike watched him, still searching, evaluating, not liking what he saw.

Too damn bad. "I have to be there. She doesn't trust the police. None of them do."

"And last I heard, you accused them of orchestrating a beating and framing you. So, I have to wonder what makes you think they'd let her talk to you?"

Maybe because he wasn't going to give them a choice?

But he had enough brain cells left not to say it out loud.

"Her name?"

"Nope."

"No name." Mike put his hands on his hips. "Description?"

"I sketched a likeness of her. I'll go home, text you the picture, bring you the original. You have to promise to take me with you. She'll talk to me. I know she will." What was begging compared to the threat of losing Kate? "Please."

Mike looked off to the side. "All right, send the pic, bring us the original. I'll talk to Chase. We'll figure how we're going to work it."

Seth raced for his car praying it would all prove unnecessary. He pulled up short when he saw Tyler leaning against Veronica, arms and ankles crossed. Waiting. "So, what's the plan?"

Why did he have a deep abiding distrust of this guy? If there was a time to put it all aside it was now. But he couldn't. "You heard them. We wait."

"Bullshit." But it lacked the heat, the fire of earlier.

Seth shrugged aside the bug under microscope feeling. He had nothing else to say to the guy.

"Right." Tyler pursed his lips and put a hand to his forehead in a mocking farewell. "See you later then."

He gritted his teeth determined not to worry about Bodnar. Seth climbed into his car. When he checked his rearview mirror, the other man was still standing in the middle of the road. Watching.

Seth dismissed him and drove away. He had bigger things on his mind. He wanted Kate back safe, and he'd do whatever it took to make that happen.

Chapter Thirteen

Tiredness ground down on Kate. She huddled on the bed, arms wrapped around her knees, petrified to close her eyes. The terrifying smells of new paint, new bedding, new levels of insane smothered her. The silence nauseated her. She'd given in and used the washroom. But other than reclaiming her grandmother's necklace, she refused to touch a thing.

Two hours into waiting she had an epiphany. Fresh-faced, hair in a ponytail, she aimed for youthful. Like in the photographs on the dresser. To foster the illusion she was still the same girl from back then. As a way to manipulate his obsession. She hoped.

She heard nothing until a key fit into the lock. Tyler slipped into the room. When the hell had he lost his mind, Kate wondered for the hundredth time? All the way lost it to the point of no return? He still looked like Tyler. Still looked a bit like the boy she'd loved and the man she'd called friend. The grin, the laugh lines, the easy grace were there. But that part of him that pushed and prodded and never let up had taken over. More narrowed eyes and smirking grins. More arrogance. More aggression.

The part of him she'd chosen to ignore.

Because it was easier to use him as a buffer that way.

And fine. That was on her.

But him seeing her as property? As someone to own? As *his*? That was on him.

How dare he lock her up? Put a chain on her? "Tyler, it's about time. You need to let me out of here."

"I can't do that, Katie. And I think you know why. I can't trust you." He leaned back against the door, crossed his arms over his chest looking for all the world like it was her fault. "You went from making good decisions to really, really fucking bad decisions. Like turning down every guy who tried anything, good decision, to handing it to some punk in front of the whole town." He thumped his chest, his lips twisting. "Do you have any idea how that made me feel?"

Completely insane. *He* couldn't trust *her*? She picked up the length of chain, opened her hand, and let it drop to the floor where it slithered into a furious, clanking heap. "Let. Me. Go."

He ignored her and dropped into the only chair undoing his tie. "You aren't going anywhere."

Kate gritted her teeth. Clearly, taking the rational route was going to get her nowhere. "You can't mean to keep me here?"

"I do." He shrugged out of his suit jacket, his smile a warning. "And I will."

She shuddered. "Don't you think people are going to get suspicious?"

He brushed her words aside. "Oh, they're plenty suspicious. They're busy bracing themselves for the worst. Wandering around in the woods searching for your body. Or thinking you and your kidnapper are long gone. Why would they think to look here?" He put a hand over his heart. "Upstanding citizen that I am. Dedicated searcher. Heartbroken and grieving over your disappearance."

"You cannot be serious?" She filled her words with all the disdain and contempt her failing hope could manage.

"Oh, I'm serious." He emphasized the word *serious*. "That's the first thing you need to figure out. How very serious I am."

If hope was a spark, fear was a bonfire. "What have you done, Tyler?"

"Created a clean slate for us." His voice was casual but the grooves carved in his forehead deepened.

The despair she battled won a major victory. She lifted her chin at his tone even though she wanted to bow her head. "What's that supposed to mean?"

Smiling he dug his phone out of his pocket. He pushed a couple of buttons and turned it around to show her. She caught sight of flames. The smothering rush of foreboding dragged her where she didn't want to go. "What is this?"

"Kate's Closet burning to the ground." He announced it like you announced a sale for tires.

She lifted her eyes to his as the screaming in her head pounded at the borders of her skull.

"I know, Katie." His words echoed, hazy and muffled. "But it's going to be okay. You'll see."

"*No*."

Not in her head. That keening, wailing sound was coming out of her mouth. The bed dipped and arms wrapped around her. Whispered hushes brushed against her ear. She reared back, pushing at his arms. It didn't do any good. She started to gag. Tyler picked her up and carried her to the bathroom.

"That's it. Let it all out." He rubbed a hand over

her back as she heaved into the toilet.

She rested her head against the cool porcelain. Everything she'd worked for gone. "You burnt it down?" she whispered.

"All but the brick." He tugged her to her feet. "Come on. You need your rest."

Numb she wrapped protective arms around her stomach. He guided her to the bed. "A clean break. It's what we need."

She swallowed, tried to think and think fast.

Tyler dipped down to her eye level. "I promise you. Things will get better."

In that second she knew they never would. The thought was terrifying. "You're insane."

He leaned in to grab her chin. "This arrangement is going to go a lot smoother if we go over some ground rules."

Her head was pinned in place, but she would have stayed put without the force of his fingers. "You drove me to this, Katie. If you'd turned to me after the break-in like you were supposed to, none of this would be happening. If you'd confided in me after the prank phone calls, shared your concerns about Parsons, any of it…If you had chosen me, you wouldn't be chained to a wall."

"What?" She fought to clear her head. "You were the one who broke into Kate's Closet?"

His grip on her chin tightened. "Pay attention. You're not getting the big picture."

She was going to be sick again.

"I sat with you through the night when you were sick. What thanks did I get? You whispering another man's name. That's when I knew building this room as

338

a backup plan was the right idea."

"Tyler, please." Her whole body trembled. His arm was warm under her hand. She could do this, she could. "You don't need to do this. Go to all this trouble. I'm yours. I always have been."

His eyes softened, and he leaned in closer. "Do I look stupid to you?"

"No," she whispered. She tried again. "I'm yours. I promise."

"One more thing. You try and contact Stone, and I will put a bullet in his brain. If you try and contact anybody? He. Will. Die.

Seth.

"If you hurt him…" Kate's fists clenched.

"Oh, he's hurting plenty, Katie. You should see him. All churned up. Running here. Running there." He stuck out his bottom lip in an exaggerated pout. "I don't know how he's going to live without you. Then again, I don't really care. I just know that's the way it's going to be."

"There is no way you're going to get away with keeping me hostage."

"Hostage?" He backed up. "Who said anything about being a hostage? No." Tyler shook his head. "I'm protecting what's mine. Till death do us part, Katie."

She was done with the whole shivering, cringing, sniveling business. "There is no us, Tyler. There hasn't been for a long time. You need to let me go before this situation escalates. Before there's no undoing it."

"I'm sensing you need convincing. Proof I'll follow through on my promises. Then maybe you'll start to trust my intentions."

"No." She didn't want to see what other horrible

things he'd done.

"Oh, you'll like this. Don't worry. The man who threatened you on the steps of the library this morning? There was no way I could let him live, Katie. Not after he practically accosted you right in front of me." The chair creaked under his shifting weight, smug and purposeful all at once. Kate held her breath. "He's buried in the woods."

The room tilted. She braced a hand against the wall words failing her.

"Do you want to know where?" Like he couldn't wait to tell her. And he didn't. "On lover boy's property. Killed with some stupid carving tool right out of his very own workshop. Buried in a grave dug with his shovel. Brilliant, right? Two birds with one shovel."

He braced his hands on the side of the chair and rose. "God knows what the police will think if they find the body." He held up a finger and faked a surprised smile. "Oh, yeah. They'll think he's a murderer."

He crossed to the door, lifted the key from a chain around his neck. "But if you're a good girl and behave it could be years before they find the body."

It was too much. She leaped from the bed but ended up tangled in the chain. Tyler opened the door. "Sweet dreams, Katie."

The door shut in her face. She slapped her hands against the cool surface of the floor again and again. The air rang with her efforts. Hands numb, she slumped to the floor.

She ran a hand over her stomach. A secret. But for how long? And what would he do when he found out?

Escape.

It was the one thing she couldn't afford to screw

up.

****

Seth's head was a fucking mess. Throbbing with every painful agonizing beat of his heart. Replaying every horrifying worst-case scenario. It was chaos in there. There was no escaping it. How was it he could still feel her in his arms? Had that been only hours ago?

Was she hurt? Terrified?

Alive?

His fingers fumbled over the keyboard, but he hit send, and his sketch was in the hands of the police. He sat in the silence and knew if he stayed it would drive him insane. He grabbed the original and headed for his truck.

Back at the scene, he held vigil with Bill Logan and Stan Knight while the fire crews worked into the night to contain the blaze. They waited, cold coffee in hand, for good news or bad. In the distance, the Abbey sat silent. Its rooms lit as officers searched. There was no word of Kate.

Night still black as pitch, they headed home for a couple of hours of rest before the official search including volunteers began at first light. A bout of blessed numbness set in. It lasted through his shower. It disappeared when he settled back and closed his eyes. All he smelled was smoke. All he saw were flames. All he felt was panic.

He blocked images, overlapped them with better ones. Positive ones. It didn't help him sleep. Ironic that exhaustion made that impossible. He willed his body to relax. They'd find her. They absolutely would.

He jerked awake at the sound of the doorbell. He tossed the mangled blankets aside and ran for the door.

Karyn Good

Mike and Chase stood on the threshold dawn breaking behind them.

"We need to talk to you."

Seth swallowed. He clenched his shaking hands into fists and prepared for the worst. "Did you find her?"

"No. Not yet. But we did find some evidence at the fire scene that points to the Shepherd of the Valley Church." Chase sighed. "We're on our way to the compound. We need you to do a sketch of William Killborne. Can you do that?"

"No problem." The guy's image was burned into his brain. "I'm coming with you."

Chase gave Mike a look, and he nodded on a sigh. "Stay out of the way."

He had the sketch complete by the time they passed over the cattle guard at the entrance to the compound.

They parked in front of a large two-story house with a veranda running along the front. The faint light of early morning silence greeted them. On alert Chase motioned him over. They spared a moment to look around. The house sat on a massive yard protected on three sides by eight-foot high hedges. The usual assortment of outbuildings were off to the side: a large steel Quonset, a broken down barn, and a collection of old wooden granaries. Beyond that sat several modular homes.

Not a person in sight. The front door of the house banged open, and a mountain of a man stepped out onto the porch. He crossed his arms and blocked the door.

"Morning," said Mike, sounding both unintimidated and unimpressed. "Constables Davenport and Porter. This is Seth Stone. We're here to speak with

Matthew Parsons."

"You're trespassing."

"We'd like to come in and talk to you." Mike continued, "We're conducting an investigation into the disappearance of a local woman. Have you seen this man?" He held up Seth's sketch.

You didn't have to be a cop to catch his flinch of recognition. "I know my rights. I'm under no obligation to invite you in. Or speak to you."

Chase nodded in agreement. "True. Yet you stepped outside. And opened your mouth. Take a second and think about it, then answer the question."

At the challenge in Chase's voice some of the man's bravado evaporated. It was fascinating to watch the wheels turn…and turn…and…nothing. He was squaring his shoulders when a woman rushed out of the house knocking him forward.

Too stupid to know better he reached out. "Keep your trap shut, woman."

Mike was faster. "Stand back."

"Help." She wrung her hands in her faded apron. With a nervous glance at the man behind her, she rushed the words out. "We got a man needs medical help inside."

"Shut up," the man hissed, and made another grab for her.

Mike held him off as Chase moved the woman down the veranda. "Ma'am, is anyone else in the house?"

"He's the only one here besides me and my daughter and Matthew." She headed back inside motioning them to hurry. "Come quick."

The man moved to intercept. "You can't go in

there."

"You might want to reread the Canadian Charter of Rights and Freedoms. There seems to be gaps in your knowledge." Mike pointed at Seth. "Stay put."

Seth lost sight of Mike. The big man was left huffing and puffing and none too happy. Seth didn't give a shit about his sensibilities.

Chase beat him to it. "The local woman who disappeared last night? What do you know about it?"

He crossed his arms and stared off into the distance.

Chase shot him a warning glare. "Withholding information is a crime. That's very bad news for you if we decide you're hindering our investigation."

His forehead wrinkled and his lips curled. "There hasn't been no crime, and I don't know nothing about no missing woman."

Chase responded to the crackle of his radio, then announced, "Ambulance is on its way."

The door opened and out slipped the girl and her mother. The woman put a protective hand on her shoulder. "I'm Connie. This is my daughter, Trinity. Can you help us leave here?"

"Constable Porter." Chase moved them down the porch. Seth followed. "We'll get you out of here. Don't you worry."

Connie cast a nervous glance at the man still standing guard. Trinity's hands twisted around the straps of a ragged backpack. But she squared her shoulders, stuck out her chin. "I don't want him to hurt her anymore. My Mom. He hurts her."

Connie cleared her throat. "Trinity, this isn't about our personal situation. They're looking for a missing town woman."

Trinity glanced back at her mother. "I don't want him to hurt her either."

"Shut her up, Connie."

"Do not move another inch." Chase signaled for the man to stay in place. When he didn't Chase was forced to leave them with Seth.

"He can't hurt you anymore. But we're worried he hurt Kate. You remember her? The woman from town? The one you've been trying to help?" Seth offered a smile. It did nothing to put her at ease. She backed closer into her mother. Seth gave her a little more space.

"Not another word, little girl. Remember what the preacher says—"

Seth didn't look back to see what was happening. He didn't take his eyes of Trinity. "I won't let him hurt you. Not anymore."

She turned her face into her mother's faded shirt. Seth hunkered down in front of her, hoping to seem smaller and less intimidating. "I promise."

She peeked out at him. Seth reached into his back pocket and pulled out another copy of a sketch he'd drawn. He unfolded it and offered it to her. "I drew this. After that day on the street. Do you remember that day? The first time you tried to help her?"

She nodded, eyes huge in her face. "That's me."

"That's right. Kate, she likes you too."

She reached for the picture. "Her window always looks so pretty. The Preacher doesn't like her, same as he doesn't like me. My mom said it's not right, that he shouldn't bother her like that."

"Your mom is pretty smart. I bet she loves you a

lot."

The girl nodded again.

Her mother wrapped an arm around her daughter's shoulders. "He left here last night ranting and raving, but under it all I think he's real worried about William. He couldn't find him, didn't know where he was. He didn't want him doing anything stupid. Anything that would force us to move again."

"You're talking about the situation in Montana? William was responsible for some of the unrest?"

She nodded. "And worse. Matthew only had himself to blame. Pushing and prodding and agitating until it was impossible to rein him in. And it was starting to happen all over again here. He set William on her. Had him watching her. Following her. Until he was obsessed with her."

"And last night?"

"Parsons and some of the men left to look for William around eight o'clock. Then he showed up here just after midnight. Burned and in pain. Mumbling about the usual, whores and rescuing the damned and some fool stuff about fire breathing demons. He's been slipping in and out of consciousness ever since. Shock, I think. Those fools are out there praying for him. But he needs more than prayers, he needs a doctor."

He didn't want to scare Trinity, but he needed them to know. "Kate's Closet burned down last night and now Kate's missing. Did he say anything about Kate? About where she might be?"

The blare of sirens split the air. An ambulance and a second and third police cruiser pulled into the compound. Followers spilled out of the huge steel garage.

Pandemonium broke out. Men pushed to join their brother. The women tried to get to their men. Scared children clung to skirts. RCMP officers held people back. But six against a horde with no preacher to lead them? Seth didn't care for the odds.

Trinity slipped her hand into his. He looked down at her looking up at him. He squeezed her hand. "Don't worry. It's all going to work out. We'll get you out of here."

With the law on their side, Mike and Chase took charge. The power of expertise and experience won out over chaos and confusion. The members of the Shepherd of the Valley church were used to obeying orders, and those that protested were arrested. Including the man on the porch. Seth kept Connie and Trinity close and out of the way.

Matthew Parsons was loaded into the ambulance. Five of his minions sat in police cruisers. The rest of his followers, now rudderless, huddled together in messy groups whispering, crying, chanting. Mike held out a hand to Trinity and her mother. "Time to get you out of here. We'll make further arrangements at the station."

"I'm not leaving. Kate might be here somewhere. I can help you search." The small hand in his squeezed and hung on tighter.

"Not happening, Seth."

He opened his mouth.

"No." Mike didn't waste time explaining.

Trinity tugged on Seth's hand. "She's not here."

Her mother put a hand on her chin and lifted her head up. "Trinity, sweetie, you can't know that for sure. Not for sure."

"Yes, I can," she insisted.

Seth looked to Connie for help. She shook her head. "Trinity's made it her business to keep track of Parsons. Makes it easier to avoid him. Or hide when needed. Even without her spying, I can tell you Parsons isn't likely to have your woman hidden anywhere on the compound." She lifted her chin at the crowd on the lawn. "Those fools can't keep a secret to save their souls. He would never bring her here. But I don't think he'd take her away. And he'd never leave his flock."

"And William?"

She gave him a pitying look. "He's capable of anything."

At the police detachment Seth hunted up a pad of paper and a pencil. He helped put Trinity at ease so they could get as much as possible out of her. But it was Connie who was the real font of information. After her husband died Trinity's mother had become the "second" wife of Matthew Parsons. With no money, she was no better off than an indentured servant, forced to work for their room and board. Worse, fingermark type bruises covered Trinity's arms. Not put there by Parsons, but by his "first" wife.

To say she was pissed was an understatement. She spilled every secret. Some Parsons didn't realize she knew. It was more than enough for a search warrant. Seth bet it would also lead to some calls being placed to the local law enforcement of Landslide, Montana.

Ash stopped by before her shift. He needed a vehicle, and she'd arranged for a ride out to the cabin to get his truck. She brought him the keys and a huge to-go cup of coffee.

She handed it to him. "You look like crap."

"Thanks." He lifted the lid and blew across the cup

inhaling the smell of caffeine.

"When was the last time you slept?"

He shrugged, not wanting to go there.

She sighed. "Okay. My shift is only four hours today. After that I'll hang out with you, make you something to eat."

An attempt at humor seemed called for, a way to ease the hammering blows of futility shattering the hope he clutched at in desperation. "Because I don't feel bad enough?"

"Hey, I make a mean charred grilled cheese."

He hooked an arm around her shoulders. "Thanks, Ash."

"Just returning the favor, bro." She bumped her hip into his. "Love you."

"Likewise."

She dropped the funny act and hugged him. "They're going to find her. You need to believe that."

"I do," he lied. He brushed a kiss against her cheek. "See you later."

The day slipped into late afternoon with no news and no progress. Nothing had turned up in the search of the compound. There was nothing left to do at the station so Seth made plans to join the volunteer search. If he stopped moving, he was done for.

On his way out, Tyler Bodnar was coming in. He spotted Seth. "What the hell is going on? Where have you been? I've been looking all over for you, and then I hear some wild rumor about those crazies from out of town having something to do with the fire last night?"

Seth frowned at him, stepping between him and the rest of the group exiting the building. "Take it easy. Keep your voice down."

"Apparently, taking it easy is your job. I'm trying to be proactive and find Kate. Remember her?"

Seth gritted his teeth as Trinity pressed against his side. Seth hunkered down in front of her. Her eyes were huge in her pale face. Seth tried to tug his hand free. "Why don't you wait here? I'll only be a minute."

Trinity kept her eyes glued on Tyler and shook her head. Seth gave her hand a reassuring squeeze. "I promise."

She relented and Seth pulled Tyler outside. "What the hell is wrong with you?"

Bodnar wasn't listening. "Is that one of those weirdoes from the compound? What's she doing here? What the hell is going on?"

Seth wanted him gone. "We found Matthew Parsons at the compound early this morning. Burns all over his hands, arms, and face. Thankfully, he was still alive when we found him. They're hoping he can tell them more when he wakes up."

Bodnar's mouth opened, and Seth waited. He ran a hand over his jaw without saying anything. Seth frowned, and Bodnar blinked before asking, "He was there? At Kate's?"

"Looks like it." Seth expected a rant, an I-told-you-so, anything but shock. "They're searching the compound and questioning members right now."

"That's good," muttered Tyler looking away. "And the girl? What's she got to do with it?"

Exhaustion made him paranoid. Seth brushed his questions aside. "Long story."

"So, he was there." Tyler lifted a hand, let it drop.

Something was off. Very, very off. "Yeah, he was there. Why is this a surprise?"

"It's not." Bodnar scowled. "It's nothing. Never mind."

But it didn't seem like nothing. It seemed like something big that Seth wasn't getting. "It's not *nothing*. What's going on?"

Tyler ignored him. "That's good right? Means they're closer to finding Kate?"

Seth hesitated. A warning buzzed in his head. "I don't know. I hope so."

"Great. Good. I'll be in touch."

On that ominous promise Seth moved in close. "What the fuck is up with you?"

Bodnar shoved him back. "Nothing. What the hell is wrong with *you*, man?"

Seth didn't believe him. But he backed down. He needed time and space to figure out why without Bodnar getting suspicious. "Forget it. It's been a long twenty-four hours, you know?"

"Yeah, well. Shit to do." Then he was striding away stuffing his big black hat further onto his head.

Seth didn't watch him leave. He was too busy wondering why all of a sudden he smelled Kate like she was right there. God, he was losing his mind. Searching with the others would help. More than anything he needed her back. He breathed in deep but her scent was gone. Like it had never been there except in his imagination.

Chapter Fourteen

The door shot open startling Kate awake. She blinked, confused until the awful, haunting rattle of the chain around her ankle brought reality back into focus.

There was a clock on the wall. Watching it made her crazy. With no windows, six o'clock in the evening meant nothing. Time was suspended. The same number of minutes stretching into an hour with those minutes becoming thinner and thinner until she feared time would stop altogether.

Tyler entered the room with a tray. He left it on the tiny table than sat in the only chair. "How's my beautiful girl?"

She cringed at his use of the word *girl*. It sucked them into a perverted, reverse time warp. Kate shuffled away from Tyler.

"It's only temporary, you know." He smoothed a finger over her ankle cuff. "When I know I can trust you, I'll take it off."

"Gee, something to look forward to." She made a point out of moving her foot away from his hand.

"Play nice, Katie." His hand slipped under the material of the dress she refused to take off. Her calf muscles contracted.

She gritted her teeth. Inflated her resolve. Lit a blaze of heat under it. She would rise to the occasion. She would do whatever she had to, to protect her child.

"I can do that. I can play nice. But it's going to require a gesture of good faith." She gripped his roaming fingers. "Get rid of the chain."

"Not yet. But soon." He twisted his hand and threaded his fingers through hers. The way lovers held hands. He kissed her knuckles. She wanted him pacified so she resisted the urge to shudder. "First I need to fill you in on what's happening."

"Okay," she said, trying her best to appear cooperative, even though dread spread like thick tar. Please, let Seth be okay. "What's going on?"

"Nothing I can't handle." He shrugged. "And actually, the more I think it over the more it's going to help us. That damned preacher was at Kate's Closet last night. They found him this morning. A little charred around the edges but alive."

At his casual tone her eyes closed. The best thing to say was nothing at all.

"Poor sucker." So casual. So...psychotic. He laughed. "Always showing up where he doesn't belong. Right now he's the prime suspect. Here's hoping he doesn't make it. That would be the ideal situation. But even if he does and he saw something, the cops are never going to believe him. I mean, come on. The guy's obviously crazy."

No, she was looking at crazy. Crazy had clear blue eyes, tousled hair, and a clear conscience. "Tyler, don't say things like that."

"Why not? Because it disturbs you? I spent months avoiding anything that might upset your delicate sensibilities and look where it got us? Look around. You think I want this?" He lifted the chain, let it drop. "Do you think I want to have to go into town and deal with some long-haired artist freak who had the nerve to put his hands on my girl?"

"I am your girl." The lie was a foreign object lodged in her throat.

"You don't mean that, but you will. Someday your words won't be a lie. They'll be the truth. And we'll be happy."

"Tyler, we can be all those things. Out in the open. I promise you I'm yours." Her heart broke even though her words were confident. Selling her soul was going to cost him. "You don't need to keep me chained up like an animal. Take off the chain."

"I've known you your whole life." The thinning of his lips, the lowering of his voice, the minute shake of his head spelled out his disappointment. "You don't think I know when you're lying, Katie?"

"I'm not," she insisted, to stubborn to cave at the first obstacle.

"You're playing me and I don't like it." He yanked her foot closer. "When you stop I'll take this off."

"When you take this off..." she taunted, because it worked both ways. They *had* known each other forever and while she'd underestimated him she also knew what he wanted: her submission. He was going to pay for trying to take it. "You'll get what you want."

"This isn't a negotiation." Once again his hand slithered up her leg.

Once again she blocked his hand from going further. "You're not a rapist, Tyler. If I know anything about you, I know that."

Appealing to his ego failed. He pushed her back and crawled on top of her. He laid his mouth next to her ear. "You're wrong, Katie. I'll be whatever I have to be to win."

****

Seth ended up at home when the search parties spilt up at dusk. In the shower, he let the hot water beat against his numb skin. The cold crept back in the moment he stepped out of the glassed enclosure. He grabbed clothes and slipped them on. His back to the headboard he picked up his sketch pad. He flipped through the drawings he and Trinity had made that afternoon.

He braced himself then turned to the sketches of Kate. His fingers came away smudged with charcoal. The next sketch was of the rink parking lot the night he'd confronted Tyler. He'd written Green Glue off to the side. He frowned, remembering the buckets of the stuff. More than willing to grasp at any straw, he looked around for his computer. The sound of the doorbell had him shoving up off his bed.

"Seth."

Ash's voice drifted up the stairs seconds before the sound of her footsteps followed. He met her on the steps. "Who is it?"

She made a face and whispered, "That asshole cowboy is downstairs."

Just what he didn't need. He put a hand on her shoulder. "What's he want?"

"Didn't say. Wants to talk to you."

"Why don't you hang out in my room for a while?"

"Thanks." She grabbed his hand on the way by, held on. "Be careful. There's something about this guy…"

He squeezed her fingers and let go. "I know what you mean. Go on up. I'll get rid of him."

Tyler was standing in front of the big windows facing the lake, hat in hand. He looked over when Seth came to stand beside him. His eyes lifted toward the loft area. "Cozy."

Seth figured he was insinuating at more than the surroundings. Why had he let this asshole get to him? "Something I can do for you?"

"Figured I'd stop in. Get an update."

An update his ass. Seth lifted his hands and let them drop in an I-got-nothing gesture. "Sorry, man."

"You seemed pretty tight with that kid? She shedding any light on things?"

He ignored the question. "Saturday afternoon? You didn't see William again, did you?"

"No." He gave Seth a curious look that turned hard at the edges. "Why?"

"No reason. Just…trying to tie all the different pieces together, I guess."

"That girl? And her mother? Where'd you say they were staying?"

"They didn't say." The lie came easily. For some reason Seth was getting a bad feeling. He had no way to know if it was legitimate or his feelings for the guy were coloring his perceptions. Either way he wasn't telling him anything. He'd have to beg for the information the same way Seth had. "Guess they didn't figure it was any of my business."

"Figures." He shook his head, but his eyes never left Seth's. "Cops, right?"

"Yeah." Seth didn't buy it for a minute.

"But you'll let me know if you hear anything?"

He'd heard somewhere direct eye contact implied you were telling the truth. "Sure, of course."

He stuffed his hat on his head. "Your grandparents left you a nice place. When my parents moved into town they left the old farmhouse to me. The whole place needs updating."

"Renovations are hell." He thought of the supplies in Tyler's truck the night he confronted him. "You working on it?"

"Don't have time for that shit right now. Some of us have to work for a living." He slapped Seth on the shoulder. "But maybe someday. See you around."

Seth raised his chin in acknowledgement. "Yeah. See you around."

He stood on the small stoop and watched Tyler Bodnar jog down the steps to the gravel driveway and into his truck. When his lights were swinging down the road, he closed it on a soft click.

Not Matthew Parsons' usual MO.

Personal items of Kate's missing. Not random. Meaningful ones. Ones only someone close to her would know the significance of. He headed for his laptop. He typed in the words *Green Glue*.

He stared at the words: *Noiseproof Your Life.* He grabbed his phone and his keys.

****

Kate had no plan. What she had was morning sickness so severe she slumped down by the toilet and stayed there. The upside was its untimely arrival had saved her from Tyler. At least, she hoped it was morning sickness. She rested a hand against her stomach. "We can do this, little one. We can."

Since she was already on her knees she prayed she was right. Then she rose and opened the tap, grabbed for the glass at the side and filled it. When the sip of water stayed down she swallowed another. How was she going to do this trapped in a room? By herself? What if there was no way out of here? Her stomach heaved. She wasn't going there, wasn't going to think those kinds of thoughts.

Someone would figure it out. Seth would come for her. Tyler would relax his guard. Slip up. And she'd be ready. With a plan.

A hundred best-case scenarios shattered at the sound of the key in the lock and deadbolts sliding back. Kate stumbled into her tiny prison in time to see Felicity poke her head past the door.

"Holy shit, Kate. What the hell?" Eyes wide and disbelieving she surveyed the room. "Everyone's going out of their minds looking for you."

Kate almost fainted in relief. "Felicity, thank God."

Felicity's wild eyes landed on Kate and she repeated, "What the *hell*? I knew he was up to something. But this…"

Kate stumbled in haste. "He's lost his mind. We have to hurry."

Felicity's jaw dropped when the chain around her ankle clanked. "Holy shit!"

"Yes, yes. Move. You have to help me get out of here." Kate sank down to the floor. "We need to find the key."

"Right." Felicity spun in a full circle. There was no mistaking her panic. "Any idea where it would be? Did he say? Give me a clue here."

"Where'd you find that one?" Kate pointed to the lanyard clutched in Felicity's hand.

"I swiped it out of his truck. It was the only one there." She swallowed, looking panicked. "He must have the key to that stashed somewhere else."

Kate pressed a hand to her forehead. She had no idea. "Forget the key for now. Call nine-one-one."

"Shit. Okay. Right." She pulled out her phone, held it up. "No service down here. I have to go upstairs."

Not the end of the world. She'd be back. Kate cringed. "Go. Hurry."

Felicity whirled and charged for the door. "I'll be right back."

Kate stared at the open door. If she could just…She shuffled forward. The chain stretched exactly to the doorway.

"Felicity," she called. There was no way to stem the panic when she didn't answer. She tried again, louder. "Felicity."

There were footsteps on the stairs, and then she raced around the corner. "They're on their way."

"Okay." Kate breathed in deep.

"That's the good news."

She'd hit her bad news limit about forty hours ago, but she asked anyway, "What?"

"Tyler's coming up the lane." Sympathy eased the panic in her features. "Kate, I have to go back up there."

Kate grabbed for her. "No."

Felicity put a shaky hand on her arm. "My truck's out there. He knows I'm here. The cops are on their way. I promise. I'm going to shut the door. But I'll leave it unlocked. Okay? You with me? I'm going to stall him until they get here."

She nodded, not sure at all and wanting to hold onto her and hold her there. "Get back up there. We don't want him to suspect anything."

Felicity risked one glance back before shutting the door behind her.

It was going to be okay. Felicity was going to be okay. Tyler wouldn't suspect anything. They were safe. Saved. She should breathe. Breathing was good.

But a minute later the door crashed open and Tyler shoved in, chest heaving, reeking of rage. "Did you think I wouldn't have a video feed? Alarms. Some way of keeping track of you when I wasn't here?"

Kate backed up. "Felicity? Where is she?"

"Move." He shoved her back onto the bed and grabbed her ankle. She kicked at him and his hands slid off. The air left her lungs in a whoosh, his weight crushing her. When the cuff fell off, he yanked her to her feet.

She beat at any part of him she could get her hands on. "Tyler. Where is she? What have you done with Felicity?"

She landed a hit and he grunted. Not enough to slow him down. He shoved her toward the door. "This way."

No way. He was going to have to drag her out of here.

"Move." Tyler turned to face her. "Now."

Kate struggled against his efforts to pick her up, arms and legs flailing. She screamed, and wailed and did whatever she needed to do.

Boots pounded on the stairs. Distracted, they both hesitated. Tyler recovered first and dropped her. He spun around.

A moving force slammed into him and Tyler grunted. Kate expected to see a police officer. But there was no mistaking Seth's shape. He grabbed onto

360

Tyler's jacket to hold him in place and threw a punch.

Tyler stumbled. Kate gasped at the sound of fist on bone and scrambled to get out of the way.

Seth spared her a glance. Disbelief and fury pinned her in place. It was an advantage Tyler didn't need. His fist hit Seth square in the face. Kate pushed up onto all fours and screamed his name.

Seth staggered back on a roar. Tyler swung again. Seth twisted and the blow landed on his shoulder. Before Tyler could pull back Seth grabbed him around the waist and pushed him back.

"Kate, run." Seth fought to hang on and give her time. Tyler clasped his fists together and brought them down on Seth's back.

Kate tripped in a tangle of fabric and fear. Seth grunted. Her knees hit the cement floor.

"Bastard," Seth growled.

Black spots blurred her vision. She blinked. They retreated. Seth called her name a second time before sending Tyler skidding across the floor. He slammed into an old wardrobe across from her. It rocked and Kate held her breath. Seth stepped in front of her.

"She's." Tyler rushed him. "Mine."

"Not now." Seth met his challenge. "Not ever."

"Tell him, Katie," raged Tyler. "Tell him the truth."

There was a flash of movement and a dull thud. Tyler pitched forward. He landed in a heap at her feet. Kate stared at the blood leaking from his skull and dribbling to the floor.

Seth pried the baseball bat out of Felicity's raised hands. "It's okay. He's down."

"Jesus, Kate." Then he was beside her. In the

Karyn Good

sudden silence she heard the sirens, more pounding of boots upstairs and on the stairs. Shouting. Warnings. Relief.

"Down here," Seth called, his hands sliding and slipping over her body in feather touches. "Are you hurt?"

"No." But she clung to him in case she was lying and didn't know it. "I'm fine."

"He had a bad habit of underestimating, not to mention under appreciating, me." Felicity dropped down beside Kate. Blood trickled from a cut on the side of her temple. Kate couldn't help it. A laugh bubbled out. But it wasn't the cleansing, therapeutic kind.

Seth hugged her close. "It's okay. I've got you."

Armed police officers moved in and got them out. Seth refused to let her go. Or was it the other way around? Didn't matter, she was exactly where she needed to be, in Seth's arms. Lights flashed in the drizzle and the dark. She felt Chase's hand on her arm, heard Mike's voice. But her face was buried in Seth's neck. He refused to put her down until they reached the ambulance.

"She's freezing."

Kate shivered in confirmation. Seth handed her over to the ambulance attendants. She clung to his hand and brushed at his bloody knuckles. They lost contact when they ushered Felicity in beside her.

Chapter Fifteen

Kate's doctor stepped into her cubicle in the ER and the nurse ushered everybody else out. They were keeping her overnight for observation and to rehydrate her. She'd confided her suspicions about her pregnancy to him earlier. With Seth, her family and friends waiting outside the room, he confirmed what she already knew. She stumbled over how to take it all in.

She was homeless.

Out of work.

And pregnant.

When the doctor finished up, the police were waiting to talk to her. Thankfully, it wasn't Chase and Mike. They were dealing with Tyler. It made her story easier to tell. After the police left they transferred her from the small trauma/emergency area to a room.

It gave her some precious moments to think. She slumped back against the hard mattress and awful pillow bracing for the invasion of family and friends. She'd come back to Aspen Lake to rebuild her life. Now look at her. Her life was unrecognizable. Again.

She curled up into a ball on the bed. Much like she had those first days in rehab. When she walked out of here she had no home to go to, nothing to do the next day but deal with the loss of her dreams. How pathetic was that thought? How pathetic was she? If rehab had taught her anything, it was not to give up. If she hadn't given up in her tiny prison, she wasn't giving up now. She pressed a hand against her stomach. Not for anything.

Rebuilding while growing a baby wasn't going to be easy. She reached over for a cracker to nibble on. But it wasn't impossible.

A baby.

She stuffed the rest of the cracker in her mouth.

God.

Seth.

She closed her eyes and breathed in deep. Time to forge ahead. Starting with Seth and telling him the truth. She wanted him involved. More than involved. She wanted them to think about the possibility of being a couple. A family.

Wasn't that the dream of every twenty-two year old guy who'd known you for a month?

Her chest got tight, her breathing sped up. She didn't want to think about what had happened in Tyler's basement. She couldn't relive it and keep it together. To calm herself she reached for another cracker. When it stayed down, she reached for the ginger ale a nurse had brought her. Against her will, her fingers tensed around the can. She closed her eyes but all she saw was that room. And Tyler.

Not again.

No more falling apart. She was done with that. She concentrated on ugly hospital gowns, crackers, and Seth. It failed. Her breath hitched. How could she have been so wrong about a man she'd known practically her whole life?

The first stunning blow of what had happened hit her. The can slipped through her fingers. The rolling and fizz of soda filled her ears. She struggled to breathe. To stop the tears.

Tyler had terrorized her. Hurt her. Her heart shouldn't ache. Not because of him. Her hands shouldn't shake. So badly they couldn't rest steady against her forehead.

Tears slipped down despite her forbidding it to happen. She curled up tighter willing it all to stop. A nurse's cool hand slipped across her forehead, her words soothing.

Not that it helped.

"Katie." Her father gathered her up. She hated that he needed to.

"I didn't see it." She gasped, tried to breathe through the need to weep. "Why didn't I see it?"

He smoothed his big hands over her hair, her back. "None of us did."

"I made it worse," she whispered as she leaned into him, inhaled the same scent he'd sported the last twenty-nine years, sawdust and shaving cream. "That's what I do."

"Come now, sweetie. That's not true." He swiped a tissue from the side table and handed it to her. "He's not worth this. He might have been once, but that was a long time ago. He made his choices. Bad ones. And now he has to be a man and pay for them."

She sensed Seth hovering and turned to see him, hands shoved in pockets, shoulders hunched, in the background. She watched him turn and walk out of the room.

****

Seth paced the hallway outside Kate's room. He wasn't done hitting things. Nope. Not. At. All. He wanted back in that dingy basement beating his fists against Tyler Bodnar. Why Kate was wasting more tears over that asshole he had no idea.

Sunni put a hand on his arm. "She's in shock."

"Right." He knew that.

"It's going to take her some time to work through everything that's happened."

He knew that too.

"And if you expect her to let go of what happened out at that farm, you need to do the same."

No. Fucking. Way.

"If you can't…you aren't the man she needs by her side right now."

Well, score a hit for honesty. It blew a hole right through his chest.

"She's going to have a lot on her plate the next little while, and she needs to know you have her back."

Seth bowed his head. "If I had her back, we wouldn't be here."

"Seth—"

But he was done listening. "I need coffee."

An hour later he came back to find Kate dozing. Sunni closed her magazine and tugged a reluctant Bill Logan out of his chair. He gave Seth a glare on his way out. Seth still had no idea what was up with him, and he didn't care.

"Ignore him," Kate whispered.

Seth dropped into the vacated chair and reached for her hand, brought her fingers to his lips. "I'm glad you're okay."

"Me too."

He set a to-go cup down on the side table. "I brought you coffee."

She grimaced at the cup as she sat up, straightening her shoulders. "There's something I have to tell you."

He tucked a strand of hair behind her ear but didn't quite meet her eyes. Worked on keeping his shit together. If that son of a bitch had touched her, or worse…He squeezed her hand. He'd take it like a man and be there for her without going off the deep end. "Okay."

She braced, and it broke his heart. He prepared for the worst. She swallowed. "I'm pregnant."

He was going to kill that fucker with his bare hands. He was going to break into the jail—"Jesus, I'm so sorry. So sorry he hurt you. That he—" Seth couldn't get the words out.

"What? No." She stared at him, surprise widening her beautiful swollen, red-rimmed eyes. Then she blinked and stuttered out something before clearing her throat and trying again. "I'm pregnant. You're the father. Not Tyler." Her whole face flushed. Her hand let go of his to flutter around. "He didn't…touch me…like that. Or anything like what you're thinking."

His jaw dropped open. He shut it. Opened it. Shut it again. Then that would mean…"What?"

"I'm pregnant," she repeated, like that clarified things.

"With my baby?" That's what she was saying. *Oh God*…that's exactly what she was saying.

"Well, with *my* baby. But you're right. Our baby, technically. But I don't expect…" She stopped when he held up a hand. Then she kept talking and Seth's head kept spinning. "I'm making a mess of this."

But he'd stopped listening. He was too busy thinking it couldn't be true. And how had they gone from one worst-case scenario to another worst-case scenario? "I'm sorry. But how can that be? You said…you said you were on the pill?"

She said something, a rather lengthy explanation but he didn't hear that either. "I just spent the last forty hours worried you were dead."

"I know." She was rubbing his back, smoothing a hand over his cheek, doing everything but taking his vitals. Which might be a good idea because he was pretty sure he was having some kind of attack. "I'm sorry."

One thing was perfectly clear. "But you're not dead, you're pregnant."

More patting, more instructions. "It's okay. It's going to be okay. Just breathe."

Just breathe? Who had time for that shit? "It's true. I heard you say it."

"Seth."

He pushed out of the chair and held onto his head. "Holy *shit*."

"Seth, it's going to be okay."

"*Holy* shit."

"Seth, listen to me."

"This can't be happening."

She opened her mouth.

He wasn't done. She deserved to know. Right now before anyone thought anything different. "I don't know anything about babies."

"Neither do I," she offered. To comfort him he was sure. It didn't work.

"That's just great. Great. Holy shit." He put a hand over his heart and bunched up the material of his shirt. "We're screwed. This *baby* is screwed."

"Seth, calm down," she ordered.

"I can't calm down," he insisted. "I'm too busy having a stroke."

"I know this is a shock, especially on top of everything else. But we'll work it out."

"How? How are we going to work this out? All I wanted was a little peace and quiet. A place to concentrate on my art. To be alone. And then I met you," he accused.

She raised a brow. "I didn't make this baby by myself."

"No. But you just had to be the most beautiful woman I've ever met. Everything about you pulled me in until I couldn't think straight. I didn't want to resist you. Now we're having a baby. A *baby*. I can't put a baby in Veronica."

"You do realize these words are coming out of your mouth, right? That I can hear you?"

Then he looked at her. Really looked at her and everything about him sagged. "What are we going to do?"

"First, sit down before you fall down."

"Sitting down is not going to help."

"Well, it'll help me."

He sat.

"Let's try this again." She held out her hand and motioned for him to put his in hers. When his hand was wrapped up in hers, she squeezed. "I'm having a baby. I want this baby. I just spent the last forty hours promising her she'd be okay."

"She?"

"I'm assuming."

Girl babies. He knew less about them than the

other kind. He stared at her wondering why all of a sudden she was so calm. Serene almost. Despite the tired, cautious eyes and dark circles. "I don't know if I can do this."

"That's the only thing I'm sure about. You can do this. You're going to make a great dad. Whether we're together as a couple or not. But maybe for right now you need to take the night to let things sink in."

"Oh no. No. No. No. You're not kicking me out. I'm not leaving. Something bad always happens when I walk away from you." It was that simple. It was also honest. And if they were going to be any kind of parents, they needed full disclosure. "Kate, I don't know what the future's going to hold. For us. As a couple. Or a family. I wish I did."

Kate sighed. "Neither of us do."

"I'm still not letting you out of my sight. Not anytime soon. As for *our* baby." His heart stuttered. "Let's take it one step at a time. See how it goes."

"Sounds good to me."

"Move over," he ordered.

She didn't question him, just scooted over and made as much room for him as she could.

He toed off his shoes and climbed onto the bed. "We need to talk about what happened with Tyler."

"Tomorrow," she murmured.

"Tomorrow," he agreed.

Her eyes were already drooping. "You came for me. I knew you would."

He pressed against her back. Close enough to feel her breathing and wrapped an arm around her waist. His palm spread out over her stomach. Rested there. Warm and protective. "Not soon enough."

She put her hand over his, snuggled in closer. "You're the best thing to happen to me in a long, long time."

He closed his eyes. "Same goes, princess."

Epilogue

"Kate, hurry up." Seth arranged his daughter on his hip as he tossed formula, bottles, and a smiley-faced container of Cheerios into a bag.

"Be right down," Kate called from upstairs.

He glanced down at his watch trying to guess at how long "be right down" could take. Then he kissed the top of Chloe's head. "Pray it means sooner rather than later."

"Did you pack her cereal?"

He grabbed another box off the counter and tossed it into the bag. "Yes."

"Her bib, her—"

"Princess, get your ass down here so we can go or I'm gonna be late for work." He rolled his eyes at his daughter and bent to kiss her nose. "It makes Grandpa grumpy. And when Grandpa's grumpy everyone's grumpy."

"Okay, okay. I'm coming."

Then he waited like he did every single day and looked to the stairs knowing today was bound to be spectacular. He was right. At the sight of her his heart turned over. The grand opening of the new and expanded Kate's Closet was today. She also sold infant and toddler clothing. God help him.

"She better be wearing the outfit I set out for her and not something with Pearl Jam stamped on it. Or have little baby boy jeans on."

"What's wrong with jeans and a t-shirt?" he asked Chloe, who answered by jamming her fist in her mouth. Then there was the click of heels on the stairs. First came the shoes, then her legs, and then the rest of her. And like always he couldn't believe his good fortune.

Seth appreciated the tight skirt and the off-the-shoulder blouse. But the outfit was nothing without the attitude. Or her personality or the giant well of determination that fed it. He let the look of her slide through him. Until he noticed the giant duffel bag clumping down the stairs behind her. "Kate, she's only going to be gone for one night, not two weeks."

"Funny." She struggled to get the bag down the stairs.

He hadn't been going for funny. He'd been going for reasonable. Chloe giggled as Seth stooped to buckle her into her car seat. "Seriously. What is in there?"

"Outfits."

"Outfits? As in plural?"

"Yes, Seth. Plural. Twenty-four hours require outfits. And she's a girl so she needs plural outfits. And seeing as this is her first sleepover she needs stuff. Sunni needs her to have stuff."

Seth set the car seat on the floor and wrapped his arms around Kate. "She's going to be fine."

Kate avoided his look and sniffed. "I know."

"Look at me."

She lifted her head. "What?"

God bless her prissy attitude. "I promise to distract you later."

Kate wrapped her arms around his neck. "I have a special outfit to change into later too."

He wasn't sure his heart could take one of Kate's special outfits. He rested his forehead against hers. "You know I love you right?"

She nodded against him.

"Then can we please get our asses out the door, so we can get the work part of this day over with, so I can come home, and you can show me your outfit, and I'll take it off you, and we can spend the next ten hours having sex?" Seth thought of the ring box tucked into the back of his nightstand. Tonight was the night.

"What if she can't get to sleep over there?"

"Kate, she doesn't sleep here." He dropped a kiss on her glossy pink lips, picked up Chloe, and headed for the door. "It's time she kept someone else up all night."

Kate followed. "Ten hours? Of sex? That thought's a little...overwhelming."

"You've got all day to come to terms with it." But he'd settle for an hour of sex and eight hours of uninterrupted sleep. God, he loved his baby girl, but she wasn't a big fan of sleeping. She'd rather be socializing at two o'clock in the morning than traipsing through dreamland. Not that he'd trade her for anything, but he was willing to lend her out for twenty-four hours. Especially to people who loved and adored her like her Grandpa and Sunni. If they ever got out the door.

A word about the author...

Karyn Good grew up on a farm in the middle of Canada's breadbasket. Under the canopy of crisp blue prairie skies she read books. Lots and lots of books. Eventually, she migrated to the city, fell in love, married and started a family. When the time was right, what to write was never the issue—romance and the gut-wrenching journey toward forever.

http://www.karyngood.com